THE ELRIC SAGA
Part One

THE ELRIC SAGA

Part One

ELRIC OF MELNIBONÉ
THE SAILOR ON THE SEAS OF FATE
THE WEIRD OF THE WHITE WOLF

Michael Moorcock

Nelson Doubleday, Inc.
Garden City, New York

Contents

THE ELRIC SAGA
Part One

ELRIC OF MELNIBONÉ

To Poul Anderson for *The Broken Sword* and *Three Hearts and Three Lions.* To the late Fletcher Pratt for *The Well of the Unicorn.* To the late Bertolt Brecht for *The Threepenny Opera* which, for obscure reasons, I link with the other books as being one of the chief influences on the first Elric stories.

CONTENTS

Contents

BOOK ONE

On the island kingdom of Melniboné all the old
rituals are still observed, though the nation's
power has waned for five hundred years, and
now her way of life is maintained only by her
trade with the Young Kingdoms and the fact that
the city of Imrryr has become the meeting place
of merchants. Are those rituals no longer useful;
can the rituals be denied and doom avoided? One
who would rule in Emperor Elric's stead prefers
to think not. He says that Elric will bring destruction to Melniboné by his refusal to honour all the
rituals (Elric honours many). And now opens the
tragedy which will close many years from now
and precipitate the destruction of this world.

1 A Melancholy King: A Court Strives to Honour Him

It is the colour of a bleached skull, his flesh; and the long hair which flows below his shoulders is milk-white. From the tapering, beautiful head stare two slanting eyes, crimson and moody, and from the loose sleeves of his yellow gown emerge two slender hands, also the colour of bone, resting on each arm of a seat which has been carved from a single, massive ruby.

The crimson eyes are troubled and sometimes one hand will rise to finger the light helm which sits upon the white locks: a helm made from some dark, greenish alloy and exquisitely moulded into the likeness of a dragon about to take wing. And on the hand which absently caresses the crown there is a ring in which is set a single rare Actorios stone whose core sometimes shifts sluggishly and reshapes itself, as if it were sentient smoke and as restless in its jewelled prison as the young albino on his Ruby Throne.

He looks down the long flight of quartz steps to where his court disports itself, dancing with such delicacy and whispering grace that it might be a court of ghosts. Mentally he debates moral issues and in itself this activity divides him from the great majority of his subjects, for these people are not human.

These are the people of Melniboné, the Dragon Isle, which ruled the world for ten thousand years and has ceased to rule it for less than five hundred years. And they are cruel and clever and to them 'morality' means little more than a proper respect for the traditions of a hundred centuries.

To the young man, four hundred and twenty-eighth in direct line of descent from the first Sorcerer Emperor of Melniboné, their assumptions seem not only arrogant but foolish; it is plain that the Dragon Isle has lost most of her power and will soon be threatened, in another century or two, by a direct conflict with the emerging human nations whom they call, somewhat patronisingly, the Young Kingdoms. Already pirate fleets have made unsuccessful attacks on Imrryr the Beautiful, the Dreaming City, capital of the Dragon Isle of Melniboné.

Yet even the emperor's closest friends refuse to discuss the prospect of Melniboné's fall. They are not pleased when he mentions the idea, considering his remarks not only unthinkable, but also a singular breach of good taste.

So, alone, the emperor broods. He mourns that his father, Sadric the Eighty-Sixth, did not sire more children, for then a more suitable monarch might have been available to take his place on the Ruby Throne. Sadric has been dead a year; whispering a glad welcome to that which came to claim his soul. Through most of his life Sadric had never known another woman than his wife, for the Empress had died bringing her sole thin-blooded issue into the world. But, with Melnibonéan emotions (oddly different from those of the human newcomers), Sadric had loved his wife and had been unable to find pleasure in any other company, even that of the son who had killed her and who was all that was left of her. By magic potions and the chanting of runes, by rare herbs had her son been nurtured, his strength sustained artificially by every art known to the Sorcerer Kings of Melniboné. And he had lived—still lives—thanks to sorcery alone, for he is naturally lassitudinous and, without his drugs, would barely be able to raise his hand from his side through most of a normal day.

If the young emperor has found any advantage in his lifelong weakness it must be in that, perforce, he has read much. Before he was fifteen he had read every book in his father's library, some more than once. His sorcerous powers, learned initially from Sadric, are now greater than any possessed by his ancestors for many a generation. His knowledge of the world beyond the shores of Melniboné is profound, though he has as yet had little direct experience of it. If he wishes he could resurrect the Dragon Isle's former might and rule both his own land and the Young Kingdoms as an invulnerable tyrant. But his reading has also taught him to question the uses to which power is put, to question his motives, to question whether his own power should be used at all, in any cause. His reading has led him to this 'morality', which, still, he barely understands. Thus, to his subjects, he is an enigma and, to some, he is a threat, for he neither thinks nor acts in accordance with their conception of how a true Melnibonéan (and a Melnibonéan emperor, at that) should think and act. His cousin Yyrkoon, for instance, has been heard more than once to voice strong doubts concerning the emperor's right to rule the people of Melniboné. 'This feeble scholar will bring doom to us all,' he said one night to Dyvim Tvar, Lord of the Dragon Caves.

Dyvim Tvar is one of the emperor's few friends and he had duly reported the conversation, but the youth had dismissed the remarks as 'only a trivial treason', whereas any of his ancestors would have rewarded such sentiments with a very slow and exquisite public execution

The emperor's attitude is further complicated by the fact that Yyrkoon, who is even now making precious little secret of his feelings that he should be emperor, is the brother of Cymoril, a girl whom the albino considers the closest of his friends, and who will one day become his empress.

Down on the mosaic floor of the court Prince Yyrkoon can be seen in all his finest silks and furs, his jewels and his brocades, dancing with a hundred women, all of whom are rumoured to have been mistresses of his at one time or another. His dark features, at once handsome and saturnine, are framed by long black hair, waved and oiled, and his expression, as ever, is sardonic while his bearing is arrogant. The heavy brocade cloak swings this way and that, striking other dancers with some force. He wears it almost as if it is armour or, perhaps, a weapon. Amongst many of the courtiers there is more than a little respect for Prince Yyrkoon. Few resent his arrogance and those who do keep silent, for Yyrkoon is known to be a considerable sorcerer himself. Also his behaviour is what the court expects and welcomes in a Melnibonéan noble; it is what they would welcome in their emperor.

The emperor knows this. He wishes he could please his court as it strives to honour him with its dancing and its wit, but he cannot bring himself to take part in what he privately considers a wearisome and irritating sequence of ritual posturings. In this he is, perhaps, somewhat more arrogant than Yyrkoon who is, at least, a conventional boor.

From the galleries, the music grows louder and more complex as the slaves, specially trained and surgically operated upon to sing but one perfect note each, are stimulated to more passionate efforts. Even the young emperor is moved by the sinister harmony of their song which in few ways resembles anything previously uttered by the human voice. Why should their pain produce such marvellous beauty? he wonders. Or is all beauty created through pain? Is that the secret of great art, both human and Melnibonéan?

The Emperor Elric closes his eyes.

There is a stir in the hall below. The gates have opened and the dancing courtiers cease their motion, drawing back and bowing low as soldiers enter. The soldiers are clad all in light blue, their ornamental helms cast in fantastic shapes, their long, broad-bladed lances decorated with jewelled ribbons. They surround a young woman whose blue dress matches their uniforms and whose bare arms are encircled by five or six bracelets of diamonds, sapphires and gold. Strings of diamonds and sapphires are wound into her hair. Unlike most of the women of the court, her face has no designs painted upon the eyelids or cheekbones. Elric smiles. This is Cymoril. The soldiers are her personal ceremonial guard who, according to tradition, must escort her into the court. They ascend the steps leading to the Ruby Throne. Slowly Elric rises and stretches out his hands.

'Cymoril. I thought you had decided not to grace the court tonight?'

She returns his smile. 'My emperor, I found that I was in the mood for conversation, after all.'

Elric is grateful. She knows that he is bored and she knows, too, that she is one of the few people of Melniboné whose conversation interests him. If protocol allowed, he would offer her the throne, but as it is she must sit on the topmost step at his feet.

'Please sit, sweet Cymoril.' He resumes his place upon the throne and leans forward as she seats herself and looks into his eyes with a mixed expression of humour and tenderness. She speaks softly as her guard withdraws to mingle at the sides of the steps with Elric's own guard. Her voice can be heard only by Elric.

'Would you ride out to the wild region of the island with me tomorrow, my lord?'

'There are matters to which I must give my attention . . .' He is attracted by the idea. It is weeks since he left the city and rode with her, their escort keeping a discreet distance away.

'Are they urgent?'

He shrugs. 'What matters are urgent in Melniboné? After ten thousand years, most problems may be seen in a certain perspective.' His smile is almost a grin, rather like that of a young scholar who plans to play truant from his tutor. 'Very well—early in the morning, we'll leave, before the others are up.'

'The air beyond Imrryr will be clear and sharp. The sun will be warm for the season. The sky will be blue and unclouded.'

Elric laughs. 'Such sorcery you must have worked!'

Cymoril lowers her eyes and traces a pattern on the marble of the dais. 'Well, perhaps a little. I am not without friends among the weakest of the elementals . . .'

Elric stretches down to touch her fine, fair hair. 'Does Yyrkoon know?'

'No.'

Prince Yyrkoon has forbidden his sister to meddle in magical matters. Prince Yyrkoon's friends are only among the darker of the supernatural beings and he knows that they are dangerous to deal with; thus he assumes that all sorcerous dealings bear a similar element of danger. Besides this, he hates to think that others possess the power that he possesses. Perhaps this is what, in Elric, he hates most of all.

'Let us hope that all Melniboné needs fine weather for tomorrow,' says Elric. Cymoril stares curiously at him. She is still a Melnibonéan. It has not occurred to her that her sorcery might prove unwelcome to some. Then she shrugs her lovely shoulders and touches her lord lightly upon the hand.

'This "guilt",' she says. 'This searching of the conscience. Its purpose is beyond my simple brain.'

'And mine, I must admit. It seems to have no practical function. Yet more than one of our ancestors predicted a change in the nature of our earth. A spiritual as well as a physical change. Perhaps I have glimmerings of this change when I think my stranger, un-Melnibonéan, thoughts?'

The music swells. The music fades. The courtiers dance on, though many eyes are upon Elric and Cymoril as they talk at the top of the dais. There is speculation. When will Elric announce Cymoril as his empress-to-be? Will Elric revive the custom that Sadric dismissed, of sacrificing twelve brides and their bridegrooms to the Lords of Chaos in order to ensure a good marriage for the rulers of Melniboné? It was obvious that Sadric's refusal to allow the custom to continue brought misery upon him and death upon his wife; brought him a sickly son and threatened the very continuity of the monarchy. Elric must revive the custom. Even Elric must fear a repetition of the doom which visited his father. But some say that Elric will do nothing in accordance with tradition and that he threatens not only his own life, but the existence of Melniboné itself and all it stands for. And those who speak thus are often seen to be on good terms with Prince Yyrkoon who dances on, seemingly unaware of their conversation or, indeed, unaware that his sister talks quietly with the cousin who sits on the Ruby Throne; who sits on the edge of the seat, forgetful of his dignity, who exhibits none of the ferocious and disdainful pride which has, in the past, marked virtually every other emperor of Melniboné; who chats animatedly, forgetful that the court is supposed to be dancing for his entertainment.

And then suddenly Prince Yyrkoon freezes in midpirouette and raises his dark eyes to look up at his emperor. In one corner of the hall, Dyvim Tvar's attention is attracted by Yyrkoon's calculated and dramatic posture and the Lord of the Dragon Caves frowns. His hand falls to where his sword would normally be, but no swords are worn at a court ball. Dyvim Tvar looks warily and intently at Prince Yyrkoon as the tall nobleman begins to ascend the stairs to the Ruby Throne. Many eyes follow the emperor's cousin and now hardly anyone dances, though the music grows wilder as the masters of the music slaves goad their charges to even greater exertions.

Elric looks up to see Yyrkoon standing one step below that on which Cymoril sits. Yyrkoon makes a bow which is subtly insulting.

'I present myself to my emperor,' he says.

2 An Upstart Prince: He Confronts His Cousin

'And how do you enjoy the ball, cousin?' Elric asked, aware that Yyr-koon's melodramatic presentation had been designed to catch him off-guard and, if possible, humiliate him. 'Is the music to your taste?'

Yyrkoon lowered his eyes and let his lips form a secret little smile. 'Everything is to my taste, my liege. But what of yourself? Does something displease you? You do not join the dance.'

Elric raised one pale finger to his chin and stared at Yyrkoon's hidden eyes. 'I enjoy the dance, cousin, nonetheless. Surely it is possible to take pleasure in the pleasure of others?'

Yyrkoon seemed genuinely astonished. His eyes opened fully and met Elric's. Elric felt a slight shock and then turned his own gaze away, indicating the music galleries with a languid hand. 'Or perhaps it is the pain of others which brings me pleasure. Fear not, for my sake, cousin. I am pleased. I am pleased. You may dance on, assured that your emperor enjoys the ball.'

But Yyrkoon was not to be diverted from his object. 'Surely, if his subjects are not to go away saddened and troubled that they have not pleased their ruler, the emperor should demonstrate his enjoyment . . . ?'

'I would remind you, cousin,' said Elric quietly, 'that the emperor has no duty to his subjects at all, save to rule them. Their duty is to him. That is the tradition of Melniboné.'

Yyrkoon had not expected Elric to use such arguments against him, but he rallied with his next retort. 'I agree, my lord. The emperor's duty is to rule his subjects. Perhaps that is why so many of them do not, themselves, enjoy the ball as much as they might.'

'I do not follow you, cousin.'

Cymoril had risen and stood with her hands clenched on the step above her brother. She was tense and anxious, worried by her brother's bantering tone, his disdainful bearing.

'Yyrkoon . . .' she said.

He acknowledged her presence. 'Sister. I see you share our emperor's reluctance to dance.'

'Yyrkoon,' she murmured, 'you are going too far. The emperor is tolerant, but . . .'

'Tolerant? Or is he careless? Is he careless of the traditions of our great race? Is he contemptuous of that race's pride?'

Dyvim Tvar was now mounting the steps. It was plain that he, too, sensed that Yyrkoon had chosen this moment to test Elric's power.

Cymoril was aghast. She said urgently: 'Yyrkoon. If you would live . . .'

'I would not care to live if the soul of Melniboné perished. And the guardianship of our nation's soul is the responsibility of the emperor. And what if we should have an emperor who failed in that responsibility? An emperor who was weak? An emperor who cared nothing for the greatness of the Dragon Isle and its folk?'

'A hypothetical question, cousin.' Elric had recovered his composure and his voice was an icy drawl. 'For such an emperor has never sat upon the Ruby Throne and such an emperor never shall.'

Dyvim Tvar came up, touching Yyrkoon on the shoulder. 'Prince, if you value your dignity and your life . . .'

Elric raised his hand. 'There is no need for that, Dyvim Tvar. Prince Yyrkoon merely entertains us with an intellectual debate. Fearing that I was bored by the music and the dance—which I am not—he thought he would provide the subject for a stimulating discourse. I am certain that we are most stimulated, Prince Yyrkoon.' Elric allowed a patronising warmth to colour his last sentence.

Yyrkoon flushed with anger and bit his lip.

'But go on, dear cousin Yyrkoon,' Elric said. 'I am interested. Enlarge further on your argument.'

Yyrkoon looked around him, as if for support. But all his supporters were on the floor of the hall. Only Elric's friends, Dyvim Tvar and Cymoril, were nearby. Yet Yyrkoon knew that his supporters were hearing every word and that he would lose face if he did not retaliate. Elric could tell that Yyrkoon would have preferred to have retired from this confrontation and choose another day and another ground on which to continue the battle, but that was not possible. Elric, himself, had no wish to continue the foolish banter which was, no matter how disguised, a little better than the quarrelling of two little girls over who should play with the slaves first. He decided to make an end to it.

Yyrkoon began: 'Then let me suggest that an emperor who was physically weak might also be weak in his will to rule as befitted . . .'

And Elric raised his hand. 'You have done enough, dear cousin. More than enough. You have wearied yourself with this conversation when you would have preferred to dance. I am touched by your concern. But now I, too, feel weariness steal upon me.' Elric signaled for his old servant Tanglebones who stood on the far side of the throne dais, amongst the soldiers. 'Tanglebones! My cloak.'

Elric stood up. 'I thank you again for your thoughtfulness, cousin.' He addressed the court in general. 'I was entertained. Now I retire.'

Tanglebones brought the cloak of white fox fur and placed it around his master's shoulders. Tanglebones was very old and much taller than Elric, though his back was stooped and all his limbs seemed knotted and twisted back on themselves, like the limbs of a strong, old tree.

Elric walked across the dais and through the door which opened onto a corridor which led to his private apartments.

Yyrkoon was left fuming. He whirled round on the dais and opened his mouth as if to address the watching courtiers. Some, who did not support him, were smiling quite openly. Yyrkoon clenched his fists at his sides and glowered. He glared at Dyvim Tvar and opened his thin lips to speak. Dyvim Tvar coolly returned the glare, daring Yyrkoon to say more.

Then Yyrkoon flung back his head so that the locks of his hair, all curled and oiled, swayed against his back. And Yyrkoon laughed.

The harsh sound filled the hall. The music stopped. The laughter continued.

Yyrkoon stepped up so that he stood on the dais. He dragged his heavy cloak round him so that it engulfed his body.

Cymoril came forward. 'Yyrkoon, please do not . . .' He pushed her back with a motion of his shoulder.

Yyrkoon walked stiffly towards the Ruby Throne. It became plain that he was about to seat himself in it and thus perform one of the most traitorous actions possible in the code of Melniboné. Cymoril ran the few steps to him and pulled at his arm.

Yyrkoon's laughter grew. 'It is Yyrkoon they would wish to see on the Ruby Throne,' he told his sister. She gasped and looked in horror at Dyvim Tvar whose face was grim and angry.

Dyvim Tvar signed to the guards and suddenly there were two ranks of armoured men between Yyrkoon and the throne.

Yyrkoon glared back at the Lord of the Dragon Caves. 'You had best hope you perish with your master,' he hissed.

'This guard of honour will escort you from the hall,' Dyvim Tvar said evenly. 'We were all stimulated by your conversation this evening, Prince Yyrkoon.'

Yyrkoon paused, looked about him, then relaxed. He shrugged. 'There's time enough. If Elric will not abdicate, then he must be deposed.'

Cymoril's slender body was rigid. Her eyes blazed. She said to her brother:

'If you harm Elric in any way, I will slay you myself, Yyrkoon.'

He raised his tapering eyebrows and smiled. At that moment he seemed to hate his sister even more than he hated his cousin. 'Your loyalty to that creature has ensured your own doom, Cymoril. I would rather you died than that you should give birth to any progeny of his. I will not have the blood of our house diluted, tainted—even touched—by his blood. Look to your own life, sister, before you threaten mine.'

And he stormed down the steps, pushing through those who came up to congratulate him. He knew that he had lost and the murmurs of his sycophants only irritated him further.

The great doors of the hall crashed together and closed. Yyrkoon was gone from the hall.

Dyvim Tvar raised both his arms. 'Dance on, courtiers. Pleasure yourselves with all that the hall provides. It is what will please the emperor most.'

But it was plain there would be little more dancing done tonight. Courtiers were already deep in conversation as, excitedly, they debated the events.

Dyvim Tvar turned to Cymoril. 'Elric refuses to understand the danger, Princess Cymoril. Yyrkoon's ambition could bring disaster to all of us.'

'Including Yyrkoon.' Cymoril sighed.

'Aye, including Yyrkoon. But how can we avoid this, Cymoril, if Elric will not give orders for your brother's arrest?'

'He believes that such as Yyrkoon should be allowed to say what they please. It is part of his philosophy. I can barely understand it, but it seems integral to his whole belief. If he destroys Yyrkoon, he destroys the basis on which his logic works. That at any rate, Dragon Master, is what he has tried to explain to me.'

Dyvim Tvar sighed and he frowned. Though unable to understand Elric, he was afraid that he could sometimes sympathise with Yyrkoon's viewpoint. At least Yyrkoon's motives and arguments were relatively straightforward. He knew Elric's character too well, however, to believe that Elric acted from weakness or lassitude. The paradox was that Elric tolerated Yyrkoon's treachery because he was strong, because he had the power to destroy Yyrkoon whenever he cared. And Yyrkoon's own character was such that he must constantly be testing that strength of Elric's, for he knew instinctively that if Elric did weaken and order him slain, then he would have won. It was a complicated situation and Dyvim Tvar dearly wished that he was not embroiled in it. But his loyalty to the royal line of Melniboné was strong and his personal loyalty to Elric was great. He considered the idea of having Yyrkoon secretly assassinated, but he knew that such a plan would almost certainly come to nothing. Yyrkoon was a sorcerer of immense power and doubtless would be forewarned of any attempt on his life.

'Princess Cymoril,' said Dyvim Tvar, 'I can only pray that your brother swallows so much of his rage that it eventually poisons him.'

'I will join you in that prayer, Lord of the Dragon Caves.'

Together, they left the hall.

3 Riding Through the Morning: A Moment of Tranquillity

The light of the early morning touched the tall towers of Imrryr and made them scintillate. Each tower was of a different hue; there were a thousand soft colours. There were rose pinks and pollen yellows, there were purples and pale greens, mauves and browns and oranges, hazy blues, whites and powdery golds, all lovely in the sunlight. Two riders left the Dreaming City behind them and rode away from the walls, over the green turf towards a pine forest where, among the shadowy trunks, a little of the night seemed to remain. Squirrels were stirring and foxes crept homeward; birds were singing and forest flowers opened their petals and filled the air with delicate scent. A few insects wandered sluggishly aloft. The contrast between life in the nearby city and this lazy rusticity was very great and seemed to mirror some of the contrasts existing in the mind of at least one of the riders, who now dismounted and led his horse, walking knee-deep through a mass of blue flowers. The other rider, a girl, brought her own horse to a halt but did not dismount. Instead, she leaned casually on her high Melnibonéan pommel and smiled at the man, her lover.

'Elric? Would you stop so near to Imrryr?'

He smiled back at her, over his shoulder. 'For the moment. Our flight was hasty. I would collect my thoughts before we ride on.'

'How did you sleep last night?'

'Well enough, Cymoril, though I must have dreamed without knowing it, for there were—there were little intimations in my head when I awoke. But then, the meeting with Yyrkoon was not pleasant . . .'

'Do you think he plots to use sorcery against you?'

Elric shrugged. 'I would know if he brought a large sorcery against me. And he knows my power. I doubt if he would dare employ wizardry.'

'He has reason to believe you might not use your power. He has worried at your personality for so long—is there not a danger he will begin to worry at your skills? Testing your sorcery as he has tested your patience?'

Elric frowned. 'Yes, I suppose there is that danger. But not yet, I should have thought.'

'He will not be happy until you are destroyed, Elric.'

'Or is destroyed himself, Cymoril.' Elric stooped and picked one of the flowers. He smiled. 'Your brother is inclined to absolutes, is he not? How the weak hate weakness.'

Cymoril took his meaning. She dismounted and came towards him. Her thin gown matched, almost perfectly, the colour of the flowers through which she moved. He handed her the flower and she accepted it, touching its petals with her perfect lips. 'And how the strong hate strength, my love. Yyrkoon is my kin and yet I give you this advice— use your strength against him.'

'I could not slay him. I have not the right.' Elric's face fell into familiar, brooding lines.

'You could exile him.'

'Is not exile the same as death to a Melnibonéan?'

'You, yourself, have talked of travelling in the lands of the Young Kingdoms.'

Elric laughed somewhat bitterly. 'But perhaps I am not a true Melnibonéan. Yyrkoon has said as much—and others echo his thoughts.'

'He hates you because you are contemplative. Your father was contemplative and no one denied that he was a fitting emperor.'

'My father chose not to put the results of his contemplation into his personal actions. He ruled as an emperor should. Yyrkoon, I must admit, would also rule as an emperor should. He, too, has the opportunity to make Melniboné great again. If he were emperor, he would embark on a campaign of conquest to restore our trade to its former volume, to extend our power across the earth. And that is what the majority of our folk would wish. Is it my right to deny that wish?'

'It is your right to do what you think, for you are the emperor. All who are loyal to you think as I do.'

'Perhaps their loyalty is misguided. Perhaps Yyrkoon is right and I will betray that loyalty, bring doom to the Dragon Isle?' His moody, crimson eyes looked directly into hers. 'Perhaps I should have died as I left my mother's womb. Then Yyrkoon would have become emperor. Has Fate been thwarted?'

'Fate is never thwarted. What has happened has happened because Fate willed it thus—if, indeed, there is such a thing as Fate and if men's actions are not merely a response to other men's actions.'

Elric drew a deep breath and offered her an expression tinged with irony. 'Your logic leads you close to heresy, Cymoril, if we are to believe the traditions of Melniboné. Perhaps it would be better if you forgot your friendship with me.'

She laughed. 'You begin to sound like my brother. Are you testing my love for you, my lord?'

He began to remount his horse. 'No, Cymoril, but I would advise you to test your love yourself, for I sense there is tragedy implicit in our love.'

As she swung herself back into her saddle she smiled and shook her head. 'You see doom in all things. Can you not accept the good gifts granted you? They are few enough, my lord.'

'Aye. I'll agree with that.'

They turned in their saddles, hearing hoofbeats behind them. Some distance away they saw a company of yellow-clad horsemen riding about in confusion. It was their guard, which they had left behind, wishing to ride alone.

'Come!' cried Elric. 'Through the woods and over yonder hill and they'll never find us!'

They spurred their steeds through the sun-speared wood and up the steep sides of the hill beyond, racing down the other side and away across a plain where noidel bushes grew, their lush, poison fruit glimmering a purplish blue, a night-colour which even the light of day could not disperse. There were many such peculiar berries and herbs on Melniboné and it was to some of them that Elric owed his life. Others were used for sorcerous potions and had been sown generations before by Elric's ancestors. Now few Melnibonéans left Imrryr even to collect these harvests. Only slaves visited the greater part of the island, seeking the roots and the shrubs which made men dream monstrous and magnificent dreams, for it was in their dreams that the nobles of Melniboné found most of their pleasures; they had ever been a moody, inward-looking race and it was for this quality that Imrryr had come to be named the Dreaming City. There, even the meanest slaves chewed berries to bring them oblivion and thus were easily controlled, for they came to depend on their dreams. Only Elric himself refused such drugs, perhaps because he required so many others simply to ensure his remaining alive.

The yellow-clad guards were lost behind them and once across the plain where the noidel bushes grew they slowed their flight and came at length to cliffs and then the sea.

The sea shone brightly and languidly washed the white beaches below the cliffs. Seabirds wheeled in the clear sky and their cries were distant, serving only to emphasise the sense of peace which both Elric and Cymoril now had. In silence the lovers guided their horses down steep paths to the shore and there they tethered the steeds and began to walk across the sand, their hair—his white, hers jet black—waving in the wind which blew from the east.

They found a great, dry cave which caught the sounds the sea made and replied in a whispering echo. They removed their silken garments and made love tenderly in the shadows of the cave. They lay in each other's arms as the day warmed and the wind dropped. Then they went to bathe in the waters, filling the empty sky with their laughter.

When they were dry and were dressing themselves they noticed a darkening of the horizon and Elric said: 'We shall be wet again before we return to Imrryr. No matter how fast we ride, the storm will catch us.'

'Perhaps we should remain in the cave until it is past?' she suggested, coming close and holding her soft body against him.

'No,' he said. 'I must return soon, for there are potions in Imrryr I must take if my body is to retain its strength. An hour or two longer and I shall begin to weaken. You have seen me weak before, Cymoril.'

She stroked his face and her eyes were sympathetic. 'Aye. I've seen you weak before, Elric. Come, let's find the horses.'

By the time they reached the horses the sky was grey overhead and full of boiling blackness not far away in the east. They heard the grumble of thunder and the crash of lightning. The sea was threshing as if infected by the sky's hysteria. The horses snorted and pawed at the sand, anxious to return. Even as Elric and Cymoril climbed into their saddles large spots of rain began to fall on their heads and spread over their cloaks.

Then, suddenly, they were riding at full tilt back to Imrryr while the lightning flashed around them and the thunder roared like a furious giant, like some great old Lord of Chaos attempting to break through, unbidden, into the Realm of Earth.

Cymoril glanced at Elric's pale face, illuminated for a moment by a flash of sky-fire, and she felt a chill come upon her then and the chill had nothing to do with the wind or the rain, for it seemed to her in that second that the gentle scholar she loved had been transformed by the elements into a hell-driven demon, into a monster with barely a semblance of humanity. His crimson eyes had flared from the whiteness of his skull like the very flames of the Higher Hell; his hair had been whipped upward so that it had become the crest of a sinister warhelm and, by a trick of the stormlight, his mouth had seemed twisted in a mixture of rage and agony.

And suddenly Cymoril knew.

She knew, profoundly, that their morning's ride was the last moment of peace the two of them would ever experience again. The storm was a sign from the gods themselves—a warning of storms to come.

She looked again at her lover. Elric was laughing. He had turned his face upward so that the warm rain fell upon it, so that the water splashed into his open mouth. The laughter was the easy, unsophisticated laughter of a happy child.

Cymoril tried to laugh back, but then she had to turn her face away so that he should not see it. For Cymoril had begun to weep.

She was weeping still when Imrryr came in sight—a black and grotesque silhouette against a line of brightness which was the as yet untainted western horizon.

4   Prisoners: Their Secrets
Are Taken from Them

The men in yellow armour saw Elric and Cymoril as the two approached the smallest of the eastern gates.

'They have found us at last,' smiled Elric through the rain, 'but somewhat belatedly, eh, Cymoril?'

Cymoril, still embattled with her sense of doom, merely nodded and tried to smile in reply.

Elric took this as an expression of disappointment, nothing more, and called to his guards: 'Ho, men! Soon we shall all be dry again!'

But the captain of the guard rode up urgently, crying: 'My lord emperor is needed at Monshanjik Tower where spies are held.'

'Spies?'

'Aye, my lord.' The man's face was pale. Water cascaded from his helm and darkened his thin cloak. His horse was hard to control and kept sidestepping through pools of water, which had gathered wherever the road was in disrepair. 'Caught in the maze this morning. Southern barbarians, by their chequered dress. We are holding them until the emperor himself can question them.'

Elric waved his hand. 'Then lead on, captain. Let's see the brave fools who dare Melniboné's sea-maze.'

The tower of Monshanjik had been named for the wizard-architect who had designed the sea-maze millennia before. The maze was the only means of reaching the great harbour of Imrryr and its secrets had been carefully guarded, for it was their greatest protection against sudden attack. The maze was complicated and pilots had to be specially trained to steer ships through it. Before the maze had been built, the harbour had been a kind of inland lagoon, fed by the sea which swept in through a system of natural caverns in the towering cliff which rose between lagoon and ocean. There were five separate routes through the sea-maze

and any individual pilot knew but one. In the outer wall of the cliff
there were five entrances. Here Young Kingdom ships waited until a
pilot came aboard. Then one of the gates to one of the entrances would
be lifted, all aboard the ship would be blindfolded and sent below save
for the oar-master and the steersman who would also be masked in
heavy steel helms so that they could see nothing, do nothing but obey
the complicated instructions of the pilot. And if a Young Kingdom ship
should fail to obey any of those instructions and should crush itself
against the rock walls, well Melniboné did not mourn for it and any
survivors from the crew would be taken as slaves. All who sought to
trade with the Dreaming City understood the risks, but scores of merchants came every month to dare the dangers of the maze and trade
their own poor goods for the splendid riches of Melniboné.

The Tower of Monshanjik stood overlooking the harbour and the
massive mole which jutted out into the middle of the lagoon. It was a
sea-green tower and was squat compared with most of those in Imrryr,
though still a beautiful and tapering construction, with wide windows
so that the whole of the harbour could be seen from it. From Monshanjik Tower most of the business of the harbour was done and in its
lower cellars were kept any prisoners who had broken any of the myriad rules governing the functioning of the harbour. Leaving Cymoril to
return to the palace with a guard, Elric entered the tower, riding
through the great archway at the base, scattering not a few merchants
who were waiting for permission to begin their bartering, for the whole
of the ground floor was full of sailors, merchants and Melnibonéan
officials engaged in the business of trade, though it was not here that the
actual wares were displayed. The great echoing babble of a thousand
voices engaged in a thousand separate aspects of bargaining slowly
stilled as Elric and his guard rode arrogantly through to another dark
arch at the far end of the hall. This arch opened onto a ramp which
sloped and curved down into the bowels of the tower.

Down this ramp clattered the horsemen, passing slaves, servants and
officials who stepped hastily aside, bowing low as they recognised the
emperor. Great brands illuminated the tunnel, guttering and smoking
and casting distorted shadows onto the smooth, obsidian walls. A chill
was in the air now, and a dampness, for water washed about the outer
walls below the quays of Imrryr. And still the emperor rode on and still
the ramp struck lower through the glassy rock. And then a wave of heat
rose to meet them and shifting light could be seen ahead and they
passed into a chamber that was full of smoke and the scent of fear.
From the low ceiling hung chains and from eight of the chains, swinging by their feet, hung four people. Their clothes had been torn from

them, but their bodies were clothed in blood from tiny wounds, precise but severe, made by the artist who stood, scalpel in hand, surveying his handiwork.

The artist was tall and very thin, almost like a skeleton in his stained, white garments. His lips were thin, his eyes were slits, his fingers were thin, his hair was thin and the scalpel he held was thin, too, almost invisible save when it flashed in the light from the fire which erupted from a pit on the far side of the cavern. The artist was named Doctor Jest and the art he practised was a performing art rather than a creative one (though he could argue otherwise with some conviction): the art of drawing secrets from those who kept them. Doctor Jest was the Chief Interrogator of Melniboné. He turned sinuously as Elric entered, the scalpel held between the thin thumb and the thin forefinger of his right hand; he stood poised and expectant, almost like a dancer, and then bowed from the waist.

'My sweet emperor!' His voice was thin. It rushed from his thin throat as if bent on escape and one was inclined to wonder if one had heard the words at all, so quickly had they come and gone.

'Doctor. Are these the southlanders caught this morning?'

'Indeed they are, my lord.' Another sinuous bow. 'For your pleasure.'

Coldly Elric inspected the prisoners. He felt no sympathy for them. They were spies. Their actions had led them to this pass. They had known what would happen to them if caught. But one of them was a boy and another a woman, it appeared, though they writhed so in their chains it was quite difficult to tell at first. It seemed a shame. Then the woman snapped what remained of her teeth at him and hissed: 'Demon!' And Elric stepped back, saying:

'Have they informed you of what they were doing in our maze, doctor?'

'They still tantalise me with hints. They have a fine sense of drama. I appreciate that. They are here, I would say, to map a route through the maze which a force of raiders might then follow. But they have so far withheld the details. That is the game. We all understand how it must be played.'

'And when will they tell you, Doctor Jest?'

'Oh, very soon, my lord.'

'It would be best to know if we are to expect attackers. The sooner we know, the less time we shall lose dealing with the attack when it comes. Do you not agree, doctor?'

'I do, my lord.'

'Very well.' Elric was irritated by this break in his day. It had spoile the pleasure of the ride, it had brought him face to face with his duties too quickly.

Doctor Jest returned to his charges and, reaching out with his free hand, expertly seized the genitals of one of the male prisoners. The scalpel flashed. There was a groan. Doctor Jest tossed something onto the fire. Elric sat in the chair prepared for him. He was bored rather than disgusted by the rituals attendant upon the gathering of information and the discordant screams, the clash of the chains, the thin whisperings of Doctor Jest, all served to ruin the feeling of well-being he had retained even as he reached the chamber. But it was one of his kingly duties to attend such rituals and attend this one he must until the information was presented to him and he could congratulate his Chief Interrogator and issue orders as to the means of dealing with any attack and even when that was over he must confer with admirals and with generals, probably through the rest of the night, choosing between arguments, deciding on the deposition of men and ships. With a poorly disguised yawn he leaned back and watched as Doctor Jest ran fingers and scalpel, tongue, tongs and pincers over the bodies. He was soon thinking of other matters: philosophical problems which he had still failed to resolve.

It was not that Elric was inhumane; it was that he was, still, a Melnibonéan. He had been used to such sights since childhood. He could not have saved the prisoners, even if he had desired, without going against every tradition of the Dragon Isle. And in this case it was a simple matter of a threat being met by the best methods available. He had become used to shutting off those feelings which conflicted with his duties as emperor. If there had been any point in freeing the four who danced now at Doctor Jest's pleasure he would have freed them, but there was no point and the four would have been astonished if they had received any other treatment than this. Where moral decisions were concerned Elric was, by and large, practical. He would make his decision in the context of what action he could take. In this case, he could take no action. Such a reaction had become second nature to him. His desire was not to reform Melniboné but to reform himself, not to initiate action but to know the best way of responding to the actions of others. Here, the decision was easy to make. A spy was an aggressor. One defended oneself against aggressors in the best possible way. The methods employed by Doctor Jest were the best methods.

'My lord?'

Absently, Elric looked up.

'We have the information now, my lord.' Doctor Jest's thin voice whispered across the chamber. Two sets of chains were now empty and slaves were gathering things up from the floor and flinging them on the fire. The two remaining shapeless lumps reminded Elric of meat carefully prepared by a chef. One of the lumps still quivered a little, but the other was still.

Doctor Jest slid his instruments into a thin case he carried in a pouch at his belt. His white garments were almost completely covered in stains.

'It seems there have been other spies before these,' Doctor Jest told his master. 'These came merely to confirm the route. If they do not return in time, the barbarians will still sail.'

'But surely they will know that we expect them?' Elric said.

'Probably not, my lord. Rumours have been spread amongst the Young Kingdom merchants and sailors that four spies were seen in the maze and were speared—slain whilst trying to escape.'

'I see.' Elric frowned. 'Then our best plan will be to lay a trap for the raiders.'

'Aye, my lord.'

'You know the route they have chosen?'

'Aye, my lord.'

Elric turned to one of his guards. 'Have messages sent to all our generals and admirals. What's the hour?'

'The hour of sunset is just past, my liege.'

'Tell them to assemble before the Ruby Throne at two hours past sunset.'

Wearily, Elric rose. 'You have done well, as usual, Doctor Jest.'

The thin artist bowed low, seeming to fold himself in two. A thin and somewhat unctuous sigh was his reply.

5   A Battle: The King
Proves His War-Skill

Yyrkoon was the first to arrive, all clad in martial finery, accompanied by two massive guards, each holding one of the prince's ornate war-banners.

'My emperor!' Yyrkoon's shout was proud and disdainful. 'Would you let me command the warriors? It will relieve you of that care when, doubtless, you have many other concerns with which to occupy your time.'

Elric replied impatiently: 'You are most thoughtful, Prince Yyrkoon, but fear not for me. I shall command the armies and the navies of Melniboné, for that is the duty of the emperor.'

Yyrkoon glowered and stepped to one side as Dyvim Tvar, Lord of the Dragon Caves, entered. He had no guard whatsoever with him and it seemed he had dressed hastily. He carried his helmet under his arm.

'My emperor—I bring news of the dragons . . .'

'I thank you, Dyvim Tvar, but wait until all my commanders are assembled and impart that news to them, too.'

Dyvim Tvar bowed and went to stand on the opposite side of the hall to that on which Prince Yyrkoon stood.

Gradually the warriors arrived until a score of great captains waited at the foot of the steps which led to the Ruby Throne where Elric sat. Elric himself still wore the clothes in which he had gone riding that morning. He had not had time to change and had until a little while before been consulting maps of the maze—maps which only he could read and which, at normal times, were hidden by magical means from any who might attempt to find them.

'Southlanders would steal Imrryr's wealth and slay us all,' Elric began. 'They believe they have found a way through our sea-maze. A fleet of a hundred warships sails on Melniboné even now. Tomorrow it will wait below the horizon until dusk, then it will sail to the maze and enter. By midnight it expects to reach the harbour and to have taken the Dreaming City before dawn. Is that possible, I wonder?'

'No!' Many spoke the single word.

'No.' Elric smiled. 'But how shall we best enjoy this little war they offer us?'

Yyrkoon, as ever, was first to shout. 'Let us go to meet them now, with dragons and with battle-barges. Let us pursue them to their own land and take their war to them. Let us attack their nations and burn their cities! Let us conquer them and thus ensure our own security!'

Dyvim Tvar spoke up again:

'No dragons,' he said.

'What?' Yyrkoon whirled. 'What?'

'No dragons, prince. They will not be awakened. The dragons sleep in their caverns, exhausted by their last engagement on your behalf.'

'Mine?'

'You would use them in our conflict with the Vilmirian pirates. I told you that I would prefer to save them for a larger engagement. But you flew them against the pirates and you burned their little boats and now the dragons sleep.'

Yyrkoon glowered. He looked up at Elric. 'I did not expect . . .'

Elric raised his hand. 'We need not use our dragons until such a time as we really need them. This attack from the southlander fleet is nothing. But we will conserve our strength if we bide our time. Let them think we are unready. Let them enter the maze. Once the whole hundred are through, we close in, blocking off all routes in or out of the maze. Trapped, they will be crushed by us.'

Yyrkoon looked pettishly at his feet, evidently wishing he could think of some flaw in the plan. Tall, old Admiral Magum Colim in his seagreen armour stepped forward and bowed. 'The golden battle-barges of Imrryr are ready to defend their city, my liege. It will take time, however, to manoeuvre them into position. It is doubtful if all will fit into the maze at once.'

'Then sail some of them out now and hide them around the coast, so that they can wait for any survivors that may escape our attack,' Elric instructed him.

'A useful plan, my liege.' Magum Colim bowed and sank back into the crowd of his peers.

The debate continued for some time and then they were ready and about to leave. But then Prince Yyrkoon bellowed once more:

'I repeat my offer to the emperor. His person is too valuable to risk in battle. My person—it is worthless. Let me command the warriors of both land and sea while the emperor may remain at the palace, untroubled by the battle, confident that it will be won and the south-landers trounced—perhaps there is a book he wishes to finish?'

Elric smiled. 'Again I thank you for your concern, Prince Yyrkoon. But an emperor must exercise his body as well as his mind. I will command the warriors tomorrow.'

When Elric arrived back at his apartments it was to discover that Tanglebones had already laid out his heavy, black wargear. Here was the armour which had served a hundred Melnibonéan emperors; an armour which was forged by sorcery to give it a strength unequalled on the Realm of Earth, which could, so rumour went, even withstand the bite of the mythical runeblades, Stormbringer and Mournblade, which had been wielded by the wickedest of Melniboné's many wicked rulers before being seized by the Lords of the Higher Worlds and hidden forever in a realm where even those Lords might rarely venture.

The face of the tangled man was full of joy as he touched each piece of armour, each finely balanced weapon, with his long, gnarled fingers. His seamed face looked up to regard Elric's care-ravaged features. 'Oh, my lord! Oh, my king! Soon you will know the joy of the fight!'

'Aye, Tanglebones—and let us hope it will be a joy.'

'I taught you all the skills—the art of the sword and the poignard—the art of the bow—the art of the spear, both mounted and on foot. And you learned well, for all they say you are weak. Save one, there's no better swordsman in Melniboné.'

'Prince Yyrkoon could be better than me,' Elric said reflectively. 'Could he not?'

'I said "save one", my lord.'

'And Yyrkoon is that one. Well, one day perhaps we'll be able to test the matter. I'll bathe before I don all that metal.'

'Best make speed, master. From what I hear, there is much to do.'

'And I'll sleep after I've bathed.' Elric smiled at his old friend's consternation. 'It will be better thus, for I cannot personally direct the barges into position. I am needed to command the fray—and that I will do better when I've rested.'

'If you think it good, lord king, then it is good.'

'And you are astonished. You are too eager, Tanglebones, to get me into all that stuff and see me strut about in it as if I were Arioch himself . . .'

Tanglebones's hand flew to his mouth as if he had spoken the words, not his master, and he was trying to block them. His eyes widened.

Elric laughed. 'You think I speak bold heresies, eh? Well, I've spoken worse without any ill befalling me. On Melniboné, Tanglebones, the emperors control the demons, not the reverse.'

'So you say, my liege.'

'It is the truth.' Elric swept from the room, calling for his slaves. The war-fever filled him and he was jubilant.

Now he was in all his black gear: the massive breastplate, the padded jerkin, the long greaves, the mail gauntlets. At his side was a five-foot broadsword which, it was said, had belonged to a human hero called Aubec. Resting on the deck against the golden rail of the bridge was the great round warboard, his shield, bearing the sign of the swooping dragon. And a helm was on his head; a black helm, with a dragon's head craning over the peak, and dragon's wings flaring backward above it, and a dragon's tail curling down the back. All the helm was black, but within the helm there was a white shadow from which glared two crimson orbs, and from the sides of the helm strayed wisps of milk-white hair, almost like smoke escaping from a burning building. And, as the helm turned in what little light came from the lantern hanging at the base of the mainmast, the white shadow sharpened to reveal features —fine, handsome features—a straight nose, curved lips, up-slanting eyes. The face of Emperor Elric of Melniboné peered into the gloom of the maze as he listened for the first sounds of the sea-raiders' approach.

He stood on the high bridge of the great golden battle-barge which, like all its kind, resembled a floating ziggurat equipped with masts and sails and oars and catapults. The ship was called *The Son of the Pyaray* and it was the flagship of the fleet. The Grand Admiral Magum Colim stood beside Elric. Like Dyvim Tvar, the admiral was one of Elric's few close friends. He had known Elric all his life and had encouraged him to learn all he could concerning the running of fighting ships and fighting fleets. Privately Magum Colim might fear that Elric was too scholarly and introspective to rule Melniboné, but he accepted Elric's right to rule and was made angry and impatient by the talk of the likes of Yyrkoon. Prince Yyrkoon was also aboard the flagship, though at this moment he was below, inspecting the war-engines.

The Son of the Pyaray lay at anchor in a huge grotto, one of hundreds built into the walls of the maze when the maze itself was built, and designed for just this purpose—to hide a battle-barge. There was just enough height for the masts and enough width for the oars to move freely. Each of the golden battle-barges was equipped with banks of oars, each bank containing between twenty and thirty oars on either side. The banks were four, five or six decks high and, as in the case of *The Son of the Pyaray,* might have three independent steering systems, fore and aft. Being armoured all in gold, the ships were virtually inde-structible, and, for all their massive size, they could move swiftly and manoeuvre delicately when occasion demanded. It was not the first time they had waited for their enemies in these grottoes. It would not be the last (though when next they waited it would be in greatly different circumstances).

The battle-barges of Melniboné were rarely seen on the open seas these days, but once they had sailed the oceans of the world like fearsome floating mountains of gold and they had brought terror whenever they were sighted. The fleet had been larger then, comprising hundreds of craft. Now there were less than forty ships. But forty would suffice. Now, in damp darkness, they awaited their enemies.

Listening to the hollow slap of the water against the sides of the ship, Elric wished that he had been able to conceive a better plan than this. He was sure that this one would work, but he regretted the waste of lives, both Melnibonéan and barbarian. It would have been better if some way could have been devised of frightening the barbarians away rather than trapping them in the sea-maze. The southlander fleet was not the first to have been attracted by Imrryr's fabulous wealth. The southlander crews were not the first to entertain the belief that the Melnibonéans, because they never now ventured far from the Dreaming City, had become decadent and unable to defend their treasures. And so the southlanders must be destroyed in order to make the lesson clear. Melniboné was still strong. She was strong enough, in Yyrkoon's view, to resume her former dominance of the world—strong in sorcery if not in soldiery.

'Hist!' Admiral Magum Colim craned forward. 'Was that the sound of an oar?'

Elric nodded. 'I think so.'

Now they heard regular splashes, as of rows of oars dipping in and out of the water, and they heard the creak of timbers. The southlanders were coming. *The Son of the Pyaray* was the ship nearest to the entrance and it would be the first to move out, but only when the last of the southlanders' ships had passed them. Admiral Magum Colim bent and extinguished the lantern, then, quickly, quietly, he descended to inform his crew of the raiders' coming.

Not long before, Yyrkoon had used his sorcery to summon a peculiar mist, which hid the golden barges from view, but through which those on the Melnibonéan ships could peer. Now Elric saw torches burning in the channel ahead as carefully the reavers negotiated the maze. Within the space of a few minutes ten of the galleys had passed the grotto. Admiral Magum Colim rejoined Elric on the bridge and now Prince Yyrkoon was with him. Yyrkoon, too, wore a dragon helm, though less magnificent than Elric's, for Elric was chief of the few surviving Dragon

Princes of Melniboné. Yyrkoon was grinning through the gloom and his eyes gleamed in anticipation of the bloodletting to come. Elric wished that Prince Yyrkoon had chosen another ship than this, but it was Yyrkoon's right to be aboard the flagship and he could not deny it.

Now half the hundred vessels had gone past.

Yyrkoon's armour creaked as, impatiently, he waited, pacing the bridge, his gauntletted hand on the hilt of his broadsword. 'Soon' he kept saying to himself. 'Soon.'

And then their anchor was groaning upwards and their oars were plunging into the water as the last southland ship went by and they shot from the grotto into the channel ramming the enemy galley amidships and smashing it in two.

A great yell went up from the barbarian crew. Men were flung in all directions. Torches danced erratically on the remains of the deck as men tried to save themselves from slipping into the dark, chill waters of the channel. A few brave spears rattled against the sides of the Melnibonéan flag-galley as it began to turn amongst the debris it had created. But Imrryrian archers returned the shots and the few survivors went down.

The sound of this swift conflict was the signal to the other battle-barges. In perfect order they came from both sides of the high rock walls and it must have seemed to the astonished barbarians that the great golden ships had actually emerged from solid stone—ghost ships filled with demons who rained spears, arrows and brands upon them. Now the whole of the twisting channel was confusion and a medley of war-shouts echoed and boomed and the clash of steel upon steel was like the savage hissing of some monstrous snake, and the raiding fleet itself resembled a snake which had been broken into a hundred pieces by the tall, implacable golden ships of Melniboné. These ships seemed almost serene as they moved against their enemies, their grappling irons flashing out to catch wooden decks and rails and draw the galleys nearer so that they might be destroyed.

But the southlanders were brave and they kept their heads after their initial astonishment. Three of their galleys headed directly for *The Son of the Pyaray,* recognising it as the flagship. Fire arrows sailed high and dropped down into the decks which were wooden and not protected by the golden armour, starting fires wherever they fell, or else bringing blazing death to the men they struck.

Elric raised his shield above his head and two arrows struck it, bouncing, still flaring, to a lower deck. He leapt over the rail, following the arrows, jumping down to the widest and most exposed deck where his warriors were grouping, ready to deal with the attacking galleys.

Catapults thudded and balls of blue fire swished through the blackness, narrowly missing all three galleys. Another volley followed and one mass of flame struck the far galley's mast and then burst upon the deck, scattering huge flames wherever it touched. Grapples snaked out and seized the first galley, dragging it close and Elric was amongst the first to leap down onto the deck, rushing forward to where he saw the southland captain, dressed all in crude, chequered armour, a chequered surcoat over that, a big sword in both his huge hands, bellowing at his men to resist the Melnibonéan dogs.

As Elric approached the bridge three barbarians armed with curved swords and small, oblong shields ran at him. Their faces were full of fear, but there was determination there as well, as if they knew they must die but planned to wreak as much destruction as they could before their souls were taken.

Shifting his war-board onto his arm, Elric took his own broadsword in both hands and charged the sailors, knocking one off his feet with the lip of the shield and smashing the collar-bone of another. The remaining barbarian skipped aside and thrust his curved sword at Elric's face. Elric barely escaped the thrust and the sharp edge of the sword grazed his cheek, bringing out a drop or two of blood. Elric swung the broadsword like a scythe and it bit deep into the barbarian's waist, almost cutting him in two. He struggled for a moment, unable to believe that he was dead but then, as Elric yanked the sword free, he closed his eyes and dropped. The man who had been struck by Elric's shield was staggering to his feet as Elric whirled, saw him, and smashed the broadsword into his skull. Now the way was clear to the bridge. Elric began to climb the ladder, noting that the captain had seen him and was waiting for him at the top.

Elric raised his shield to take the captain's first blow. Through all the noise he thought he heard the man shouting at him.

'Die, you white-faced demon! Die! You have no place in this earth any longer!'

Elric was almost diverted from defending himself by these words. They rang true to him. Perhaps he really had no place on the earth. Perhaps that was why Melniboné was slowly collapsing, why fewer children were born every year, why the dragons themselves were no longer breeding. He let the captain strike another blow at the shield, then he reached under it and swung at the man's legs. But the captain had anticipated the move and jumped backwards. This, however, gave Elric time to run up the few remaining steps and stand on the deck, facing the captain.

The man's face was almost as pale as Elric's. He was sweating and he was panting and his eyes had misery in them as well as a wild fear.

'You should leave us alone,' Elric heard himself saying. 'We offer you no harm, barbarian. When did Melniboné last sail against the Young Kingdoms?'

'You offer us harm by your very presence, Whiteface. There is your sorcery. There are your customs. And there is your arrogance.'

'Is that why you came here? Was your attack motivated by disgust for us? Or would you help yourselves to our wealth? Admit it, captain—greed brought you to Melniboné.'

'At least greed is an honest quality, an understandable one. But you creatures are not human. Worse—you are not gods, though you behave as if you were. Your day is over and you must be wiped out, your city destroyed, your sorceries forgotten.'

Elric nodded. 'Perhaps you are right, captain.'

'I am right. Our holy men say so. Our seers predict your downfall. The Chaos Lords whom you serve will themselves bring about that downfall.'

'The Chaos Lords no longer have any interest in the affairs of Melniboné. They took away their power nearly a thousand years since.' Elric watched the captain carefully, judging the distance between them. 'Perhaps that is why our own power waned. Or perhaps we merely became tired of power.'

'Be that as it may,' the captain said, wiping his sweating brow, 'your time is over. You must be destroyed once and for all.' And then he groaned, for Elric's broadsword had come under his chequered breastplate and gone up through his stomach and into his lungs.

One knee bent, one leg stretched behind him, Elric began to withdraw the long sword, looking up into the barbarian's face which had now assumed an expression of reconciliation. 'That was unfair, Whiteface. We had barely begun to talk and you cut the conversation short. You are most skillful. May you writhe forever in the Higher Hell. Farewell.'

Elric hardly knew why, after the captain had fallen face down on the deck, he hacked twice at the neck until the head rolled off the body, rolled to the side of the bridge and was then kicked over the side so that it sank into the cold, deep water.

And then Yyrkoon came up behind Elric and he was still grinning.

'You fight fiercely and well, my lord emperor. That dead man was right.'

'Right?' Elric glared at his cousin. 'Right?'

'Aye—in his assessment of your prowess.' And, chuckling, Yyrkoon went to supervise his men who were finishing off the few remaining raiders.

Elric did not know why he had refused to hate Yyrkoon before. But now he did hate Yyrkoon. At that moment he would gladly have slain him. It was as if Yyrkoon had looked deeply into Elric's soul and expressed contempt for what he had seen there.

Suddenly Elric was overwhelmed by an angry misery and he wished with all his heart that he was not a Melnibonéan, that he was not an emperor and that Yyrkoon had never been born.

6   Pursuit: A Deliberate Treachery

Like haughty Leviathans the great golden battle-barges swam through the wreckage of the reaver fleet. A few ships burned and a few were still sinking, but most had sunk into the unplumbable depths of the channel. The burning ships sent strange shadows dancing against the dank walls of the sea-caverns, as if the ghosts of the slain offered a last salute before departing to the sea-depths where, it was said, a Chaos king still ruled, crewing his eerie fleets with the souls of all who died in conflict upon the oceans of the world. Or perhaps they went to a gentler doom, serving Straasha, Lord of the Water Elementals, who ruled the upper reaches of the sea.

But a few had escaped. Somehow the southland sailors had got past the massive battle-barges, sailed back through the channel and must even now have reached the open sea. This was reported to the flagship where Elric, Magum Colim and Prince Yyrkoon now stood together again on the bridge, surveying the destruction they had wreaked.

'Then we must pursue them and finish them,' said Yyrkoon. He was sweating and his dark face glistened; his eyes were alight with fever. 'We must follow them.'

Elric shrugged. He was weak. He had brought no extra drugs with him to replenish his strength. He wished to go back to Imrryr and rest. He was tired of bloodletting, tired of Yyrkoon and tired, most of all, of himself. The hatred he felt for his cousin was draining him still further —and he hated the hatred; that was the worst part. 'No,' he said. 'Let them go.'

'Let them go? Unpunished? Come now, my lord king! That is not our way!' Prince Yyrkoon turned to the aging admiral. 'Is that our way, Admiral Magum Colim?'

Magum Colim shrugged. He, too, was tired, but privately he agreed with Prince Yyrkoon. An enemy of Melniboné should be punished for daring even to think of attacking the Dreaming City. Yet he said: 'The emperor must decide.'

'Let them go,' said Elric again. He leant heavily against the rail. 'Let them carry the news back to their own barbarian land. Let them say how the Dragon Princes defeated them. The news will spread. I believe we shall not be troubled by raiders again for some time.'

'The Young Kingdoms are full of fools,' Yyrkoon replied. 'They will not believe the news. There will always be raiders. The best way to warn them will be to make sure that not one southlander remains alive or uncaptured.'

Elric drew a deep breath and tried to fight the faintness which threatened to overwhelm him. 'Prince Yyrkoon, you are trying my patience . . .'

'But, my emperor, I think only of the good of Melniboné. Surely you do not want your people to say that you are weak, that you fear a fight with but five southland galleys?'

This time Elric's anger brought him strength. 'Who will say that Elric is weak? Will it be you, Yyrkoon?' He knew that his next statement was senseless, but there was nothing he could do to stop it. 'Very well, let us pursue these poor little boats and sink them. And let us make haste. I am weary of it all.'

There was a mysterious light in Yyrkoon's eyes as he turned away to relay the orders.

The sky was turning from black to grey when the Melnibonéan fleet reached the open sea and turned its prows south towards the Boiling Sea and the southern continent beyond. The barbarian ships would not sail through the Boiling Sea—no mortal ship could do that, it was said —but would sail around it. Not that the barbarian ships would even reach the edges of the Boiling Sea, for the huge battle-barges were fast-sailing vessels. The slaves who pulled the oars were full of a drug which increased their speed and their strength for a score or so of hours, before it slew them. And now the sails billowed out, catching the breeze. Golden mountains, skimming rapidly over the sea, these ships; their method of construction was a secret lost even to the Melnibonéans (who had forgotten so much of their lore). It was easy to imagine how men of the Young Kingdoms hated Melniboné and its inventions, for it did seem that the battle-barges belonged to an older, alien age, as they bore down upon the fleeing galleys now sighted on the horizon.

The Son of the Pyaray was in the lead of the rest of the fleet and was priming its catapults well before any of its fellows had seen the enemy. Perspiring slaves gingerly manhandled the viscous stuff of the fireballs, getting them into the bronze cups of the catapults by means of long, spoon-ended tongs. It flickered in the pre-dawn gloom.

Now slaves climbed the steps to the bridge and brought wine and food on platinum platters for the three Dragon Princes who had remained there since the pursuit had begun. Elric could not summon the strength to eat, but he seized a tall cup of yellow wine and drained it. The stuff was strong and revived him a trifle. He had another cup poured and drank that as swiftly as the other. He peered ahead. It was almost dawn. There was a line of purple light on the horizon. 'At the first sign of the sun's disc,' Elric said, 'let loose the fireballs.'

'I will give the order,' said Magum Colim, wiping his lips and putting down the meat bone on which he had been chewing. He left the bridge. Elric heard his feet striking the steps heavily. All at once the albino felt surrounded by enemies. There had been something strange in Magum Colim's manner during the argument with Prince Yyrkoon. Elric tried to shake off such foolish thoughts. But the weariness, the self-doubt, the open mockery of his cousin, all succeeded in increasing the feeling that he was alone and without friends in the world. Even Cymoril and Dyvim Tvar were, finally, Melnibonéans and could not understand the peculiar concerns which moved him and dictated his actions. Perhaps it would be wise to renounce everything Melnibonéan and wander the world as an anonymous soldier of fortune, serving whoever needed his aid?

The dull red semicircle of the sun showed above the black line of the distant water. There came a series of booming sounds from the forward decks of the flagship as the catapults released their fiery shot; there was a whistling scream, fading away, and it seemed that a dozen meteors leapt through the sky, hurtling towards the five galleys which were now little more than thirty ship-lengths away.

Elric saw two galleys flare, but the remaining three began to sail a zig-zag course and avoided the fireballs which landed on the water and burned fitfully for a while before sinking (still burning) into the depths.

More fireballs were prepared and Elric heard Yyrkoon shout from the other side of the bridge, ordering the slaves to greater exertions. Then the fleeing vessels changed their tactics, evidently realising that they could not save themselves for long, and, spreading out, sailed towards *The Son of the Pyaray,* just as the other ships had done in the sea-maze. It was not merely their courage that Elric admired but their manoeuvring skill and the speed at which they had arrived at this logical, if hopeless, decision.

The sun was behind the southland ships as they turned. Three brave silhouettes drew nearer to the Melnibonéan flagship as scarlet stained the sea, as if in anticipation of the bloodletting to come.

Another volley of fireballs was flung from the flagship and the leading galley tried to tack round and avoid it, but two of the fiery globes spattered directly on its deck and soon the whole ship was alive with flame. Burning men leapt into the water. Burning men shot arrows at the flagship. Burning men fell slowly from their positions in the rigging. The burning men died, but the burning ship came on; someone had lashed the steering arm and directed the galley at *The Son of the Pyaray*. It crashed into the golden side of the battle-barge and some of the fire splashed on the deck where the main catapults were in position. A cauldron containing the firestuff caught and immediately men were running from all quarters of the ship to try to douse the flame. Elric grinned as he saw what the barbarians had done. Perhaps that ship had deliberately allowed itself to be fired. Now the majority of the flagship's complement was engaged with putting out the blaze—while the southland ships drew alongside, threw up their own grapples, and began to board.

' 'Ware boarders!' Elric shouted, long after he might have warned his crew. 'Barbarians attack.'

He saw Yyrkoon whirl round, see the situation, and rush down the steps from the bridge. 'You stay there, my lord king,' he flung at Elric as he disappeared. 'You are plainly too weary to fight.'

And Elric summoned all that was left of his strength and stumbled after his cousin, to help in the defense of the ship.

The barbarians were not fighting for their lives—they knew those to be taken already. They were fighting for their pride. They wanted to take one Melnibonéan ship down with them and that ship must be the flagship itself. It was hard to be contemptuous of such men. They knew that even if they took the flagship the other ships of the golden fleet would soon overwhelm them.

But the other ships were still some distance away. Many lives would be lost before they reached the flagship.

On the lowest deck Elric found himself facing a pair of tall barbarians, each armed with a curved blade and a small, oblong shield. He lunged forward, but his armour seemed to drag at his limbs, his own shield and sword were so heavy that he could barely lift them. Two swords struck his helm, almost simultaneously. He lunged back and caught a man in the arm, rammed the other with his shield. A curved blade clanged on his backplate and he all but lost his footing. There was choking smoke everywhere, and heat, and the tumult of battle. Desperately he swung about him and felt his broadsword bite deep into flesh.

One of his opponents fell, gurgling, with blood spouting from his mouth and nose. The other lunged. Elric stepped backwards, fell over the corpse of the man he had slain, and went down, his broadsword held out before him in one hand. And as the triumphant barbarian leapt forward to finish the albino, Elric caught him on the point of the broadsword, running him through. The dead man fell towards Elric who did not feel the impact, for he had already fainted. Not for the first time had his deficient blood, no longer enriched by drugs, betrayed him.

He tasted salt and thought at first it was blood. But it was sea water. A wave had risen over the deck and momentarily revived him. He struggled to crawl from under the dead man and then he heard a voice he recognised. He twisted his head and looked up.

Prince Yyrkoon stood there. He was grinning. He was full of glee at Elric's plight. Black, oily smoke still drifted everywhere, but the sounds of the fight had died.

'Are—are we victorious, cousin?' Elric spoke painfully.

'Aye. The barbarians are all dead now. We are about to sail for Imrryr.'

Elric was relieved. He would begin to die soon if he could not get to his store of potions.

His relief must have been evident, for Yyrkoon laughed. 'It is as well the battle did not last longer, my lord, or we should have been without our leader.'

'Help me up, cousin.' Elric hated to ask Prince Yyrkoon any favour, but he had no choice. He stretched out his empty hand. 'I am fit enough to inspect the ship.'

Yyrkoon came forward as if to take the hand, but then he hesitated, still grinning. 'But, my lord, I disagree. You will be dead by the time this ship turns eastward again.'

'Nonsense. Even without the drugs I can live for a considerable time, though movement is difficult. Help me up, Yyrkoon, I command you.'

'You cannot command me, Elric. I am emperor now, you see.'

'Be wary, cousin. I can overlook such treachery, but others will not. I shall be forced to . . .'

Yyrkoon swung his legs over Elric's body and went to the rail. Here were bolts which fixed one section of the rail in place when it was not used for the gangplank. Yyrkoon slowly released the bolts and kicked the section of rail into the water.

Now Elric's efforts to free himself became more desperate. But he could hardly move at all.

Yyrkoon, on the other hand, seemed possessed of unnatural strength. He bent and easily flung the corpse away from Elric.

'Yyrkoon,' said Elric, 'this is unwise of you.'

'I was never a cautious man, cousin, as well as you know.' Yyrkoon placed a booted foot against Elric's ribs and began to shove. Elric slid towards the gap in the rail. He could see the black sea heaving below. 'Farewell, Elric. Now a true Melnibonéan shall sit upon the Ruby Throne. And, who knows, might even make Cymoril his queen? It has not been unheard of . . .'

And Elric felt himself rolling, felt himself fall, felt himself strike the water, felt his armour pulling him below the surface. And Yyrkoon's last words drummed in Elric's ears like the persistent booming of the waves against the sides of the golden battle-barge.

BOOK TWO

Less certain of himself or his destiny than ever, the albino king must perforce bring his powers of sorcery into play, conscious that he has embarked upon a course of action by no means at one with his original conception of the way he wished to live his life. And now matters must be settled. He must begin to rule. He must become cruel. But even in this he will find himself thwarted.

BOOK TWO

1   The Caverns of the Sea King

Elric sank rapidly, desperately trying to keep the last of his breath in his body. He had no strength to swim and the weight of the armor denied any hope of his rising to the surface and being sighted by Magum Colim or one of the others still loyal to him.

The roaring in his ears gradually faded to a whisper so that it sounded as if little voices were speaking to him, the voices of the water elementals with whom, in his youth, he had had a kind of friendship. And the pain in his lungs faded; the red mist cleared from his eyes and he thought he saw the face of his father, Sadric, of Cymoril and, fleetingly, of Yyrkoon. Stupid Yyrkoon: for all that he prided himself that he was a Melnibonéan, he lacked the Melnibonéan subtlety. He was as brutal and direct as some of the Young Kingdom barbarians he so much despised. And now Elric began to feel almost grateful to his cousin. His life was over. The conflicts which tore his mind would no longer trouble him. His fears, his torments, his loves and his hatreds all lay in the past and only oblivion lay before him. As the last of his breath left his body, he gave himself wholly to the sea; to Straasha, Lord of all the Water Elementals, once the comrade of the Melnibonéan folk. And as he did this he remembered the old spell which his ancestors had used to summon Straasha. The spell came unbidden into his dying brain.

> *Waters of the sea, thou gave us birth*
> *And were our milk and mother both*
> *In days when skies were overcast*
> *You who were first shall be the last.*
>
> *Sea-rulers, fathers of our blood,*
> *Thine aid is sought, thine aid is sought,*
> *Your salt is blood, our blood your salt,*
> *Your blood the blood of Man.*

Straasha, eternal king, eternal sea
Thine aid is sought by me;
For enemies of thine and mine
Seek to defeat our destiny, and drain
away our sea.

Either the words had an old, symbolic meaning or they referred to some incident in Melnibonéan history which even Elric had not read about. The words meant very little to him and yet they continued to repeat themselves as his body sank deeper and deeper into the green waters. Even when blackness overwhelmed him and his lungs filled with water, the words continued to whisper through the corridors of his brain. It was strange that he should be dead and still hear the incantation.

It seemed a long while later that his eyes opened and revealed swirling water and, through it, huge, indistinct figures gliding towards him. Death, it appeared, took a long time to come and, while he died, he dreamed. The leading figure had a turquoise beard and hair, pale green skin that seemed made of the sea itself and, when he spoke, a voice that was like a rushing tide. He smiled at Elric.

'*Straasha answers thy summons, mortal. Our destinies are bound together. How may I aid thee, and, in aiding thee, aid myself?*'

Elric's mouth was filled with water and yet he still seemed capable of speech (thus proving he dreamed).

He said:

'King Straasha. The paintings in the Tower of D'a'rputna—in the library. When I was a boy I saw them, King Straasha.'

The sea-king stretched out his sea-green hands. '*Aye. You sent the summons. You need our aid. We honour our ancient pact with your folk.*'

'No. I did not mean to summon you. The summons came unbidden to my dying mind. I am happy to drown, King Straasha.'

'*That cannot be. If your mind summoned us it means you wish to live. We will aid you.*' King Straasha's beard streamed in the tide and his deep, green eyes were gentle, almost tender, as they regarded the albino.

Elric closed his own eyes again. 'I dream,' he said. 'I deceive myself with fantasies of hope.' He felt the water in his lungs and he knew he no longer breathed. It stood to reason, therefore, that he was dead. 'But if you were real, old friend, and you wished to aid me, you would return me to Melniboné so that I might deal with the usurper, Yyrkoon, and save Cymoril, before it is too late. That is my only regret—the torment which Cymoril will suffer if her brother becomes Emperor of Melniboné.'

'Is that all you ask of the water elementals?' King Straasha seemed almost disappointed.

'I do not even ask that of you. I only voice what I would have wished, had this been reality and I was speaking, which I know is impossible. Now I shall die.'

'That cannot be, Lord Elric, for our destinies are truly intertwined and I know that it is not yet your destiny to perish. Therefore I will aid you as you have suggested.'

Elric was surprised at the sharpness of detail of this fantasy. He said to himself. 'What a cruel torment I subject myself to. Now I must set about admitting my death . . .'

'You cannot die. Not yet.'

Now it was as if the sea-king's gentle hands had picked him up and bore him through twisting corridors of a delicate coral pink texture, slightly shadowed, no longer in water. And Elric felt the water vanish from his lungs and stomach and he breathed. Could it be that he had actually been brought to the legendary plane of the elemental folk—a plane which intersected that of the earth and in which they dwelled, for the most part?

In a huge, circular cavern, which shone with pink and blue mother-of-pearl, they came to rest at last. The sea-king laid Elric down upon the floor of the cavern, which seemed to be covered with fine, white sand which was yet not sand for it yielded and then sprang back when he moved.

When King Straasha moved, it was with a sound like the tide drawing itself back over shingle. The sea-king crossed the white sand, walking towards a large throne of milky jade. He seated himself upon this throne and placed his green head on his green fist, regarding Elric with puzzled, yet compassionate, eyes.

Elric was still physically weak, but he could breathe. It was as if the sea water had filled him and then cleansed him when it was driven out. He felt clear-headed. And now he was much less sure that he dreamed.

'I still find it hard to know why you saved me, King Straasha,' he murmured from where he lay on the sand.

'The rune. We heard it on this plane and we came. That is all.'

'Aye. But there is more to sorcery-working than that. There are chants, symbols, rituals of all sorts. Previously that has always been true.'

'Perhaps the rituals take the place of urgent need of the kind which sent out your summons to us. Though you say you wished to die, it was

evident you did not really want to die or the summoning would not have been so clear and have reached us so swiftly. Forget all this now. When you have rested, we shall do what you have requested of us.'

Painfully, Elric raised himself into a sitting position. 'You spoke earlier of "intertwined destinies". Do you, then, know something of my destiny?'

'A little, I think. Our world grows old. Once the elementals were powerful on your plane and the people of Melniboné all shared that power. But now our power wanes, as does yours. Something is changing. There are intimations that the Lords of the Higher Worlds are again taking an interest in your world. Perhaps they fear that the folk of the Young Kingdoms have forgotten them. Perhaps the folk of the Young Kingdoms threaten to bring in a new age, where gods and beings such as myself no longer shall have a place. I suspect there is a certain unease upon the planes of the Higher Worlds.'

'You know no more?'

King Straasha raised his head and looked directly into Elric's eyes. *'There is no more I can tell you, son of my old friends, save that you would be happier if you gave yourself up entirely to your destiny when you understand it.'*

Elric sighed. 'I think I know of what you speak, King Straasha. I shall try to follow your advice.'

'And now that you have rested, it is time to return.'

The sea-king rose from his throne of milky jade and flowed towards Elric, lifting him up in strong, green arms.

'We shall meet again before your life ends, Elric. I hope that I shall be able to aid you once more. And remember that our brothers of the air and of fire will try to aid you also. And remember the beasts—they, too, can be of service to you. There is no need to suspect their help. But beware of gods, Elric. Beware of the Lords of the Higher Worlds and remember that their aid and their gifts must always be paid for.'

These were the last words Elric heard the sea-king speak before they rushed again through the sinuous tunnels of this other plane, moving at such a speed that Elric could distinguish no details and, at times, did not know whether they remained in King Straasha's kingdom or had returned to the depths of his own world's sea.

2   A New Emperor and an Emperor Renewed

Strange clouds filled the sky and the sun hung heavy and huge and red behind them and the ocean was black as the golden galleys swept homeward before their battered flagship *The Son of the Pyaray* which moved slowly with dead slaves at her oars and her tattered sails limp at their masts and smoke-begrimed men on her decks and a new emperor upon her war-wrecked bridge. The new emperor was the only jubilant man in the fleet and he was jubilant indeed. It was his banner now, not Elric's, which took pride of place on the flagmast, for he had lost no time in proclaiming Elric slain and himself ruler of Melniboné.

To Yyrkoon, the peculiar sky was an omen of change, of a return to the old ways and the old power of the Dragon Isle. When he issued orders, his voice was a veritable croon of pleasure, and Admiral Magum Colim, who had ever been wary of Elric but who now had to obey Yyrkoon's orders, wondered if, perhaps, it would not have been preferable to have dealt with Yyrkoon in the manner in which (he suspected) Yyrkoon had dealt with Elric.

Dyvim Tvar leaned on the rail of his own ship, *Terhali's Particular Satisfaction,* and he also paid attention to the sky, though he saw omens of doom, for he mourned for Elric and considered how he might take vengeance on Prince Yyrkoon, should it emerge that Yyrkoon had murdered his cousin for possession of the Ruby Throne.

Melniboné appeared on the horizon, a brooding silhouette of crags, a dark monster squatting in the sea, calling her own back to the heated pleasures of her womb, the Dreaming City of Imrryr. The great cliffs loomed, the central gate to the sea-maze opened, water slapped and gasped as the golden prows disturbed it and the golden ships were swallowed into the murky dankness of the tunnels where bits of wreckage still floated from the previous night's encounter; where white, bloated corpses could still be seen when the brandlight touched them.

The prows nosed arrogantly through the remains of their prey, but there was no joy aboard the golden battle-barges, for they brought news of their old emperor's death in battle (Yyrkoon had told them what had happened). Next night and for seven nights in all the Wild Dance of Melniboné would fill the streets. Potions and petty spells would ensure that no-one slept, for sleep was forbidden to any Melnibonéan, old or young, while a dead emperor was mourned. Naked, the Dragon Princes would prowl the city, taking any young woman they found and filling her with their seed for it was traditional that if an emperor died then the nobles of Melniboné must create as many children of aristocratic blood as was possible. Music-slaves would howl from the top of every tower. Other slaves would be slain and some eaten. It was a dreadful dance, the Dance of Misery, and it took as many lives as it created. A tower would be pulled down and a new one erected during those seven days and the tower would be called for Elric VIII, the Albino Emperor, slain upon the sea, defending Melniboné against the southland pirates.

Slain upon the sea and his body taken by the waves. That was not a good portent, for it meant that Elric had gone to serve Pyaray, the Tentacled Whisperer of Impossible Secrets, the Chaos Lord who commanded the Chaos Fleet—dead ships, dead sailors, forever in his thrall—and it was not fitting that such a fate should befall one of the Royal Line of Melniboné. Ah, but the mourning would be long, thought Dyvim Tvar. He had loved Elric, for all that he had sometimes disapproved of his methods of ruling the Dragon Isle. Secretly he would go to the Dragon Caves that night and spend the period of mourning with the sleeping dragons who, now that Elric was dead, were all he had left to love. And Dyvim Tvar then thought of Cymoril, awaiting Elric's return.

The ships began to emerge into the half-light of the evening. Torches and braziers already burned on the quays of Imrryr which were deserted save for a small group of figures who stood around a chariot which had been driven out to the end of the central mole. A cold wind blew. Dyvim Tvar knew that it was the Princess Cymoril who waited, with her guards, for the fleet.

Though the flagship was the last to pass through the maze, the rest of the ships had to wait until it could be towed into position and dock first. If this had not been the required tradition, Dyvim Tvar would have left his ship and gone to speak to Cymoril, escort her from the quay and tell her what he knew of the circumstances of Elric's death. But it was impossible. Even before *Terhali's Particular Satisfaction* had dropped anchor, the main gangplank of *The Son of the Pyaray* had been lowered and the Emperor Yyrkoon, all swaggering pride, had stepped down it, his arms raised in triumphant salute to his sister who could be seen, even now, searching the decks of the ships for a sign of her beloved albino.

Suddenly Cymoril knew that Elric was dead and she suspected that Yyrkoon had, in some way, been responsible for Elric's death. Either Yyrkoon had allowed Elric to be borne down by a group of southland reavers or else he had managed to slay Elric himself. She knew her brother and she recognised his expression. He was pleased with himself as he always had been when successful in some form of treachery or another. Anger flashed in her tear-filled eyes and she threw back her head and shouted at the shifting, ominous sky:

'Oh! Yyrkoon has destroyed him!'

Her guards were startled. The captain spoke solicitously. 'Madam?'

'He is dead—and that brother slew him. Take Prince Yyrkoon, captain. Kill Prince Yyrkoon, captain.'

Unhappily, the captain put his right hand on the hilt of his sword. A young warrior, more impetuous, drew his blade, murmuring: 'I will slay him, princess, if that is your desire.' The young warrior loved Cymoril with considerable and unthinking intensity.

The captain offered the warrior a cautionary glance, but the warrior was blind to it. Now two others slid swords from scabbards as Yyrkoon, a red cloak wound about him, his dragon crest catching the light from the brands guttering in the wind, stalked forward and cried:

'Yyrkoon is emperor now!'

'No!' shrieked Yyrkoon's sister. 'Elric! Elric! Where are you?'

'Serving his new master, Pyaray of Chaos. His dead hands pull at the sweep of a Chaos ship, sister. His dead eyes see nothing at all. His dead ears hear only the crack of Pyaray's whips and his dead flesh cringes, feeling nought but that unearthly scourge. Elric sank in his armour to the bottom of the sea.'

'Murderer! Traitor!' Cymoril began to sob.

The captain, who was a practical man, said to his warriors in a low voice: 'Sheath your weapons and salute your new emperor.'

Only the young guardsman who loved Cymoril disobeyed. 'But he slew the emperor! My lady Cymoril said so!'

'What of it? He is emperor now. Kneel or you'll be dead within the minute.'

The young warrior gave a wild shout and leapt towards Yyrkoon, who stepped back, trying to free his arms from the folds of his cloak. He had not expected this.

But it was the captain who leapt forward, his own sword drawn, and hacked down the youngster so that he gasped, half-turned, then fell at Yyrkoon's feet.

This demonstration of the captain's was confirmation of his real power and Yyrkoon almost smirked with satisfaction as he looked down at the corpse. The captain fell to one knee, the bloody sword still in his hand. 'My emperor,' he said.

'You show a proper loyalty, captain.'

'My loyalty is to the Ruby Throne.'

'Quite so.'

Cymoril shook with grief and rage, but her rage was impotent. She knew now that she had no friends.

Leering, the Emperor Yyrkoon presented himself before her. He reached out his hand and he caressed her neck, her cheek, her mouth. He let his hand fall so that it grazed her breast. 'Sister,' he said, 'thou art mine entirely now.'

And Cymoril was the second to fall at his feet, for she had fainted.

'Pick her up,' Yyrkoon said to the guard. 'Take her back to her own tower and there be sure she remains. Two guards will be with her at all times, in even her most private moments they must observe her, for she may plan treachery against the Ruby Throne.'

The captain bowed and signed to his men to obey the emperor. 'Aye, my lord. It shall be done.'

Yyrkoon looked back at the corpse of the young warrior. 'And feed that to her slaves tonight, so that he can continue serving her.' He smiled.

The captain smiled, too, appreciating the joke. He felt it was good to have a proper emperor in Melniboné again. An emperor who knew how to behave, who knew how to treat his enemies and who accepted un-swerving loyalty as his right. The captain fancied that fine, martial times lay ahead for Melniboné. The golden battle-barges and the war-riors of Imrryr could go a-spoiling again and instil in the barbarians of the Young Kingdoms a sweet and satisfactory sense of fear. Already, in his mind, the captain helped himself to the treasures of Lormyr, Argimiliar and Pikarayd, of Ilmiora and Jadmar. He might even be made governor, say, of the Isle of the Purple Towns. What luxuries of torment would he bring to those upstart sealords, particularly Count Smiorgan Baldhead who was even now beginning to try to make the isle a rival to Melniboné as a trading port. As he escorted the limp body of the Princess Cymoril back to her tower, the captain looked on that body and felt the swellings of lust within him. Yyrkoon would reward his loyalty, there was no doubt of that. Despite the cold wind, the captain began to sweat in his anticipation. He, himself, would guard the Princess Cymoril. He would relish it.

Marching at the head of his army, Yyrkoon strutted for the Tower of D'a'rputna, the Tower of Emperors, and the Ruby Throne within. He preferred to ignore the litter which had been brought for him and to go on foot, so that he might savour every small moment of his triumph. He approached the tower, tall among its fellows at the very centre of Imrryr, as he might approach a beloved woman. He approached it with a sense of delicacy and without haste, for he knew that it was his.

He looked about him. His army marched behind him. Magum Colim and Dyvim Tvar led the army. People lined the twisting streets and bowed low to him. Slaves prostrated themselves. Even the beasts of burden were made to kneel as he strode by. Yyrkoon could almost taste the power as one might taste a luscious fruit. He drew deep breaths of the air. Even the air was his. All Imrryr was his. All Melniboné. Soon would all the world be his. And he would squander it all. How he would squander it! Such a grand terror would he bring back to the earth; such a munificence of fear! In ecstasy, almost blindly, did the Emperor Yyrkoon enter the tower. He hesitated at the great doors of the throne room. He signed for the doors to be opened and as they opened he deliberately took in the scene tiny bit by tiny bit. The walls, the banners, the trophies, the galleries, all were his. The throne room was empty now, but soon he would fill it with colour and celebration and true, Melnibonéan entertainments. It had been too long since blood had sweetened the air of this hall. Now he let his eyes linger upon the steps leading up to the Ruby Throne itself, but, before he looked at the throne, he heard Dyvim Tvar gasp behind him and his gaze went suddenly to the Ruby Throne and his jaw slackened at what he saw. His eyes widened in incredulity.

'An illusion!'

'An apparition,' said Dyvim Tvar with some satisfaction.

'Heresy!' cried the Emperor Yyrkoon, staggering forward, finger pointing at the robed and cowled figure which sat so still upon the Ruby Throne. 'Mine! Mine!'

The figure made no reply.

'Mine! Begone! The throne belongs to Yyrkoon. Yyrkoon is emperor now! What are you? Why would you thwart me thus?'

The cowl fell back and a bone-white face was revealed, surrounded by flowing, milk-white hair. Crimson eyes looked coolly down at the shrieking, stumbling thing which came towards them.

'You are dead, Elric! I know that you are dead!'

The apparition made no reply, but a thin smile touched the white lips.

'You *could* not have survived. You drowned. You cannot come back. Pyaray owns your soul!'

'There are others who rule in the sea,' said the figure on the Ruby Throne. 'Why did you slay me, cousin?'

Yyrkoon's guile had deserted him, making way for terror and confusion. 'Because it is my right to rule! Because you were not strong enough, nor cruel enough, nor humorous enough . . .'

'Is this not a good joke, cousin?'

'Begone! Begone! Begone! I shall not be ousted by a spectre! A dead emperor cannot rule Melniboné!'

'We shall see,' said Elric, signing to Dyvim Tvar and his soldiers.

3   A Traditional Justice

'Now indeed I shall rule as you would have had me rule, cousin.' Elric watched as Dyvim Tvar's soldiers surrounded the would-be usurper and seized his arms, relieving him of his weapons.

Yyrkoon panted like a captured wolf. He glared around him as if hoping to find support from the assembled warriors, but they stared back at him either neutrally or with open contempt.

'And you, Prince Yyrkoon, will be the first to benefit from this new rule of mine. Are you pleased?'

Yyrkoon lowered his head. He was trembling now. Elric laughed. 'Speak up, cousin.'

'May Arioch and all the Dukes of Hell torment you for eternity,' growled Yyrkoon. He flung back his head, his wild eyes rolling, his lips curling: 'Arioch! Arioch! Curse this feeble albino! Arioch! Destroy him or see Melniboné fall!'

Elric continued to laugh. 'Arioch does not hear you. Chaos is weak upon the earth now. It needs a greater sorcery than yours to bring the Chaos Lords back to aid you as they aided our ancestors. And now, Yyrkoon, tell me—where is the Lady Cymoril?'

But Yyrkoon had lapsed, again, into a sullen silence.

'She is at her own tower, my emperor,' said Magum Colim.

'A creature of Yyrkoon's took her there,' said Dyvim Tvar. 'The captain of Cymoril's own guard, he slew a warrior who tried to defend his mistress against Yyrkoon. It could be that Princess Cymoril is in danger, my lord.'

'Then go quickly to the tower. Take a force of men. Bring both Cymoril and the captain of her guard to me.'

'And Yyrkoon, my lord?' asked Dyvim Tvar.

'Let him remain here until his sister returns.'

Dyvim Tvar bowed and, selecting a body of warriors, left the throne room. All noticed that Dyvim Tvar's step was lighter and his expression less grim than when he had first approached the throne room at Prince Yyrkoon's back.

Yyrkoon straightened his head and looked about the court. For a moment he seemed like a pathetic and bewildered child. All the lines of hate and anger had disappeared and Elric felt sympathy for his cousin growing again within him. But this time Elric quelled the feeling.

'Be grateful, cousin, that for a few hours you were totally powerful, that you enjoyed domination over all the folk of Melniboné.'

Yyrkoon said in a small, puzzled voice: 'How did you escape? You had no time for making a sorcery, no strength for it. You could barely move your limbs and your armour must have dragged you deep to the bottom of the sea so that you should have drowned. It is unfair, Elric. You should have drowned.'

Elric shrugged, 'I have friends in the sea. They recognise my royal blood and my right to rule if you do not.'

Yyrkoon tried to disguise the astonishment he felt. Evidently his respect for Elric had increased, as had his hatred for the albino emperor. 'Friends.'

'Aye,' said Elric with a thin grin.

'I—I thought, too, you had vowed not to use your powers of sorcery.'

'But you thought that a vow which was unbefitting for a Melnibonéan monarch to make, did you not? Well, I agree with you. You see, Yyrkoon, you have won a victory, after all.'

Yyrkoon stared narrowly at Elric, as if trying to divine a secret meaning behind Elric's words. 'You will bring back the Chaos Lords?'

'No sorcerer, however powerful, can summon the Chaos Lords or, for that matter, the Lords of Law, if they do not wish to be summoned. That you know. You must know it, Yyrkoon. Have you not, yourself, tried. And Arioch did not come, did he? Did he bring you the gift you sought—the gift of the two black swords?'

'You know that?'

'I did not. I guessed. Now I know.'

Yyrkoon tried to speak but his voice would not form words, so angry was he. Instead, a strangled growl escaped his throat and for a few moments he struggled in the grip of his guards.

Dyvim Tvar returned with Cymoril. The girl was pale but she was smiling. She ran into the throne room. 'Elric!'

'Cymoril! Are you harmed?'

Cymoril glanced at the crestfallen captain of her guard who had been brought with her. A look of disgust crossed her fine face. Then she shook her head. 'No. I am not harmed.'

The captain of Cymoril's guard was shaking with terror. He looked pleadingly at Yyrkoon as if hoping that his fellow prisoner could help him. But Yyrkoon continued to stare at the floor.

'Have that one brought closer.' Elric pointed at the captain of the guard. The man was dragged to the foot of the steps leading to the Ruby Throne. He moaned. 'What a petty traitor you are,' said Elric. 'At least Yyrkoon had the courage to attempt to slay me. And his ambitions were high. Your ambition was merely to become one of his pet curs. So you betrayed your mistress and slew one of your own men. What is your name?'

The man had difficulty speaking, but at last he murmured, 'It is Valharik, my name. What could I do? I serve the Ruby Throne, whoever sits upon it.'

'So the traitor claims that loyalty motivated him. I think not.'

'It was, my lord. It was.' The captain began to whine. He fell to his knees. 'Slay me swiftly. Do not punish me more.'

Elric's impulse was to heed the man's request, but he looked at Yyrkoon and then remembered the expression on Cymoril's face when she had looked at the guard. He knew that he must make a point now, whilst making an example of Captain Valharik. So he shook his head. 'No. I will punish you more. Tonight you will die here according to the traditions of Melniboné, while my nobles feast to celebrate this new era of my rule.'

Valharik began to sob. Then he stopped himself and got slowly to his feet, a Melnibonéan again. He bowed low and stepped backward, giving himself into the grip of his guards.

'I must consider a way in which your fate may be shared with the one you wished to serve,' Elric went on. 'How did you slay the young warrior who sought to obey Cymoril?'

'With my sword. I cut him down. It was a clean stroke. But one.'

'And what became of the corpse.'

'Prince Yyrkoon told me to feed it to Princess Cymoril's slaves.'

'I understand. Very well, Prince Yyrkoon, you may join us at the feast tonight while Captain Valharik entertains us with his dying.'

Yyrkoon's face was almost as pale as Elric's. 'What do you mean?'

'The little pieces of Captain Valharik's flesh which our Doctor Jest will carve from his limbs will be the meat on which you feast. You may give instructions as to how you wish the captain's flesh prepared. We should not expect you to eat it raw, cousin.'

Even Dyvim Tvar looked astonished at Elric's decision. Certainly it was in the spirit of Melniboné and a clever irony improving on Prince Yyrkoon's own idea, but it was unlike Elric—or, at least, it was unlike the Elric he had known up until a day earlier.

As he heard his fate, Captain Valharik gave a great scream of terror and glared at Prince Yyrkoon as if the would-be usurper were already tasting his flesh. Yyrkoon tried to turn away, his shoulders shaking.

'And that will be the beginning of it,' said Elric. 'The feast will start at midnight. Until that time, confine Yyrkoon to his own tower.'

After Prince Yyrkoon and Captain Valharik had been led away, Dyvim Tvar and Princess Cymoril came and stood beside Elric who had sunk back in his great throne and was staring bitterly into the middle-distance.

'That was a clever cruelty,' Dyvim Tvar said.

Cymoril said: 'It is what they both deserve.'

'Aye,' murmured Elric. 'It is what my father would have done. It is what Yyrkoon would have done had our positions been reversed. I but follow the traditions. I no longer pretend that I am my own man. Here I shall stay until I die, trapped upon the Ruby Throne—serving the Ruby Throne as Valharik claimed to serve it.'

'Could you not kill them both quickly?' Cymoril asked. 'You know that I do not plead for my brother because he is my brother. I hate him most of all. But it might destroy you, Elric, to follow through with your plan.'

'What if it does? Let me be destroyed. Let me merely become an unthinking extension of my ancestors. The puppet of ghosts and memories, dancing to strings which extend back through time for ten thousand years.'

'Perhaps if you slept . . .' Dyvim Tvar suggested.

'I shall not sleep, I feel, for many nights after this. But your brother is not going to die, Cymoril. After his punishment—after he has eaten the flesh of Captain Valharik—I intend to send him into exile. He will go alone into the Young Kingdoms and he will not be allowed to take his grimoires with him. He must make his way as best he can in the lands of the barbarian. That is not too severe a punishment, I think.'

'It is too lenient,' said Cymoril. 'You would be best advised to slay him. Send soldiers now. Give him no time to consider counterplots.'

'I do not fear his counterplots.' Elric rose wearily. 'Now I should like it if you would both leave me, until an hour or so before the feasting begins. I must think.'

'I will return to my tower and prepare myself for tonight,' said Cymoril. She kissed Elric lightly upon his pale forehead. He looked up, filled with love and tenderness for her. He reached out and touched her hair and her cheek. 'Remember that I love you, Elric,' she said.

'I will see that you are safely escorted homeward,' Dyvim Tvar said to her. 'And you must choose a new commander of your guard. Can I assist in that?'

'I should be grateful, Dyvim Tvar.'

They left Elric still upon the Ruby Throne, still staring into space. The hand that he lifted from time to time to his pale head shook a little and now the torment showed in his strange, crimson eyes.

Later, he rose up from the Ruby Throne and walked slowly, head bowed, to his own apartments, followed by his guards. He hesitated at the door which led onto the steps going up to the library. Instinctively he sought the consolation and forgetfulness of a certain kind of knowledge, but at that moment he suddenly hated his scrolls and his books. He blamed them for his ridiculous concerns regarding 'morality' and 'justice'; he blamed them for the feelings of guilt and despair which now filled him as a result of his decision to behave as a Melnibonéan monarch was expected to behave. So he passed the door to the library and went on to his apartments, but even his apartments displeased him now. They were austere. They were not furnished according to the luxurious tastes of all Melnibonéans (save for his father) with their delight in lush mixtures of colour and bizarre design. He would have them changed as soon as possible. He would give himself up to those ghosts who ruled him. For some time he stalked from room to room, trying to push back that part of him which demanded he be merciful to Valharik and to Yyrkoon—at very least to slay them and be done with it or, better, to send them both into exile. But it was impossible to reverse his decision now.

At last he lowered himself to a couch which rested beside a window looking out over the whole of the city. The sky was still full of turbulent cloud, but now the moon shone through, like the yellow eye of an unhealthy beast. It seemed to stare with a certain triumphant irony at him, as if relishing the defeat of his conscience. Elric sank his head into his arms.

Later the servants came to tell him that the courtiers were assembling for the celebration feast. He allowed them to dress him in his yellow robes of state and to place the dragon crown upon his head and then he returned to the throne room to be greeted by a mighty cheer, more wholehearted than any he had ever received before. He acknowledged the greeting and then seated himself in the Ruby Throne, looking out over the banqueting tables which now filled the hall. A table was brought and set before him and two extra seats were brought, for

Dyvim Tvar and Cymoril would sit beside him. But Dyvim Tvar and Cymoril were not yet here and neither had the renegade Valharik been brought. And where was Yyrkoon? They should, even now, be at the centre of the hall—Valharik in chains and Yyrkoon seated beneath him. Doctor Jest was there, heating his brazier on which rested his cooking pans, testing and sharpening his knives. The hall was filled with excited talk as the court waited to be entertained. Already the food was being brought in, though no one might eat until the emperor ate first.

Elric signed to the commander of his own guard. 'Has the Princess Cymoril or Lord Dyvim Tvar arrived at the tower yet?'

'No, my lord.'

Cymoril was rarely late and Dyvim Tvar never. Elric frowned. Perhaps they did not relish the entertainment.

'And what of the prisoners?'

'They have been sent for, my lord.'

Doctor Jest looked up expectantly, his thin body tensed in anticipation.

And then Elric heard a sound above the din of the conversation. A groaning sound which seemed to come from all around the tower. He bent his head and listened closely.

Others were hearing it now. They stopped talking and also listened intently. Soon the whole hall was in silence and the groaning increased.

Then, all at once, the doors of the throne room burst open and there was Dyvim Tvar, gasping and bloody, his clothes slashed and his flesh gashed. And following him in came a mist—a swirling mist of dark purples and unpleasant blues and it was this mist that groaned.

Elric sprang from his throne and knocked the table aside. He leapt down the steps towards his friend. The groaning mist began to creep further into the throne room, as if reaching out for Dyvim Tvar.

Elric took his friend in his arms. 'Dyvim Tvar! What is this sorcery?'

Dyvim Tvar's face was full of horror and his lips seemed frozen until at last he said:

'It is Yyrkoon's sorcery. He conjured the groaning mist to aid him in his escape. I tried to follow him from the city but the mist engulfed me and I lost my senses. I went to his tower to bring him and his accessory here, but the sorcery had already been accomplished.'

'Cymoril? Where is she?'

'He took her, Elric. She is with him. Valharik is with him and so are a hundred warriors who remained secretly loyal to him.'

'Then we must pursue him. We shall soon capture him.'

'You can do nothing against the groaning mist. Ah! It comes!'

And sure enough the mist was beginning to surround them. Elric tried to disperse it by waving his arms, but then it had gathered thickly around him and its melancholy groaning filled his ears, its hideous colours blinded his eyes. He tried to rush through it, but it remained with him. And now he thought he heard words amongst the groans. 'Elric is weak. Elric is foolish. Elric must die!'

'Stop this!' he cried. He bumped into another body and fell to his knees. He began to crawl, desperately trying to peer through the mist. Now faces formed in the mist—frightful faces, more terrifying than any he had ever seen, even in his worst nightmares.

'Cymoril!' he cried. 'Cymoril!'

And one of the faces became the face of Cymoril—a Cymoril who leered at him and mocked him and whose face slowly aged until he saw a filthy crone and, ultimately, a skull on which the flesh rotted. He closed his eyes, but the image remained.

'Cymoril,' whispered the voices. 'Cymoril.'

And Elric grew weaker as he became more desperate. He cried out for Dyvim Tvar, but heard only a mocking echo of the name, as he had heard Cymoril's. He shut his lips and he shut his eyes and, still crawling, tried to free himself from the groaning mist. But hours seemed to pass before the groans became whines and the whines became faint strands of sound and he tried to rise, opening his eyes to see the mist fading, but then his legs buckled and he fell down against the first step which led to the Ruby Throne. Again he had ignored Cymoril's advice concerning her brother—and again she was in danger. Elric's last thought was a simple one:

'I am not fit to live,' he thought.

4   To Call the Chaos Lord

As soon as he recovered from the blow which had knocked him unconscious and thus wasted even more time, Elric sent for Dyvim Tvar. He was eager for news. But Dyvim Tvar could report nothing. Yyrkoon had summoned sorcerous aid to free him, sorcerous aid to effect his escape. 'He must have had some magical means of leaving the island, for he could not have gone by ship,' said Dyvim Tvar.

'You must send out expeditions,' said Elric. 'Send a thousand detachments if you must. Send every man in Melniboné. Strive to wake the dragons that they might be used. Equip the golden battle-barges. Cover the world with our men if you must, but find Cymoril.'

'All those things I have already done,' said Dyvim Tvar, 'save that I have not yet found Cymoril.'

A month passed and Imrryrian warriors marched and rode through the Young Kingdoms seeking news of their renegade countrymen.

'I worried more for myself than for Cymoril and I called that "morality",' thought the albino. 'I tested my sensibilities, not my conscience.'

A second month passed and Imrryrian dragons sailed the skies to South and East, West and North, but though they flew across mountains, and seas, and forests and plains and, unwittingly, brought terror to many a city, they found no sign of Yyrkoon and his band.

'For, finally, one can only judge oneself by one's actions,' thought Elric. 'I have looked at what I have done, not at what I meant to do or thought I would like to do, and what I have done has, in the main, been foolish, destructive and with little point. Yyrkoon was right to despise me and that was why I hated him so.'

A fourth month came and Imrryrian ships stopped in remote ports and Imrryrian sailors questioned other travelers and explorers for news of Yyrkoon. But Yyrkoon's sorcery had been strong and none had seen him (or remembered seeing him).

'I must now consider the implications of all these thoughts,' said Elric to himself.

Wearily, the swiftest of the soldiers began to return to Melniboné, bearing their useless news. And as faith disappeared and hope faded, Elric's determination increased. He made himself strong, both physically and mentally. He experimented with new drugs which would increase his energy rather than replenish the energy he did not share with other men. He read much in the library, though this time he read only certain grimoires and he read those over and over again.

These grimoires were written in the High Speech of Melniboné—the ancient language of sorcery with which Elric's ancestors had been able to communicate with the supernatural beings they had summoned. And at last Elric was satisfied that he understood them fully, though what he read sometimes threatened to stop him in his present course of action.

And when he was satisfied—for the dangers of misunderstanding the implications of the things described in the grimoires were catastrophic—he slept for three nights in a drugged slumber.

And then Elric was ready. He ordered all slaves and servants from his quarters. He placed guards at the doors with instructions to admit no one, no matter how urgent their business. He cleared one great chamber of all furniture so that it was completely empty save for one grimoire which he had placed in the very centre of the room. Then he seated himself beside the book and began to think.

When he had meditated for more than five hours Elric took a brush and a jar of ink and began to paint both walls and floor with complicated symbols, some of which were so intricate that they seemed to disappear at an angle to the surface on which they had been laid. At last this was done and Elric spreadeagled himself in the very centre of his huge rune, face down, one hand upon his grimoire, the other (with the Actorios upon it) stretched palm down. The moon was full. A shaft of its light fell directly upon Elric's head, turning the hair to silver. And then the Summoning began.

Elric sent his mind into twisting tunnels of logic, across endless plains of ideas, through mountains of symbolism and endless universes of alternate truths; he sent his mind out further and further and as it went he sent with it the words which issued from his writhing lips—words that few of his contemporaries would understand, though their very sound would chill the blood of any listener. And his body heaved as he forced it to remain in its original position and from time to time a groan would escape him. And through all this a few words came again and again.

One of these words was a name, 'Arioch.'

Arioch, the patron demon of Elric's ancestors; one of the most powerful of all the Dukes of Hell, who was called Knight of the Swords, Lord of the Seven Darks, Lord of the Higher Hell and many more names besides.

'Arioch!'

It was on Arioch whom Yyrkoon had called, asking the Lord of Chaos to curse Elric. It was Arioch whom Yyrkoon had sought to summon to aid him in his attempt upon the Ruby Throne. It was Arioch who was known as the Keeper of the Two Black Swords—the swords of unearthly manufacture and infinite power which had once been wielded by emperors of Melniboné.

'Arioch! I summon thee.'

Runes, both rhythmic and fragmented, howled now from Elric's throat. His brain had reached the plane on which Arioch dwelt. Now it sought Arioch himself.

'Arioch! It is Elric of Melniboné who summons thee.'

Elric glimpsed an eye staring down at him. The eye floated, joined another. The two eyes regarded him.

'Arioch! My Lord of Chaos! Aid me!'

The eyes blinked—and vanished.

'Oh, Arioch! Come to me! Come to me! Aid me and I will serve you!'

A silhouette that was not a human form, turned slowly until a black, faceless head looked down upon Elric. A halo of red light gleamed behind the head.

Then that, too, vanished.

Exhausted, Elric let the image fade. His mind raced back through plane upon plane. His lips no longer chanted the runes and the names. He lay exhausted upon the floor of his chamber, unable to move, in silence.

He was certain that he had failed.

There was a small sound. Painfully he raised his weary head.

A fly had come into the chamber. It buzzed about erratically, seeming almost to follow the lines of the runes Elric had so recently painted.

The fly settled first upon one rune and then on another.

It must have come in through the window, thought Elric. He was annoyed by the distraction but still fascinated by it.

The fly settled on Elric's forehead. It was a large, black fly and its buzz was loud, obscene. It rubbed its forelegs together, and it seemed to be taking a particular interest in Elric's face as it moved over it. Elric shuddered, but he did not have the strength to swat it. When it came into his field of vision, he watched it. When it was not visible he felt its legs covering every inch of his face. Then it flew up and, still buzzing loudly, hovered a short distance from Elric's nose. And then Elric could see the fly's eyes and recognise something in them. They were the eyes —and yet not the eyes—he had seen on that other plane.

It began to dawn on him that this fly was no ordinary creature. It had features that were in some way faintly human.

The fly smiled at him.

From his hoarse throat and through his parched lips Elric was able to utter but one word:

'Arioch?'

And a beautiful youth stood where the fly had hovered. The beautiful youth spoke in a beautiful voice—soft and sympathetic and yet manly. He was clad in a robe that was like a liquid jewel and yet which did not dazzle Elric, for in some way no light seemed to come from it. There was a slender sword at the youth's belt and he wore no helm, but a circlet of red fire. His eyes were wise and his eyes were old and when they were looked at closely they could be seen to contain an ancient and confident evil.

'Elric.'

That was all the youth said, but it revived the albino so that he could raise himself to his knees.

'Elric.'

And Elric could stand. He was filled with energy.

The youth was taller, now, than Elric. He looked down at the Emperor of Melniboné and he smiled the smile that the fly had smiled. 'You alone are fit to serve Arioch. It is long since I was invited to this plane, but now that I am here I shall aid you, Elric. I shall become your patron. I shall protect you and give you strength and the source of strength, though master I be and slave you be.'

'How must I serve you, Duke Arioch?' Elric asked, having made a monstrous effort of self-control, for he was filled with terror by the implications of Arioch's words.

'You will serve me by serving yourself for the moment. Later a time will come when I shall call upon you to serve me in specific ways, but (for the moment) I ask little of you, save that you swear to serve me.'

Elric hesitated.

'You must swear that,' said Arioch reasonably, 'or I cannot help you in the matter of your cousin Yyrkoon or his sister Cymoril.'

'I swear to serve you,' said Elric. And his body was flooded with ecstatic fire and he trembled with joy and he fell to his knees.

'Then I can tell you that, from time to time, you can call on my aid and I will come if your need is truly desperate. I will come in whichever form is appropriate, or no form at all if that should prove appropriate. And now you may ask me one question before I depart.'

'I need the answers to two questions.'

'Your first question I cannot answer. I will not answer. You must accept that you have now sworn to serve me. I will not tell you what the future holds. But you need not fear, if you serve me well.'

'Then my second question is this: Where is Prince Yyrkoon.'

'Prince Yyrkoon is in the south, in a land of barbarians. By sorcery and by superior weapons and intelligence he has effected the conquest of two mean nations, one of which is called Oin and the other of which is called Yu. Even now he trains the men of Oin and the men of Yu to march upon Melniboné, for he knows that your forces are spread thinly across the earth, searching for him.'

'How has he hidden?'

'He has not. But he has gained possession of the Mirror of Memory— a magical device whose hiding place he discovered by his sorceries. Those who look into this mirror have their memories taken. The mirror contains a million memories: the memories of all who have looked into it. Thus anyone who ventures into Oin or Yu or travels by sea to the capital which serves both is confronted by the mirror and forgets that he has seen Prince Yyrkoon and his Imrryrians in those lands. It is the best way of remaining undiscovered.'

'It is.' Elric drew his brows together. 'Therefore it might be wise to consider destroying the mirror. But what would happen then, I wonder?'

Arioch raised his beautiful hand. 'Although I have answered further questions which are, one could argue, part of the same question, I will answer no more. It could be in your interest to destroy the mirror, but it might be better to consider other means of countering its effects, for it does, I remind you, contain many memories, some of which have been imprisoned for thousands of years. Now I must go. And you must go— to the lands of Oin and Yu which lie several months' journey from here, to the south and well beyond Lormyr. They are best reached by the Ship Which Sails Over Both Land and Sea. Farewell, Elric.'

And a fly buzzed for a moment upon the wall before vanishing.

Elric rushed from the room, shouting for his slaves.

5   The Ship Which Sails Over Land and Sea

'And how many dragons still sleep in the caverns?' Elric paced the gallery overlooking the city. It was morning, but no sun came through the dull clouds which hung low upon the towers of the Dreaming City. Imrryr's life continued unchanged in the streets below, save for the absence of the majority of her soldiers who had not yet returned home from their fruitless quests and would not be home for many months to come.

Dyvim Tvar leaned on the parapet of the gallery and stared unseeingly into the streets. His face was tired and his arms were folded on his chest as if he sought to contain what was left of his strength.

'Two perhaps. It would take a great deal to wake them and even then I doubt if they'd be useful to us. What is this "Ship Which Sails Over Land and Sea" which Arioch spoke of?'

'I've read of it before—in the Silver Grimoire and in other tomes. A magic ship. Used by a Melnibonéan hero even before there was Melniboné and the empire. But where it exists, and if it exists, I do not know.'

'Who would know?' Dyvim Tvar straightened his back and turned it on the scene below.

'Arioch?' Elric shrugged. 'But he would not tell me.'

'What of your friends the Water Elementals. Have they not promised you aid? And would they not be knowledgeable in the matter of ships?'

Elric frowned, deepening the lines which now marked his face. 'Aye —Straasha might know. But I'm loath to call on his aid again. The Water Elementals are not the powerful creatures that the Lords of Chaos are. Their strength is limited and, moreover, they are inclined to be capricious, in the manner of the elements. What is more, Dyvim Tvar, I hesitate to use sorcery, save where absolutely imperative . . .'

'You are a sorcerer, Elric. You have but lately proved your greatness in that respect, involving the most powerful of all sorceries, the sum-moning of a Chaos Lord—and you still hold back? I would suggest, my lord king, that you consider such logic and that you judge it unsound. You decided to use sorcery in your pursuit of Prince Yyrkoon. The die is already cast. It would be wise to use sorcery now.'

'You cannot conceive of the mental and physical effort involved . . .'

'I can conceive of it, my lord. I am your friend. I do not wish to see you pained—and yet . . .'

'There is also the difficulty, Dyvim Tvar, of my physical weakness,' Elric reminded his friend. 'How long can I continue in the use of these overstrong potions that now sustain me? They supply me with energy, aye—but they do so by using up my few resources. I might die before I find Cymoril.'

'I stand rebuked.'

But Elric came forward and put his white hand on Dyvim Tvar's butter-coloured cloak. 'But what have I to lose, eh? No. You are right. I am a coward to hesitate when Cymoril's life is at stake. I repeat my stupidities—the stupidities which first brought this pass upon us all. I'll do it. Will you come with me to the ocean?'

'Aye.'

Dyvim Tvar began to feel the burden of Elric's conscience settling upon him also. It was a peculiar feeling to come to a Melnibonéan and Dyvim Tvar knew very well that he liked it not at all.

Elric had last ridden these paths when he and Cymoril were happy. It seemed a long age ago. He had been a fool to trust that happiness. He turned his white stallion's head towards the cliffs and the sea beyond them. A light rain fell. Winter was descending swiftly on Melniboné.

They left their horses on the cliffs, lest they be disturbed by Elric's sorcery-working, and clambered down to the shore. The rain fell into the sea. A mist hung over the water little more than five ship lengths from the beach. It was deathly still and, with the tall, dark cliffs behind them and the wall of mist before them, it seemed to Dyvim Tvar that they had entered a silent netherworld where might easily be encoun-tered the melancholy souls of those who, in legend, had committed suicide by a process of slow self-mutilation. The sound of the two men's boots on shingle was loud and yet was at once muffled by the mist which seemed to suck at noise and swallow it greedily as if it sustained its life on sound.

'Now,' Elric murmured. He seemed not to notice the brooding and depressive surroundings. 'Now I must recall the rune which came so easily, unsummoned, to my brain not many months since.' He left

Dyvim Tvar's side and went down to the place where the chill water lapped the land and there, carefully, he seated himself, cross-legged. His eyes stared, unseeingly, into the mist.

To Dyvim Tvar the tall albino appeared to shrink as he sat down. He seemed to become like a vulnerable child and Dyvim Tvar's heart went out to Elric as it might go out to a brave, nervous boy, and Dyvim Tvar had it in mind to suggest that the sorcery be done with and they seek the lands of Oin and Yu by ordinary means.

But Elric was already lifting his head as a dog lifts its head to the moon. And strange, thrilling words began to tumble from his lips and it became plain that, even if Dyvim Tvar did speak now, Elric would not hear him.

Dyvim Tvar was no stranger to the High Speech—as a Melnibonéan noble he had been taught it as a matter of course—but the words seemed nonetheless strange to him, for Elric used peculiar inflections and emphases, giving the words a special and secret weight and chanting them in a voice which ranged from bass groan to falsetto shriek. It was not pleasant to listen to such noises coming from a mortal throat and now Dyvim Tvar had some clear understanding of why Elric was reluctant to use sorcery. The Lord of the Dragon Caves, Melnibonéan though he was, found himself inclined to step backward a pace or two, even to retire to the cliff-tops and watch over Elric from there, and he had to force himself to hold his ground as the summoning continued.

For a good space of time the rune-chanting went on. The rain beat harder upon the pebbles of the shore and made them glisten. It dashed most ferociously into the still, dark sea, lashed about the fragile head of the chanting, pale-haired figure, and caused Dyvim Tvar to shiver and draw his cloak more closely about his shoulders.

'Straasha—Straasha—Straasha . . .'

The words mingled with the sound of the rain. They were now barely words at all but sounds which the wind might make or a language which the sea might speak.

'*Straasha* . . .'

Again Dyvim Tvar had the impulse to move, but this time he desired to go to Elric and tell him to stop, to consider some other means of reaching the lands of Oin and Yu.

'*Straasha!*'

There was a cryptic agony in the shout.

'*Straasha!*'

Elric's name formed on Dyvim Tvar's lips, but he found that he could not speak it.

'*Straasha!*'

The cross-legged figure swayed. The word became the calling of the wind through the Caverns of Time.

'*Straasha!*'

It was plain to Dyvim Tvar that the rune was, for some reason, not working and that Elric was using up all his strength to no effect. And yet there was nothing the Lord of the Dragon Caves could do. His tongue was frozen. His feet seemed frozen. His feet seemed frozen to the ground.

He looked at the mist. Had it crept closer to the shore? Had it taken on a strange, almost luminous, green tinge? He peered closely.

There was a massive disturbance of the water. The sea rushed up the beach. The shingle crackled. The mist retreated. Vague lights flickered in the air and Dyvim Tvar thought he saw the shining silhouette of a gigantic figure emerging from the sea and he realised that Elric's chant had ceased.

'King Straasha,' Elric was saying in something approaching his normal tone. 'You have come. I thank you.'

The silhouette spoke and the voice reminded Dyvim Tvar of slow, heavy waves rolling beneath a friendly sun.

'*We elementals are concerned, Elric, for there are rumours that you have invited Chaos Lords back to your plane and the elementals have never loved the Lords of Chaos. Yet I know that if you have done this it is because you are fated to do it and therefore we hold no enmity against you.*'

'The decision was forced upon me, King Straasha. There was no other decision I could make. If you are therefore reluctant to aid me, I shall understand that and call on you no more.'

'*I will help you, though helping you is harder now, not for what happens in the immediate future but what is hinted will happen in years to come. Now you must tell me quickly how we of the water can be of service to you.*'

'Do you know aught of the Ship Which Sails Over Land and Sea? I need to find that ship if I am to fulfil my vow to find my love, Cymoril.'

'*I know much of that ship, for it is mine. Grome also lays claim to it. But it is mine. Fairly, it is mine.*'

'Grome of the Earth?'

'*Grome of the Land Below the Roots. Grome of the Ground and all that lives under it. My brother. Grome. Long since, even as we elementals count time. Grome and I built that ship so that we could travel between the realms of Earth and Water whenever we chose. But we quarrelled (may we be cursed for such foolishness) and we fought. There were earth-*

quakes, tidal waves, volcanic eruptions, typhoons and battles in which all the elementals joined, with the result that new continents were flung up and old ones drowned. It was not the first time we had fought each other, but it was the last. And finally, lest we destroy each other completely, we made a peace. I gave Grome part of my domain and he gave me the Ship Which Sails Over Land and Sea. But he gave it somewhat unwillingly and thus it sails the sea better than it sails the land, for Grome thwarts its progress whenever he can. Still, if the ship is of use to you, you shall have it.'

'I thank you, King Straasha. Where shall I find it?'

'It will come. And now I grow weary, for the further from my own realm I venture, the harder it is to sustain my mortal form. Farewell, Elric—and be cautious. You have a greater power than you know and many would make use of it to their own ends.'

'Shall I wait here for the Ship Which Sails Over Land and Sea?'

'No . . .' the Sea King's voice was fading as his form faded. Grey mist drifted back where the silhouette and the green lights had been. The sea again was still. *'Wait. Wait in your tower . . . It will come . . .'*

A few wavelets lapped the shore and then it was as if the king of the Water Elementals had never been there at all. Dyvim Tvar rubbed his eyes. Slowly at first he began to move to where Elric still sat. Gently he bent down and offered the albino his hand. Elric looked up in some surprise. 'Ah, Dyvim Tvar. How much time has passed?'

'Some hours, Elric. It will soon be night. What little light there is begins to wane. We had best ride back for Imrryr.'

Stiffly Elric rose to his feet, with Dyvim Tvar's assistance. 'Aye . . .' he murmured absently. 'The Sea King said . . .'

'I heard the Sea King, Elric. I heard his advice and I heard his warning. You must remember to heed both. I like too little the sound of this magic boat. Like most things of sorcerous origin, the ship appears to have vices as well as virtues, like a double-bladed knife which you raise to stab your enemy and which, instead, stabs you . . .'

'That must be expected where sorcery is concerned. It was you who urged me on, my friend.'

'Aye,' said Dyvim Tvar almost to himself as he led the way up the cliff-path towards the horses. 'Aye. I have not forgotten that, my lord king.'

Elric smiled wanly and touched Dyvim Tvar's arm. 'Worry not. The summoning is over and now we have the vessel we need to take us swiftly to Prince Yyrkoon and the lands of Oin and Yu.'

'Let us hope so.' Dyvim Tvar was privately sceptical about the benefits they would gain from the Ship Which Sails Over Land and Sea. They reached the horses and he began to wipe the water off the flanks of his own roan. 'I regret,' he said, 'that we have once again allowed the dragons to expend their energy on a useless endeavour. With a squadron of my beasts, we could do much against Prince Yyrkoon. And it would be fine and wild, my friend, to ride the skies again, side by side, as we used to.'

'When all this is done and Princess Cymoril brought home, we shall do that,' said Elric, hauling himself wearily into the saddle of his white stallion. 'You shall blow the Dragon Horn and our dragon brothers will hear it and you and I shall sing the *Song of the Dragon Masters* and our goads shall flash as we straddle Flamefang and his mate Sweetclaw. Ah, that will be like the days of old Melniboné, when we no longer equate freedom with power, but let the Young Kingdoms go their own way and be certain that they let us go ours!'

Dyvim Tvar pulled on his horse's reins. His brow was clouded. 'Let us pray that day will come, my lord. But I cannot help this nagging thought which tells me that Imrryr's days are numbered and that my own life nears its close . . .'

'Nonsense, Dyvim Tvar. You'll survive me. There's little doubt of that, though you be my elder.'

Dyvim Tvar said, as they galloped back through the closing day: 'I have two sons. Did you know that, Elric?'

'You have never mentioned them.'

'They are by old mistresses.'

'I am happy for you.'

'They are fine Melnibonéans.'

'Why do you mention this, Dyvim Tvar?' Elric tried to read his friend's expression.

'It is that I love them and would have them enjoy the pleasures of the Dragon Isle.'

'And why should they not?'

'I do not know.' Dyvim Tvar looked hard at Elric. 'I could suggest that it is your responsibility, the fate of my sons, Elric.'

'Mine?'

'It seems to me, from what I gathered from the Water Elemental's words, that your decisions could decide the fate of the Dragon Isle. I ask you to remember my sons, Elric.'

'I shall, Dyvim Tvar. I am certain they shall grow into superb Dragon Masters and that one of them shall succeed you as Lord of the Dragon Caves.'

'I think you miss my meaning, my lord emperor.'

And Elric looked solemnly at his friend and shook his head. 'I do not miss your meaning, old friend. But I think you judge me harshly if you fear I'll do aught to threaten Melniboné and all she is.'

'Forgive me, then.' Dyvim Tvar lowered his head. But the expression in his eyes did not change.

In Imrryr they changed their clothes and drank hot wine and had spiced food brought. Elric, for all his weariness, was in better spirits than he had been for many a month. And yet there was still a tinge of something behind his surface mood which suggested he encouraged himself to speak gaily and put vitality into his movements. Admittedly, thought Dyvim Tvar, the prospects had improved and soon they would be confronting Prince Yyrkoon. But the dangers ahead of them were unknown, the pitfalls probably considerable. Still, he did not, out of sympathy for his friend, want to dispel Elric's mood. He was glad, in fact, that Elric seemed in a more positive frame of mind. There was talk of the equipment they would need in their expedition to the mysterious lands of Yu and Oin, speculation concerning the capacity of the Ship Which Sails Over Land and Sea—how many men it would take, what provisions they should put aboard and so on.

When Elric went to his bed, he did not walk with the dragging tiredness which had previously accompanied his step and again, bidding him goodnight, Dyvim Tvar was struck by the same emotion which had filled him on the beach, watching Elric begin his rune. Perhaps it was not by chance that he had used the example of his sons when speaking to Elric earlier that day, for he had a feeling that was almost protective, as if Elric were a boy looking forward to some treat which might not bring him the joy he expected.

Dyvim Tvar dismissed the thoughts, as best he could, and went to his own bed. Elric might blame himself for all that had occurred in the question of Yyrkoon and Cymoril, but Dyvim Tvar wondered if he, too, were not to blame in some part. Perhaps he should have offered his advice more cogently—more vehemently, even—earlier and made a stronger attempt to influence the young emperor. And then, in the Melnibonéan manner, he dismissed such doubts and questions as pointless. There was only one rule—seek pleasure however you would. But had that always been the Melnibonéan way? Dyvim Tvar wondered suddenly if Elric might not have regressive rather than deficient blood. Could Elric be a reincarnation of one of their most distant ancestors? Had it always been in the Melnibonéan character to think only of oneself and one's own gratification?

And again Dyvim Tvar dismissed the questions. What use was there in questions, after all? The world was the world. A man was a man. Before he sought his own bed he went to visit both his old mistresses, waking them up and insisting that he see his sons, Dyvim Slorm and Dyvim Mav and when his sons, sleepy-eyed, bewildered, had been brought to him, he stared at them for a long while before sending them back. He had said nothing to either, but he had brought his brows together frequently and rubbed at his face and shaken his head and, when they had gone, had said to Niopal and Saramal, his mistresses, who were as bewildered as their offspring, 'Let them be taken to the Dragon Caves tomorrow and begin their learning.'

'So soon, Dyvim Tvar?' said Niopal.

'Aye. There's little time left, I fear.'

He would not amplify on this remark because he could not. It was merely a feeling he had. But it was a feeling that was growing almost to the point where it was becoming an obsession with him.

In the morning Dyvim Tvar returned to Elric's tower and found the emperor pacing the gallery above the city, asking eagerly for any news of a ship sighted off the coast of the island. But no such ship had been seen. Servants answered earnestly that if their emperor could describe the ship, it would be easier for them to know for what to look, but he could not describe the ship, and could only hint that it might not be seen on water at all, but might appear on land. He was all dressed up in his black war gear and it was plain to Dyvim Tvar that Elric was indulging in even larger quantities of the potions which replenished his blood. The crimson eyes gleamed with a hot vitality, the speech was rapid and the bone-white hands moved with unnatural speed when Elric made even the lightest gesture.

'Are you well this morning, my lord?' asked the Dragon Master.

'In excellent spirits, thank you, Dyvim Tvar.' Elric grinned. 'Though I'd feel even better if the Ship Which Sails Over Land and Sea were here now.' He went to the balustrade and leaned upon it, peering over the towers and beyond the city walls, looking first to the sea and then to the land. 'Where can it be? I wish that King Straasha had been able to be more specific.'

'I'll agree with that.' Dyvim Tvar, who had not breakfasted, helped himself from the variety of succulent foods laid upon the table. It was evident that Elric had eaten nothing.

Dyvim Tvar began to wonder if the volume of potions had not affected his old friend's brain; perhaps madness, brought about by his involvement with complicated sorcery, his anxiety for Cymoril, his hatred of Yyrkoon, had begun to overwhelm Elric.

'Would it not be better to rest and to wait until the ship is sighted?' he suggested quietly as he wiped his lips.

'Aye—there's reason in that,' Elric agreed. 'But I cannot. I have an urge to be off, Dyvim Tvar, to come face to face with Yyrkoon, to have my revenge on him, to be united with Cymoril again.'

'I understand that. Yet, still . . .'

Elric's laugh was loud and ragged. 'You fret like Tanglebones over my well-being. I do not need two nursemaids, Lord of the Dragon Caves.'

With an effort Dyvim Tvar smiled. 'You are right. Well, I pray that this magical vessel—what is that?' He pointed out across the island. 'A movement in yonder forest. As if the wind passes through it. But there is no sign of wind elsewhere.'

Elric followed his gaze. 'You are right. I wonder . . .'

And then they saw something emerge from the forest and the land itself seemed to ripple. It was something which glinted white and blue and black. It came closer.

'A sail,' said Dyvim Tvar. 'It is your ship, I think, my lord.'

'Aye,' Elric whispered, craning forward. 'My ship. Make yourself ready, Dyvim Tvar. By midday we shall be gone from Imrryr.'

6   What the Earth God Desired

The ship was tall and slender and she was delicate. Her rails, masts and
bulwarks were exquisitely carved and obviously not the work of a mortal craftsman. Though built of wood, the wood was not painted but
naturally shone blue and black and green and a kind of deep smoky red;
and her rigging was the colour of sea-weed and there were veins in the
planks of her polished deck, like the roots of trees, and the sails on her
three tapering masts were as fat and white and light as clouds on a fine
summer day. The ship was everything that was lovely in nature; few
could look upon her and not feel delighted, as they might be delighted
upon sighting a perfect view. In a word, the ship radiated harmony, and
Elric could think of no finer vessel in which to sail against Prince Yyrkoon and the dangers of the lands of Oin and Yu.

The ship sailed gently in the ground as if upon the surface of a river
and the earth beneath the keel rippled as if turned momentarily to
water. Wherever the keel of the ship touched, and a few feet around it,
this effect became evident, though, after the ship had passed, the ground
would return to its usual stable state. This was why the trees of the
forest had swayed as the ship passed through them, parting before the
keel as the ship sailed towards Imrryr.

The Ship Which Sails Over Land and Sea was not particularly large.
Certainly she was considerably smaller than a Melnibonéan battle-barge
and only a little bigger than a southern galley. But the grace of her; the
curve of her line; the pride of her bearing—in these, she had no rival at
all.

Already her gangplanks had been lowered down to the ground and
she was being made ready for her journey. Elric, hands on his slim hips,
stood looking up at King Straasha's gift. From the gates of the city wall
slaves were bearing provisions and arms and carrying them up the gang-
ways. Meanwhile Dyvim Tvar was assembling the Imrryrian warriors

and assigning them their ranks and duties while on the expedition. There were not many warriors. Only half the available strength could come with the ship, for the other half must remain behind under the command of Admiral Magum Colim and protect the city. It was unlikely that there would be any large attack on Melniboné after the punishment meted out to the barbarian fleet, but it was wise to take precautions, particularly since Prince Yyrkoon had vowed to conquer Imrryr. Also, for some strange reason that none of the onlookers could divine, Dyvim Tvar had called for volunteers—veterans who shared a common disability—and made up a special detachment of these men who, so the onlookers thought, could be of no use at all on the expedition. Still, neither were they of use when it came to defending the city, so they might as well go. These veterans were led aboard first.

Last to climb the gangway was Elric himself. He walked slowly, heavily, a proud figure in his black armour, until he reached the deck. Then he turned, saluted his city, and ordered the gangplank raised.

Dyvim Tvar was waiting for him on the poop-deck. The Lord of the Dragon Caves had stripped off one of his gauntlets and was running his naked hand over the oddly coloured wood of the rail. 'This is not a ship made for war, Elric,' he said. 'I should not like to see it harmed.'

'How can it be harmed?' Elric asked lightly as Imrryrians began to climb the rigging and adjust the sails. 'Would Straasha let it be destroyed? Would Grome? Fear not for the Ship Which Sails Over Land and Sea, Dyvim Tvar. Fear only for our own safety and the success of our expedition. Now, let us consult the charts. Remembering Straasha's warning concerning his brother Grome, I suggest we travel by sea for as far as possible, calling in here . . .' he pointed to a sea-port on the western coast of Lormyr—'to get our bearings and learn what we can of the lands of Oin and Yu and how those lands are defended.'

'Few travellers have ever ventured beyond Lormyr. It is said that the edge of the world lies not far from that country's most southerly borders.' Dyvim Tvar frowned. 'Could not this whole mission be a trap, I wonder? Arioch's trap? What if he is in league with Prince Yyrkoon and we have been completely deceived into embarking upon an expedition which will destroy us?'

'I have considered that,' said Elric. 'But there is no other choice. We must trust Arioch.'

'I suppose we must.' Dyvim Tvar smiled ironically. 'Another matter now occurs to me. How does the ship move? I saw no anchors we could raise and there are no tides that I know of that sweep across the land. The wind fills the sails—see.' It was true. The sails were billowing and the masts creaked slightly as they took the strain.

Elric shrugged and spread his hands. 'I suppose we must tell the ship,' he suggested. 'Ship—we are ready to sail.'

Elric took some pleasure in Dyvim Tvar's expression of astonishment as, with a lurch, the ship began to move. It sailed smoothly, as over a calm sea, and Dyvim Tvar instinctively clutched the rail, shouting: 'But we are heading directly for the city wall!'

Elric crossed quickly to the centre of the poop where a large lever lay, horizontally attached to a ratchet which in turn was attached to a spindle. This was almost certainly the steering gear. Elric grasped the lever as one might grasp an oar and pushed it round a notch or two. Immediately the ship responded—and turned towards another part of the wall! Elric hauled back on the lever and the ship leaned, protesting a little as she yawed around and began to head out across the island. Elric laughed in delight. 'You see, Dyvim Tvar, it is easy? A slight effort of logic was all it took!'

'Nonetheless,' said Dyvim Tvar suspiciously. 'I'd rather we rode dragons. At least they are beasts and may be understood. But this sorcery, it troubles me.'

'Those are not fitting ..ords for a noble of Melniboné!' Elric shouted above the sound of the wind in the rigging, the creaking of the ship's timbers, the slap of the great white sails.

'Perhaps not,' said Dyvim Tvar. 'Perhaps that explains why I stand beside you now, my lord.'

Elric darted his friend a puzzled look before he went below to find a helmsman whom he could teach how to steer the ship.

The ship sped swiftly over rocky slopes and up gorse-covered hills; she cut her way through forests and sailed grandly over grassy plains. She moved like a low-flying hawk which keeps close to the ground but progresses with incredible speed and accuracy as it searches for its prey, altering its course with an imperceptible flick of a wing. The soldiers of Imrryr crowded her decks, gasping in amazement at the ship's progress over the land, and many of the men had to be clouted back to their positions at the sails or elsewhere about the ship. The huge warrior who acted as bosun seemed the only member of the crew unaffected by the miracle of the ship. He was behaving as he would normally behave aboard one of the golden battle-barges; going solidly about his duties and seeing to it that all was done in a proper seamanly manner. The helmsman Elric had selected was, on the other hand, wide-eyed and somewhat nervous of the ship he handled. You could see that he felt he was, at any moment, going to be dashed against a slab of rock or smash the ship apart in a tangle of thick-trunked pines. He was forever wetting his lips and wiping sweat from his brow, even though the air was sharp and his breath steamed as it left his throat. Yet he was a good helmsman and gradually he became used to handling the ship, though his movements were, perforce, more rapid, for there was little time to deliberate upon a decision, the ship travelled with such speed over the land. The speed was breathtaking; they sped more swiftly than any horse—were swifter, even, than Dyvim Tvar's beloved dragons. Yet the motion was exhilarating, too, as the expressions on the faces of all the Imrryrians told.

Elric's delighted laughter rang through the ship and infected many another member of the crew.

'Well, if Grome of the Roots is trying to block our progress, I hesitate to guess how fast we shall travel when we reach water!' he called to Dyvim Tvar.

Dyvim Tvar had lost some of his earlier mood. His long, fine hair streamed around his face as he smiled at his friend. 'Aye—we shall all be whisked off the deck and into the sea!'

And then, as if in answer to their words, the ship began suddenly to buck and at the same time sway from side to side, like a ship caught in powerful cross-currents. The helmsman went white and clung to his lever, trying to get the ship back under control. There came a brief, terrified yell and a sailor fell from the highest cross-tree in the main mast and crashed onto the deck, breaking every bone in his body. And then the ship swayed once or twice and the turbulence was behind them and they continued on their course.

Elric stared at the body of the fallen sailor. Suddenly the mood of gaiety left him completely and he gripped the rail in his black gauntleted hands and he gritted his strong teeth and his crimson eyes glowed and his lips curled in self-mockery. 'What a fool I am. What a fool I am to tempt the gods so!'

Still, though the ship moved almost as swiftly as it had done, there seemed to be something dragging at it, as if Grome's minions clung on to the bottom as barnacles might cling in the sea. And Elric sensed something around him in the air, something in the rustling of the trees through which they passed, something in the movement of the grass and the bushes and the flowers over which they crossed, something in the weight of the rocks, of the angle of the hills. And he knew that what he sensed was the presence of Grome of the Ground—Grome of the Land Below the Roots—Grome, who desired to own what he and his brother Straasha had once owned jointly, what they had had made as a sign of the unity between them and over which they had then fought. Grome wanted very much to take back the Ship Which Sails Over Land and Sea. And Elric, staring down at the black earth, became afraid.

7 King Grome

But at last, with the land tugging at their keel, they reached the sea, sliding into the water and gathering speed with every moment, until Melniboné was gone behind them and they were sighting the thick clouds of steam which hung forever over the Boiling Sea. Elric thought it unwise to risk even this magical vessel in those peculiar waters, so the vessel was turned and headed for the coast of Lormyr, sweetest and most tranquil of the Young Kingdom nations, and the port of Ramasaz on Lormyr's western shore. If the southern barbarians with whom they had so recently fought had been from Lormyr, Elric would have considered making for some other port, but the barbarians had almost certainly been from the South-East on the far side of the continent, beyond Pikarayd. The Lormyrians, under their fat, cautious King Fadan, were not likely to join a raid unless its success were completely assured. Sailing slowly into Ramasaz, Elric gave instructions that their ship be moored in a conventional way and treated like any ordinary ship. It attracted attention, nonetheless, for its beauty, and the inhabitants of the port were astonished to find Melnibonéans crewing the vessel. Though Melnibonéans were disliked throughout the Young Kingdoms, they were also feared. Thus, outwardly at any rate, Elric and his men were treated with respect and were served reasonably good food and wine in the hostelries they entered.

In the largest of the waterfront inns, a place called *Heading Outward and Coming Safely Home Again,* Elric found a garrulous host who had, until he bought the inn, been a prosperous fisherman and who knew the southernmost shores reasonably well. He certainly knew the lands of Oin and Yu, but he had no respect for them at all.

'You think they could be massing for war, my lord.' He raised his eyebrows at Elric before hiding his face in his wine-mug. Wiping his lips, he shook his red head. "Then they must war against sparrows. Oin and Yu are barely nations at all. Their only halfway decent city is Dhoz-Kam—and that is shared between them, half being on one side of the River Ar and half being on the other. As for the rest of Oin and Yu—it is inhabited by peasants who are for the most part so ill-educated and superstition-ridden that they are poverty-striken. Not a potential soldier among 'em.'

'You've heard nothing of a Melnibonéan renegade who has conquered Oin and Yu and set about training these peasants to make war?' Dyvim Tvar leaned on the bar next to Elric. He sipped fastidiously from a thick cup of wine. 'Prince Yyrkoon is the renegade's name.'

'Is that whom you seek?' The innkeeper became more interested. 'A dispute between the Dragon Princes, eh?'

'That's our business,' said Elric haughtily.

'Of course, my lords.'

'You know nothing of a great mirror which steals men's memories?' Dyvim Tvar asked.

'A magical mirror!' The innkeeper threw back his head and laughed heartily. 'I doubt if there's one decent mirror in the whole of Oin or Yu! No, my lords, I think you are misled if you fear danger from those lands!"

'Doubtless you are right,' said Elric, staring down into his own un-tasted wine. 'But it would be wise if we were to check for ourselves—and it would be in Lormyr's interests, too, if we were to find what we seek and warn you accordingly.'

'Fear not for Lormyr. We can deal easily with any silly attempt to make war from that quarter. But if you'd see for yourselves, you must follow the coast for three days until you come to a great bay. The River Ar runs into that bay and on the shores of the river lies Dhoz-Kam—a seedy sort of city, particularly for a capital serving two nations. The inhabitants are corrupt, dirty and disease-ridden, but fortunately they are also lazy and thus afford little trouble, especially if you keep a sword by you. When you have spent an hour in Dhoz-Kam, you will realise the impossibility of such folk becoming a menace to anyone else, unless they should get close enough to you to infect you with one of their several plagues!' Again the innkeeper laughed hugely at his own wit. As he ceased shaking, he added: 'Or unless you fear their navy. It consists of a dozen or so filthy fishing boats, most of which are so unseaworthy they dare only fish the shallows of the estuary.'

Elric pushed his wine-cup aside. 'We thank you, landlord.' He placed a Melnibonéan silver piece upon the counter.

'This will be hard to change,' said the innkeeper craftily.

'There is no need to change it on our account,' Elric told him.

'I thank you, masters. Would you stay the night at my establishment. I can offer you the finest beds in Ramasaz.'

'I think not,' Elric told him. 'We shall sleep aboard our ship tonight, that we might be ready to sail at dawn.'

The landlord watched the Melnibonéans depart. Instinctively he bit at the silver piece and then, suspecting he tasted something odd about it, removed it from his mouth. He stared at the coin, turning it this way and that. Could Melnibonéan silver be poisonous to an ordinary mortal? he wondered. It was best not to take risks. He tucked the coin into his purse and collected up the two wine-cups they had left behind. Though he hated waste, he decided it would be wiser to throw the cups out lest they should have become tainted in some way.

The Ship Which Sails Over Land and Sea reached the bay at noon on the following day and now it lay close inshore, hidden from the distant city by a short isthmus on which grew thick, near-tropical foliage. Elric and Dyvim Tvar waded through the clear, shallow water to the beach and entered the forest. They had decided to be cautious and not make their presence known until they had determined the truth of the innkeeper's contemptuous description of Dhoz-Kam. Near the tip of the isthmus was a reasonably high hill and growing on the hill were several good-sized trees. Elric and Dyvim Tvar used their swords to clear a path through the undergrowth and made their way up the hill until they stood under the trees, picking out the one most easily climbed. Elric selected a tree whose trunk bent and then straightened out again. He sheathed his sword, got his hands onto the trunk and hauled himself up, clambering along until he reached a succession of thick branches which would bear his weight. In the meantime Dyvim Tvar climbed another nearby tree until at last both men could get a good view across the bay where the city of Dhoz-Kam could be clearly seen. Certainly the city itself deserved the innkeeper's description. It was squat and grimy and evidently poor. Doubtless this was why Yyrkoon had chosen it, for the lands of Oin and Yu could not have been hard to conquer with the help of a handful of well-trained Imrryrians and some of Yyrkoon's sorcerous allies. Indeed, few would have bothered to conquer such a place, since its wealth was plainly virtually non-existent and its geographical position of no strategic importance. Yyrkoon had chosen well, for purposes of secrecy if nothing else. But the landlord had been wrong about Dhoz-Kam's fleet. Even from here Elric and Dyvim Tvar could make out a good thirty good-sized warships in the harbour and there seemed to be more anchored up-river. But the ships did not interest them as much as the thing which flashed and glittered above the city—something which had been mounted on huge pillars which supported an axle which, in turn, supported a vast, circular mirror set in a frame whose workmanship was as plainly non-mortal as that of the ship which had brought the Melnibonéans here. There was no doubt that they looked upon the Mirror of Memory and that any who had sailed into the harbour after it had been erected must have had their memory of what they had seen stolen from them instantly.

'It seems to me, my lord,' said Dyvim Tvar from his perch a yard or two away from Elric, 'that it would be unwise of us to sail directly into the harbour of Dhoz-Kam. Indeed, we could be in danger if we entered the bay. I think that we look upon the mirror, even now, only because it is not pointed directly at us. But you notice there is machinery to turn it in any direction its user chooses—save one. It cannot be turned inland, behind the city. There is no need for it, for who would approach Oin and Yu from the wastelands beyond their borders and who but the inhabitants of Oin or Yu would need to come overland to their capital?'

'I think I take your meaning, Dyvim Tvar. You suggest that we would be wise to make use of the special properties of our ship and . . .'

'. . . and go overland to Dhoz-Kam, striking suddenly and making full use of those veterans we brought with us, moving swiftly and ignoring Prince Yyrkoon's new allies—seeking the prince himself, and his renegades. Could we do that, Elric? Dash into the city—seize Yyrkoon, rescue Cymoril—then speed out again and away?'

'Since we have too few men to make a direct assault, it is all we can do, though it's dangerous. The advantage of surprise would be lost, of course, once we had made the attempt. If we failed in our first attempt it would become much harder to attack a second time. The alternative is to sneak into the city at night and hope to locate Yyrkoon and Cymoril alone, but then we should not be making use of our one important weapon, the Ship Which Sails Over Land and Sea. I think your plan is the best one, Dyvim Tvar. Let us turn the ship inland, now, and hope that Grome takes his time in finding us—for I still worry lest he try seriously to wrest the ship from our possession.' Elric began to climb down towards the ground.

Standing once more upon the poop-deck of the lovely ship, Elric ordered the helmsman to turn the vessel once again towards the land. Under half-sail the ship moved gracefully through the water and up the curve of the bank and the flowering shrubs of the forest parted before its prow and then they were sailing through the green dark of the jungle, while startled birds cawed and shrilled and little animals paused in

astonishment and peered down from the trees at the Ship Which Sails
Over Land and Sea and some almost lost their balance as the graceful
boat progressed calmly over the floor of the forest, turning aside for
only the thickest of the trees.

And thus they made their way to the interior of the land called Oin,
which lay to the north of the River Ar, which marked the border between Oin and the land called Yu with which Oin shared a single capital.

Oin was a country consisting largely of jungle and infertile plains
where the inhabitants farmed, for they feared the forest and would not
go into it, even though that was where Oin's wealth might be found.

The ship sailed well enough through the forest and out over the plain
and soon they could see a large lake glinting ahead of them and Dyvim
Tvar, glancing at the crude map with which he had furnished himself in
Ramasaz, suggested that they begin to turn towards the south again and
approach Dhoz-Kam by means of a wide semi-circle. Elric agreed and
the ship began to tack round.

It was then that the land began to heave again and huge waves of
grassy earth this time rolled around the ship and blotted out the surrounding view. The ship pitched wildly up and down and from side to
side. Two more Imrryrians fell from the rigging and were killed on the
deck below. The bosun was shouting loudly—though in fact all this
upheaval was happening in silence—and the silence made the situation
seem that much more menacing. The bosun yelled to his men to tie
themselves to their positions. 'And all those not doing anything—get
below at once!' he added.

Elric had wound a scarf around the rail and tied the other end to his
wrist. Dyvim Tvar had used a long belt for the same purpose. But still
they were flung in all directions, often losing their footing as the ship
bucked this way and that, and every bone in Elric's body seemed about
to crack and every inch of his flesh seemed bruised. And the ship was
creaking and protesting and threatening to break up under the awful
strain of riding the heaving land.

'Is this Grome's work, Elric?' Dyvim Tvar panted. 'Or is it some
sorcery of Yyrkoon's?'

Elric shook his head. 'Not Yyrkoon. It is Grome. And I know no
way to placate him. Not Grome, who thinks least of all the Kings of the
Elements, yet, perhaps, is the most powerful.'

'But surely he breaks his bargain with his brother by doing this to
us?'

'No. I think not. King Straasha warned us this might happen. We can only hope that Grome expends all his energy and that the ship survives, as it might survive a natural storm at sea.'

'This is worse than a sea-storm, Elric!'

Elric nodded his agreement but could say nothing, for the deck was tilting at a crazy angle and he had to cling to the rails with both hands in order to retain any kind of footing.

And now the silence stopped.

Instead they heard a rumbling and a roaring that seemed to have something of the character of laughter.

'King Grome!' Elric shouted. 'King Grome! Let us be! We have done you no harm!'

But the laughter increased and it made the whole ship quiver as the land rose and fell around it, as trees and hills and rocks rushed towards the ship and then fell away again, never quite engulfing them, for Grome doubtless wanted his ship intact.

'Grome! You have no quarrel with mortals!' Elric cried again. 'Let us be! Ask a favour of us if you must, but grant us this favour in return!'

Elric was shouting almost anything that came into his head. Really, he had no hope of being heard by the earth god and he did not expect King Grome to bother to listen even if the elemental did hear. But there was nothing else to do.

'*Grome! Grome! Grome!* Listen to me!'

Elric's only response was in the louder laughter which made every nerve in him tremble. And the earth heaved higher and dropped lower and the ship spun round and round until Elric was sure he would lose his senses entirely.

'*King Grome! King Grome!* Is it just to slay those who have never done you harm?'

And then, slowly, the heaving earth subsided and the ship was still and a huge, brown figure stood looking down at the ship. The figure was the colour of earth and looked like a vast, old oak. His hair and his beard were the colour of leaves and his eyes were the colour of gold ore and his teeth were the colour of granite and his feet were like roots and his skin seemed covered in tiny green shoots in place of hair and he smelled rich and musty and good and he was King Grome of the Earth Elementals. He sniffed and he frowned and he said in a soft, mighty voice that was yet coarse and grumpy: 'I want my ship.'

'It is not our ship to give, King Grome,' said Elric.

Grome's tone of petulance increased. 'I want my ship,' he said slowly. 'I want the thing. It is mine.'

'Of what use is it to you, King Grome?'

'Use? It is mine.'

Grome stamped and the land rippled.

Elric said desperately: 'It is your brother's ship, King Grome. It is King Straasha's ship. He gave you part of his domain and you allowed him to keep the ship. That was the bargain.'

'I know nothing of a bargain. The ship is mine.'

'You know that if you take the ship then King Straasha will have to take back the land he gave you.'

'I want my ship.' The huge figure shifted its position and bits of earth fell from it, landing with distinctly heard thuds on the ground below and on the deck of the ship.

'Then you must kill us to obtain it,' Elric said.

'Kill? Grome does not kill mortals. He kills nothing. Grome builds. Grome brings to life.'

'You have already killed three of our company,' Elric pointed out. 'Three are dead, King Grome, because you made the land-storm.'

Grome's great brows drew together and he scratched his great head, causing an immense rustling noise to sound. 'Grome does not kill,' he said again.

'King Grome has killed,' said Elric reasonably. 'Three lives lost.'

Grome grunted. 'But I want my ship.'

'The ship is lent to us by your brother. We cannot give it to you. Besides, we sail in it for a purpose—a noble purpose, I think. We . . .'

'I know nothing of "purposes"—and care nothing for you. I want my ship. My brother should not have lent it to you. I had almost forgotten it. But now that I remember it, I want it.'

'Will you not accept something else in place of the ship, King Grome?' said Dyvim Tvar suddenly. 'Some other gift.'

Grome shook his monstrous head. 'How could a mortal give me something? It is mortals who take from me all the time. They steal my bones and my blood and my flesh. Could you give me back all that your kind has taken?'

'Is there not one thing?' Elric said.

Grome closed his eyes.

'Precious metals? Jewels?' suggested Dyvim Tvar. 'We have many such in Melniboné.'

'I have plenty,' said King Grome.

Elric shrugged in despair. 'How can we bargain with a god, Dyvim Tvar?' He gave a bitter smile. 'What can the Lord of the Soil desire? More sun, more rain? These are not ours to give.'

'I am a rough sort of god,' said Grome, 'if indeed god I am. But I did not mean to kill your comrades. I have an idea. Give me the bodies of the slain. Bury them in my earth.'

Elric's heart leapt. 'That is all you wish of us.'

'It would seem much to me.'

'And for that you will let us sail on?'

'On water, aye,' growled Grome. 'But I do not see why I should allow you to sail over my land. It is too much to expect of me. You can go to yonder lake, but from now this ship will only possess the properties bestowed upon it by my brother Straasha. No longer shall it cross my domain.'

'But, King Grome, we need this ship. We are upon urgent business. We need to sail to the city yonder.' Elric pointed in the direction of Dhoz-Kam.

'You may go to the lake, but after that the ship will sail only on water. Now give me what I ask.'

Elric called down to the bosun who, for the first time, seemed amazed by what he was witnessing. 'Bring up the bodies of the three dead men.'

The bodies were brought up from below. Grome stretched out one of his great, earthy hands and picked them up.

'I thank you,' he growled. 'Farewell.'

And slowly Grome began to descend into the ground, his whole huge frame becoming, atom by atom, absorbed with the earth until he was gone.

And then the ship was moving again, slowly towards the lake, on the last short voyage it would ever make upon the land.

'And thus our plans are thwarted,' said Elric.

Dyvim Tvar looked miserably towards the shining lake. 'Aye. So much for that scheme. I hesitate to suggest this to you, Elric, but I fear we must resort to sorcery again if we are to stand any chance of achieving our goal.'

Elric sighed.

'I fear we must,' he said.

8   The City and the Mirror

Prince Yyrkoon was pleased. His plans went well. He peered through the high fence which enclosed the flat roof of his house (three storeys high and the finest in Dhoz-Kam); he looked out towards the harbour at his splendid, captured fleet. Every ship which had come to Dhoz-Kam and which had not flown the standard of a powerful nation had been easily taken after its crew had looked upon the great mirror which squatted on its pillars above the city. Demons had built those pillars and Prince Yyrkoon had paid them for their work with the souls of all those in Oin and Yu who had resisted him. Now there was one last ambition to fulfil and then he and his new followers would be on their way to Melniboné . . .

He turned and spoke to his sister. Cymoril lay on a wooden bench, staring unseeingly at the sky, clad in the filthy tatters of the dress she had been wearing when Yyrkoon abducted her from her tower.

'See our fleet, Cymoril! While the golden barges are scattered we shall sail unhampered into Imrryr and declare the city ours. Elric cannot defend himself against us now. He fell so easily into my trap. He is a fool! And you were a fool to give him your affection!'

Cymoril made no response. Through all the months she had been away, Yyrkoon had drugged her food and drink and produced in her a lassitude which rivalled Elric's undrugged condition. Yyrkoon's own experiments with his sorcerous powers had turned him gaunt, wild-eyed and somewhat mangy; he ceased to take any pains with his physical appearance. But Cymoril had a wasted, haunted look to her, for all that beauty remained. It was as if Dhoz-Kam's rundown seediness had infected them both in different ways.

'Fear not for your own future, however, my sister,' Yyrkoon continued. He chuckled. 'You shall still be empress and sit beside the emperor on his Ruby Throne. Only I shall be emperor and Elric shall die for many days and the manner of his death will be more inventive than anything he thought to do to me.'

Cymoril's voice was hollow and distant. She did not turn her head when she spoke. 'You are insane, Yyrkoon.'

'Insane? Come now, sister, is that a word that a true Melnibonéan should use? We Melnibonéans judge nothing sane or insane. What a man is—he is. What he does—he does. Perhaps you have stayed too long in the Young Kingdoms and its judgments are becoming yours. But that shall soon be righted. We shall return to the Dragon Isle in triumph and you will forget all this, just as if you yourself had looked into the Mirror of Memory.' He darted a nervous glance upwards, as if he half-expected the mirror to be turned on him.

Cymoril closed her eyes. Her breathing was heavy and very slow; she was bearing this nightmare with fortitude, certain that Elric must eventually rescue her from it. That hope was all that had stopped her from destroying herself. If the hope went altogether, then she would bring about her own death and be done with Yyrkoon and all his horrors.

'Did I tell you that last night I was successful? I raised demons, Cymoril. Such powerful, dark demons. I learned from them all that was left for me to learn. And I opened the Shade Gate at last. Soon I shall pass through it and there I shall find what I seek. I shall become the most powerful mortal on earth. Did I tell you all this, Cymoril?'

He had, in fact, repeated himself several times that morning, but Cymoril had paid no more attention to him than she did now. She felt so tired. She tried to sleep. She said slowly, as if to remind herself of something: 'I hate you, Yyrkoon.'

'Ah, but you shall love me soon, Cymoril. Soon.'

'Elric will come . . .'

'Elric! Ha! He sits twiddling his thumbs in his tower, waiting for news that will never come—save when I bring it to him!'

'Elric will come,' she said.

Yyrkoon snarled. A brute-faced Oinish girl brought him his morning wine. Yyrkoon seized the cup and sipped the stuff. Then he spat it at the girl who, trembling, ducked away. Yyrkoon took the jug and emptied it onto the white dust of the roof. 'This is Elric's thin blood. This is how it will flow away!'

But again Cymoril was not listening. She was trying to remember her albino lover and the few sweet days they had spent together since they were children.

Yyrkoon hurled the empty jug at the girl's head, but she was adept at dodging him. As she dodged, she murmured her standard response to all his attacks and insults. 'Thank you, Demon Lord,' she said. 'Thank you, Demon Lord.'

Yyrkoon laughed. 'Aye. Demon Lord. Your folk are right to call me that, for I rule more demons than I rule men. My power increases every day!'

The Oinish girl hurried away to fetch more wine, for she knew he would be calling for it in a moment. Yyrkoon crossed the roof to stare through the slats in the fence at the proof of his power, but as he looked upon his ships he heard sounds of confusion from the other side of the roof. Could the Yurits and the Oinish be fighting amongst themselves? Where were their Imrryrian centurions. Where was Captain Valharik?

He almost ran across the roof, passing Cymoril who appeared to be sleeping, and peered down into the streets.

'Fire?' he murmured. 'Fire?'

It was true that the streets appeared to be on fire. And yet it was not an ordinary fire. Balls of fire seemed to drift about, igniting rush-thatched roofs, doors, anything which would easily burn—as an invading army might put a village to the torch.

Yyrkoon scowled, thinking at first that he had been careless and some spell of his had turned against him, but then he looked over the burning houses at the river and he saw a strange ship sailing there, a ship of great grace and beauty, that somehow seemed more a creation of nature than of man—and he knew they were under attack. But who would attack Dhoz-Kam? There was no loot worth the effort. It could not be Imrryrians . . .

It could not be Elric.

'It must not be Elric,' he growled. 'The Mirror. It must be turned upon the invaders.'

'And upon yourself, brother?' Cymoril had risen unsteadily and leaned against a table. She was smiling. 'You were too confident, Yyrkoon. Elric comes.'

'Elric! Nonsense! Merely a few barbarian raiders from the interior. Once they are in the centre of the city, we shall be able to use the Mirror of Memory upon them.' He ran to the trapdoor which led down into his house. 'Captain Valharik! Valharik where are you?'

Valharik appeared in the room below. He was sweating. There was a blade in his gloved hand, though he did not seem to have been in any fighting as yet.

'Make the mirror ready, Valharik. Turn it upon the attackers.'

'But, my lord, we might . . .'

'Hurry! Do as I say. We'll soon have these barbarians added to our own strength—along with their ships.'

'Barbarians, my lord? Can barbarians command the fire elementals? These things we fight are flame spirits. They cannot be slain any more than fire itself can be slain.'

'Fire can be slain by water,' Prince Yyrkoon reminded his lieutenant. 'By water, Captain Valharik. Have you forgotten?'

'But, Prince Yyrkoon, we have tried to quench the spirits with water —and the water will not move from our buckets. Some powerful sorcerer commands the invaders. He has the aid of the spirits of fire *and* water.'

'You are mad, Captain Valharik,' said Yyrkoon firmly. 'Mad. Prepare the mirror and let us have no more of these stupidities.'

Valharik wetted his dry lips. 'Aye, my lord.' He bowed his head and went to do his master's bidding.

Again Yyrkoon went to the fence and looked through. There were men in the streets now, fighting his own warriors, but smoke obscured his view, he could not make out the identities of any of the invaders. 'Enjoy your petty victory,' Yyrkoon chuckled, 'for soon the mirror will take away your minds and you will become my slaves.'

'It is Elric,' said Cymoril quietly. She smiled. 'Elric comes to take vengeance on you, brother.'

Yyrkoon sniggered. 'Think you? Think you? Well, should that be the case, he'll find me gone, for I still have a means of evading him—and he'll find you in a condition which will not please him (though it will cause him considerable anguish). But it is not Elric. It is some crude shaman from the steppes to the east of here. He will soon be in my power.'

Cymoril, too, was peering through the fence.

'Elric,' she said. 'I can see his helm.'

'What?' Yyrkoon pushed her aside. There, in the streets, Imrryrian fought Imrryrian, there was no longer any doubt of that. Yyrkoon's men—Imrryrian, Oinish and Yurit—were being pushed back. And at the head of the attacking Imrryrians could be seen a black dragon helm such as only one Melnibonéan wore. It was Elric's helm. And Elric's sword, that had once belonged to Earl Aubec of Malador, rose and fell and was bright with blood which glistened in the morning sunshine.

For a moment Yyrkoon was overwhelmed with despair. He groaned. 'Elric. Elric. Elric. Ah, how we continue to underestimate each other. What curse is on us?'

Cymoril had flung back her head and her face had come to life again. 'I said he would come, brother!'

Yyrkoon whirled on her. 'Aye—he has come—and the mirror will rob him of his brain and he will turn into my slave, believing anything I

care to put in his skull. This is even sweeter than I planned, sister. Ha!'
He looked up and then flung his arms across his eyes as he realised what
he had done. 'Quickly—below—into the house—the mirror begins to
turn.' There came a great creaking of gears and pulleys and chains as
the terrible Mirror of Memory began to focus on the streets below. 'It
will be only a little while before Elric has added himself and his men to
my strength. What a splendid irony!' Yyrkoon hurried his sister down
the steps leading from the roof and he closed the trapdoor behind him.
'Elric himself will help in the attack on Imrryr. He will destroy his own
kind. He will oust himself from the Ruby Throne!'

'Do you not think that Elric has anticipated the threat of the Mirror
of Memory, brother?' Cymoril said with relish.

'Anticipate it, aye—but resist it he cannot. He must see to fight. He
must either be cut down or open his eyes. No man with eyes can be safe
from the power of the mirror.' He glanced around the crudely furnished
room. 'Where is Valharik? Where is the cur?'

Valharik came running in. 'The mirror is being turned, my lord, but it
will affect our own men, too. I fear . . .'

'Then cease to fear. What if our own men are drawn under its influence? We can soon feed what they need to know back into their brains—
at the same time as we feed our defeated foes. You are too nervous,
Captain Valharik.'

'But Elric leads them . . .'

'And Elric's eyes *are* eyes—though they look like crimson stones. He
will fare no better than his men.'

In the streets around Prince Yyrkoon's house Elric, Dyvim Tvar and
their Imrryrians pushed on, forcing back their demoralised opponents.
The attackers had lost barely a man, whereas many Oinish and Yurits
lay dead in the streets, beside a few of their renegade Imrryrian commanders. The flame elementals, whom Elric had summoned with some
effort, were beginning to disperse, for it cost them dear to spend so
much time entirely within Elric's plane, but the necessary advantage
had been gained and there was now little question of who would win as
a hundred or more houses blazed throughout the city, igniting others
and requiring attention from the defenders lest the whole squalid place
burn down about their ears. In the harbour, too, ships were burning.

Dyvim Tvar was the first to notice the mirror beginning to swing into
focus on the streets. He pointed a warning finger, then turned, blowing
on his war-horn and ordering forward the troops who, up to now, had
played no part in the fighting. 'Now you must lead us!' he cried, and he

lowered his helm over his face. The eyeholes of the helm had been blocked so that he could not see through.

Slowly Elric lowered his own helm until he was in darkness. The sound of fighting continued however, as the veterans who had sailed with them from Melniboné, set to work in their place and the other troops fell back. The leading Imrryrians had not blocked their eyeholes.

Elric prayed that the scheme would work.

Yyrkoon, peeking cautiously through a chink in a heavy curtain, said querulously: 'Valharik? They fight on. Why is that? Is not the mirror focussed?'

'It should be, my lord.'

'Then, see for yourself, the Imrryrians continue to forge through our defenders—and our men are beginning to come under the influence of the mirror. What is wrong, Valharik? What is wrong?'

Valharik drew air between his teeth and there was a certain admiration in his expression as he looked upon the fighting Imrryrians.

'They are blind,' he said. 'They fight by sound and touch and smell. They are blind, my lord emperor—and they lead Elric and his men whose helms are so designed they can see nothing.'

'Blind?' Yyrkoon spoke almost pathetically, refusing to understand. 'Blind?'

'Aye. Blind warriors—men wounded in earlier wars, but good fighters nonetheless. That is how Elric defeats our mirror, my lord.'

'Agh! No! No!' Yyrkoon beat heavily on his captain's back and the man shrank away. 'Elric is not cunning. He is not cunning. Some powerful demon gives him these ideas.'

'Perhaps, my lord. But are there demons more powerful than those who have aided you?'

'No,' said Yyrkoon. 'There are none. Oh, that I could summon some of them now. But I have expended my powers in opening the Shade Gate. I should have anticipated . . . I could not anticipate . . . Oh Elric! I shall yet destroy you, when the runeblades are mine!' Then Yyrkoon frowned. 'But how could he have been prepared? What demon . . . ? Unless he summoned Arioch himself? But he has not the power to summon Arioch. I could not summon him . . .'

And then, as if in reply, Yyrkoon heard Elric's battle song sounding from the nearby streets. And that song answered the question.

'Arioch! Arioch! Blood and souls for my lord Arioch!'

'Then I must have the runeblades. I must pass through the Shade Gate. There I still have allies—supernatural allies who shall deal easily with

Elric, if need be. But I need time . . .' Yyrkoon mumbled to himself as
he paced about the room. Valharik continued to watch the fighting.

'They come closer,' said the captain.

Cymoril smiled. 'Closer, Yyrkoon? Who is the fool now? Elric? Or
you?'

'Be still! I think. I think . . .' Yyrkoon fingered his lips.

Then a light came into his eye and he looked cunningly at Cymoril
for a second before turning his attention to Captain Valharik.

'Valharik, you must destroy the Mirror of Memory.'

'Destroy it? But it is our only weapon, my lord?'

'Exactly—but is it not useless now?'

'Aye.'

'Destroy it and it will serve us again.' Yyrkoon flicked a long finger in
the direction of the door. 'Go. Destroy the mirror.'

'But, Prince Yyrkoon—emperor, I mean—will that not have the effect of robbing us of our only weapon?'

'Do as I say, Valharik! Or perish!'

'But how shall I destroy it, my lord?'

'Your sword. You must climb the column *behind* the face of the
mirror. Then, without looking into the mirror itself, you must swing
your sword against it and smash it. It will break easily. You know the
precautions I have had to take to make sure that it was not harmed.'

'Is that all I must do?'

'Aye. Then you are free from my service—you may escape or do
whatever else you wish to do.'

'Do we not sail against Melniboné?'

'Of course not. I have devised another method of taking the Dragon
Isle.'

Valharik shrugged. His expression showed that he had never really
believed Yyrkoon's assurances. But what else had he to do but follow
Yyrkoon, when fearful torture awaited him at Elric's hands? With
shoulders bowed, the captain slunk away to do his prince's work.

'And now, Cymoril . . .' Yyrkoon grinned like a ferret as he reached
out to grab his sister's soft shoulders. 'Now to prepare you for your
lover, Elric.'

One of the blind warriors cried: 'They no longer resist us, my lord. They
are limp and allow themselves to be cut down where they stand. Why is
this?'

'The mirror has robbed them of their memories,' Elric called, turning
his own blind head towards the sound of the warrior's voice. 'You can

lead us into a building now—where, with luck, we shall not glimpse the mirror.'

At last they stood within what appeared to Elric, as he lifted his helm, to be a warehouse of some kind. Luckily it was large enough to hold their entire force and when they were all inside Elric had the doors shut while they debated their next action.

'We should find Yyrkoon,' Dyvim Tvar said. 'Let us interrogate one of those warriors . . .'

'There'll be little point in that, my friend,' Elric reminded him. 'Their minds are gone. They'll remember nothing at all. They do not at present remember even what they are, let alone who. Go to the shutters yonder, where the mirror's influence cannot reach, and see if you can see the building most likely to be occupied by my cousin.'

Dyvim Tvar crossed swiftly to the shutters and looked cautiously out. 'Aye—there's a building larger than the rest and I see some movement within, as if the surviving warriors were regrouping. It's likely that's Yyrkoon's stronghold. It should be easily taken.'

Elric joined him. 'Aye. I agree with you. We'll find Yyrkoon there. But we must hurry, lest he decides to slay Cymoril. We must work out the best means of reaching the place and instruct our blind warriors as to how many streets, how many houses and so forth, we must pass.'

'What is that strange sound?' One of the blind warriors raised his head. 'Like the distant ringing of a gong.'

'I hear it too,' said another blind man.

And now Elric heard it. A sinister noise. It came from the air above them. It shivered through the atmosphere.

'The mirror!' Dyvim Tvar looked up. 'Has the mirror some property we did not anticipate?'

'Possibly . . .' Elric tried to remember what Arioch had told him. But Arioch had been vague. He had said nothing of this dreadful, mighty sound, this shattering clangour as if . . . 'He is breaking the mirror!' he said. 'But why?' There was something more now, something brushing at his brain. As if the sound were, itself, sentient.

'Perhaps Yyrkoon is dead and his magic dies with him,' Dyvim Tvar began. And then he broke off with a groan.

The noise was louder, more intense, bringing sharp pain to his ears.

And now Elric knew. He blocked his ears with his gauntleted hands. The memories in the mirror. They were flooding into his mind. The mirror had been smashed and was releasing all the memories it had stolen over the centuries—the aeons, perhaps. Many of those memories were not mortal. Many were the memories of beasts and intelligent creatures which had existed even before Melniboné. And the memories

warred for a place in Elric's skull—in the skulls of all the Imrryrians—
in the poor, tortured skulls of the men outside whose pitiful screams
could be heard rising from the streets—and in the skull of Captain
Valharik, the turncoat, as he lost his footing on the great column and
fell with the shards from the mirror to the ground far below.

But Elric did not hear Captain Valharik scream and he did not hear
Valharik's body crash first to a roof-top and then into the street where it
lay all broken beneath the broken mirror.

Elric lay upon the stone floor of the warehouse and he writhed, as his
comrades writhed, trying to clear his head of a million memories that
were not his own—of loves, of hatreds, of strange experiences and ordinary experiences, of wars and journeys, of the faces of relatives who
were not his relatives, of men and women and children, of animals, of
ships and cities, of fights, of lovemaking, of fears and desires—and the
memories fought each other for possession of his crowded skull, threatening to drive his own memories (and thus his own character) from his
head. And as Elric writhed upon the ground, clutching at his ears, he
spoke a word over and over again in an effort to cling to his own
identity.

'Elric. Elric. Elric.'

And gradually, by an effort which he had experienced only once
before when he had summoned Arioch to the plane of the Earth, he
managed to extinguish all those alien memories and assert his own
until, shaken and feeble, he lowered his hands from his ears and no
longer shouted his own name. And then he stood up and looked about
him.

More than two thirds of his men were dead, blind or otherwise. The
big bosun was dead, his eyes wide and staring, his lips frozen in a
scream, his right eyesocket raw and bleeding from where he had tried to
drag his eye from it. All the corpses lay in unnatural positions, all had
their eyes open (if they had eyes) and many bore the marks of self-
mutilation, while others had vomited and others had dashed their
brains against the wall. Dyvim Tvar was alive, but curled up in a corner, mumbling to himself and Elric thought he might be mad. Some of
the other survivors were, indeed, mad, but they were quiet, they af-
forded no danger. Only five, including Elric, seemed to have resisted the
alien memories and retained their own sanity. It seemed to Elric, as he
stumbled from corpse to corpse, that most of the men had had their
hearts fail.

'Dyvim Tvar?' Elric put his hand on his friend's shoulder. 'Dyvim
Tvar?'

Dyvim Tvar took his head from his arm and looked into Elric's eyes.

In Dyvim Tvar's own eyes was the experience of a score of millennia and there was irony there, too. 'I live, Elric.'

'Few of us live now.'

A little later they left the warehouse, no longer needing to fear the mirror, and found that all the streets were full of the dead who had received the mirror's memories. Stiff bodies reached out hands to them. Dead lips formed silent pleas for help. Elric tried not to look at them as he pressed through them, but his desire for vengeance upon his cousin was even stronger now.

They reached the house. The door was open and the ground floor was crammed with corpses. There was no sign of Prince Yyrkoon.

Elric and Dyvim Tvar led the few Imrryrians who were still sane up the steps, past more imploring corpses, until they reached the top floor of the house.

And here they found Cymoril.

She was lying upon a couch and she was naked. There were runes painted on her flesh and the runes were, in themselves, obscene. Her eyelids were heavy and she did not at first recognise them. Elric rushed to her side and cradled her body in his arms. The body was oddly cold.

'He—he makes me—sleep . . .' said Cymoril. 'A sorcerous sleep—from which—only he can wake me . . .' She gave a great yawn. 'I have stayed awake—this long—by an effort of—will—for Elric comes . . .'

'Elric is here,' said her lover, softly. 'I am Elric, Cymoril.'

'Elric?' She relaxed in his arms. 'You—you must find Yyrkoon—for only he can wake me . . .'

'Where has he gone?' Elric's face had hardened. His crimson eyes were fierce. 'Where?'

'To find the two black swords—the runeswords—of—our ancestors —Mournblade . . .'

'And Stormbringer,' said Elric grimly. 'Those swords are cursed. But where has he gone, Cymoril? How has he escaped us?'

'Through—through—through the—Shade Gate—he conjured it—he made the most fearful pacts with demons to go through . . . The—other—room . . .'

Now Cymoril slept, but there seemed to be a certain peace on her face.

Elric watched as Dyvim Tvar crossed the room, sword in hand, and flung the door open. A dreadful stench came from the next room, which was in darkness. Something flickered on the far side.

'Aye—that's sorcery, right enough,' said Elric. 'And Yyrkoon has thwarted me. He conjured the Shade Gate and passed through it into

some netherworld. Which one, I'll never know, for there is an infinity of
them. Oh, Arioch, I would give much to follow my cousin!'

'*Then follow him you shall,*' said a sweet, sardonic voice in Elric's
head.

At first the albino thought it was a vestige of a memory still fighting
for possession of his head, but then he knew that Arioch spoke to him.

'*Dismiss your followers that I may speak with thee,*' said Arioch.

Elric hesitated. He wished to be alone—but not with Arioch. He
wished to be with Cymoril, for Cymoril was making him weep. Tears
already flowed from his crimson eyes.

'*What I have to say could result in Cymoril being restored to her
normal state,*' said the voice. '*And, moreover, it will help you defeat
Yyrkoon and be revenged upon him. Indeed, it could make you the most
powerful mortal there has ever been.*'

Elric looked up at Dyvim Tvar. 'Would you and your men leave me
alone for a few moments?'

'Of course.' Dyvim Tvar led his men away and shut the door behind
him.

Arioch stood leaning against the same door. Again he had assumed
the shape and poise of a handsome youth. His smile was friendly and
open and only the ancient eyes belied his appearance.

'It is time to seek the black swords yourself, Elric,' said Arioch. 'Lest
Yyrkoon reach them first. I warn you of this—with the runeblades
Yyrkoon will be so powerful he will be able to destroy half the world
without thinking of it. That is why your cousin risks the dangers of the
world beyond the Shade Gate. If Yyrkoon possesses those swords before you find them, it will mean the end of you, of Cymoril, of the
Young Kingdoms and, quite possibly, the destruction of Melniboné,
too. I will help you enter the netherworld to seek for the twin runeswords.'

Elric said musingly: 'I have often been warned of the dangers of
seeking the swords—and the worse dangers of owning them. I think I
must consider another plan, my lord Arioch.'

'There is no other plan. Yyrkoon desires the swords if you do not.
With Mournblade in one hand and Stormbringer in the other, he will be
invincible, for the swords give their user power. Immense power.' Arioch paused.

'You must do as I say. It is to your advantage.'

'And to yours, Lord Arioch?'

'Aye—to mine. I am not entirely selfless.'

Elric shook his head. 'I am confused. There has been too much of the

supernatural about this affair. I suspect the gods of manipulating us
. . .'

'The gods serve only those who are willing to serve them. And the
gods serve destiny, also.'

'I like it not. To stop Yyrkoon is one thing, to assume his ambitions
and take the swords myself—that is another thing.'

'It is your destiny.'

'Cannot I change my destiny?'

Arioch shook his head. 'No more than can I.'

Elric stroked sleeping Cymoril's hair. 'I love her. She is all I desire.'

'You shall not wake her if Yyrkoon finds the blades before you do.'

'And how shall I find the blades?'

'Enter the Shade Gate—I have kept it open, though Yyrkoon thinks
it closed—then you must seek the Tunnel Under the Marsh which leads
to the Pulsing Cavern. In that chamber the runeswords are kept. They
have been kept there ever since your ancestors relinquished them . . .'

'Why were they relinquished?'

'Your ancestors lacked courage.'

'Courage to face what?'

'Themselves.'

'You are cryptic, my lord Arioch.'

'That is the way of the Lords of the Higher Worlds. Hurry. Even I
cannot keep the Shade Gate open long.'

'Very well. I will go.'

And Arioch vanished immediately.

Elric called in a hoarse, cracking voice for Dyvim Tvar. Dyvim Tvar
entered at once.

'Elric? What has happened in here? Is it Cymoril? You look   .'

'I am going to follow Yyrkoon—alone, Dyvim Tvar. You must make
your way back to Melniboné with those of our men who remain. Take
Cymoril with you. If I do not return in reasonable time, you must
declare her empress. If she still sleeps, then you must rule as regent
until she wakes.'

Dyvim Tvar said softly: 'Do you know what you do, Elric?'

Elric shook his head.

'No, Dyvim Tvar, I do not.'

He got to his feet and staggered towards the other room where the
Shade Gate waited for him.

BOOK THREE

And now there is no turning back at all. Elric's
destiny has been forged and fixed as surely as
the hellswords were forged and fixed aeons before. Was there ever a point where he might have
turned off this road to despair, damnation and
destruction? Or has he been doomed since before
his birth? Doomed through a thousand incarnations to know little else but sadness and struggle,
loneliness and remorse—eternally the champion
of some unknown cause?

1   Through the Shade Gate

And Elric stepped into a shadow and found himself in a world of shadows. He turned, but the shadow through which he had entered now faded and was gone. Old Aubec's sword was in Elric's hand, the black helm and the black armour were upon his body and only these were familiar, for the land was dark and gloomy as if contained in a vast cave whose walls, though invisible, were oppressive and tangible. And Elric regretted the hysteria, the weariness of brain, which had given him the impulse to obey his patron demon Arioch and plunge through the Shade Gate. But regret was useless now, so he forgot it.

Yyrkoon was nowhere to be seen. Either Elric's cousin had had a steed awaiting him or else, more likely, he had entered this world at a slightly different angle (for all the planes were said to turn about each other) and was thus either nearer or farther from their mutual goal. The air was rich with brine—so rich that Elric's nostrils felt as if they had been packed with salt—it was almost like walking under water and just being able to breathe the water itself. Perhaps this explained why it was so difficult to see any great distance in any direction, why there were so many shadows, why the sky was like a veil which hid the roof of a cavern. Elric sheathed his sword, there being no evident danger present at that moment, and turned slowly, trying to get some kind of bearing.

It was possible that there were jagged mountains in what he judged the east, and perhaps a forest to the west. Without sun, or stars, or moon, it was hard to gauge distance or direction. He stood on a rocky plain over which whistled a cold and sluggish wind, which tugged at his cloak as if it wished to possess it. There were a few stunted, leafless trees standing in a clump about a hundred paces away. It was all that relieved the bleak plain, save for a large, shapeless slab of rock which stood a fair way beyond the trees. It was a world which seemed to have been drained of all life, where Law and Chaos had once battled and, in their conflict, destroyed all. Were there many planes such as this one? Elric wondered. And for a moment he was filled with a dreadful presentiment concerning the fate of his own rich world. He shook this mood off at once and began to walk towards the trees and the rock beyond.

He reached the trees and passed them, and the touch of his cloak on a branch broke the brittle thing which turned almost at once to ash which was scattered on the wind. Elric drew the cloak closer about his body.

As he approached the rock he became conscious of a sound which seemed to emanate from it. He slowed his pace and put his hand upon the pommel of his sword.

The noise continued—a small, rhythmic noise. Through the gloom Elric peered carefully at the rock, trying to locate the source of the sound.

And then the noise stopped and was replaced by another—a soft scuffle, a padding footfall, and then silence. Elric took a pace backward and drew Aubec's sword. The first sound had been that of a man sleeping. The second sound was that of a man waking and preparing himself either for attack or to defend himself.

Elric said: 'I am Elric of Melniboné. I am a stranger here.'

And an arrow slid past his helm almost at the same moment as a bowstring sounded. Eric flung himself to one side and sought about for cover, but there was no cover save the rock behind which the archer hid.

And now a voice came from behind the rock. It was a firm, rather bleak voice. It said:

'That was not meant to harm you but to display my skill in case you considered harming me. I have had my fill of demons in this world and you look like the most dangerous demon of all, Whiteface.'

'I am mortal,' said Elric, straightening up and deciding that if he must die it would be best to die with some sort of dignity.

'You spoke of Melniboné. I have heard of the place. An isle of demons.'

'Then you have not heard enough of Melniboné. I am mortal as are all my folk. Only the ignorant think us demons.'

'I am not ignorant, my friend. I am a Warrior Priest of Phum, born to that caste and the inheritor of all its knowledge and, until recently, the Lords of Chaos themselves were my patrons. Then I refused to serve them longer and was exiled to this plane by them. Perhaps the same fate befell you, for the folk of Melniboné serve Chaos do they not?'

'Aye. And I know of Phum—it lies in the unmapped East—beyond the Weeping Waste, beyond the Sighing Desert, beyond even Elwher. It is one of the oldest of the Young Kingdoms.'

'All that is so—though I dispute that the East is unmapped, save by the savages of the West. So you are, indeed, to share my exile, it seems.'

'I am not exiled. I am upon a quest. When the quest is done, I shall return to my own world.'

'Return, say you? That interests me, my pale friend. I had thought return impossible.'

'Perhaps it is and I have been tricked. And if your own powers have not found you a way to another plane, perhaps mine will not save me either.'

'Powers? I have none since I relinquished my servitude to Chaos. Well, friend, do you intend to fight me?'

'There is only one upon this plane I would fight and it is not you, Warrior Priest of Phum.' Elric sheathed his sword and at the same moment the speaker rose from behind the rock, replacing a scarlet-fletched arrow in a scarlet quiver.

'I am Rackhir,' said the man. 'Called the Red Archer for, as you see, I affect scarlet dress. It is a habit of the Warrior Priests of Phum to choose but a single colour to wear. It is the only loyalty to tradition I still possess.' He had on a scarlet jerkin, scarlet breeks, scarlet shoes and a scarlet cap with a scarlet feather in it. His bow was scarlet and the pommel of his sword glowed ruby-red. His face, which was aquiline and gaunt, as if carved from fleshless bone, was weather-beaten, and that was brown. He was tall and he was thin, but muscles rippled on his arms and torso. There was irony in his eyes and something of a smile upon his thin lips, though the face showed that it had been through much experience, little of it pleasant.

'An odd place to choose for a quest,' said the Red Archer, standing with hands on hips and looking Elric up and down. 'But I'll strike a bargain with you if you're interested.'

'If the bargain suits me, archer, I'll agree to it, for you seem to know more of this world than do I.'

'Well—you must find something here and then leave, whereas I have nothing at all to do here and wish to leave. If I help you in your quest, will you take me with you when you return to our own plane?'

'That seems a fair bargain, but I cannot promise what I have no power to give. I will say only this—if it is possible for me to take you back with me to our own plane, either before or after I have finished my quest, I will do it.'

'That is reasonable,' said Rackhir the Red Archer. 'Now—tell me what you seek.'

'I seek two swords, forged millennia ago by immortals, used by my ancestors but then relinquished by them and placed upon this plane.

The swords are large and heavy and black and they have cryptic runes carved into their blades. I was told that I would find them in the Pulsing Cavern which is reached through the Tunnel Under the Marsh. Have you heard of either of these places?'

'I have not. Nor have I heard of the two black swords.' Rackhir rubbed his bony chin. 'Though I remember reading something in one of the Books of Phum and what I read disturbed me . . .'

'The swords are legendary. Many books make some small reference to them—almost always mysterious. There is said to be one tome which records the history of the swords and all who have used them—and all who will use them in the future—a timeless book which contains all time. Some call it the Chronicle of the Black Sword and in it, it is said, men may read their whole destinies.'

'I know nothing of that, either. It is not one of the Books of Phum. I fear, Comrade Elric, that we shall have to venture to the City of Ameeron and ask your questions of the inhabitants there.'

'There is a city upon this plane?'

'Aye—a city. I stayed but a short time in it, preferring the wilderness. But with a friend, it might be possible to bear the place a little longer.'

'Why is Ameeron unsuited to your taste?'

'Its citizens are not happy. Indeed, they are a most depressed and depressing group, for they are all, you see, exiles or refugees or travelers between the worlds who lost their way and never found it again. No one lives in Ameeron by choice.'

'A veritable City of the Damned.'

'As the poet might remark, aye.' Rackhir offered Elric a sardonic wink. 'But I sometimes think all cities are that.'

'What is the nature of this plane where are, as far as I can tell, no planets, no moon, no sun. It has something of the air of a great cavern.'

'There is, indeed, a theory that it is a sphere buried in an infinity of rock. Others say that it lies in the future of our own Earth—a future where the universe has died. I heard a thousand theories during the short space of time I spent in the City of Ameeron. All, it seemed to me, were of equal value. All, it seemed to me, could be correct. Why not? There are some who believe that everything is a Lie. Conversely, everything could be the Truth.'

It was Elric's turn to remark ironically: 'You are a philosopher, then, as well as an archer, friend Rackhir of Phum?'

Rackhir laughed. 'If you like! It is such thinking that weakened my loyalty to Chaos and led me to this pass. I have heard that there is a city called Tanelorn which may sometimes be found on the shifting shores of the Sighing Desert. If I ever return to our own world, Comrade Elric,

I shall seek that city, for I have heard that peace may be found there—that such debates as the nature of Truth are considered meaningless. That men are content merely to exist in Tanelorn.'

'I envy those who dwell in Tanelorn,' said Elric.

Rackhir sniffed. 'Aye. But it would probably prove a disappointment, if found. Legends are best left as legends and attempts to make them real are rarely successful. Come—yonder lies Ameeron and that, sad to say, is more typical of most cities one comes across—on any plane.'

The two tall men, both outcasts in their different ways, began to trudge through the gloom of that desolate wasteland.

2   In the City of Ameeron

The city of Ameeron came in sight and Elric had never seen such a place before. Ameeron made Dhoz-Kam seem like the cleanest and most well-run settlement there could be. The city lay below the plain of rocks, in a shallow valley over which hung perpetual smoke: a filthy, tattered cloak meant to hide the place from the sight of men and gods.

The buildings were mostly in a state of semi-ruin or else were wholly ruined and shacks and tents erected in their place. The mixture of architectural styles—some familiar, some most alien—was such that Elric was hard put to see one building which resembled another. There were shanties and castles, cottages, towers and forts, plain, square villas and wooden huts heavy with carved ornamentation. Others seemed merely piles of rock with a jagged opening at one end for a door. But none looked well—could not have looked well in that landscape under that perpetually gloomy sky.

Here and there red fires sputtered, adding to the smoke, and the smell as Elric and Rackhir reached the outskirts was rich with a great variety of stinks.

'Arrogance, rather than pride, is the paramount quality of most of Ameeron's residents,' said Rackhir, wrinkling his hawklike nose. 'Where they have any qualities of character left at all.'

Elric trudged through filth. Shadows scuttled amongst the close-packed buildings. 'Is there an inn, perhaps, where we can enquire after the Tunnel Under the Marsh and its whereabouts?'

'No inn. By and large the inhabitants keep themselves to themselves . . .'

'A city square where folk meet?'

'This city has no centre. Each resident or group of residents built their own dwelling where they felt like it, or where there was space, and they come from all planes and all ages, thus the confusion, the decay and the oldness of many of the places. Thus the filth, the hopelessness, the decadence of the majority.'

'How do they live?'

'They live off each other, by and large. They trade with demons who occasionally visit Ameeron from time to time . . .'

'Demons?'

'Aye. And the bravest hunt the rats which dwell in the caverns below the city.'

'What demons are these?'

'Just creatures, mainly minor minions of Chaos, who want something that the Ameeronese can supply—a stolen soul or two, a baby, perhaps (though few are born here)—you can imagine what else, if you've knowledge of what demons normally demand from sorcerers.'

'Aye. I can imagine. So Chaos can come and go on this plane as it pleases.'

'I'm not sure it's quite as easy. But it is certainly easier for the demons to travel back and forth here than it would be for them to travel back and forth in our plane.'

'Have you seen any of these demons?'

'Aye. The usual bestial sort. Coarse, stupid and powerful—many of them were once human before electing to bargain with Chaos. Now they are mentally and physically warped into foul, demon shapes.'

Elric found Rackhir's words not to his taste. 'Is that ever the fate of those who bargain with Chaos?' he said.

'You should know, if you come from Melniboné. I know that in Phum it is rarely the case. But it seems that the higher the stakes the subtler are the changes a man undergoes when Chaos agrees to trade with him.'

Elric sighed. 'Where shall we enquire of our Tunnel Under the Marsh?'

'There was an old man . . .' Rackhir began, and then a grunt behind him made him pause.

Another grunt.

A face with tusks in it emerged from a patch of darkness formed by a fallen slab of masonry. The face grunted again.

'Who are you?' said Elric, his sword-hand ready.

'Pig,' said the face with tusks in it. Elric was not certain whether he was being insulted or whether the creature was describing himself.

'Pig.'

Two more faces with tusks in them came out of the patch of darkness. 'Pig,' said one.

'Pig,' said another.

'Snake,' said a voice behind Elric and Rackhir. Elric turned while Rackhir continued to watch the pigs. A tall youth stood there. Where his head would have been sprouted the bodies of about fifteen good-sized snakes. The head of each snake glared at Elric. The tongues flickered and they all opened their mouths at exactly the same moment to say again:

'Snake.'

'Thing,' said anothei voice. Elric glanced in that direction, gasped, drew his sword and felt nausea sweep through him.

Then Pigs, Snake and Thing were upon them.

Rackhir took one Pig before it could move three paces. His bow was off his back and strung and a red-fletched arrow nocked and shot, all in a second. He had time to shoot one more Pig and then drop his bow to draw his sword. Back to back he and Elric prepared to defend themselves against the demons' attack. Snake was bad enough, with its fifteen darting heads hissing and snapping with teeth which dripped venom, but Thing kept changing its form—first an arm would emerge, then a face would appear from the shapeless, heaving flesh which shuffled implacably closer.

'Thing!' it shouted. Two swords slashed at Elric who was dealing with the last Pig and missed his stroke so that instead of running the Pig through the heart, he took him in a lung. Pig staggered backward and slumped to the ground in a pool of muck. He crawled for a moment, but then collapsed. Thing had produced a spear and Elric barely managed to deflect the cast with the flat of his sword. Now Rackhir was engaged with Snake and the two demons closed on the men, eager to make a finish of them. Half the heads of Snake lay writhing on the ground and Elric had managed to slice one hand off Thing, but the demon still seemed to have three other hands ready. It seemed to be created not from one creature but from several. Elric wondered if, through his bargaining with Arioch, this would ultimately be his fate, to be turned into a demon—a formless monster. But wasn't he already something of a monster? Didn't folk already mistake him for a demon?

These thoughts gave him strength. He yelled as he fought. 'Elric!'

And: 'Thing!' replied his adversary, also eager to assert what he regarded as the essence of his being.

Another hand flew off as Aubec's sword bit into it. Another javelin jabbed out and was knocked aside; another sword appeared and came down on Elric's helm with a force which dazed him and sent him reeling back against Rackhir who missed his thrust at Snake and was almost bitten by four of the heads. Elric chopped at the arm and the tentacle which held the sword and saw them part from the body but then become reabsorbed again. The nausea returned. Elric thrust his sword into the mass and the mass screamed: 'Thing! Thing! Thing!'

Elric thrust again and four swords and two spears waved and clashed and tried to deflect Aubec's blade.

'Thing!'

'This is Yyrkoon's work,' said Elric, 'without a doubt. He has heard that I have followed him and seeks to stop us with his demon allies.' He gritted his teeth and spoke through them. 'Unless one of these is Yyrkoon himself! Are you my cousin Yyrkoon, Thing?'

'Thing . . .' The voice was almost pathetic. The weapons waved and clashed but they no longer darted so fiercely at Elric.

'Or are you some other old, familiar friend?'

'Thing . . .'

Elric stabbed again and again into the mass. Thick, reeking blood spurted and fell upon his armour. Elric could not understand why it had become so easy to take the attack to the demon.

'Now!' shouted a voice from above Elric's head. 'Quickly!'

Elric glanced up and saw a red face, a white beard, a waving arm. 'Don't look at me you fool! Now—strike!'

And Elric put his two hands above his sword hilt and drove the blade deep into the shapeless creature which moaned and wept and said in a small whisper 'Frank . . .' before it died.

Rackhir thrust at the same moment and his blade went under the remaining snake heads and plunged into the chest and thence into the heart of the youth-body and his demon died, too.

The white-haired man came clambering down from the ruined archway on which he had been perched. He was laughing. 'Niun's sorcery still has some effect, even here, eh? I heard the tall one call his demon friends and instruct them to set upon you. It did not seem fair to me that five should attack two—so I sat upon that wall and I drew the many-armed demon's strength out of it. I still can. I still can. And now I have his strength (or a fair part of it) and feel considerably better than I have done for many a moon (if such a thing exists).'

'It said "Frank",' said Elric frowning. 'Was that a name, do you think? Its name before?'

'Perhaps,' said old Niun, 'perhaps. Poor creature. But still, it is dead now. You are not of Ameeron, you two—though I've seen you here before, red one.'

'And I've seen you,' said Rackhir with a smile. He wiped Snake's blood from his blade, using one of Snake's heads for the purpose. 'You are Niun Who Knew All.'

'Aye. Who Knew All but who now knows very little. Soon it will be over, when I have forgotten everything. Then I may return from this awful exile. It is the pact I made with Orland of the Staff. I was a fool who wished to know everything and my curiosity led me into an adventure concerning this Orland. Orland showed me the error of my ways and sent me here to forget. Sadly, as you noticed, I still remember some of my powers and my knowledge from time to time. I know you seek the Black Swords. I know you are Elric of Melniboné. I know what will become of you.'

'You know my destiny?' said Elric eagerly. 'Tell me what it is, Niun Who Knew All!'

Niun opened his mouth as if to speak but then firmly shut it again. 'No,' he said. 'I have forgotten.'

'No!' Elric made as if to seize the old man. 'No! You remember! I can see that you remember!'

'I have forgotten.' Niun lowered his head.

Rackhir took hold of Elric's arm. 'He has forgotten, Elric.'

Elric nodded. 'Very well.' Then he said, 'But have you remembered where lies the Tunnel Under the Marsh?'

'Yes. It is only a short distance from Ameeron, the Marsh itself. You go that way. Then you look for a monument in the shape of an eagle carved in black marble. At the base of the monument is the entrance to the tunnel.' Niun repeated this information parrot-fashion and when he looked up his face was clearer. 'What did I just tell you?'

Elric said: 'You gave us instructions on how to reach the entrance to the Tunnel Under the Marsh.'

'Did I?' Niun clapped his old hands. 'Splendid. I have forgotten that now, too. Who are you?'

'We are best forgotten,' said Rackhir with a gentle smile. 'Farewell, Niun and thanks.'

'Thanks for what?'

'Both for remembering and for forgetting.'

They walked on through the miserable City of Ameeron, away from the happy old sorcerer, sighting the odd face staring at them from a doorway or a window, doing their best to breathe as little of the foul air as possible.

'I think perhaps that I envy Niun alone of all the inhabitants of this desolate place,' said Rackhir.

'I pity him,' said Elric.

'Why so?'

'It occurs to me that when he has forgotten everything, he may well forget that he is allowed to leave Ameeron.'

Rackhir laughed and slapped the albino upon his black armoured back. 'You are a gloomy comrade, friend Elric. Are all your thoughts so hopeless?'

'They tend in that direction, I fear,' said Elric with a shadow of a smile.

3   The Tunnel Under the Marsh

And on they travelled through that sad and murky world until at last they came to the marsh.

The marsh was black. Black spiky vegetation grew in clumps here and there upon it. It was cold and it was dank; a dark mist swirled close to the surface and through the mist sometimes darted low shapes. From the mist rose a solid black object which could only be the monument described by Niun.

'The monument,' said Rackhir, stopping and leaning on his bow. 'It's well out into the marsh and there's no evident pathway leading to it. Is this a problem, do you think, Comrade Elric?'

Elric waded cautiously into the edge of the marsh. He felt the cold ooze drag at his feet. He stepped back with some difficulty.

'There must be a path,' said Rackhir, fingering his bony nose. 'Else how would your cousin cross?'

Elric looked over his shoulder at the Red Archer and he shrugged. 'Who knows? He could be travelling with sorcerous companions who have no difficulty where marshes are concerned.'

Suddenly Elric found himself sitting down upon the damp rock. The stink of brine from the marsh seemed for a moment to have over-whelmed him. He was feeling weak. The effectiveness of his drugs, last taken just as he stepped through the Shade Gate, was beginning to fade.

Rackhir came and stood by the albino. He smiled with a certain amount of bantering sympathy. 'Well, Sir Sorcerer, cannot you summon similar aid?'

Elric shook his head. 'I know little that is practical concerning the raising of small demons. Yyrkoon has all his grimoires, his favourite spells, his introductions to the demon worlds. We shall have to find a path of the ordinary kind if we wish to reach yonder monument, War-rior Priest of Phum.'

The Warrior Priest of Phum drew a red kerchief from within his tunic and blew his nose for some time. When he had finished he put down a hand, helped Elric to his feet, and began to walk along the rim of the marsh, keeping the black monument ever in sight.

It was some time later that they found a path at last and it was not a natural path but a slab of black marble extending out into the gloom of the mire, slippery to the feet and itself covered with a film of ooze.

'I would almost suspect this of being a false path—a lure to take us to our death,' said Rackhir as he and Elric stood and looked at the long slab, 'but what have we to lose now?'

'Come,' said Elric, setting foot on the slab and beginning to make his cautious way along it. In his hand he now held a torch of sorts, a bundle of sputtering reeds which gave off an unpleasant yellow light and a considerable amount of greenish smoke, but it was better than nothing.

Rackhir, testing each footstep with his unstrung bow-stave, followed behind, whistling a small, complicated tune as he went along. Another of his race would have recognised the tune as the *Song of the Son of the Hero of the High Hell who is about to Sacrifice his Life,* a popular melody in Phum, particularly amongst the caste of the Warrior Priest.

Elric found the tune irritating and distracting, but he said nothing, for he concentrated every fragment of his attention on keeping his balance upon the slippery surface of the slab, which now appeared to rock slightly, as if it floated on the surface of the marsh.

And now they were halfway to the monument whose shape could be clearly distinguished: A great eagle with spread wings and a savage beak and claws extended for the kill. An eagle in the same black marble as the slab on which they tried to keep their balance. And Elric was reminded of a tomb. Had some ancient hero been buried here? Or had the tomb been built to house the Black Swords—imprison them so that they might never enter the world of men again and steal men's souls?

The slab rocked more violently. Elric tried to remain upright but swayed first on one foot and then the other, the brand waving crazily. Both feet slid from under him and he went flying into the marsh and was instantly buried up to his knees.

He began to sink.

Somehow he had managed to keep his grip on the brand and by its light he could see the red-clad archer peering forward.

'Elric?'

'I'm here, Rackhir.'

'You're sinking?'

'The marsh seems intent on swallowing me, aye.'

'Can you lie flat?'

'I can lie forward, but my legs are trapped.' Elric tried to move his body in the ooze which pressed against it. Something rushed past him in front of his face, giving voice to a kind of muted gibbering. Elric did his best to control the fear which welled up in him. 'I think you must give me up, friend Rackhir.'

'What? And lose my means of getting out of this world? You must think me more selfless than I am, Comrade Elric. Here . . .' Rackhir carefully lowered himself to the slab and reached out his arm towards Elric. Both men were now covered in clinging slime; both shivered with cold. Rackhir stretched and stretched and Elric leaned forward as far as he could and tried to reach the hand, but it was impossible. And every second dragged him deeper into the stinking filth of the marsh.

Then Rackhir took up his bow-stave and pushed that out.

'Grab the bow, Elric. Can you?'

Leaning forward and stretching every bone and muscle in his body, Elric just managed to get a grip on the bow-stave.

'Now, I must—Ah!' Rackhir, pulling at the bow, found his own feet slipping and the slab beginning to rock quite wildly. He flung out one arm to grab the far lip of the slab and with his other hand kept a grip on the bow, 'Hurry, Elric! Hurry!'

Elric began painfully to pull himself from the ooze. The slab still rocked crazily and Rackhir's hawklike face was almost as pale as Elric's own as he desperately strove to keep his hold on both slab and bow. And then Elric, all soaked in mire, managed to reach the slab and crawl onto it, the brand still sputtering in his hand, and lie there gasping and gasping and gasping.

Rackhir, too, was short of breath, but he laughed. 'What a fish I've caught!' he said. 'The biggest yet, I'd wager!'

'I am grateful to you, Rackhir the Red Archer. I am grateful, Warrior Priest of Phum. I owe you my life,' said Elric after a while. 'And I swear that whether I'm successful in my quest or not I'll use all my powers to see you through the Shade Gate and back into the world from which we have both come.'

Rackhir said quietly: 'You are a man, Elric of Melniboné. That is why I saved you. There are few men in any world.' He shrugged and grinned. 'Now I suggest we continue towards yonder monument on our knees. Undignified it might be, but safer it is also. And it is but a short way to crawl.'

Elric agreed.

Not much more time had passed in that timeless darkness before they had reached a little moss-grown island on which stood the Monument of the Eagle, huge and heavy and towering above them into the greater gloom which was either the sky or the roof of the cavern. And at the base of the plinth they saw a low doorway. And the doorway was open.

'A trap?' mused Rackhir.

'Or does Yyrkoon assume us perished in Ameeron?' said Elric, wiping himself free of slime as best he could. He sighed. 'Let's enter and be done with it.'

And so they entered.

They found themselves in a small room. Elric cast the faint light of a brand about the place and saw another doorway. The rest of the room was featureless—each wall made of the same faintly glistening black marble. The room was filled with silence.

Neither man spoke. Both walked unfalteringly towards the next doorway and, when they found steps, began to descend the steps, which wound down and down into total darkness.

For a long time they descended, still without speaking, until eventually they reached the bottom and saw before them the entrance to a narrow tunnel which was irregularly shaped so that it seemed more the work of nature than of some intelligence. Moisture dripped from the roof of the tunnel and fell with the regularity of heartbeats to the floor, seeming to echo a deeper sound, far, far away, emanating from somewhere in the tunnel itself.

Elric heard Rackhir clear his throat.

'This is without doubt a tunnel,' said the Red Archer, 'and it unquestionably leads under the marsh.'

Elric felt that Rackhir shared his reluctance to enter the tunnel. He stood with the guttering brand held high, listening to the sound of the drops falling to the floor of the tunnel, trying to recognise that other sound which came so faintly from the depths.

And then he forced himself forward, almost running into the tunnel, his ears filled with a sudden roaring which might have come from within his head or from some other source in the tunnel. He heard Rackhir's footfalls behind him. He drew his sword, the sword of the dead hero Aubec, and he heard the hissing of his own breath echo from the walls of the tunnel which was now alive with sounds of every sort.

Elric shuddered, but he did not pause.

The tunnel was warm. The floor felt spongy beneath his feet, the smell of brine persisted. And now he could see that the walls of the tunnel were smoother, that they seemed to shiver with quick, regular movement. He heard Rackhir gasp behind him as the archer, too, noted the peculiar nature of the tunnel.

'It's like flesh,' murmured the Warrior Priest of Phum. 'Like flesh.'

Elric could not bring himself to reply. All his attention was required to force himself forward. He was consumed by terror. His whole body shook. He sweated and his legs threatened to buckle under him. His grip was so weak that he could barely keep his sword from falling to the floor. And there were hints of something in his memory, something which his brain refused to consider. Had he been here before? His trembling increased. His stomach turned. But he still stumbled on, the brand held before him.

And now the soft, steady thrumming sound grew louder and he saw ahead a small, almost circular aperture at the very end of the tunnel. He stopped, swaying.

'The tunnel ends,' whispered Rackhir. 'There is no way through.'

The small aperture was pulsing with a swift, strong beat.

'The Pulsing Cavern,' Elric whispered. 'That is what we should find at the end of the Tunnel Under the Marsh. That must be the entrance, Rackhir.'

'It is too small for a man to enter, Elric,' said Rackhir reasonably.

'No . . .'

Elric stumbled forward until he stood close to the opening. He sheathed his sword. He handed the brand to Rackhir and then, before the Warrior Priest of Phum could stop him, he had flung himself head-first through the gap, wriggling his body through—and the walls of the aperture parted for him and then closed behind him, leaving Rackhir on the other side.

Elric got slowly to his feet. A faint, pinkish light now came from the walls and ahead of him was another entrance, slightly larger than the other through which he had just come. The air was warm and thick and salty. It almost stifled him. His head throbbed and his body ached and he could barely act or think, save to force himself onward. On faltering legs he flung himself towards the next entrance as the great, muffled pulsing sounded louder and louder in his ears.

'Elric!'

Rackhir stood behind him, pale and sweating. He had abandoned the brand and followed Elric through.

Elric licked dry lips and tried to speak.

Rackhir came closer.

Elric said thickly: 'Rackhir. You should not be here.'

'I said I would help.'

'Aye, but . . .'

'Then help I shall.'

Elric had no strength for arguing, so he nodded and with his hands forced back the soft walls of the second aperture and saw that it led into a cavern whose round wall quivered to a steady pulsing. And in the centre of the cavern, hanging in the air without any support at all were two swords. Two identical swords, huge and fine and black.

And standing beneath the swords, his expression gloating and greedy, stood Prince Yyrkoon of Melniboné, reaching up for them, his lips moving but no words escaping from him. And Elric himself was able to voice but one word as he climbed through and stood upon that shuddering floor. 'No,' he said.

Yyrkoon heard the word. He turned with terror in his face. He snarled when he saw Elric and then he, too, voiced a word which was at once a scream of outrage.

'No!'

With an effort Elric dragged Aubec's blade from its scabbard. But it seemed too heavy to hold upright, it tugged his arm so that it rested on the floor, his arm hanging straight at his side. Elric drew deep breaths of heavy air into his lungs. His vision was dimming. Yyrkoon had become a shadow. Only the two black swords, standing still and cool in the very centre of the circular chamber, were in focus. Elric sensed Rackhir enter the chamber and stand beside him.

'Yyrkoon,' said Elric at last, 'those swords are mine.'

Yyrkoon smiled and reached up towards the blades. A peculiar moaning sound seemed to issue from them. A faint, black radiance seemed to emanate from them. Elric saw the runes carved into them and he was afraid.

Rackhir fitted an arrow to his bow. He drew the string back to his shoulder, sighting along the arrow at Prince Yyrkoon. 'If he must die, Elric, tell me.'

'Slay him,' said Elric.

And Rackhir released the string.

But the arrow moved very slowly through the air and then hung halfway between the archer and his intended target.

Yyrkoon turned, a ghastly grin on his face. 'Mortal weapons are useless here,' he said.

Elric said to Rackhir, 'He must be right. And your life is in danger, Rackhir. Go . . .'

Rackhir gave him a puzzled look. 'No, I must stay here and help you . . .'

Elric shook his head. 'You cannot help, you will only die if you stay. Go.'

Reluctantly the Red Archer unstrung his bow, glanced suspiciously up at the two black swords, then squeezed his way through the doorway and was gone.

'Now, Yyrkoon,' said Elric, letting Aubec's sword fall to the floor. 'We must settle this, you and I.'

4   Two Black Swords

And then the runeblades Stormbringer and Mournblade were gone from where they had hung so long.

And Stormbringer had settled into Elric's right hand. And Mourn blade lay in Prince Yyrkoon's right hand.

And the two men stood on opposite sides of the Pulsing Cavern and regarded first each other and then the swords they held.

The swords were singing. Their voices were faint but could be heard quite plainly. Elric lifted the huge blade easily and turned it this way and that, admiring its alien beauty

'Stormbringer,' he said.

And then he felt afraid.

It was suddenly as if he had been born again and that this runesword was born with him. It was as if they had never been separate.

'Stormbringer.'

And the sword moaned sweetly and settled even more smoothly into his grasp.

'Stormbringer!' yelled Elric and he leapt at his cousin.

'Stormbringer!'

And he was full of fear—so full of fear. And the fear brought a wild kind of delight—a demonic need to fight and kill his cousin, to sink the blade deep into Yyrkoon's heart. To take vengeance. To spill blood. To send a soul to hell.

And now Prince Yyrkoon's cry could be heard above the thrum of the sword-voices, the drumming of the pulse of the cavern.

'Mournblade!'

And Mournblade came up to meet Stormbringer's blow and turn that blow and thrust back at Elric who swayed aside and brought Storm-bringer round and down in a sidestroke which knocked Yyrkoon and Mournblade backward for an instant. But Stormbringer's next thrust was met again. And the next thrust was met. And the next. If the swordsmen were evenly matched, then so were the blades, which seemed possessed of their own wills, though they performed the wills of their wielders.

And the clang of the metal upon metal turned into a wild, metallic song which the swords sang. A joyful song as if they were glad at last to be back to battling, though they battled each other.

And Elric barely saw his cousin, Prince Yyrkoon, at all, save for an occasional flash of his dark, wild face. Elric's attention was given entirely to the two black swords, for it seemed that the swords fought with the life of one of the swordsmen as a prize (or perhaps the lives of both, thought Elric) and that the rivalry between Elric and Yyrkoon was nothing compared with the brotherly rivalry between the swords who seemed full of pleasure at the chance to engage again after many millennia.

And this observation, as he fought—and fought for his soul as well as his life—gave Elric pause to consider his hatred of Yyrkoon.

Kill Yyrkoon he would, but not at the will of another power. Not to give sport to these alien swords.

Mournblade's point darted at his eyes and Stormbringer rose to deflect the thrust once more.

Elric no longer fought his cousin. He fought the will of the two black swords.

Stormbringer dashed for Yyrkoon's momentarily undefended throat. Elric clung to the sword and dragged it back, sparing his cousin's life. Stormbringer whined almost petulantly, like a dog stopped from biting an intruder.

And Elric spoke through clenched teeth. 'I'll not be your puppet, runeblade. If we must be united, let it be upon a proper understanding.'

The sword seemed to hesitate, to drop its guard, and Elric was hard put to defend himself against the whirling attack of Mournblade which, in turn, seemed to sense its advantage.

Elric felt fresh energy pour up his right arm and into his body. This was what the sword could do. With it, he needed no drugs, would never be weak again. In battle he would triumph. At peace, he could rule with pride. When he travelled, it could be alone and without fear. It was as if the sword reminded him of all these things, even as it returned Mournblade's attack.

And what must the sword have in return?

Elric knew. The sword told him, without words of any sort. Stormbringer needed to fight, for that was its reason for existence. Stormbringer needed to kill, for that was its source of energy, the lives and the souls of men, demons—even gods.

And Elric hesitated, even as his cousin gave a huge, cackling yell and dashed at him so that Mournblade glanced off his helm and he was flung backwards and down and saw Yyrkoon gripping his moaning black sword in both hands to plunge the runeblade into Elric's body.

And Elric knew he would do anything to resist that fate—for his soul to be drawn into Mournblade and his strength to feed Prince Yyrkoon's strength. And he rolled aside, very quickly, and got to one knee and turned and lifted Stormbringer with one gauntleted hand upon the blade and the other upon the hilt to take the great blow Prince Yyrkoon brought upon it. And the two black swords shrieked as if in pain, and they shivered, and black radiance poured from them as blood might pour from a man pierced by many arrows. And Elric was driven, still on his knees, away from the radiance, gasping and sighing and peering here and there for sight of Yyrkoon who had disappeared.

And Elric knew that Stormbringer spoke to him again. If Elric did not wish to die by Mournblade, then Elric must accept the bargain which the Black Sword offered.

'He must not die!' said Elric. 'I will not slay him to make sport for you!'

And through the black radiance ran Yyrkoon, snarling and snapping and whirling his runesword.

Again Stormbringer darted through an opening, and again Elric made the blade pull back and Yyrkoon was only grazed.

Stormbringer writhed in Elric's hands.

Elric said: 'You shall not be my master.'

And Stormbringer seemed to understand and become quieter, as if reconciled. And Elric laughed, thinking that he now controlled the runesword and that from now on the blade would do his bidding.

'We shall disarm Yyrkoon,' said Elric. 'We shall not kill him.'

Elric rose to his feet.

Stormbringer moved with all the speed of a needle-thin rapier. It feinted, it parried, it thrust. Yyrkoon, who had been grinning in triumph, snarled and staggered back, the grin dropping from his sullen features.

Stormbringer now worked for Elric. It made the moves that Elric wished to make. Both Yyrkoon and Mournblade seemed disconcerted by this turn of events. Mournblade shouted as if in astonishment at its brother's behaviour. Elric struck at Yyrkoon's sword-arm, pierced cloth —pierced flesh—pierced sinew—pierced bone. Blood came, soaking Yyrkoon's arm and dripping down onto the hilt of the sword. The blood was slippery. It weakened Yyrkoon's grip on his runesword. He took it in both hands, but he was unable to hold it firmly.

Elric, too, took Stormbringer in both hands. Unearthly strength surged through him. With a gigantic blow he dashed Stormbringer against Mournblade where blade met hilt. The runesword flew from Yyrkoon's grasp. It sped across the Pulsing Cavern.

Elric smiled. He had defeated his own sword's will and, in turn, had defeated the brother sword.

Mournblade fell against the wall of the Pulsing Cavern and for a moment was still.

A groan then seemed to escape the defeated runesword. A high-pitched shriek filled the Pulsing Cavern. Blackness flooded over the eery pink light and extinguished it.

When the light returned Elric saw that a scabbard lay at his feet. The scabbard was black and of the same alien craftsmanship as the rune-sword. Elric saw Yyrkoon. The prince was on his knees and he was sobbing, his eyes darting about the Pulsing Cavern seeking Mournblade, looking at Elric with fright as if he knew he must now be slain.

'Mournblade?' Yyrkoon said hopelessly. He knew he was to die.

Mournblade had vanished from the Pulsing Cavern.

'Your sword is gone,' said Elric quietly.

Yyrkoon whimpered and tried to crawl towards the entrance of the cavern. But the entrance had shrunk to the size of a small coin. Yyr-koon wept.

Stormbringer trembled, as if thirsty for Yyrkoon's soul. Elric stooped.

Yyrkoon began to speak rapidly. 'Do not slay me, Elric—not with that runeblade. I will do anything you wish. I will die in any other way.'

Elric said: 'We are victims, cousin, of a conspiracy—a game played by gods, demons and sentient swords. They wish one of us dead. I suspect they wish you dead more than they wish me dead. And that is the reason why I shall not slay you here.' He picked up the scabbard. He forced Stormbringer into it and at once the sword was quiet. Elric took off his old scabbard and looked around for Aubec's sword, but that, too, was gone. He dropped the old scabbard and hooked the new one to his belt. He rested his left hand upon the pommel of Stormbringer and he looked not without sympathy upon the creature that was his cousin.

'You are a worm, Yyrkoon. But is that your fault?'

Yyrkoon gave him a puzzled glance.

'I wonder, if you had all your desire, would you cease to be a worm, cousin?'

Yyrkoon raised himself to his knees. A little hope began to show in his eyes.

Elric smiled and drew a deep breath. 'We shall see,' he said. 'You must agree to wake Cymoril from her sorcerous slumber.'

'You have humbled me, Elric,' said Yyrkoon in a small, pitiful voice. 'I will wake her. Or would . . .'

'Can you not undo your spell?'

'We cannot escape from the Pulsing Cavern. It is past the time . . .'

'What's this?'

'I did not think you would follow me. And then I thought I would easily finish you. And now it is past the time. One can keep the entrance open for only a little while. It will admit anyone who cares to enter the Pulsing Cavern, but it will let no-one out after the power of the spell dies. I gave much to know that spell.'

'You have given too much for everything,' said Elric. He went to the entrance and peered through. Rackhir waited on the other side. The Red Archer had an anxious expression. Elric said: 'Warrior Priest of Phum, it seems that my cousin and I are trapped in here. The entrance will not part for us.' Elric tested the warm, moist stuff of the wall. It would not open more than a tiny fraction. 'It seems that you can join us or else go back. If you do join us, you share our fate.'

'It is not much of a fate if I go back,' said Rackhir. 'What chances have you?'

'One,' said Elric. 'I can invoke my patron.'

'A Lord of Chaos?' Rackhir made a wry face.

'Exactly,' said Elric. 'I speak of Arioch.'

'Arioch, eh? Well, he does not care for renegades from Phum.'

'What do you choose to do?'

Rackhir stepped forward. Elric stepped back. Through the opening came Rackhir's head, followed by his shoulders, followed by the rest of him. The entrance closed again immediately. Rackhir stood up and untangled the string of his bow from the stave, smoothing it. 'I agreed to share your fate—to gamble all on escaping from this plane,' said the Red Archer. He looked surprised when he saw Yyrkoon. 'Your enemy is still alive?'

'Aye.'

'You are merciful indeed!'

'Perhaps. Or obstinate. I would not slay him merely because some supernatural agency used him as a pawn, to be killed if I should win. The Lords of the Higher Worlds do not as yet control me completely—nor will they if I have any power at all to resist them.'

Rackhir grinned. 'I share your view—though I'm not optimistic about its realism. I see you have one of those black swords at your belt. Will that not hack a way through the cavern?'

'No,' said Yyrkoon from his place against the wall. 'Nothing can harm the stuff of the Pulsing Cavern.'

'I'll believe you,' said Elric, 'for I do not intend to draw this new sword of mine often. I must learn how to control it first.'

'So Arioch must be summoned.' Rackhir sighed.

'If that is possible,' said Elric.

'He will doubtless destroy me,' said Rackhir, looking to Elric in the hope that the albino would deny this statement.

Elric looked grave. 'I might be able to strike a bargain with him. It will also test something.'

Elric turned his back on Rackhir and on Yyrkoon. He adjusted his mind. He sent it out through vast spaces and complicated mazes. And he cried:

'Arioch! Arioch! Aid me, Arioch!'

He had a sense of something listening to him.

'Arioch!'

Something shifted in the places where his mind went.

'Arioch . . .'

And Arioch heard him. He knew it was Arioch.

Rackhir gave a horrified yell. Yyrkoon screamed. Elric turned and saw that something disgusting had appeared near the far wall. It was black and it was foul and it slobbered and its shape was intolerably alien. Was this Arioch? How could it be? Arioch was beautiful. But perhaps, thought Elric, this was Arioch's true shape. Upon this plane, in this peculiar cavern, Arioch could not deceive those who looked upon him.

But then the shape had disappeared and a beautiful youth with ancient eyes stood looking at the three mortals.

'You have won the sword, Elric,' said Arioch, ignoring the others. 'I congratulate you. And you have spared your cousin's life. Why so?'

'More than one reason,' said Elric. 'But let us say he must remain alive in order to wake Cymoril.'

Arioch's face bore a little, secret smile for a moment and Elric realised that he had avoided a trap. If he had killed Yyrkoon, Cymoril would never have woken again.

'And what is this little traitor doing with you?' Arioch turned a cold eye on Rackhir who did his best to stare back at the Chaos Lord.

'He is my friend,' said Elric. 'I made a bargain with him. If he aided me to find the Black Sword, then I would take him back with me to our own plane.'

'That is impossible. Rackhir is an exile here. That is his punishment.'

'He comes back with me,' said Elric. And now he unhooked the scabbard holding Stormbringer from his belt and he held the sword out before him. 'Or I do not take the sword with me. Failing that, we all three remain here for eternity.'

'That is not sensible, Elric. Consider your responsibilities.'

'I have considered them. That is my decision.'

Arioch's smooth face had just a tinge of anger. 'You must take the sword. It is your destiny.'

'So you say. But I now know that the sword may only be borne by me. You cannot bear it, Arioch, or you would. Only I—or another mortal like me—can take it from the Pulsing Cavern. Is that not so?'

'You are clever, Elric of Melniboné.' Arioch spoke with sardonic admiration. 'And you are a fitting servant of Chaos. Very well—that traitor can go with you. But he would be best warned to tread warily. The Lords of Chaos have been known to bear malice . . .'

Rackhir said hoarsely: 'So I have heard, My Lord Arioch.'

Arioch ignored the archer. 'The man of Phum is not, after all, important. And if you wish to spare your cousin's life, so be it. It matters little. Destiny can contain a few extra threads in her design and still accomplish her original aims.'

'Very well then,' said Elric. 'Take us from this place.'

'Where to?'

'Why, to Melniboné, if you please.'

With a smile that was almost tender Arioch looked down on Elric and a silky hand stroked Elric's cheek. Arioch had grown to twice his original size. 'Oh, you are surely the sweetest of all my slaves,' said the Lord of Chaos.

And there was a whirling. There was a sound like the roar of the sea. There was a dreadful sense of nausea. And three weary men stood on the floor of the great throne room in Imrryr. The throne room was deserted, save that in one corner a black shape, like smoke, writhed for a moment and then was gone.

Rackhir crossed the floor and seated himself carefully upon the first step to the Ruby Throne. Yyrkoon and Elric remained where they were, staring into each other's eyes. Then Elric laughed and slapped his scabbarded sword. 'Now you must fulfil your promises to me, cousin. Then I have a proposition to put to you.'

'It is like a market place,' said Rackhir, leaning on one elbow and inspecting the feather in his scarlet hat. 'So many bargains!'

5 The Pale King's Mercy

Yyrkoon stepped back from his sister's bed. He was worn and his features were drawn and there was no spirit in him as he said: 'It is done.' He turned away and looked through the window at the towers of Imrryr, at the harbour where the returned golden battle-barges rode at anchor, together with the ship which had been King Straasha's gift to Elric. 'She will wake in a moment,' added Yyrkoon absently.

Dyvim Tvar and Rackhir the Red Archer looked inquiringly at Elric who kneeled by the bed, staring into the face of Cymoril. Her face grew peaceful as he watched and for one terrible moment he suspected Prince Yyrkoon of tricking him and of killing Cymoril. But then the eyelids moved and the eyes opened and she saw him and she smiled. 'Elric? The dreams . . . You are safe?'

'I am safe, Cymoril. As are you.'

'Yyrkoon . . . ?'

'He woke you.'

'But you swore to slay him . . .'

'I was as much subject to sorcery as you. My mind was confused. It is still confused where some matters are concerned. But Yyrkoon is changed now. I defeated him. He does not doubt my power. He no longer lusts to usurp me.'

'You are merciful, Elric.' She brushed raven hair from her face.

Elric exchanged a glance with Rackhir.

'It might not be mercy which moves me,' said Elric. 'It might merely be a sense of fellowship with Yyrkoon.'

'Fellowship? Surely you cannot feel . . . ?'

'We are both mortal. We were both victims of a game played between the Lords of the Higher Worlds. My loyalty must, finally, be to my own kind—and that is why I ceased to hate Yyrkoon.'

'And that is mercy,' said Cymoril.

Yyrkoon walked towards the door. 'May I leave, my lord emperor?'

Elric thought he detected a strange light in his defeated cousin's eyes. But perhaps it was only humility or despair. He nodded. Yyrkoon went from the room, closing the door softly.

Dyvim Tvar said: 'Trust Yyrkoon not at all, Elric. He will betray you again.' The Lord of the Dragon Caves was troubled.

'No,' said Elric. 'If he does not fear me, he fears the sword I now carry.'

'And you should fear that sword,' said Dyvim Tvar.

'No,' said Elric. 'I am the master of the sword.'

Dyvim Tvar made to speak again but then shook his head almost sorrowfully, bowed and, together with Rackhir the Red Archer, left Elric and Cymoril alone.

Cymoril took Elric in her arms. They kissed. They wept.

There were celebrations in Melniboné for a week. Now almost all the ships and men and dragons were home. And Elric was home, having proved his right to rule so well that all his strange quirks of character (this 'mercy' of his was perhaps the strangest) were accepted by the populace.

In the throne room there was a ball and it was the most lavish ball any of the courtiers had ever known. Elric danced with Cymoril, taking a full part in the activities. Only Yyrkoon did not dance, preferring to remain in a quiet corner below the gallery of the music-slaves, ignored by the guests. Rackhir the Red Archer danced with several Melnibonéan ladies and made assignations with them all, for he was a hero now in Melniboné. Dyvim Tvar danced, too, though his eyes were often brooding when they fell upon Prince Yyrkoon.

And later, when people ate, Elric spoke to Cymoril as they sat together on the dais of the Ruby Throne.

'Would you be empress, Cymoril?'

'You know I will marry you, Elric. We have both known that for many a year, have we not?'

'So you would be my wife?'

'Aye.' She laughed for she thought he joked.

'And not be empress? For a year at least?'

'What mean you, my lord.'

'I must go away from Melniboné, Cymoril, for a year. What I have learned in recent months has made me want to travel the Young Kingdoms—see how other nations conduct their affairs. For I think Melniboné must change if she is to survive. She could become a great force for good in the world, for she still has much power.'

'For good?' Cymoril was surprised and there was a little alarm in her voice, too. 'Melniboné has never stood for good or for evil, but for herself and the satisfaction of her desires.'

'I would see that changed.'

'You intend to alter everything?'

'I intend to travel the world and then decide if there is any point to such a decision. The Lords of the Higher Worlds have ambitions in our world. Though they have given me aid, of late, I fear them. I should like to see if it is possible for men to rule their own affairs.'

'And you will go?' There were tears in her eyes. 'When?'

'Tomorrow—when Rackhir leaves. We will take King Straasha's ship and make for the Isle of the Purple Towns where Rackhir has friends. Will you come?'

'I cannot imagine—I cannot. Oh, Elric, why spoil this happiness we now have?'

'Because I feel that the happiness cannot last unless we know com pletely what we are.'

She frowned. 'Then you must discover that, if that is what you wish,' she said slowly. 'But it is for you to discover alone, Elric, for I have no such desire. You must go by yourself into those barbarian lands.'

'You will not accompany me?'

'It is not possible. I—I am Melnibonéan . . .' She sighed. 'I love you, Elric.'

'And I you, Cymoril.'

'Then we shall be married when you return. In a year.'

Elric was full of sorrow, but he knew that his decision was correct. If he did not leave, he would grow restless soon enough and if he grew restless he might come to regard Cymoril as an enemy, someone who had trapped him.

'Then you must rule as empress until I return,' he said.

'No, Elric I cannot take that responsibility.'

'Then, who . . . ? Dyvim Tvar . . .'

'I know Dyvim Tvar. He will not take such power. Magum Colim, perhaps . . .'

'No.'

'Then you must stay, Elric.'

But Elric's gaze had travelled through the crowd in the throne room below. It stopped when it reached a lonely figure seated by itself under the gallery of the music-slaves. And Elric smiled ironically and said:

'Then it must be Yyrkoon.'

Cymoril was horrified. 'No, Elric. He will abuse any power . . .'

'Not now. And it is just. He is the only one who wanted to be emperor. Now he can rule as emperor for a year in my stead. If he rules well, I may consider abdicating in his favour. If he rules badly, it will prove, once and for all, that his ambitions were misguided.'

'Elric,' said Cymoril. 'I love you. But you are a fool—a criminal, if you trust Yyrkoon again.'

'No,' he said evenly. 'I am not a fool. All I am is Elric. I cannot help that, Cymoril.'

'It is Elric that I love!' she cried. 'But Elric is doomed. We are all doomed unless you remain here now.'

'I cannot. Because I love you, Cymoril, I cannot.'

She stood up. She was weeping. She was lost.

'And I am Cymoril,' she said. 'You will destroy us both.' Her voice softened and she stroked his hair. 'You will destroy us, Elric.'

'No,' he said. 'I will build something that will be better. I will discover things. When I return we shall marry and we shall live long and we shall be happy, Cymoril.'

And now, Elric had told three lies. The first concerned his cousin Yyrkoon. The second concerned the Black Sword. The third concerned Cymoril. And upon those three lies was Elric's destiny to be built, for it is only about things which concern us most profoundly that we lie clearly and with profound conviction.

EPILOGUE

There was a port called Menii which was one of the humblest and friendliest of the Purple Towns. Like the others on the isle it was built mainly of the purple stone which gave the towns their name. And there were red roofs on the houses and there were bright-sailed boats of all kinds in the harbour as Elric and Rackhir the Red Archer came ashore in the early morning when just a few sailors were beginning to make their way down to their ships.

King Straasha's lovely ship lay some way out beyond the harbour wall. They had used a small boat to cross the water between it and the town. They turned and looked back at the ship. They had sailed it themselves, without crew, and the ship had sailed well.

'So, I must seek peace and mythic Tanelorn,' said Rackhir, with a certain amount of self-mockery. He stretched and yawned and the bow and the quiver danced on his back.

Elric was dressed in simple costume that might have marked any soldier-of-fortune of the Young Kingdoms. He looked fit and relaxed. He smiled into the sun. The only remarkable thing about his garb was the great, black runesword at his side. Since he had donned the sword, he had needed no drugs to sustain him at all.

'And I must seek knowledge in the lands I find marked upon my map,' said Elric. 'I must learn and I must carry what I learn back to Melniboné at the end of a year. I wish that Cymoril had accompanied me, but I understand her reluctance.'

'You will go back?' Rackhir said. 'When a year is over?'

'She will draw me back!' Elric laughed. 'My only fear is that I will weaken and return before my quest is finished.'

'I should like to come with you,' said Rackhir, 'for I have travelled in most lands and would be as good a guide as I was in the netherworld. But I am sworn to find Tanelorn, for all I know it does not really exist.'

'I hope that you find it, Warrior Priest of Phum,' said Elric.

'I shall never be that again,' said Rackhir. Then his eyes widened a little. 'Why, look—your ship!'

And Elric looked and saw the ship that had once been called The Ship Which Sails Over Land and Sea, and he saw that slowly it was sinking. King Straasha was taking it back.

'The elementals are friends, at least,' he said. 'But I fear their power wanes as the power of Melniboné wanes. For all that we of the Dragon Isle are considered evil by the folk of the Young Kingdoms, we share much in common with the spirits of Air, Earth, Fire and Water.'

Rackhir said, as the masts of the ship disappeared beneath the waves: 'I envy you those friends, Elric. You may trust them.'

'Aye.'

Rackhir looked at the runesword hanging on Elric's hip. 'But you would be wise to trust nothing else,' he added.

Elric laughed. 'Fear not for me, Rackhir, for I am my own master—for a year at least. And I am master of this sword now!'

The sword seemed to stir at his side and he took firm hold of its grip and slapped Rackhir on the back and he laughed and shook his white hair so that it drifted in the air and he lifted his strange, red eyes to the sky and he said:

"I shall be a new man when I return to Melniboné.'

THE SAILOR ON THE
SEAS OF FATE

For Bill Butler, Mike and Tony, and all at Unicorn Books, Wales.

CONTENTS

BOOK ONE

SAILING TO THE FUTURE

> *. . . and leaving his cousin Yyrkoon sitting as*
> *regent upon the Ruby Throne of Melniboné, leav-*
> *ing his cousin Cymoril weeping for him and de-*
> *spairing of his ever returning, Elric sailed from*
> *Imrryr, the Dreaming City, and went to seek an*
> *unknown goal in the worlds of the Young King-*
> *doms where Melnibonéans were, at best, dis-*
> *liked.*
>
> —THE CHRONICLE OF THE
> BLACK SWORD

1

It was as if the man stood in a vast cavern whose walls and roof were comprised of gloomy, unstable colors which would occasionally break and admit rays of light from the moon. That these walls were mere clouds massed above mountains and ocean was hard to believe, for all that the moonlight pierced them, stained them and revealed the black and turbulent sea washing the shore on which the man now stood.

Distant thunder rolled; distant lightning flickered. A thin rain fell. And the clouds were never still. From dusky jet to deadly white they swirled slowly, like the cloaks of men and women engaged in a trance-like and formalistic minuet: the man standing on the shingle of the grim beach was reminded of giants dancing to the music of the faraway storm and felt as one must feel who walks unwittingly into a hall where the gods are at play. He turned his gaze from the clouds to the ocean.

The sea seemed weary. Great waves heaved themselves together with difficulty and collapsed as if in relief, gasping as they struck sharp rocks.

The man pulled his hood closer about his face and he looked over his leathern shoulder more than once as he trudged closer to the sea and let the surf spill upon the toes of his knee-length black boots. He tried to peer into the cavern formed by the clouds but could see only a short distance. There was no way of telling what lay on the other side of the ocean or, indeed, how far the water extended. He put his head on one side, listening carefully, but could hear nothing but the sounds of the sky and the sea. He sighed. For a moment a moonbeam touched him and from the white flesh of his face there glowed two crimson, tormented eyes; then darkness came back. Again the man turned, plainly fearing that the light had revealed him to some enemy. Making as little sound as possible, he headed toward the shelter of the rocks on his left.

Elric was tired. In the city of Ryfel in the land of Pikarayd he had naïvely sought acceptance by offering his services as a mercenary in the army of the governor of that place. For his foolishness he had been imprisoned as a Melnibonéan spy (it was obvious to the governor that Elric could be nothing else) and had but recently escaped with the aid of bribes and some minor sorcery.

The pursuit, however, had been almost immediate. Dogs of great cunning had been employed and the governor himself had led the hunt beyond the borders of Pikarayd and into the lonely, uninhabited shale valleys of a world locally called the Dead Hills, in which little grew or tried to live.

Up the steep sides of small mountains, whose slopes consisted of gray, crumbling slate, which made a clatter to be heard a mile or more away, the white-faced one had ridden. Along dales all but grassless and whose river-bottoms had seen no water for scores of years, through cave-tunnels bare of even a stalactite, over plateaus from which rose cairns of stones erected by a forgotten folk, he had sought to escape his pursuers, and soon it seemed to him that he had left the world he knew forever, that he had crossed a supernatural frontier and had arrived in one of those bleak places of which he had read in the legends of his people, where once Law and Chaos had fought each other to a stalemate, leaving their battleground empty of life and the possibility of life.

And at last he had ridden his horse so hard that its heart had burst and he had abandoned its corpse and continued on foot, panting to the sea, to this narrow beach, unable to go farther forward and fearing to return lest his enemies should be lying in wait for him.

He thought that he would give much for a boat now. It would not be long before the dogs discovered his scent and led their masters to the beach. He shrugged. Best to die here alone, perhaps, slaughtered by those who did not even know his name. His only regret would be that Cymoril would wonder why he had not returned at the end of the year.

He had no food and few of the drugs which had of late sustained his energy. Without renewed energy he could not contemplate working a sorcery which might conjure for him some means of crossing the sea and making, perhaps, for the Isle of the Purple Towns where the people were least unfriendly to Melnibonéans.

It had been only a month since he had left behind his court and his queen-to-be, letting Yyrkoon sit on the throne of Melniboné until his return. He had thought he might learn more of the human folk of the Young Kingdoms by mixing with them, but they had rejected him either with outright hatred or wary and insincere humility. Nowhere had he found one willing to believe that a Melnibonéan (and they did not know he was the emperor) would willingly throw in his lot with the human beings who had once been in thrall to that cruel and ancient race. And now, as he stood beside a bleak sea feeling trapped and already defeated, he knew himself to be alone in a malevolent universe, bereft of friends and purpose, a useless, sickly anachronism, a fool brought low by his own insufficiencies of character, by his profound inability to believe wholly in the rightness or the wrongness of anything at all. He lacked faith in his race, in his birthright, in gods or men, and above all he lacked faith in himself.

His pace slackened; his hand fell upon the pommel of his black rune-sword Stormbringer, the blade which had so recently defeated its twin, Mournblade, in the fleshy chamber within a sunless world of Limbo. Stormbringer, seemingly half-sentient, was now his only companion, his only confidant, and it had become his neurotic habit to talk to the sword as another might talk to his horse or as a prisoner might share his thoughts with a cockroach in his cell.

"Well, Stormbringer, shall we walk into the sea and end it now?" His voice was dead, barely a whisper. "At least we shall have the pleasure of thwarting those who follow us."

He made a halfhearted movement toward the sea, but to his fatigued brain it seemed that the sword murmured, stirred against his hip, pulled back. The albino chuckled. "You exist to live and to take lives. Do I exist, then, to die and bring both those I love and hate the mercy of death? Sometimes I think so. A sad pattern, if that should be the pattern. Yet there must be more to all this. . . ."

He turned his back upon the sea, peering upward at the monstrous clouds forming and reforming above his head, letting the light rain fall upon his face, listening to the complex, melancholy music which the sea made as it washed over rocks and shingle and was carried this way and that by conflicting currents. The rain did little to refresh him. He had not slept at all for two nights and had slept hardly at all for several more. He must have ridden for almost a week before his horse collapsed.

At the base of a damp granite crag which rose nearly thirty feet above his head, he found a depression in the ground in which he could squat and be protected from the worst of the wind and the rain. Wrapping his heavy leather cloak tightly about him, he eased himself into the hole and was immediately asleep. Let them find him while he slept. He wanted no warning of his death.

Harsh, gray light struck his eyes as he stirred. He raised his neck, holding back a groan at the stiffness of his muscles, and he opened his eyes. He blinked. It was morning—perhaps even later, for the sun was invisible—and a cold mist covered the beach. Through the mist the darker clouds could still be seen above, increasing the effect of his being inside a huge cavern. Muffled a little, the sea continued to splash and hiss, though it seemed calmer than it had on the previous night, and there were now no sounds of a storm. The air was very cold.

Elric began to stand up, leaning on his sword for support, listening carefully, but there was no sign that his enemies were close by. Doubtless they had given up the chase, perhaps after finding his dead horse.

He reached into his belt pouch and took from it a sliver of smoked bacon and a vial of yellowish liquid. He sipped from the vial, replaced the stopper, and returned the vial to his pouch as he chewed on the meat. He was thirsty. He trudged farther up the beach and found a pool of rainwater not too tainted with salt. He drank his fill, staring around him. The mist was fairly thick and if he moved too far from the beach he knew he would become immediately lost. Yet did that matter? He had nowhere to go. Those who had pursued him must have realized that. Without a horse he could not cross back to Pikarayd, the most easterly of the Young Kingdoms. Without a boat he could not venture onto that sea and try to steer a course back to the Isle of the Purple Towns. He recalled no map which showed an eastern sea and he had little idea of how far he had traveled from Pikarayd. He decided that his only hope of surviving was to go north, following the coast in the trust that sooner or later he would come upon a port or a fishing village where he might trade his few remaining belongings for a passage on a boat. Yet that hope was a small one, for his food and his drugs could hardly last more than a day or so.

He took a deep breath to steel himself for the march and then regretted it; the mist cut at his throat and his lungs like a thousand tiny knives. He coughed. He spat upon the shingle.

And he heard something, something other than the moody whisperings of the sea: a regular creaking sound, as of a man walking in stiff leather. His right hand went to his left hip and the sword which rested there. He turned about, peering in every direction for the source of the noise, but the mist distorted it. It could have come from anywhere.

Elric crept back to the rock where he had sheltered. He leaned against it so that no swordsman could take him unawares from behind. He waited.

The creaking came again, but other sounds were added. He heard a clanking; a splash; perhaps a voice, perhaps a footfall on timber; and he guessed that either he was experiencing a hallucination as a side effect of the drug he had just swallowed or he had heard a ship coming toward the beach and dropping its anchor.

He felt relieved and he was tempted to laugh at himself for assuming so readily that this coast must be uninhabited. He had thought that the bleak cliffs stretched for miles—perhaps hundreds of miles—in all directions. The assumption could easily have been the subjective result of his depression, his weariness. It occurred to him that he might as easily have discovered a land not shown on maps, yet with a sophisticated culture of its own: with sailing ships, for instance, and harbors for them. Yet still he did not reveal himself.

Instead he withdrew behind the rock, peering into the mist toward the sea. And at last he discerned a shadow which had not been there the previous night. A black, angular shadow which could only be a ship. He made out the suggestion of ropes, he heard men grunting, he heard the creak and the rasp of a yard as it traveled up a mast. The sail was being furled.

Elric waited at least an hour, expecting the crew of the ship to disembark. They could have no other reason for entering this treacherous bay. But a silence had descended, as if the whole ship slept.

Cautiously Elric emerged from behind the rock and walked down to the edge of the sea. Now he could see the ship a little more clearly. Red sunlight was behind it, thin and watery, diffused by the mist. It was a good-sized ship and fashioned throughout of the same dark wood. Its design was baroque and unfamiliar, with high decks fore and aft and no evidence of rowing ports. This was unusual in a ship either of Melnibonéan or Young Kingdoms design and it tended to prove his theory that he had stumbled upon a civilization for some reason cut off from the rest of the world, just as Elwher and the Unmapped Kingdoms were cut off by the vast stretches of the Sighing Desert and the Weeping Waste. He saw no movement aboard, heard none of the sounds one might usually expect to hear on a seagoing ship, even if the larger part of the crew was resting. The mist eddied and more of the red light poured through to illuminate the vessel, revealing the large wheels on both the foredeck and the reardeck, the slender mast with its furled sail, the complicated geometrical carvings of its rails and its figurehead, the great, curving prow which gave the ship its main impression of power and strength and made Elric think it must be a warship rather than a trading vessel. But who was there to fight in such waters as these?

He cast aside his wariness and cupped his hands about his mouth, calling out:

"Hail, the ship!"

The answering silence seemed to him to take on a peculiar hesitancy as if those on board heard him and wondered if they should answer.

"Hail, the ship!"

Then a figure appeared on the port rail and, leaning over, looked casually toward him. The figure had on armor as dark and as strange as the design of his ship; he had a helmet obscuring most of his face and the main feature that Elric could distinguish was a thick, golden beard and sharp blue eyes.

"Hail, the shore," said the armored man. His accent was unknown to Elric, his tone was as casual as his manner. Elric thought he smiled. "What do you seek with us?"

"Aid," said Elric. "I am stranded here. My horse is dead. I am lost."

"Lost? Aha!" The man's voice echoed in the mist. "Lost. And you wish to come aboard?"

"I can pay a little. I can give my services in return for a passage, either to your next port of call or to some land close to the Young Kingdoms where maps are available so that I could make my own way thereafter. . . ."

"Well," said the other slowly, "there's work for a swordsman."

"I have a sword," said Elric.

"I see it. A good, big battle-blade."

"Then I can come aboard?"

"We must confer first. If you would be good enough to wait awhile . . ."

"Of course," said Elric. He was nonplussed by the man's manner, but the prospect of warmth and food on board the ship was cheering. He waited patiently until the blond-bearded warrior came back to the rail.

"Your name, sir?" said the warrior.

"I am Elric of Melniboné."

The warrior seemed to be consulting a parchment, running his finger down a list until he nodded, satisfied, and put the list into his large-buckled belt.

"Well," he said, "there was some point in waiting here, after all. I found it difficult to believe."

"What was the dispute and why did you wait?"

"For you," said the warrior, heaving a rope ladder over the side so that its end fell into the sea. "Will you board now, Elric of Melniboné?"

2

Elric was surprised by how shallow the water was and he wondered by what means such a large vessel could come so close to the shore. Shoulder-deep in the sea he reached up to grasp the ebony rungs of the ladder. He had great difficulty heaving himself from the water and was further hampered by the swaying of the ship and the weight of his runesword, but eventually he had clambered awkwardly over the side and stood on the deck with the water running from his clothes to the timbers and his body shivering with cold. He looked about him. Shining, red-tinted mist clung about the ship's dark yards and rigging, white mist spread itself over the roofs and sides of the two large cabins set fore and aft of the mast, and this mist was not of the same character as the mist beyond the ship. Elric, for a moment, had the fanciful notion that the mist traveled permanently wherever the ship traveled. He smiled to himself, putting the dreamlike quality of his experience down to lack of food and sleep. When the ship sailed into sunnier waters he would see it for the relatively ordinary vessel it was.

The blond warrior took Elric's arm. The man was as tall as Elric and massively built. Within his helm he smiled, saying:

"Let us go below."

They went to the cabin forward of the mast and the warrior drew back a sliding door, standing aside to let Elric enter first. Elric ducked his head and went into the warmth of the cabin. A lamp of red-gray glass gleamed, hanging from four silver chains attached to the roof, revealing several more bulky figures, fully dressed in a variety of armors, seated about a square and sturdy sea-table. All faces turned to regard Elric as he came in, followed by the blond warrior who said:

"This is he."

One of the occupants of the cabin, who sat in the farthest corner and whose features were completely hidden by the shadow, nodded. "Aye," he said. "That is he."

"You know me, sir," said Elric, seating himself at the end of the bench and removing his sodden leather cloak. The warrior nearest him passed him a metal cup of hot wine and Elric accepted it gratefully, sipping at the spiced liquid and marveling at how quickly it dispersed the chill within him.

"In a sense," said the man in the shadows. His voice was sardonic and at the same time had a melancholy ring, and Elric was not offended, for the bitterness in the voice seemed directed more at the owner than at any he addressed.

The blond warrior seated himself opposite Elric. "I am Brut," he said, "once of Lashmar, where my family still holds land, but it is many a year since I have been there."

"From the Young Kingdoms, then?" said Elric.

"Aye. Once."

"This ship journeys nowhere near those nations?" Elric asked.

"I believe it does not," said Brut. "It is not so long, I think, since I myself came aboard. I was seeking Tanelorn, but found this craft, instead."

"Tanelorn?" Elric smiled. "How many must seek that mythical place? Do you know of one called Rackhir, once a warrior priest of Phum? We adventured together quite recently. He left to look for Tanelorn."

"I do not know him," said Brut of Lashmar.

"And these waters," said Elric, "do they lie far from the Young Kingdoms?"

"Very far," said the man in the shadows.

"Are you from Elwher, perhaps?" asked Elric. "Or from any other of what we in the west call the Unmapped Kingdoms?"

"Most of our lands are not on your maps," said the man in the shadows. And he laughed. Again Elric found that he was not offended. And he was not particularly troubled by the mysteries hinted at by the man in the shadows. Soldiers of fortune (as he deemed these men to be) were fond of their private jokes and references; it was usually all that united them save a common willingness to hire their swords to whomever could pay.

Outside the anchor was rattling and the ship rolled. Elric heard the yard being lowered and he heard the smack of the sail as it was unfurled. He wondered how they hoped to leave the bay with so little wind available. He noticed that the faces of the other warriors (where their faces were visible) had taken on a rather set look as the ship began to move. He looked from one grim, haunted face to another and he wondered if his own features bore the same cast.

"For where do we sail?" he asked.

Brut shrugged. "I know only that we had to stop to wait for you, Elric of Melniboné."

"You knew I would be there?"

The man in the shadows stirred and helped himself to more hot wine from the jug set into a hole in the center of the table. "You are the last one we need," he said. "I was the first taken aboard. So far I have not regretted my decision to make the voyage."

"Your name, sir?" Elric decided he would no longer be at that particular disadvantage.

"Oh, names? Names? I have so many. The one I favor is Erekosë. But I have been called Urlik Skarsol and John Daker and Ilian of Garathorm to my certain knowledge. Some would have me believe that I have been Elric Womanslayer. . . ."

"Womanslayer? An unpleasant nickname. Who is this other Elric?"

"That I cannot completely answer," said Erekosë. "But I share a name, it seems, with more than one aboard this ship. I, like Brut, sought Tanelorn and found myself here instead."

"We have that in common," said another. He was a black-skinned warrior, the tallest of the company, his features oddly enhanced by a scar running like an inverted V from his forehead and over both eyes, down his cheeks to his jawbones. "I was in a land called Ghaja-Ki, a most unpleasant, swampy place, filled with perverse and diseased life. I had heard of a city said to exist there and I thought it might be Tanelorn. It was not. And it was inhabited by a blue-skinned, hermaphroditic race who determined to cure me of what they considered my malformations of hue and sexuality. This scar you see was their work. The pain of their operation gave me strength to escape them and I ran naked into the swamps, floundering for many a mile until the swamp became a lake feeding a broad river over which hung black clouds of insects which set upon me hungrily. This ship appeared and I was more than glad to seek its sanctuary. I am Otto Blendker, once a scholar of Brunse, now a hireling sword for my sins."

"This Brunse? Does it lie near Elwher?" said Elric. He had never heard of such a place, nor such an outlandish name, in the Young Kingdoms.

The black man shook his head. "I know naught of Elwher."

"Then the world is a considerably larger place than I imagined," said Elric.

"Indeed it is," said Erekosë. "What would you say if I offered you the theory that the sea on which we sail spans more than one world?"

"I would be inclined to believe you." Elric smiled. "I have studied such theories. More, I have experienced adventures in worlds other than my own."

"It is a relief to hear it," said Erekosë. "Not all on board this ship are willing to accept my theory."

"I come closer to accepting it," said Otto Blendker, "though I find it terrifying."

"It is that," agreed Erekosë. "More terrifying than you can imagine, friend Otto."

Elric leaned across the table and helped himself to a further mug of wine. His clothes were already drying and physically he had a sense of well-being. "I'll be glad to leave this misty shore behind."

"The shore has been left already," said Brut, "but as for the mist, it is ever with us. Mist appears to follow the ship—or else the ship creates the mist wherever it travels. It is rare that we see land at all and when we do see it, as we saw it today, it is usually obscured, like a reflection in a dull and buckled shield."

"We sail on a supernatural sea," said another, holding out a gloved hand for the jug. Elric passed it to him. "In Hasghan, where I come from, we have a legend of a Bewitched Sea. If a mariner finds himself sailing in those waters he may never return and will be lost for eternity."

"Your legend contains at least some truth, I fear, Terndrik of Hasghan," Brut said.

"How many warriors are on board?" Elric asked.

"Sixteen other than the Four," said Erekosë. "Twenty in all. The crew numbers about ten and then there is the captain. You will see him soon, doubtless."

"The Four? Who are they?"

Erekosë laughed. "You and I are two of them. The other two occupy the aft cabin. And if you wish to know *why* we are called the Four, you must ask the captain, though I warn you his answers are rarely satisfying."

Elric realized that he was being pressed slightly to one side. "The ship makes good speed," he said laconically, "considering how poor the wind was."

"Excellent speed," agreed Erekosë. He rose from his corner, a broad-shouldered man with an ageless face bearing the evidence of considerable experience. He was handsome and he had plainly seen much conflict, for both his hands and his face were heavily scarred, though not disfigured. His eyes, though deep-set and dark, seemed of no particular color and yet were familiar to Elric. He felt that he might have seen those eyes in a dream once.

"Have we met before?" Elric asked him.

"Oh, possibly—or shall meet. What does it matter? Our fates are the same. We share an identical doom. And possibly we share more than that."

"More? I hardly comprehend the first part of your statement."

"Then it is for the best," said Erekosë, inching past his comrades and emerging on the other side of the table. He laid a surprisingly gentle hand on Elric's shoulder. "Come, we must seek audience with the captain. He expressed a wish to see you shortly after you came aboard."

Elric nodded and rose. "This captain—what is his name?"

"He has none he will reveal to us," said Erekosë. Together they emerged onto the deck. The mist was if anything thicker and of the same deathly whiteness, no longer tinted by the sun's rays. It was hard to see to the far ends of the ship and for all that they were evidently moving rapidly, there was no hint of a wind. Yet it was warmer than Elric might have expected. He followed Erekosë forward to the cabin set under the deck on which one of the ship's twin wheels stood, tended by a tall man in sea-coat and leggings of quilted deerskin who was so still as to resemble a statue. The red-haired steersman did not look around or down as they advanced toward the cabin, but Elric caught a glimpse of his face.

The door seemed built of some kind of smooth metal possessing a sheen almost like the healthy coat of an animal. It was reddish-brown and the most colorful thing Elric had so far seen on the ship. Erekosë knocked softly upon the door. "Captain," he said. "Elric is here."

"Enter," said a voice at once melodious and distant.

The door opened. Rosy light flooded out, half-blinding Elric as he walked in. As his eyes adapted, he could see a very tall, pale-clad man standing upon a richly hued carpet in the middle of the cabin. Elric heard the door close and realized that Erekosë had not accompanied him inside.

"Are you refreshed, Elric?" said the captain.

"I am, sir, thanks to your wine."

The captain's features were no more human than were Elric's. They were at once finer and more powerful than those of the Melnibonéan, yet bore a slight resemblance in that the eyes were inclined to taper, as did the face, toward the chin. The captain's long hair fell to his shoulders in red-gold waves and was kept back from his brow by a circlet of blue jade. His body was clad in buff-colored tunic and hose and there were sandals of silver and silver-thread laced to his calves. Apart from his clothing, he was twin to the steersman Elric had recently seen.

"Will you have more wine?"

The captain moved toward a chest on the far side of the cabin, near the porthole, which was closed.

"Thank you," said Elric. And now he realized why the eyes had not focused on him. The captain was blind. For all that his movements were deft and assured, it was obvious that he could not see at all. He poured the wine from a silver jug into a silver cup and began to cross toward Elric, holding the cup out before him. Elric stepped forward and accepted it.

"I am grateful for your decision to join us," said the captain. "I am much relieved, sir."

"You are courteous," said Elric, "though I must add that my decision was not difficult to make. I had nowhere else to go."

"I understand that. It is why we put into shore when and where we did. You will find that all your companions were in a similar position before they, too, came aboard."

"You appear to have considerable knowledge of the movements of many men," said Elric. He held the wine untasted in his left hand.

"Many," agreed the captain, "on many worlds. I understand that you are a person of culture, sir, so you will be aware of something of the nature of the sea upon which my ship sails."

"I think so."

"She sails between the worlds, for the most part—between the planes of a variety of aspects of the same world, to be a little more exact." The captain hesitated, turning his blind face away from Elric. "Please know that I do not deliberately mystify you. There are some things I do not understand and other things which I may not completely reveal. It is a trust I have and I hope you feel you can respect it."

"I have no reason as yet to do otherwise," replied the albino. And he took a sip of the wine.

"I find myself with a fine company," said the captain. "I hope that you continue to think it worthwhile honoring my trust when we reach our destination."

"And what is that, Captain?"

"An island indigenous to these waters."

"That must be a rarity."

"Indeed, it is, and once undiscovered, uninhabited by those we must count our enemies. Now that they have found it and realize its power, we are in great danger."

"We? You mean your race or those aboard your ship?"

The captain smiled. "I have no race, save myself. I speak, I suppose, of all humanity."

"These enemies are not human, then?"

"No. They are inextricably involved in human affairs, but this fact has not instilled in them any loyalty to us. I use 'humanity,' of course, in its broader sense, to include yourself and myself."

"I understood," said Elric. "What is this folk called?"

"Many things," said the captain. "Forgive me, but I cannot continue longer now. If you will ready yourself for battle I assure you that I will reveal more to you as soon as the time is right."

Only when Elric stood again outside the reddish-brown door, watching Erekosë advancing up the deck through the mist, did the albino wonder if the captain had charmed him to the point where he had forgotten all common sense. Yet the blind man had impressed him and he had, after all, nothing better to do than to sail on to the island. He shrugged. He could always alter his decision if he discovered that those upon the island were not, in his opinion, enemies.

"Are you more mystified or less, Elric?" said Erekosë, smiling.

"More mystified in some ways, less in others," Elric told him. "And, for some reason, I do not care."

"Then you share the feeling of the whole company," Erekosë told him.

It was only when Erekosë led him to the cabin aft of the mast that Elric realized he had not asked the captain what the significance of the Four might be.

3

Save that it faced in the opposite direction, the other cabin resembled the first in almost every detail. Here, too, were seated some dozen men, all experienced soldiers of fortune by their features and their clothing. Two sat together at the center of the table's starboard side. One was bareheaded, fair, and careworn, the other had features resembling Elric's own and he seemed to be wearing a silver gauntlet on his left hand while the right hand was naked; his armor was delicate and outlandish. He looked up as Elric entered and there was recognition in his single eye (the other was covered by a brocade-work patch).

"Elric of Melniboné!" he exclaimed. "My theories become more meaningful!" He turned to his companion. "See, Hawkmoon, this is the one of whom I spoke."

"You know me, sir?" Elric was nonplussed.

"You recognize me, Elric. You must! At the Tower of Voilodion Ghagnasdiak? With Erekosë—though a different Erekosë."

"I know of no such tower, no name which resembles that, and this is the first I have seen of Erekosë. You know me and you know my name, but I do not know you. I find this disconcerting, sir."

"I, too, had never met Prince Corum before he came aboard," said Erekosë, "yet he insists we fought together once. I am inclined to believe him. Time on the different planes does not always run concurrently. Prince Corum might well exist in what we would term the future."

"I had thought to find some relief from such paradoxes here," said Hawkmoon, passing his hand over his face. He smiled bleakly. "But it seems there is none at this present moment in the history of the planes. Everything is in flux and even our identities, it seems, are prone to alter at any moment."

"We were Three," said Corum. "Do you not recall it, Elric? The Three Who Are One?"

Elric shook his head.

Corum shrugged, saying softly to himself, "Well, now we are Four. Did the captain say anything of an island we are supposed to invade?"

"He did," said Elric. "Do you know who these enemies might be?"

"We know no more or less than do you, Elric," said Hawkmoon. "I seek a place called Tanelorn and two children. Perhaps I seek the Runestaff, too. Of that I am not entirely sure."

"We found it once," said Corum. "We three. In the Tower of Voilodion Ghagnasdiak. It was of considerable help to us."

"As it might be to me," Hawkmoon told him. "I served it once. I gave it a great deal."

"We have much in common," Erekosë put in, "as I told you, Elric. Perhaps we share masters in common, too?"

Elric shrugged. "I serve no master but myself."

And he wondered why they all smiled in the same strange way.

Erekosë said quietly, "On such ventures as these one is inclined to forget much, as one forgets a dream."

"This *is* a dream," said Hawkmoon. "Of late I've dreamed many such."

"It is all dreaming, if you like," said Corum. "All existence."

Elric was not interested in such philosophizing. "Dream or reality, the experience amounts to the same, does it not?"

"Quite right," said Erekosë with a wan smile.

They talked on for another hour or two until Corum stretched and yawned and commented that he was feeling sleepy. The others agreed that they were all tired and so they left the cabin and went aft and below where there were bunks for all the warriors. As he stretched himself out in one of the bunks, Elric said to Brut of Lashmar, who had climbed into the bunk above:

"It would help to know when this fight begins."

Brut looked over the edge, down at the prone albino. "I think it will be soon," he said.

Elric stood alone upon the deck, leaning upon the rail and trying to make out the sea, but the sea, like the rest of the world, was hidden by white curling mist. Elric wondered if there were waters flowing under the ship's keel at all. He looked up to where the sail was tight and swollen at the mast, filled with a warm and powerful wind. It was light, but again it was not possible to tell the hour of the day. Puzzled by Corum's comments concerning an earlier meeting, Elric wondered if there had been other dreams in his life such as this might be—dreams he had forgotten completely upon awakening. But the uselessness of such speculation became quickly evident and he turned his attention to more immediate matters, wondering at the origin of the captain and his strange ship sailing on a stranger ocean.

"The captain," said Hawkmoon's voice, and Elric turned to bid good morning to the tall, fair-haired man who bore a strange, regular scar in the center of his forehead, "has requested that we four visit him in his cabin."

The other two emerged from the mist and together they made their way to the prow, knocking on the reddish-brown door and being at once admitted into the presence of the blind captain, who had four silver wine-cups already poured for them. He gestured them toward the great chest on which the wine stood. "Please help yourselves, my friends."

They did so, standing there with the cups in their hands, four tall, doom-haunted swordsmen, each of a strikingly different cast of features, yet each bearing a certain stamp which marked them as being of a like kind. Elric noticed it, for all that he was one of them, and he tried to recall the details of what Corum had told him on the previous evening.

"We are nearing our destination," said the captain. "It will not be long before we disembark. I do not believe our enemies expect us, yet it will be a hard fight against those two."

"Two?" said Hawkmoon. "Only two?"

"Only two." The captain smiled. "A brother and a sister. Sorcerers from quite another universe than ours. Due to recent disruptions in the fabric of our worlds—of which you know something, Hawkmoon, and you, too, Corum—certain beings have been released who would not otherwise have the power they now possess. And possessing great power, they crave for more—for all the power that there is in our universe. These beings are amoral in a way in which the Lords of Law or Chaos are not. They do not fight for influence upon the Earth, as those gods do; their only wish is to convert the essential energy of our universe to their own uses. I believe they foster some ambition in their particular universe which would be furthered if they could achieve their wish. At present, in spite of conditions highly favorable to them, they have not attained their full strength, but the time is not far off before they do attain it. Agak and Gagak is how they are called in human tongue and they are outside the power of any of our gods, so a more powerful group has been summoned—yourselves. The Champion Eternal in four of his incarnations (and four is the maximum number we can risk with precipitating further unwelcome disruptions among the planes of Earth)—Erekosë, Elric, Corum, and Hawkmoon. Each of you will command four others, whose fates are linked with your own and who are great fighters in their own right, though they do not share your destinies in every sense. You may each pick the four with whom you wish to fight. I think you will find it easy enough to decide. We make landfall quite shortly now."

"You will lead us?" Hawkmoon said.

"I cannot. I can only take you to the island and wait for those who survive—if any survive."

Elric frowned. "This fight is not mine, I think."

"It is yours," said the captain soberly. "And it is mine. I would land with you if that were permitted me, but it is not."

"Why so?" asked Corum.

"You will learn that one day. I have not the courage to tell you. I bear you nothing but goodwill, however. Be assured of that."

Erekosë rubbed his jaw. "Well, since it is my destiny to fight, and since I, like Hawkmoon, continue to seek Tanelorn, and since I gather there is some chance of my fulfilling my ambition if I am successful, I for one agree to go against these two. Agak and Gagak."

Hawkmoon nodded. "I go with Erekosë, for similar reasons."

"And I," said Corum.

"Not long since," said Elric, "I counted myself without comrades. Now I have many. For that reason alone I will fight with them."

"It is perhaps the best of reasons," said Erekosë approvingly.

"There is no reward for this work, save my assurance that your success will save the world much misery," said the captain. "And for you, Elric, there is less reward than the rest may hope for."

"Perhaps not," said Elric.

"As you say." The captain gestured toward the jug of wine. "More wine, my friends?"

They each accepted, while the captain continued, his blind face staring upward at the roof of the cabin.

"Upon this island is a ruin—perhaps it was once a city called Tanelorn—and at the center of the ruin stands one whole building. It is this building which Agak and his sister use. It is that which you must attack. You will recognize it, I hope, at once."

"And we must slay this pair?" said Erekosë.

"If you can. They have servants who help them. These must be slain, also. Then the building must be fired. This is important." The captain paused. "Fired. It must be destroyed in no other way."

Elric smiled a dry smile. "There are few other ways of destroying buildings, Sir Captain."

The captain returned his smile and made a slight bow of acknowledgment. "Aye, it's so. Nonetheless, it is worth remembering what I have said."

"Do you know what these two look like, these Agak and Gagak?" Corum asked.

"No. It is possible that they resemble creatures of our own worlds; it is possible that they do not. Few have seen them. It is only recently that they have been able to materialize at all."

"And how may they best be overwhelmed?" asked Hawkmoon.

"By courage and ingenuity," said the captain.

"You are not very explicit, sir," said Elric.

"I am as explicit as I can be. Now, my friends, I suggest you rest and prepare your arms."

As they returned to their cabins, Erekosë sighed.

"We are fated," he said. "We have little free will, for all we deceive ourselves otherwise. If we perish or live through this venture, it will not count for much in the overall scheme of things."

"I think you are of a gloomy turn of mind, friend," said Hawkmoon.

The mist snaked through the branches of the mast, writhing in the rigging, flooding the deck. It swirled across the faces of the other three men as Elric looked at them.

"A realistic turn of mind," said Corum.

The mist massed more thickly upon the deck, mantling each man like a shroud. The timbers of the ship creaked and to Elric's ears took on the sound of a raven's croak. It was colder now. In silence they went to their cabins to test the hooks and buckles of their armor, to polish and to sharpen their weapons and to pretend to sleep.

"Oh, I've no liking for sorcery," said Brut of Lashmar, tugging at his golden beard, "for sorcery it was resulted in my shame." Elric had told him all that the captain had said and had asked Brut to be one of the four who fought with him when they landed.

"It is all sorcery here," Otto Blendker said. And he smiled wanly as he gave Elric his hand. "I'll fight beside you, Elric."

His sea-green armor shimmering faintly in the lantern light, another rose, his casque pushed back from his face. It was a face almost as white as Elric's, though the eyes were deep and near-black. "And I," said Hown Serpent-tamer, "though I fear I'm little use on still land."

The last to rise, at Elric's glance, was a warrior who had said little during their earlier conversations. His voice was deep and hesitant. He wore a plain iron battle-cap and the red hair beneath it was braided. At the end of each braid was a small fingerbone which rattled on the shoulders of his byrnie as he moved. This was Ashnar the Lynx, whose eyes were rarely less than fierce. "I lack the eloquence or the breeding of you other gentlemen," said Ashnar. "And I've no familiarity with sorcery or those other things of which you speak, but I'm a good soldier and my joy is in fighting. I'll take your orders, Elric, if you'll have me."

"Willingly," said Elric.

"There is no dispute, it seems," said Erekosë to the remaining four who had elected to join him. "All this is doubtless preordained. Our destinies have been linked from the first."

"Such philosophy can lead to unhealthy fatalism," said Terndrik of Hasghan. "Best believe our fates are our own, even if the evidence denies it."

"You must think as you wish," said Erekosë. "I have led many lives, though all, save one, are remembered but faintly." He shrugged. "Yet I deceive myself, I suppose, in that I work for a time when I shall find this Tanelorn and perhaps be reunited with the one I seek. That ambition is what gives me energy, Terndrik."

Elric smiled. "I fight, I think, because I relish the comradeship of battle. That, in itself, is a melancholy condition in which to find oneself, is it not?"

"Aye." Erekosë glanced at the floor. "Well, we must try to rest now."

4

The outlines of the coast were dim. They waded through white water and white mist, their swords held above their heads. Swords were their only weapons. Each of the Four possessed a blade of unusual size and design, but none bore a sword which occasionally murmured to itself as did Elric's Stormbringer. Glancing back, Elric saw the captain standing at the rail, his blind face turned toward the island, his pale lips moving as if he spoke to himself. Now the water was waist-deep and the sand beneath Elric's feet hardened and became smooth rock. He waded on, wary and ready to carry any attack to those who might be defending the island. But now the mist grew thinner, as if it could gain no hold on the land, and there were no obvious signs of defenders.

Tucked into his belt, each man had a brand, its end wrapped in oiled cloth so that it should not be wet when the time came to light it. Similarly, each was equipped with a handful of smoldering tinder in a little firebox in a pouch attached to his belt, so that the brands could be instantly ignited.

"Only fire will destroy this enemy forever," the captain had said
again as he handed them their brands and their tinderboxes.

As the mist cleared, it revealed a landscape of dense shadows. The
shadows spread over red rock and yellow vegetation and they were
shadows of all shapes and dimensions, resembling all manner of things.
They seemed cast by the huge blood-colored sun which stood at perpetual noon above the island, but what was disturbing about them was that
the shadows themselves seemed without a source, as if the objects they
represented were invisible or existed elsewhere than on the island itself.
The sky, too, seemed full of these shadows, but whereas those on the
island were still, those in the sky sometimes moved, perhaps when the
clouds moved. And all the while the red sun poured down its bloody
light and touched the twenty men with its unwelcome radiance just as it
touched the land.

And at times, as they advanced cautiously inland, a peculiar flickering light sometimes crossed the island so that the outlines of the place
became unsteady for a few seconds before returning to focus. Elric
suspected his eyes and said nothing until Hown Serpent-tamer (who
was having difficulty finding his land-legs) remarked:

"I have rarely been ashore, it's true, but I think the quality of this
land is stranger than any other I've known. It shimmers. It distorts."

Several voices agreed with him.

"And from whence come all these shadows?" Ashnar the Lynx
stared around him in unashamed superstitious awe. "Why cannot we
see that which casts them?"

"It could be," Corum said, "that these are shadows cast by objects
existing in other dimensions of the Earth. If all dimensions meet here,
as has been suggested, that could be a likely explanation." He put his
silver hand to his embroidered eye-patch. "This is not the strangest
example I have witnessed of such a conjunction."

"Likely?" Otto Blendker snorted. "Pray let none give me an *unlikely*
explanation, if you please!"

They pressed on through the shadows and the lurid light until they
arrived at the outskirts of the ruins.

These ruins, thought Elric, had something in common with the ram-
shackle city of Ameeron, which he had visited on his quest for the
Black Sword. But they were altogether more vast—more a collection of
smaller cities, each one in a radically different architectural style.

"Perhaps this is Tanelorn," said Corum, who had visited the place,
"or, rather, all the versions of Tanelorn there have ever been. For
Tanelorn exists in many forms, each form depending upon the wishes of
those who most desire to find her."

"This is not the Tanelorn I expected to find," said Hawkmoon bitterly.

"Nor I," added Erekosë bleakly.

"Perhaps it is not Tanelorn," said Elric. "Perhaps it is not."

"Or perhaps this is a graveyard," said Corum distantly, frowning with his single eye. "A graveyard containing all the forgotten versions of that strange city."

They began to clamber over the ruins, their arms clattering as they moved, heading for the center of the place. Elric could tell by the introspective expressions in the faces of many of his companions that they, like him, were wondering if this were not a dream. Why else should they find themselves in this peculiar situation, unquestioningly risking their lives—perhaps their souls—in a fight with which none of them was identified?

Erekosë moved closer to Elric as they marched. "Have you noticed," said he, "that the shadows now represent something?"

Elric nodded. "You can tell from the ruins what some of the buildings looked like when they were whole. The shadows are the shadows of those buildings—the original buildings before they became ruined."

"Just so," said Erekosë. Together, they shuddered.

At last they approached the likely center of the place and here was a building which was not ruined. It stood in a cleared space, all curves and ribbons of metal and glowing tubes.

"It resembles a machine more than a building," said Hawkmoon.

"And a musical instrument more than a machine," Corum mused.

The party came to a halt, each group of four gathering about its leader. There was no question but that they had arrived at their goal.

Now that Elric looked carefully at the building he could see that it was in fact two buildings—both absolutely identical and joined at various points by curling systems of pipes which might be connecting corridors, though it was difficult to imagine what manner of being could utilize them.

"Two buildings," said Erekosë. "We were not prepared for this. Shall we split up and attack both?"

Instinctively Elric felt that this action would be unwise. He shook his head. "I think we should go together into one, else our strength will be weakened."

"I agree," said Hawkmoon, and the rest nodded.

Thus, there being no cover to speak of, they marched boldly toward the nearest building to a point near the ground where a black opening of irregular proportions could be discerned. Ominously, there was still no sign of defenders. The buildings pulsed and glowed and occasionally whispered, but that was all.

Elric and his party were the first to enter, finding themselves in a damp, warm passage which curved almost immediately to the right. They were followed by the others until all stood in this passage warily glaring ahead, expecting to be attacked. But no attack came.

With Elric at their head, they moved on for some moments before the passage began to tremble violently and sent Hown Serpent-tamer crashing to the floor cursing. As the man in the sea-green armor scrambled up, a voice began to echo along the passage, seemingly coming from a great distance yet nonetheless loud and irritable.

"Who? Who? Who?" shrieked the voice.

"Who? Who? Who invades me?"

The passage's tremble subsided a little into a constant quivering motion. The voice became a muttering, detached and uncertain.

"What attacks? What?"

The twenty men glanced at one another in puzzlement. At length Elric shrugged and led the party on and soon the passage had widened out into a hall whose walls, roof, and floor were damp with sticky fluid and whose air was hard to breathe. And now, somehow passing themselves through the walls of this hall, came the first of the defenders, ugly beasts who must be the servants of that mysterious brother and sister Agak and Gagak.

"Attack!" cried the distant voice. *"Destroy this. Destroy it!"*

The beasts were of a primitive sort, mostly gaping mouth and slithering body, but there were many of them oozing toward the twenty men, who quickly formed themselves into the four fighting units and prepared to defend themselves. The creatures made a dreadful slushing sound as they approached and the ridges of bone which served them as teeth clashed as they reared up to snap at Elric and his companions. Elric whirled his sword and it met hardly any resistance as it sliced through several of the things at once. But now the air was thicker than ever and a stench threatened to overwhelm them as fluid drenched the floor.

"Move on through them," Elric instructed, "hacking a path through as you go. Head for yonder opening." He pointed with his left hand.

And so they advanced, cutting back hundreds of the primitive beasts and thus decreasing the breathability of the air.

"The creatures are not hard to fight," gasped Hown Serpent-tamer, "but each one we kill robs us a little of our own chances of life."

Elric was aware of the irony. "Cunningly planned by our enemies, no doubt." He coughed and slashed again at a dozen of the beasts slithering toward him. The things were fearless, but they were stupid, too. They made no attempt at strategy.

Finally Elric reached the next passage, where the air was slightly purer. He sucked gratefully at the sweeter atmosphere and waved his companions on.

Sword-arms rising and falling, they gradually retreated back into the passage, followed by only a few of the beasts. The creatures seemed reluctant to enter the passage and Elric suspected that somewhere within it there must lie a danger which even they feared. There was nothing for it, however, but to press on and he was only grateful that all twenty had survived this initial ordeal.

Gasping, they rested for a moment, leaning against the trembling walls of the passage, listening to the tones of that distant voice, now muffled and indistinct.

"I like not this castle at all," growled Brut of Lashmar, inspecting a rent in his cloak where a creature had seized it. "High sorcery commands it."

"It is only what we knew," Ashnar the Lynx reminded him, and Ashnar was plainly hard put to control his terror. The fingerbones in his braids kept time with the trembling of the walls and the huge barbarian looked almost pathetic as he steeled himself to go on.

"They are cowards, these sorcerers," Otto Blendker said. "They do not show themselves." He raised his voice. "Is their aspect so loathsome that they are afraid lest we look upon them?" It was a challenge not taken up. As they pushed on through the passages there was no sign either of Agak or his sister Gagak. It became gloomier and brighter in turns. Sometimes the passages narrowed so that it was difficult to squeeze their bodies through, sometimes they widened into what were almost halls. Most of the time they appeared to be climbing higher into the building.

Elric tried to guess the nature of the building's inhabitants. There were no steps in the castle, no artifacts he could recognize. For no particular reason he developed an image of Agak and Gagak as reptilian in form, for reptiles would prefer gently rising passages to steps and doubtless would have little need of conventional furniture. There again it was possible that they could change their shape at will, assuming human form when it suited them. He was becoming impatient to face either one or both of the sorcerers.

Ashnar the Lynx had other reasons—or so he said—for his own lack of patience.

"They said there'd be treasure here," he muttered. "I thought to stake my life against a fair reward, but there's naught here of value." He put a horny hand against the damp material of the wall. "Not even stone or brick. What are these walls made of, Elric?"

Elric shook his head. "That has puzzled me, also, Ashnar."

Then Elric saw large, fierce eyes peering out of the gloom ahead. He heard a rattling noise, a rushing noise, and the eyes grew larger and larger. He saw a red mouth, yellow fangs, orange fur. Then the growling sounded and the beast sprang at him even as he raised Stormbringer to defend himself and shouted a warning to the others. The creature was a baboon, but huge, and there were at least a dozen others following the first. Elric drove his body forward behind his sword, taking the beast in its groin. Claws reached out and dug into his shoulders and waist. He groaned as he felt at least one set of claws draw blood. His arms were trapped and he could not pull Stormbringer free. All he could do was twist the sword in the wound he had already made. With all his might, he turned the hilt. The great ape shouted, its bloodshot eyes blazing, and it bared its yellow fangs as its muzzle shot toward Elric's throat. The teeth closed on his neck, the stinking breath threatened to choke him. Again he twisted the blade. Again the beast yelled in pain.

The fangs were pressing into the metal of Elric's gorget, the only thing saving him from immediate death. He struggled to free at least one arm, twisting the sword for the third time, then tugging it sideways to widen the wound in the groin. The growls and groans of the baboon grew more intense and the teeth tightened their hold on his neck, but now, mingled with the noises of the ape, he began to hear a murmuring and he felt Stormbringer pulse in his hand. He knew that the sword was drawing power from the ape even as the ape sought to destroy him. Some of that power began to flow into his body.

Desperately Elric put all his remaining strength into dragging the sword across the ape's body, slitting its belly wide so that its blood and entrails spilled over him as he was suddenly free and staggering backward, wrenching the sword out in the same movement. The ape, too, was staggering back, staring down in stupefied awe at its own horrible wound before it fell to the floor of the passage.

Elric turned, ready to give aid to his nearest comrade, and he was in time to see Terndrik of Hasghan die, kicking in the clutches of an even larger ape, his head bitten clean from his shoulders and his red blood gouting.

Elric drove Stormbringer cleanly between the shoulders of Terndrik's slayer, taking the ape in the heart. Beast and human victim fell together. Two others were dead and several bore bad wounds, but the remaining warriors fought on, swords and armor smeared with crimson. The narrow passage stank of ape, of sweat, and of blood. Elric pressed into the fight, chopping at the skull of an ape which grappled with Hown Serpent-tamer, who had lost his sword. Hown darted a look of thanks at Elric as he bent to retrieve his blade and together they set upon the largest of all the baboons. This creature stood much taller than Elric and had Erekosë pressed against the wall, Erekosë's sword through its shoulder.

From two sides, Hown and Elric stabbed and the baboon snarled and screamed, turning to face the new attackers, Erekosë's blade quivering in its shoulder. It rushed upon them and they stabbed again together, taking the monster in its heart and its lung so that when it roared at them blood vomited from its mouth. It fell to its knees, its eyes dimming, then sank slowly down.

And now there was silence in the passage and death lay all about them.

Terndrik of Hasghan was dead. Two of Corum's party were dead. All of Erekosë's surviving men bore major wounds. One of Hawkmoon's men was dead, but the remaining three were virtually unscathed. Brut of Lashmar's helm was dented, but he was otherwise unwounded and Ashnar the Lynx was disheveled, nothing more. Ashnar had taken two of the baboons during the fight. But now the barbarian's eyes rolled as he leaned, panting, against the wall.

"I begin to suspect this venture of being uneconomical," he said with a half-grin. He rallied himself, stepping over a baboon's corpse to join Elric. "The less time we take over it, the better. What think you, Elric?"

"I would agree." Elric returned his grin. "Come." And he led the way through the passage and into a chamber whose walls gave off a pinkish light. He had not walked far before he felt something catch at his ankle and he stared down in horror to see a long, thin snake winding itself about his leg. It was too late to use his sword; instead he seized the reptile behind its head and dragged it partially free of his leg before hacking the head from the body. The others were now stamping and shouting warnings to each other. The snakes did not appear to be venomous, but there were thousands of them, appearing, it seemed, from out of the floor itself. They were flesh-colored and had no eyes, more closely resembling earthworms than ordinary reptiles, but they were strong enough.

Hown Serpent-tamer sang a strange song now, with many liquid, hissing notes, and this seemed to have a calming effect upon the creatures. One by one at first and then in increasing numbers, they dropped back to the floor, apparently sleeping. Hown grinned at his success.

Elric said, "Now I understand how you came by your surname."

"I was not sure the song would work on these," Hown told him, "for they are unlike any serpents I have ever seen in the seas of my own world."

They waded on through mounds of sleeping serpents, noticing that the next passage rose sharply. At times they were forced to use their hands to steady themselves as they climbed the peculiar, slippery material of the floor.

It was much hotter in this passage and they were all sweating, pausing several times to rest and mop their brows. The passage seemed to extend upward forever, turning occasionally, but never leveling out for more than a few feet. At times it narrowed to little more than a tube through which they had to squirm on their stomachs and at other times the roof disappeared into the gloom over their heads. Elric had long since given up trying to relate their position to what he had seen of the outside of the castle. From time to time small, shapeless creatures rushed toward them in shoals apparently with the intention of attacking them, but these were rarely more than an irritation and were soon all but ignored by the party as it continued its climb.

For a while they had not heard the strange voice which had greeted them upon their entering, but now it began to whisper again, its tones more urgent than before.

"Where? Where? Oh, the pain!"

They paused, trying to locate the source of the voice, but it seemed to come from everywhere at once.

Grim-faced, they continued, plagued by thousands of little creatures which bit at their exposed flesh like so many gnats, yet the creatures were not insects. Elric had seen nothing like them before. They were shapeless, primitive, and all but colorless. They battered at his face as he moved; they were like a wind. Half-blinded, choked, sweating, he felt his strength leaving him. The air was so thick now, so hot, so salty, it was as if he moved through liquid. The others were as badly affected as was he; some were staggering and two men fell, to be helped up again by comrades almost as exhausted. Elric was tempted to strip off his armor, but he knew this would leave more of his flesh to the mercy of the little flying creatures.

Still they climbed and now more of the serpentine things they had seen earlier began to writhe around their feet, hampering them further, for all that Hown sang his sleeping song until he was hoarse.

"We can survive this only a little longer," said Ashnar the Lynx, moving close to Elric. "We shall be in no condition to meet the sorcerer if we ever find him or his sister."

Elric nodded a gloomy head. "My thoughts, too, yet what else may we do, Ashnar?"

"Nothing," said Ashnar in a low voice. "Nothing."

"Where? Where? Where?" The word rustled all about them. Many of the party were becoming openly nervous.

5

They had reached the top of the passage. The querulous voice was much louder now, but it quavered more. They saw an archway and beyond the archway a lighted chamber.

"Agak's room, without doubt," said Ashnar, taking a better grip on his sword.

"Possibly," said Elric. He felt detached from his body. Perhaps it was the heat and the exhaustion, or his growing sense of disquiet, but something made him withdraw into himself and hesitate before entering the chamber.

The place was octagonal and each of its eight sloping sides was of a different color and each color changed constantly. Occasionally the walls became semitransparent, revealing a complete view of the ruined city (or collection of cities) far below, and also a view of the twin castle to this one, still connected by tubes and wires.

It was the large pool in the center of the chamber which attracted their attention mostly. It seemed deep and was full of evil-smelling, viscous stuff. It bubbled. Shapes formed in it. Grotesque and strange, beautiful and familiar, the shapes seemed always upon the brink of taking permanent form before falling back into the stuff of the pool. And the voice was still louder and there was no question now that it came from the pool.

"What? What? Who invades?"

Elric forced himself closer to the pool and for a moment saw his own face staring out at him before it melted.

"Who invades? Ah! I am too weak!"

Elric spoke to the pool. "We are of those you would destroy," he said. "We are those on whom you would feed."

"Ah! Agak! Agak! I am sick! Where are you?"

Ashnar and Brut joined Elric. The faces of the warriors were filled with disgust.

"Agak," growled Ashnar the Lynx, his eyes narrowing. "At last some sign that the sorcerer is here!"

The others had all crowded in, to stand as far away from the pool as possible, but all stared, fascinated by the variety of the shapes forming and disintegrating in the viscous liquid.

"*I weaken. . . . My energy needs to be replenished. . . . We must begin now, Agak. . . . It took us so long to reach this place. I thought I could rest. But there is disease here. It fills my body. Agak. Awaken, Agak. Awaken!*"

"Some servant of Agak's, charged with the defense of the chamber?" suggested Hown Serpent-tamer in a small voice.

But Elric continued to stare into the pool as he began, he thought, to realize the truth.

"Will Agak wake?" Brut said. "Will he come?" He glanced nervously around him.

"Agak!" called Ashnar the Lynx. "Coward!"

"Agak!" cried many of the other warriors, brandishing their swords.

But Elric said nothing and he noted, too, that Hawkmoon and Corum and Erekosë all remained silent. He guessed that they must be filled with the same dawning understanding.

He looked at them. In Erekosë's eyes he saw an agony, a pity both for himself and his comrades.

"We are the Four Who Are One," said Erekosë. His voice shook.

Elric was seized by an alien impulse, an impulse which disgusted and terrified him. "No. . . ." He attempted to sheathe Stormbringer, but the sword refused to enter its scabbard.

"*Agak! Quickly!*" said the voice from the pool.

"If we do not do this thing," said Erekosë, "they will eat all our worlds. Nothing will remain."

Elric put his free hand to his head. He swayed upon the edge of that frightful pool. He moaned.

"We must do it, then." Corum's voice was an echo.

"I will not," said Elric. "I am myself."

"And I!" said Hawkmoon.

But Corum Jhaelen Irsei said, "It is the only way for us, for the single thing that we are. Do you not see that? We are the only creatures of our worlds who possess the means of slaying the sorcerers—in the only manner in which they can be slain!"

Elric looked at Corum, at Hawkmoon, at Erekosë, and again he saw something of himself in all of them.

"We are the Four Who Are One," said Erekosë. "Our united strength is greater than the sum. We must come together, brothers. We must conquer here before we can hope to conquer Agak."

"No. . . ." Elric moved away, but somehow he found himself standing at a corner of the bubbling, noxious pool from which the voice still murmured and complained, in which shapes still formed, reformed, and faded. And at each of the other three corners stood one of his companions. All had a set, fatalistic look to them.

The warriors who had accompanied the Four drew back to the walls. Otto Blendker and Brut of Lashmar stood near the doorway, listening for anything which might come up the passage to the chamber. Ashnar the Lynx fingered the brand at his belt, a look of pure horror on his rugged features.

Elric felt his arm begin to rise, drawn upward by his sword, and he saw that each of his three companions were also lifting their swords. The swords reached out across the pool and their tips met above the exact center.

Elric yelled as something entered his being. Again he tried to break free, but the power was too strong. Other voices spoke in his head.

"I understand. . . ." This was Corum's distant murmur. *"It is the only way."*

"Oh, no, no. . . ." And this was Hawkmoon, but the words came from Elric's lips.

"Agak!" cried the pool. The stuff became more agitated, more alarmed. *"Agak! Quickly! Wake!"*

Elric's body began to shake, but his hand kept a firm hold upon the sword. The atoms of his body flew apart and then united again into a single flowing entity which traveled up the blade of the sword toward the apex. And Elric was still Elric, shouting with the terror of it, sighing with the ecstasy of it.

Elric was still Elric when he drew away from the pool and looked upon himself for a single moment, seeing himself wholly joined with his three other selves.

A being hovered over the pool. On each side of its head was a face and each face belonged to one of the companions. Serene and terrible, the eyes did not blink. It had eight arms and the arms were still; it squatted over the pool on eight legs, and its armor and accouterments were of all colors blending and at the same time separate.

The being clutched a single great sword in all eight hands and both he and the sword glowed with a ghastly golden light.

Then Elric had rejoined this body and had become a different thing— himself and three others and something else which was the sum of that union.

The Four Who Were One reversed its monstrous sword so that the point was directed downward at the frenetically boiling stuff in the pool below. The stuff feared the sword. It mewled.

"*Agak, Agak. . . .*"

The being of whom Elric was a part gathered its great strength and began to plunge the sword down.

Shapeless waves appeared on the surface of the pool. Its whole color changed from sickly yellow to an unhealthy green. "*Agak, I die. . . .*"

Inexorably the sword moved down. It touched the surface.

The pool swept back and forth; it tried to ooze over the sides and onto the floor. The sword bit deeper and the Four Who Were One felt new strength flow up the blade. There came a moan; slowly the pool quieted. It became silent. It became still. It became gray.

Then the Four Who Were One descended into the pool to be absorbed.

It could see clearly now. It tested its body. It controlled every limb, every function. It had triumphed; it had revitalized the pool. Through its single octagonal eye it looked in all directions at the same time over the wide ruins of the city; then it focused all its attention upon its twin.

Agak had awakened too late, but he was awakening at last, roused by the dying cries of his sister Gagak, whose body the mortals had first invaded and whose intelligence they had overwhelmed, whose eye they now used and whose powers they would soon attempt to utilize.

Agak did not need to turn his head to look upon the being he still saw as his sister. Like hers, his intelligence was contained within the huge eight-sided eye.

"*Did you call me, sister?*"

"*I spoke your name, that is all, brother.*" There were enough vestiges of Gagak's life-force in the Four Who Were One for it to imitate her manner of speaking.

"*You cried out?*"

"*A dream.*" The Four paused and then it spoke again: "*A disease. I dreamed that there was something upon this island which made me unwell.*"

"*Is that possible? We do not know sufficient about these dimensions or the creatures inhabiting them. Yet none is as powerful as Agak and Gagak. Fear not, sister. We must begin our work soon.*"

"*It is nothing. Now I am awake.*"

Agak was puzzled. "*You speak oddly.*"

"*The dream . . .*" answered the creature which had entered Gagak's body and destroyed her.

"*We must begin,*" said Agak. "*The dimensions turn and the time has come. Ah, feel it. It waits for us to take it. So much rich energy. How we shall conquer when we go home!*"

"I feel it," replied the Four, and it did. It felt its whole universe, dimension upon dimension, swirling all about it. Stars and planets and moons through plane upon plane, all full of the energy upon which Agak and Gagak had desired to feed. And there was enough of Gagak still within the Four to make the Four experience a deep, anticipatory hunger which, now that the dimensions attained the right conjunction, would soon be satisfied.

The Four was tempted to join with Agak and feast, though it knew if it did so it would rob its own universe of every shred of energy. Stars would fade, worlds would die. Even the Lords of Law and Chaos would perish, for they were part of the same universe. Yet to possess such power it might be worth committing such a tremendous crime. . . . It controlled this desire and gathered itself for its attack before Agak became too wary.

"Shall we feast, sister?"

The Four realized that the ship had brought it to the island at exactly the proper moment. Indeed, they had almost come too late.

"Sister?" Agak was again puzzled. *"What . . . ?"*

The Four knew it must disconnect from Agak. The tubes and wires fell away from his body and were withdrawn into Gagak's.

"What's this?" Agak's strange body trembled for a moment. *"Sister?"*

The Four prepared itself. For all that it had absorbed Gagak's memories and instincts, it was still not confident that it would be able to attack Agak in her chosen form. And since the sorceress had possessed the power to change her form, the Four began to change, groaning greatly, experiencing dreadful pain, drawing all the materials of its stolen being together so that what had appeared to be a building now became pulpy, unformed flesh. And Agak, stunned, looked on.

"Sister? Your sanity . . ."

The building, the creature that was Gagak, threshed, melted, and erupted. It screamed in agony.

It attained its form.

It laughed.

Four faces laughed upon a gigantic head. Eight arms waved in triumph, eight legs began to move. And over that head it waved a single, massive sword.

And it was running.

It ran upon Agak while the alien sorcerer was still in his static form. Its sword was whirling and shards of ghastly golden light fell away from it as it moved, lashing the shadowed landscape. The Four was as large as Agak. And at this moment it was as strong.

But Agak, realizing his danger, began to suck. No longer would this be a pleasurable ritual shared with his sister. He must suck at the energy of this universe if he were to find the strength to defend himself, to gain what he needed to destroy his attacker, the slayer of his sister. Worlds died as Agak sucked.

But not enough. Agak tried cunning.

"This is the center of your universe. All its dimensions intersect here. Come, you can share the power. My sister is dead. I accept her death. You shall be my partner now. With this power we shall conquer a universe far richer than this!"

"No!" said the Four, still advancing.

"Very well, but be assured of your defeat."

The Four swung its sword. The sword fell upon the faceted eye within which Agak's intelligence-pool bubbled, just as his sister's had once bubbled. But Agak was stronger already and healed himself at once.

Agak's tendrils emerged and lashed at the Four and the Four cut at the tendrils as it sought his body. And Agak sucked more energy to himself. His body, which the mortals had mistaken for a building, began to glow burning scarlet and to radiate an impossible heat.

The sword roared and flared so that black light mingled with the gold and flowed against the scarlet. And all the while the Four could sense its own universe shrinking and dying.

"Give back, Agak, what you have stolen!" said the Four.

Planes and angles and curves, wires and tubes, flickered with deep red heat and Agak sighed. The universe whimpered.

"I am stronger than you," said Agak. *"Now."*

And Agak sucked again.

The Four knew that Agak's attention was diverted for just that short while as he fed. And the Four knew that it, too, must draw energy from its own universe if Agak were to be defeated. So the sword was raised.

The sword was flung back, its blade slicing through tens of thousands of dimensions and drawing their power to it. Then it began to swing back. It swung and black light bellowed from its blade. It swung and Agak became aware of it. His body began to alter. Down toward the sorcerer's great eye, down toward Agak's intelligence-pool swept the black blade.

Agak's many tendrils rose to defend the sorcerer against the sword, but the sword cut through them as if they were not there and it struck the eight-sided chamber which was Agak's eye and it plunged on down into Agak's intelligence-pool, deep into the stuff of the sorcerer's sensibility, drawing up Agak's energy into itself and thence into its master, the Four Who Were One. And something screamed through the universe and something sent a tremor through the universe. And the universe was dead, even as Agak began to die.

The Four did not dare wait to see if Agak were completely vanquished. It swept the sword out, back through the dimensions, and everywhere the blade touched the energy was restored. The sword rang round and round, round and round, dispersing the energy. And the sword sang its triumph and its glee.

And little shreds of black and golden light whispered away and were reabsorbed.

For a moment the universe had been dead. Now it lived and Agak's energy had been added to it.

Agak lived, too, but he was frozen. He had attempted to change his shape. Now he still half-resembled the building Elric had seen when he first came to the island, but part of him resembled the Four Who Were One—here was part of Corum's face, here a leg, there a fragment of sword-blade—as if Agak had believed, at the end, that the Four could only be defeated if its own form were assumed, just as the Four had assumed Gagak's form.

"We had waited so long. . . ." Agak sighed and then he was dead.

And the Four sheathed its sword.

Then there came a howling through the ruins of the many cities and a strong wind blustered against the body of the Four so that it was forced to kneel on its eight legs and bow its four-faced head before the gale. Then, gradually, it reassumed the shape of Gagak, the sorceress, and then it lay within Gagak's stagnating intelligence-pool and then it rose over it, hovered for a moment, withdrew its sword from the pool. Then four beings fled apart and Elric and Hawkmoon and Erekosë and Corum stood with sword-blades touching over the center of the dead brain.

The four men sheathed their swords. They stared for a second into each other's eyes and all saw terror and awe there. Elric turned away.

He could find neither thoughts nor emotions in him which would relate to what had happened. There were no words he could use. He stood looking dumbly at Ashnar the Lynx and he wondered why Ashnar giggled and chewed at his beard and scraped at the flesh of his own face with his fingernails, his sword forgotten upon the floor of the gray chamber.

"Now I have flesh again. Now I have flesh," Ashnar kept saying.

Elric wondered why Hown Serpent-tamer lay curled in a ball at Ashnar's feet, and why when Brut of Lashmar emerged from the passage he fell down and lay stretched upon the floor, stirring a little and moaning as if in disturbed slumber. Otto Blendker came into the chamber. His sword was in its scabbard. His eyes were tight shut and he hugged at himself, shivering.

Elric thought to himself: *I must forget all this or sanity will disappear forever.*

He went to Brut and helped the blond warrior to his feet. "What did you see?"

"More than I deserved, for all my sins. We were trapped—trapped in that skull. . . ." Then Brut began to weep as a small child might weep and Elric took the tall warrior in his own arms and stroked his head and could not find words or sounds with which to comfort him.

"We must go," said Erekosë. His eyes were glazed. He staggered as he walked.

Thus, dragging those who had fainted, leading those who had gone mad, leaving those who had died behind, they fled through the dead passages of Gagak's body, no longer plagued by the things she had created in her attempt to rid that body of those she had experienced as an invading disease. The passages and chambers were cold and brittle and the men were glad when they stood outside and saw the ruins, the sourceless shadows, the red, static sun.

Otto Blendker was the only one of the warriors who seemed to retain his sanity through the ordeal, when they had been absorbed, unknowingly, into the body of the Four Who Were One. He dragged his brand from his belt and he took out his tinder and ignited it. Soon the brand was flaming and the others lighted theirs from his. Elric trudged to where Agak's remains still lay and he shuddered as he recognized in a monstrous stone face part of his own features. He felt that the stuff could not possibly burn, but it did. Behind him Gagak's body blazed, too. They were swiftly consumed and pillars of growling fire jutted into the sky, sending up a smoke of white and crimson which for a little while obscured the red disk of the sun.

The men watched the corpses burn.

"I wonder," said Corum, "if the captain knew why he sent us here?"

"Or if he suspected what would happen?" said Hawkmoon. Hawkmoon's tone was near to resentful.

"Only we—only that being—could battle Agak and Gagak in anything resembling their own terms," said Erekosë. "Other means would not have been successful, no other creature could have the particular qualities, the enormous power needed to slay such strange sorcerers."

"So it seems," said Elric, and he would talk no more of it.

"Hopefully," said Corum, "you will forget this experience as you forgot—or will forget—the other."

Elric offered him a hard stare. "Hopefully, brother," he said.

Erekosë's chuckle was ironic. "Who could recall that?" And he, too, said no more.

Ashnar the Lynx, who had ceased his gigglings as he watched the fire, shrieked suddenly and broke away from the main party. He ran toward the flickering column and then veered away, disappearing among the ruins and the shadows.

Otto Blendker gave Elric a questioning stare, but Elric shook his head. "Why follow him? What can we do for him?" He looked down at Hown Serpent-tamer. He had particularly liked the man in the sea-green armor. He shrugged.

When they moved on, they left the curled body of Hown Serpent-tamer where it lay, helping only Brut of Lashmar across the rubble and down to the shore.

Soon they saw the white mist ahead and knew they neared the sea, though the ship was not in sight.

At the edge of the mist both Hawkmoon and Erekosë paused.

"I will not rejoin the ship," said Hawkmoon. "I feel I've served my passage now. If I can find Tanelorn, this, I suspect, is where I must look."

"My own feelings." Erekosë nodded his head.

Elric looked to Corum. Corum smiled. "I have already found Tanelorn. I go back to the ship in the hope that soon it will deposit me upon a more familiar shore."

"That is my hope," said Elric. His arm still supported Brut of Lashmar.

Brut whispered, "What was it? What happened to us?"

Elric increased his grip upon the warrior's shoulder. "Nothing," he said.

Then, as Elric tried to lead Brut into the mist, the blond warrior stepped back, breaking free. "I will stay," he said. He moved away from Elric. "I am sorry."

Elric was puzzled. "Brut?"

"I am sorry," Brut said again. "I fear you. I fear that ship."

Elric made to follow the warrior, but Corum put a hard silver hand upon his shoulder. "Comrade, let us be gone from this place." His smile was bleak. "It is what is back there that I fear more than the ship."

They stared over the ruins. In the distance they could see the remains of the fire and there were two shadows there now, the shadows of Gagak and Agak as they had first appeared to them.

Elric drew a cold breath of air. "With that I agree," he told Corum.

Otto Blendker was the only warrior who chose to return to the ship with them. "If that is Tanelorn, it is not, after all, the place I sought," he said.

Soon they were waist-deep in the water. They saw again the outlines of the dark ship; they saw the captain leaning on the rail, his arm raised as if in salute to someone or something upon the island.

"Captain," called Corum, "we come aboard."

"You are welcome," said the captain. "Yes, you are welcome." The blind face turned toward them as Elric reached out for the rope ladder. "Would you care to sail for a while into the silent places, the restful places?"

"I think so," said Elric. He paused, halfway up the ladder, and he touched his head. "I have many wounds."

He reached the rail and with his own cool hands the captain helped him over. "They will heal, Elric."

Elric moved closer to the mast. He leaned against it and watched the silent crew as they unfurled the sail. Corum and Otto Blendker came aboard. Elric listened to the sharp sound of the anchor as it was drawn up. The ship swayed a little.

Otto Blendker looked at Elric, then at the captain, then he turned and went into his cabin, saying nothing at all as he closed the door.

The sail filled, the ship began to move. The captain reached out and found Elric's arm. He took Corum's arm, too, and led them toward his cabin. "The wine," he said. "It will heal all the wounds."

At the door of the captain's cabin Elric paused. "And does the wine have other properties?" he asked. "Does it cloud a man's reason? Was it that which made me accept your commission, Captain?"

The captain shrugged. "What is reason?"

The ship was gathering speed. The white mist was thicker and a cold wind blew at the rags of cloth and metal Elric wore. He sniffed, thinking for a moment that he smelled smoke upon that wind.

He put his two hands to his face and touched his flesh. His face was cold. He let his hands fall to his sides and he followed the captain into the warmth of the cabin.

The captain poured wine into silver cups from his silver jug. He stretched out a hand to offer a cup to Elric and to Corum. They drank.

A little later the captain said, "How do you feel?"

Elric said, "I feel nothing."

And that night he dreamed only of shadows and in the morning he could not understand his dream at all.

BOOK TWO

SAILING TO
THE PRESENT

1

His bone-white, long-fingered hand upon a carved demon's head in black-brown hardwood (one of the few such decorations to be found anywhere about the vessel), the tall man stood alone in the ship's fo'c'sle and stared through large, slanting crimson eyes at the mist into which they moved with a speed and sureness to make any mortal mariner marvel and become incredulous.

There were sounds in the distance, incongruent with the sounds of even this nameless, timeless sea: thin sounds, agonized and terrible, for all that they remained remote—yet the ship followed them, as if drawn by them; they grew louder—pain and despair were there, but terror was predominant.

Elric had heard such sounds echoing from his cousin Yyrkoon's sardonically named "Pleasure Chambers" in the days before he had fled the responsibilities of ruling all that remained of the old Melnibonéan Empire. These were the voices of men whose very souls were under siege; men to whom death meant not mere extinction, but a continuation of existence, forever in thrall to some cruel and supernatural master. He had heard men cry so when his salvation and his nemesis, his great black battle-blade Stormbringer, drank their souls.

He did not savor the sound: he hated it, turned his back away from the source and was about to descend the ladder to the main deck when he realized that Otto Blendker had come up behind him. Now that Corum had been borne off by friends with chariots which could ride upon the surface of the water, Blendker was the last of those comrades to have fought at Elric's side against the two alien sorcerers Gagak and Agak.

Blendker's black, scarred face was troubled. The ex-scholar, turned hireling sword, covered his ears with his huge palms.

"Ach! By the Twelve Symbols of Reason, Elric, who makes that din? It's as though we sail close to the shores of Hell itself!"

Prince Elric of Melniboné shrugged. "I'd be prepared to forego an answer and leave my curiosity unsatisfied, Master Blendker, if only our ship would change course. As it is, we sail closer and closer to the source."

Blendker grunted his agreement. "I've no wish to encounter whatever it is that causes those poor fellows to scream so! Perhaps we should inform the captain."

"You think he does not know where his own ship sails?" Elric's smile had little humor.

The tall black man rubbed at the inverted V-shaped scar which ran from his forehead to his jawbones. "I wonder if he plans to put us into battle again."

"I'll not fight another for him." Elric's hand moved from the carved rail to the pommel of his runesword. "I have business of my own to attend to, once I'm back on real land."

A wind came from nowhere. There was a sudden rent in the mist. Now Elric could see that the ship sailed through rust-colored water. Peculiar lights gleamed in that water, just below the surface. There was an impression of creatures moving ponderously in the depths of the ocean and, for a moment, Elric thought he glimpsed a white, bloated face not dissimilar to his own—a Melnibonéan face. Impulsively he whirled, back to the rail, looking past Blendker as he strove to control the nausea in his throat.

For the first time since he had come aboard the Dark Ship he was able clearly to see the length of the vessel. Here were the two great wheels, one beside him on the foredeck, one at the far end of the ship on the reardeck, tended now as always by the steersman, the captain's sighted twin. There was the great mast bearing the taut black sail, and fore and aft of this, the two deck cabins, one of which was entirely empty (its occupants having been killed during their last landfall) and one of which was occupied only by himself and Blendker. Elric's gaze was drawn back to the steersman and not for the first time the albino wondered how much influence the captain's twin had over the course of the Dark Ship. The man seemed tireless, rarely, to Elric's knowledge, going below to his quarters, which occupied the stern deck as the captain's occupied the foredeck. Once or twice Elric or Blendker had tried to involve the steersman in conversation, but he appeared to be as dumb as his brother was blind.

The cryptographic, geometrical carvings covering all the ship's wood and most of its metal, from sternpost to figurehead, were picked out by the shreds of pale mist still clinging to them (and again Elric wondered if the ship actually generated the mist normally surrounding it) and, as he watched, the designs slowly turned to pale pink fire as the light from that red star, which forever followed them, permeated the overhead cloud.

A noise from below. The captain, his long red-gold hair drifting in a breeze which Elric could not feel, emerged from his cabin. The captain's circlet of blue jade, worn like a diadem, had turned to something of a violet shade in the pink light, and even his buff-colored hose and tunic reflected the hue—even the silver sandals with their silver lacing glittered with the rosy tint.

Again Elric looked upon that mysterious blind face, as unhuman, in the accepted sense, as his own, and puzzled upon the origin of the one who would allow himself to be called nothing but "Captain."

As if at the captain's summons, the mist drew itself about the ship again, as a woman might draw a froth of furs about her body. The red star's light faded, but the distant screams continued.

Did the captain notice the screams now for the first time, or was this a pantomime of surprise? His blind head tilted, a hand went to his ear. He murmured in a tone of satisfaction, "Aha!" The head lifted. "Elric?"

"Here," said the albino. "Above you."

"We are almost there, Elric."

The apparently fragile hand found the rail of the companionway. The captain began to climb.

Elric faced him at the top of the ladder. "If it's a battle . . ."

The captain's smile was enigmatic, bitter. "It was a fight—or shall be one."

". . . we'll have no part of it," concluded the albino firmly.

"It is not one of the battles in which my ship is directly involved," the blind man reassured him. "Those whom you can hear are the vanquished—lost in some future which, I think, you will experience close to the end of your present incarnation."

Elric waved a dismissive hand. "I'll be glad, Captain, if you would cease such vapid mystification. I'm weary of it."

"I'm sorry it offends you. I answer literally, according to my instincts."

The captain, going past Elric and Otto Blendker so that he could stand at the rail, seemed to be apologizing. He said nothing for a while, but listened to the disturbing and confused babble from the mist. Then he nodded, apparently satisfied.

"We'll sight land shortly. If you would disembark and seek your own world, I should advise you to do so now. This is the closest we shall ever come again to your plane."

Elric let his anger show. He cursed, invoking Arioch's name, and put a hand upon the blind man's shoulder. "What? You cannot return me directly to my own plane?"

"It is too late." The captain's dismay was apparently genuine. "The ship sails on. We near the end of our long voyage."

"But how shall I find my world? I have no sorcery great enough to move me between the spheres! And demonic assistance is denied me here."

"There is one gateway to your world," the captain told him. "That is why I suggest you disembark. Elsewhere there are none at all. Your sphere and this one intersect directly."

"But you say this lies in my future."

"Be sure—you will return to your own time. Here you are timeless. It is why your memory is so poor. It is why you remember so little of what befalls you. Seek for the gateway—it is crimson and it emerges from the sea off the coast of the island."

"Which island?"

"The one we approach."

Elric hesitated. "And where shall you go, when I have landed?"

"To Tanelorn," said the captain. "There is something I must do there. My brother and I must complete our destiny. We carry cargo as well as men. Many will try to stop us now, for they fear our cargo. We might perish, but yet we must do all we can to reach Tanelorn."

"Was that not, then, Tanelorn, where we fought Agak and Gagak?"

"That was nothing more than a broken dream of Tanelorn, Elric."

The Melnibonéan knew that he would receive no more information from the captain.

"You offer me a poor choice—to sail with you into danger and never see my own world again, or to risk landing on yonder island inhabited, by the sound of it, by the damned and those which prey upon the damned!"

The captain's blind eyes moved in Elric's direction. "I know," he said softly. "But it is the best I can offer you, nonetheless."

The screams, the imploring, terrified shouts, were closer now, but there were fewer of them. Glancing over the side, Elric thought he saw a pair of armored hands rising from the water; there was foam, red-flecked and noxious, and there was yellowish scum in which pieces of frightful flotsam drifted; there were broken timbers, scraps of canvas, tatters of flags and clothing, fragments of weapons, and, increasingly, there were floating corpses.

"But where was the battle?" Blendker whispered, fascinated and horrified by the sight.

"Not on this plane," the captain told him. "You see only the wreckage which has drifted over from one world to another."

"Then it was a supernatural battle?"

The captain smiled again. "I am not omniscient. But, yes, I believe there were supernatural agencies involved. The warriors of half a world fought in the sea-battle—to decide the fate of the multiverse. It is—or will be—one of the decisive battles to determine the fate of Mankind, to fix Man's destiny for the coming Cycle."

"Who were the participants?" asked Elric, voicing the question in spite of his resolve. "What were the issues as they understood them?"

"You will know in time, I think." The captain's head faced the sea again.

Blendker sniffed the air. "Ach! It's foul!"

Elric, too, found the odor increasingly unpleasant. Here and there now the water was lighted by guttering fires which revealed the faces of the drowning, some of whom still managed to cling to pieces of blackened driftwood. Not all the faces were human (though they had the appearance of having, once, been human): Things with the snouts of pigs and of bulls raised twisted hands to the Dark Ship and grunted plaintively for succor, but the captain ignored them and the steersman held his course.

Fires spluttered and water hissed; smoke mingled with the mist. Elric had his sleeve over his mouth and nose and was glad that the smoke and mist between them helped obscure the sights, for as the wreckage grew thicker not a few of the corpses he saw reminded him more of reptiles than of men, their pale, lizard bellies spilling something other than blood.

"If that is my future," Elric told the captain, "I've a mind to remain on board, after all."

"You have a duty, as have I," said the captain quietly. "The future must be served, as much as the past and the present."

Elric shook his head. "I fled the duties of an empire because I sought freedom," the albino told him. "And freedom I must have."

"No," murmured the captain. "There is no such thing. Not yet. Not for us. We must go through much more before we can even begin to guess what freedom is. The price for the knowledge alone is probably higher than any you would care to pay at this stage of your life. Indeed, life itself is often the price."

"I also sought release from metaphysics when I left Melniboné," said Elric. "I'll get the rest of my gear and take the land that's offered. With luck this Crimson Gate will be quickly found and I'll be back among dangers and torments which will, at least, be familiar."

"It is the only decision you could have made." The captain's blind head turned toward Blendker. "And you, Otto Blendker? What shall you do?"

"Elric's world is not mine and I like not the sound of those screams. What can you promise me, sir, if I sail on with you?"

"Nothing but a good death." There was regret in the captain's voice.

"Death is the promise we're all born with, sir. A good death is better than a poor one. I'll sail on with you."

"As you like. I think you're wise." The captain sighed. "I'll say farewell to you, then, Elric of Melniboné. You fought well in my service and I thank you."

"Fought for what?" Elric asked.

"Oh, call it Mankind. Call it Fate. Call it a dream or an ideal, if you wish."

"Shall I never have a clearer answer?"

"Not from me. I do not think there is one."

"You allow a man little faith." Elric began to descend the companionway.

"There are two kinds of faith, Elric. Like freedom, there is a kind which is easily kept but proves not worth the keeping, and there is a kind which is hard-won. I agree, I offer little of the former."

Elric strode toward his cabin. He laughed, feeling genuine affection for the blind man at that moment. "I thought I had a penchant for such ambiguities, but I have met my match in you, Captain."

He noticed that the steersman had left his place at the wheel and was swinging out a boat on its davits, preparatory to lowering it.

"Is that for me?"

The steersman nodded.

Elric ducked into his cabin. He was leaving the ship with nothing but that which he had brought aboard, only his clothing and his armor were in a poorer state of repair than they had been, and his mind was in a considerably greater state of confusion.

Without hesitation he gathered up his things, drawing his heavy cloak about him, pulling on his gauntlets, fastening buckles and thongs, then he left the cabin and returned to the deck. The captain was pointing through the mist at the dark outlines of a coast. "Can you see land, Elric?"

"I can."

"You must go quickly, then."

"Willingly."

Elric swung himself over the rail and into the boat. The boat struck the side of the ship several times, so that the hull boomed like the beating of some huge funeral drum. Otherwise there was silence now upon the misty waters and no sign of wreckage.

Blendker saluted him. "I wish you luck, comrade."

"You, too, Master Blendker."

The boat began to sink toward the flat surface of the sea, the pulleys of the davits creaking. Elric clung to the rope, letting go as the boat hit the water. He stumbled and sat down heavily upon the seat, releasing the ropes so that the boat drifted at once away from the Dark Ship. He got out the oars and fitted them into their rowlocks.

As he pulled toward the shore he heard the captain's voice calling to him, but the words were muffled by the mist and he would never know, now, if the blind man's last communication had been a warning or merely some formal pleasantry. He did not care. The boat moved smoothly through the water; the mist began to thin, but so, too, did the light fade.

Suddenly he was under a twilight sky, the sun already gone and stars appearing. Before he had reached the shore it was already completely dark, with the moon not yet risen, and it was with difficulty that he beached the boat on what seemed flat rocks, and stumbled inland until he judged himself safe enough from any inrushing tide.

Then, with a sigh, he lay down, thinking just to order his thoughts before moving on; but, almost instantly, he was asleep.

2

Elric dreamed.

He dreamed not merely of the end of his world but of the end of an entire cycle in the history of the cosmos. He dreamed that he was not only Elric of Melniboné but that he was other men, too—men who were pledged to some numinous cause which even they could not describe. And he dreamed that he had dreamed of the Dark Ship and Tanelorn and Agak and Gagak while he lay exhausted upon a beach somewhere beyond the borders of Pikarayd; and when he woke up he was smiling sardonically, congratulating himself for the possession of a grandiose imagination. But he could not clear his head entirely of the impression left by that dream.

This shore was not the same, so plainly something had befallen him —perhaps he had been drugged by slavers, then later abandoned when they found him not what they expected. . . . But, no, the explanation would not do. If he could discover his whereabouts, he might also recall the true facts.

It was dawn, for certain. He sat up and looked about him.

He was sprawled upon a dark, sea-washed limestone pavement, cracked in a hundred places, the cracks so deep that the small streams

of foaming salt water rushing through these many narrow channels
made raucous what would otherwise have been a very still morning.

Elric climbed to his feet, using his scabbarded runesword to steady
himself. His bone-white lids closed for a moment over his crimson eyes
as he sought, again, to recollect the events which had brought him here.

He recalled his flight from Pikarayd, his panic, his falling into a coma
of hopelessness, his dreams. And, because he was evidently neither dead
nor a prisoner, he could at least conclude that his pursuers had, after
all, given up the chase, for if they had found him they would have killed
him.

Opening his eyes and casting about him, he remarked the peculiar
blue quality of the light (doubtless a trick of the sun behind the gray
clouds) which made the landscape ghastly and gave the sea a dull,
metallic look.

The limestone terraces which rose from the sea and stretched above
him shone intermittently, like polished lead. On an impulse he held his
hand to the light and inspected it. The normally lusterless white of his
skin was now tinged with a faint, bluish luminosity. He found it pleas-
ing and smiled as a child might smile, in innocent wonder.

He had expected to be tired, but he now realized that he felt unusually refreshed, as if he had slept long after a good meal, and, deciding
not to question the fact of this fortunate (and unlikely) gift, he determined to climb the cliffs in the hope that he might get some idea of his
bearings before he decided which direction he would take.

Limestone could be a little treacherous, but it made easy climbing,
for there was almost always somewhere that one terrace met another.

He climbed carefully and steadily, finding many footholds, and
seemed to gain considerable height quite quickly, yet it was noon before
he had reached the top and found himself standing at the edge of a
broad, rocky plateau which fell away sharply to form a close horizon.
Beyond the plateau was only the sky. Save for sparse, brownish grass,
little grew here and there were no signs at all of human habitation. It
was now, for the first time, that Elric realized the absence of any form
of wildlife. Not a single seabird flew in the air, not an insect crept
through the grass. Instead, there was an enormous silence hanging over
the brown plain.

Elric was still remarkably untired, so he decided to make the best use
he could of his energy and reach the edge of the plateau in the hope
that, from there, he would sight a town or a village. He pressed on,
feeling no lack of food and water, and his stride was singularly ener-
getic, still; but he had misjudged his distance and the sun had begun to
set well before his journey to the edge was completed. The sky on all

sides turned a deep, velvety blue and the few clouds that there were in it were also tinged blue, and now, for the first time, Elric realized that the sun itself was not its normal shade, that it burned blackish purple, and he wondered again if he still dreamed.

The ground began to rise sharply and it was with some effort that he walked, but before the light had completely faded he was on the steep flank of a hill, descending toward a wide valley which, though bereft of trees, contained a river which wound through rocks and russet turf and bracken.

After a short rest, Elric decided to press on, although night had fallen, and see if he could reach the river where he might at least drink and, possibly, in the morning find fish to eat.

Again, no moon appeared to aid his progress and he walked for two or three hours in a darkness which was almost total, stumbling occasionally into large rocks, until the ground leveled and he felt sure he had reached the floor of the valley.

He had developed a strong thirst by now and was feeling somewhat hungry, but decided that it might be best to wait until morning before seeking the river when, rounding a particularly tall rock, he saw, with some astonishment, the light of a camp fire.

Hopefully this would be the fire of a company of merchants, a trading caravan on its way to some civilized country which would allow him to travel with it, perhaps in return for his services as a mercenary swordsman (it would not be the first time, since he had left Melniboné, that he had earned his bread in such a way).

Yet Elric's old instincts did not desert him; he approached the fire cautiously and let no one see him. Beneath an overhang of rock, made shadowy by the flame's light, he stood and observed the group of fifteen or sixteen men who sat or lay close to the fire, playing some kind of game involving dice and slivers of numbered ivory.

Gold, bronze, and silver gleamed in the firelight as the men staked large sums on the fall of a die and the turn of a slip of ivory.

Elric guessed that, if they had not been so intent on their game, these men must certainly have detected his approach, for they were not, after all, merchants. By the evidence, they were warriors, wearing scarred leather and dented metal, their weapons ready to hand, yet they belonged to no army—unless it be an army of bandits—for they were of all races and (oddly) seemed to be from various periods in the history of the Young Kingdoms.

It was as if they had looted some scholar's collection of relics. An axman of the later Lormyrian Republic, which had come to an end some two hundred years ago, lay with his shoulder rubbing the elbow of a Chalalite bowman, from a period roughly contemporary with Elric's own. Close to the Chalalite sat a short Ilmioran infantryman of a century past. Next to him was a Filkharian in the barbaric dress of that nation's earliest times. Tarkeshites, Shazarians, Vilmirians, all mingled and the only thing they had in common, by the look of them, was a villainous, hungry cast to their features.

In other circumstances Elric might have skirted this encampment and moved on, but he was so glad to find human beings of any sort that he ignored the disturbing incongruities of the group; yet he remained content to watch them.

One of the men, less unwholesome than the others, was a bulky, black-bearded, baldheaded sea-warrior clad in the casual leathers and silks of the people of the Purple Towns. It was when this man produced a large gold Melnibonéan wheel—a coin not minted, as most coins, but carved by craftsmen to a design both ancient and intricate—that Elric's caution was fully conquered by his curiosity.

Very few of those coins existed in Melniboné and none, that Elric had heard of, outside; for the coins were not used for trade with the Young Kingdoms. They were prized, even by the nobility of Melniboné.

It seemed to Elric that the baldheaded man could only have acquired the coin from another Melnibonéan traveler—and Elric knew of no other Melnibonéans who shared his penchant for exploration. His wariness dismissed, he stepped into the circle.

If he had not been completely obsessed by the thought of the Melnibonéan wheel he might have taken some satisfaction in the sudden scuffle to arms which resulted. Within seconds, the majority of the men were on their feet, their weapons drawn.

For a moment, the gold wheel was forgotten. His hand upon his runesword's pommel, he presented the other in a placatory gesture.

"Forgive the interruption, gentlemen. I am but one tired fellow soldier who seeks to join you. I would beg some information and purchase some food, if you have it to spare."

On foot, the warriors had an even more ruffianly appearance. They grinned among themselves, entertained by Elric's courtesy but not impressed by it.

One, in the feathered helmet of a Pan Tangian sea-chief, with features to match—swarthy, sinister—pushed his head forward on its long neck and said banteringly:

"We've company enough, white-face. And few here are overfond of the man-demons of Melniboné. You must be rich."

Elric recalled the animosity with which Melnibonéans were regarded in the Young Kingdoms, particularly by those from Pan Tang who envied the Dragon Isle her power and her wisdom and, of late, had begun crudely to imitate Melniboné.

Increasingly on his guard, he said evenly, "I have a little money."

"Then we'll take it, demon." The Pan Tangian presented a dirty palm just below Elric's nose as he growled, "Give it over and be on your way."

Elric's smile was polite and fastidious, as if he had been told a poor joke.

The Pan Tangian evidently thought the joke better than did Elric, for he laughed heartily and looked to his nearest fellows for approval.

Coarse laughter infected the night and only the baldheaded, black-bearded man did not join in the jest, but took a step or two backward, while all the others pressed forward.

The Pan Tangian's face was close to Elric's own; his breath was foul and Elric saw that his beard and hair were alive with lice, yet he kept his head, replying in the same equable tone:

"Give me some decent food, a flask of water—some wine, if you have it—and I'll gladly give you the money I have."

The laughter rose and fell again as Elric continued:

"But if you would take my money and leave me with naught—then I must defend myself. I have a good sword."

The Pan Tangian strove to imitate Elric's irony. "But you will note, Sir Demon, that we outnumber you. Considerably."

Softly the albino spoke: "I've noticed that fact, but I'm not disturbed by it," and he had drawn the black blade even as he finished speaking, for they had come at him with a rush.

And the Pan Tangian was the first to die, sliced through the side, his vertebrae sheared, and Stormbringer, having taken its first soul, began to sing.

A Chalalite died next, leaping with stabbing javelin poised, on the point of the runesword, and Stormbringer murmured with pleasure.

But it was not until it had sliced the head clean off a Filkharian pike-master that the sword began to croon and come fully to life, black fire flickering up and down its length, its strange runes glowing.

Now the warriors knew they battled sorcery and became more cautious, yet they scarcely paused in their attack, and Elric, thrusting and parrying, hacking and slicing, needed all of the fresh, dark energy the sword passed on to him.

Lance, sword, ax, and dirk were blocked, wounds were given and received, but the dead had not yet outnumbered the living when Elric found himself with his back against the rock and nigh a dozen sharp weapons seeking his vitals.

It was at this point, when Elric had become somewhat less than confident that he could best so many, that the baldheaded warrior, ax in one gloved hand, sword in the other, came swiftly into the firelight and set upon those of his fellows closest to him.

"I thank you, sir!" Elric was able to shout, during the short respite this sudden turn produced. His morale improved, he resumed the attack.

The Lormyrian was cleaved from hip to pelvis as he dodged a feint; a Filkharian, who should have been dead four hundred years before, fell with the blood bubbling from lips and nostrils, and the corpses began to pile one upon the other. Still Stormbringer sang its sinister battle-song and still the runesword passed its power to its master so that with every death Elric found strength to slay more of the soldiers.

Those who remained now began to express their regret for their hasty attack. Where oaths and threats had issued from their mouths, now came plaintive petitions for mercy and those who had laughed with such bold braggadocio now wept like young girls, but Elric, full of his old battle-joy, spared none.

Meanwhile the man from the Purple Towns, unaided by sorcery, put ax and sword to good work and dealt with three more of his one-time comrades, exulting in his work as if he had nursed a taste for it for some time.

"Yoi! But this is worthwhile slaughter!" cried the black-bearded one.

And then that busy butchery was suddenly done and Elric realized that none were left save himself and his new ally, who stood leaning on his ax, panting and grinning like a hound at the kill, replacing a steel skullcap upon his pate from where it had fallen during the fight, and wiping a bloody sleeve over the sweat glistening on his brow, and saying, in a deep, good-humored tone:

"Well, now, it is we who are wealthy, of a sudden."

Elric sheathed a Stormbringer still reluctant to return to its scabbard. "You desire their gold. Is that why you aided me?"

The black-bearded soldier laughed. "I owed them a debt and had been biding my time, waiting to pay. These rascals are all that were left of a pirate crew which slew everyone aboard my own ship when we wandered into strange waters—they would have slain me had I not told them I wished to join them. Now I am revenged. Not that I am above taking the gold, since much of it belongs to me and my dead brothers. It will go to their wives and their children when I return to the Purple Towns."

"How did you convince them not to kill you, too?" Elric sought among the ruins of the fire for something to eat. He found some cheese and began to chew upon it.

"They had no captain or navigator, it seemed. None were real sailors at all, but coast-huggers, based upon this island. They were stranded here, you see, and had taken to piracy as a last resort, but were too terrified to risk the open sea. Besides, after the fight, they had no ship. We had managed to sink that as we fought. We sailed mine to this shore, but provisions were already low and they had no stomach for setting sail without full holds, so I pretended that I knew this coast (may the gods take my soul if I ever see it again after this business) and offered to lead them inland to a village they might loot. They had heard of no such village, but believed me when I said it lay in a hidden valley. That way I prolonged my life while I waited for the opportunity to be revenged upon them. It was a foolish hope, I know. Yet"—grinning—"as it happened, it was well-founded, after all! Eh?"

The black-bearded man glanced a little warily at Elric, uncertain of what the albino might say, hoping, however, for comradeship, though it was well known how haughty Melnibonéans were. Elric could tell that all these thoughts went through his new acquaintance's mind; he had seen many others make similar calculations. So he smiled openly and slapped the man on the shoulder.

"You saved my life, also, my friend. We are both fortunate."

The man sighed in relief and slung his ax upon his back. "Aye—lucky's the word. But shall our luck hold, I wonder?"

"You do not know the island at all?"

"Nor the waters, either. How we came to them I'll never guess. Enchanted waters, though, without question. You've seen the color of the sun?"

"I have."

"Well"—the seaman bent to remove a pendant from around the Pan Tangian's throat—"you'd know more about enchantments and sorceries than I. How came you here, Sir Melnibonéan?"

"I know not. I fled from some who hunted me. I came to a shore and could flee no further. Then I dreamed a great deal. When next I awoke I was on the shore again, but of this island."

"Spirits of some sort—maybe friendly to you—took you to safety, away from your enemies."

"That's just possible," Elric agreed, "for we have many allies among the elementals. I am called Elric and I am self-exiled from Melniboné. I travel because I believe I have something to learn from the folk of the Young Kingdoms. I have no power, save what you see. ."

The black-bearded man's eyes narrowed in appraisal as he pointed at himself with his thumb. "I'm Smiorgan Baldhead, once a sea-lord of the Purple Towns. I commanded a fleet of merchantmen. Perhaps I still do. I shall not know until I return—if I ever do return."

"Then let us pool our knowledge and our resources, Smiorgan Baldhead, and make plans to leave this island as soon as we can."

Elric walked back to where he saw traces of the abandoned game, trampled into the mud and the blood. From among the dice and the ivory slips, the silver and the bronze coins, he found the gold Melnibonéan wheel. He picked it up and held it in his outstretched palm. The wheel almost covered the whole palm. In the old days, it had been the currency of kings.

"This was yours, friend?" he asked Smiorgan.

Smiorgan Baldhead looked up from where he was still searching the Pan Tangian for his stolen possessions. He nodded.

"Aye. Would you keep it as part of your share?"

Elric shrugged. "I'd rather know from whence it came. Who gave it you?"

"It was not stolen. It's Melnibonéan, then?"

"Yes."

"I guessed it."

"From whom did you obtain it?"

Smiorgan straightened up, having completed his search. He scratched at a slight wound on his forearm. "It was used to buy passage on our ship—before we were lost—before the raiders attacked us."

"Passage? By a Melnibonéan?"

"Maybe," said Smiorgan. He seemed reluctant to speculate.

"Was he a warrior?"

Smiorgan smiled in his beard. "No. It was a woman gave that to me."

"How came she to take passage?"

Smiorgan began to pick up the rest of the money. "It's a long tale and, in part, a familiar one to most merchant sailors. We were seeking new markets for our goods and had equipped a good-sized fleet, which I commanded as the largest shareholder." He seated himself casually upon the big corpse of the Chalalite and began to count the money. "Would you hear the tale or do I bore you already?"

"I'd be glad to listen."

Reaching behind him, Smiorgan pulled a wine-flask from the belt of the corpse and offered it to Elric, who accepted it and drank sparingly of a wine which was unusually good.

Smiorgan took the flask when Elric had finished. "That's part of our cargo," he said. "We were proud of it. A good vintage, eh?"

"Excellent. So you set off from the Purple Towns?"

"Aye. Going east toward the Unknown Kingdoms. We sailed due east for a couple of weeks, sighting some of the bleakest coasts I have ever seen, and then we saw no land at all for another week. That was when we entered a stretch of water we came to call the Roaring Rocks —like the Serpent's Teeth off Shazar's coast, but much greater in expanse, and larger, too. Huge volcanic cliffs which rose from the sea on every side and around which the waters heaved and boiled and howled with a fierceness I've rarely experienced. Well, in short, the fleet was dispersed and at least four ships were lost on those rocks. At last we were able to escape those waters and found ourselves becalmed and alone. We searched for our sister ships for a while and then decided to give ourselves another week before turning for home, for we had no liking to go back into the Roaring Rocks again. Low on provisions, we sighted land at last—grassy cliffs and hospitable beaches and, inland, some signs of cultivation, so we knew we had found civilization again. We put into a small fishing port and satisfied the natives—who spoke no tongue used in the Young Kingdoms—that we were friendly. And that was when the woman approached us."

"The Melnibonéan woman?"

"If Melnibonéan she was. She was a fine-looking woman, I'll say that. We were short of provisions, as I told you, and short of any means of purchasing them, for the fishermen desired little of what we had to trade. Having given up our original quest, we were content to head westward again."

"The woman?"

"She wished to buy passage to the Young Kingdoms—and was content to go with us as far as Menii, our home port. For her passage she gave us two of those wheels. One was used to buy provisions in the town —Graghin, I think it was called—and after making repairs we set off again."

"You never reached the Purple Towns?"

"There were more storms—strange storms. Our instruments were useless, our lodestones were of no help to us at all. We became even more completely lost than before. Some of my men argued that we had gone beyond our own world altogether. Some blamed the woman, saying she was a sorceress who had no intention of going to Menii. But I believed her. Night fell and seemed to last forever until we sailed into a calm dawn beneath a blue sun. My men were close to panic—and it takes much to make my men panic—when we sighted the island. As we headed for it those pirates attacked us in a ship which belonged to history—it should have been on the bottom of the ocean, not on the surface. I've seen pictures of such craft in murals on a temple wall in

Tarkesh. In ramming us, she stove in half her port side and was sinking even when they swarmed aboard. They were desperate, savage men, Elric—half-starved and blood-hungry. We were weary after our voyage, but fought well. During the fighting the woman disappeared, killed herself, maybe, when she saw the stamp of our conquerors. After a long fight only myself and one other, who died soon after, were left. That was when I became cunning and decided to wait for revenge."

"The woman had a name?"

"None she would give. I have thought the matter over and suspect that, after all, we were used by her. Perhaps she did not seek Menii and the Young Kingdoms. Perhaps it was this world she sought, and, by sorcery, led us here."

"This world? You think it different from our own?"

"If only because of the sun's strange color. Do you not think so, too? You, with your Melnibonéan knowledge of such things, must believe it."

"I have dreamed of such things," Elric admitted, but he would say no more.

"Most of the pirates thought as I—they were from all the ages of the Young Kingdoms. That much I discovered. Some were from the earliest years of the era, some from our own time—and some were from the future. Adventurers, most of them, who, at some stage in their lives, sought a legendary land of great riches which lay on the other side of an ancient gateway, rising from the middle of the ocean; but they found themselves trapped here, unable to sail back through this mysterious gate. Others had been involved in sea-fights, thought themselves drowned and woken up on the shores of the island. Many, I suppose, had once had reasonable virtues, but there is little to support life on the island and they had become wolves, living off one another or any ship unfortunate enough to pass, inadvertently, through this gate of theirs."

Elric recalled part of his dream. "Did any call it the 'Crimson Gate'?"

"Several did, aye."

"And yet the theory is unlikely, if you'll forgive my skepticism," Elric said. "As one who has passed through the Shade Gate to Ameeron . . ."

"You know of other worlds, then?"

"I've never heard of this one. And I am versed in such matters. That is why I doubt the reasoning. And yet, there was the dream. . . ."

"Dream?"

"Oh, it was nothing. I am used to such dreams and give them no significance."

"The theory cannot seem surprising to a Melnibonéan, Elric!" Smiorgan grinned again. "It's I who should be skeptical, not you."

And Elric replied, half to himself: "Perhaps I fear the implications more." He lifted his head, and with the shaft of a broken spear, began to poke at the fire. "Certain ancient sorcerers of Melniboné proposed that an infinite number of worlds coexist with our own. Indeed, my dreams, of late, have hinted as much!" He forced himself to smile. "But I cannot afford to believe such things. Thus, I reject them."

"Wait for the dawn," said Smiorgan Baldhead. "The color of the sun shall prove the theory."

"Perhaps it will prove only that we both dream," said Elric. The smell of death was strong in his nostrils. He pushed aside those corpses nearest to the fire and settled himself to sleep.

Smiorgan Baldhead had begun to sing a strong yet lilting song in his own dialect, which Elric could scarcely follow.

"Do you sing of your victory over your enemies?" the albino asked.

Smiorgan paused for a moment, half-amused. "No, Sir Elric, I sing to keep the shades at bay. After all, these fellows' ghosts must still be lurking nearby, in the dark, so little time has passed since they died."

"Fear not," Elric told him. "Their souls are already eaten."

But Smiorgan sang on, and his voice was louder, his song more intense, than ever it had been before.

Just before he fell asleep, Elric thought he heard a horse whinny, and he meant to ask Smiorgan if any of the pirates had been mounted, but he fell asleep before he could do so.

3

Recalling little of his voyage on the Dark Ship, Elric would never know how he came to reach the world in which he now found himself. In later years he would recall most of these experiences as dreams, and indeed they seemed dreamlike even as they occurred.

He slept uneasily, and in the morning the clouds were heavier, shining with that strange, leaden light, though the sun itself was obscured. Smiorgan Baldhead of the Purple Towns was pointing upward, already on his feet, speaking with quiet triumph:

"Will that evidence suffice to convince you, Elric of Melniboné?"

"I am convinced of a quality about the light—possibly about this terrain—which makes the sun appear blue," Elric replied. He glanced with distaste around him at the carnage. The corpses made a wretched sight and he was filled with a nebulous misery that was neither remorse nor pity.

Smiorgan's sigh was sardonic. "Well, Sir Skeptic, we had best retrace my steps and seek my ship. What say you?"

"I agree," the albino told him.

"How far had you marched from the coast when you found us?"

Elric told him.

Smiorgan smiled. "You arrived in the nick of time, then. I should have been most embarrassed by today if the sea had been reached and I could show my pirate friends no village! I shall not forget this favor you have done me, Elric. I am a count of the Purple Towns and have much influence. If there is any service I can perform for you when we return, you must let me know."

"I thank you," Elric said gravely. "But first we must discover a means of escape."

Smiorgan had gathered up a satchel of food, some water and some wine. Elric had no stomach to make his breakfast among the dead, so he slung the satchel over his shoulder. "I'm ready," he said.

Smiorgan was satisfied. "Come—we go this way."

Elric began to follow the sea-lord over the dry, crunching turf. The steep sides of the valley loomed over them, tinged with a peculiar and unpleasant greenish hue, the result of the brown foliage being stained by the blue light from above. When they reached the river, which was narrow and ran rapidly through boulders giving easy means of crossing, they rested and ate. Both men were stiff from the previous night's fighting; both were glad to wash the dried blood and mud from their bodies in the water.

Refreshed, the pair climbed over the boulders and left the river behind, ascending the slopes, speaking little so that their breath was saved for the exertion. It was noon by the time they reached the top of the valley and observed a plain not unlike the one which Elric had first crossed. Elric now had a fair idea of the island's geography: it resembled the top of a mountain, with an indentation near the center which was the valley. Again he became sharply aware of the absence of any wildlife and remarked on this to Count Smiorgan, who agreed that he had seen nothing—no bird, fish, nor beast since he had arrived.

"It's a barren little world, friend Elric, and a misfortune for a mariner to be wrecked upon its shores."

They moved on, until the sea could be observed meeting the horizon in the far distance.

It was Elric who first heard the sound behind them, recognizing the steady thump of the hooves of a galloping horse, but when he looked back over his shoulder he could see no sign of a rider, nor anywhere that a rider could hide. He guessed that, in his tiredness, his ears were betraying him. It had been thunder that he had heard.

Smiorgan strode implacably onward, though he, too, must have heard the sound.

Again it came. Again, Elric turned. Again he saw nothing.

"Smiorgan? Did you hear a rider?"

Smiorgan continued to walk without looking back. "I heard," he grunted.

"You have heard it before?"

"Many times since I arrived. The pirates heard it, too, and some believed it their nemesis—an Angel of Death seeking them out for retribution."

"You don't know the source?"

Smiorgan paused, then stopped, and when he turned his face was grim. "Once or twice I have caught a glimpse of a horse, I think. A tall horse—white—richly dressed—but with no man upon his back. Ignore it, Elric, as I do. We have larger mysteries with which to occupy our minds!"

"You are afraid of it, Smiorgan?"

He accepted this. "Aye. I confess it. But neither fear nor speculation will rid us of it. Come!"

Elric was bound to see the sense of Smiorgan's statement and he accepted it; yet when the sound came again, about an hour later, he could not resist turning. Then he thought he glimpsed the outline of a large stallion, caparisoned for riding, but that might have been nothing more than an idea Smiorgan had put in his mind.

The day grew colder and in the air was a peculiar, bitter odor. Elric remarked on the smell to Count Smiorgan and learned that this, too, was familiar.

"The smell comes and goes, but it is usually here in some strength."

"Like sulfur," said Elric.

Count Smiorgan's laugh had much irony in it, as if Elric made reference to some private joke of Smiorgan's own. "Oh, aye! Sulfur right enough!"

The drumming of hooves grew louder behind them as they neared the coast and at last Elric, and Smiorgan too, turned around again, to look.

And now a horse could be seen plainly—riderless, but saddled and bridled, its dark eyes intelligent, its beautiful white head held proudly.

"Are you still convinced of the absence of sorcery here, Sir Elric?" Count Smiorgan asked with some satisfaction. "The horse was invisible. Now it is visible." He shrugged the battle-ax on his shoulder into a better position. "Either that, or it moves from one world to another with ease, so that all we mainly hear are its hoofbeats."

"If so," said Elric sardonically, eyeing the stallion, "it might bear us back to our own world."

"You admit, then, that we are marooned in some Limbo?"

"Very well, yes. I admit the possibility."

"Have you no sorcery to trap the horse?"

"Sorcery does not come so easily to me, for I have no great liking for it," the albino told him.

As they spoke, they approached the horse, but it would let them get no closer. It snorted and moved backward, keeping the same distance between them and itself.

At last, Elric said, "We waste time, Count Smiorgan. Let's get to your ship with speed and forget blue suns and enchanted horses as quickly as we may. Once aboard the ship I can doubtless help you with a little incantation or two, for we'll need aid of some sort if we're to sail a large ship by ourselves."

They marched on, but the horse continued to follow them. They came to the edge of the cliffs, standing high above a narrow, rocky bay in which a battered ship lay at anchor. The ship had the high, fine lines of a Purple Towns merchantman, but its decks were piled with shreds of torn canvas, pieces of broken rope, shards of timber, torn-open bales of cloth, smashed wine-jars, and all manner of other refuse, while in several places her rails were smashed and two or three of her yards had splintered. It was evident that she had been through both storms and sea-fights and it was a wonder that she still floated.

"We'll have to tidy her up as best we can, using only the mains'l for motion," mused Smiorgan. "Hopefully we can salvage enough food to last us . . ."

"Look!" Elric pointed, sure that he had seen someone in the shadows near the afterdeck. "Did the pirates leave any of their company behind?"

"None "

"Did you see anyone on the ship, just then?"

"My eyes play filthy tricks on my mind," Smiorgan told him. "It is this damned blue light. There is a rat or two aboard, that's all. And that's what you saw."

"Possibly." Elric looked back. The horse appeared to be unaware of them as it cropped the brown grass. "Well, let's finish the journey."

They scrambled down the steeply sloping cliff-face and were soon on the shore, wading through the shallows for the ship, clambering up the slippery ropes which still hung over the sides, and, at last, setting their feet with some relief upon the deck.

"I feel more secure already," said Smiorgan. "This ship was my home for so long!" He searched through the scattered cargo until he found an unbroken wine-jar, carved off the seal, and handed it to Elric. Elric lifted the heavy jar and let a little of the good wine flow into his mouth. As Count Smiorgan began to drink, Elric was sure he saw another movement near the afterdeck, and he moved closer.

Now he was certain that he heard strained, rapid breathing—like the breathing of one who sought to stifle his need for air rather than be detected. They were slight sounds, but the albino's ears, unlike his eyes, were sharp. His hand ready to draw his sword, he stalked toward the source of the sound, Smiorgan now behind him.

She emerged from her hiding place before he reached her. Her hair hung in heavy, dirty coils about her pale face; her shoulders were slumped and her soft arms hung limply at her sides, and her dress was stained and ripped.

As Elric approached, she fell on her knees before him. "Take my life," she said humbly, "but I beg you—do not take me back to Saxif D'Aan, though I know you must be his servant or his kinsman."

"It's she!" cried Smiorgan in astonishment. "It's our passenger. She must have been in hiding all this time."

Elric stepped forward, lifting up the girl's chin so that he could study her face. There was a Melnibonéan cast about her features, but she was, to his mind, of the Young Kingdoms; she lacked the pride of a Melnibonéan woman, too. "What name was that you used, girl?" he asked kindly. "Did you speak of Saxif D'Aan? Earl Saxif D'Aan of Melniboné?"

"I did, my lord."

"Do not fear me as his servant," Elric told her. "And as for being a kinsman, I suppose you could call me that, on my mother's side—or rather my great-grandmother's side. He was an ancestor. He must have been dead for two centuries, at least!"

"No," she said. "He lives, my lord."

"On this island?"

"This island is not his home, but it is in this plane that he exists. I sought to escape him through the Crimson Gate. I fled through the gate in a skiff, reached the town where you found me, Count Smiorgan, but he drew me back once I was aboard your ship. He drew me back and the ship with me. For that, I have remorse—and for what befell your crew. Now I know he seeks me. I can feel his presence growing nearer

"Is he invisible?" Smiorgan asked suddenly. "Does he ride a white horse?"

She gasped. "You see! He *is* near! Why else should the horse appear on this island?"

"He rides it?" Elric asked.

"No, no! He fears the horse almost as much as I fear him. The horse pursues him!"

Elric produced the Melnibonéan gold wheel from his purse. "Did you take this from Earl Saxif D'Aan?"

"I did."

The albino frowned.

"Who is this man, Elric?" Count Smiorgan asked. "You describe him as an ancestor—yet he lives in this world. What do you know of him?"

Elric weighed the large gold wheel in his hand before replacing it in his pouch. "He was something of a legend in Melniboné. His story is part of our literature. He was a great sorcerer—one of the greatest—and he fell in love. It's rare enough for Melnibonéans to fall in love, as others understand the emotion, but rarer for one to have such feelings for a girl who was not even of our own race. She was half-Melnibonéan, so I heard, but from a land which was, in those days, a Melnibonéan possession, a western province close to Dharijor. She was bought by him in a batch of slaves he planned to use for some sorcerous experiment, but he singled her out, saving her from whatever fate it was the others suffered. He lavished his attention upon her, giving her everything. For her, he abandoned his practices, retired to live quietly away from Imrryr, and I think she showed him a certain affection, though she did not seem to love him. There was another, you see, called Carolak, as I recall, and also half-Melnibonéan, who had become a mercenary in Shazar and risen in the favor of the Shazarian court. She had been pledged to this Carolak before her abduction. . . ."

"She loved him?" Count Smiorgan asked.

"She was pledged to marry him, but let me finish my story. . . ." Elric continued: "Well, at length Carolak, now a man of some substance, second only to the king in Shazar, heard of her fate and swore to rescue her. He came with raiders to Melniboné's shores, and aided by sorcery, sought out Saxif D'Aan's palace. That done, he sought the girl, finding her at last in the apartments Saxif D'Aan had set aside for her use. He told her that he had come to claim her as his bride, to rescue her from persecution. Oddly, the girl resisted, suggesting that she had been too long a slave in the Melnibonéan harem to readapt to the life of a princess in the Shazarian court. Carolak scoffed at this and seized her. He managed to escape the castle and had the girl over the saddle of his horse and was about to rejoin his men on the coast when Saxif D'Aan detected them. Carolak, I think, was slain, or else a spell was put on him, but Saxif D'Aan, in his terrible jealousy and certain that the girl had planned the escape with a lover, ordered her to die upon the Wheel of Chaos—a machine rather like that coin in design. Her limbs were broken slowly and Saxif D'Aan sat and watched, through long days, while she died. Her skin was peeled from her flesh, and Earl Saxif D'Aan observed every detail of her punishment. Soon it was evident that the drugs and sorcery used to sustain her life were failing and Saxif D'Aan ordered her taken from the Wheel of Chaos and laid upon a couch. 'Well,' he said, 'you have been punished for betraying me and I am glad. Now you may die.' And he saw that her lips, blood-caked and frightful, were moving, and he bent to hear her words."

"Those words? Revenge? An oath?" asked Smiorgan.

"Her last gesture was an attempt to embrace him. And the words were those she had never uttered to him before, much as he had hoped that she would. She said simply, over and over again, until the last breath left her: 'I love you. I love you. I love you.' And then she died."

Smiorgan rubbed at his beard. "Gods! What then? What did your ancestor do?"

"He knew remorse."

"Of course!"

"Not so, for a Melnibonéan. Remorse is a rare emotion with us. Few have ever experienced it. Torn by guilt, Earl Saxif D'Aan left Melniboné, never to return. It was assumed that he had died in some remote land, trying to make amends for what he had done to the only creature he had ever loved. But now, it seems, he sought the Crimson Gate, perhaps thinking it an opening into Hell."

"But why should he plague me!" the girl cried. "I am not she! My name is Vassliss. I am a merchant's daughter, from Jharkor. I was voyaging to visit my uncle in Vilmir when our ship was wrecked. A few of us escaped in an open boat. More storms seized us. I was flung from the boat and was drowning when"—she shuddered—"when *his* galley found me. I was grateful, then . . ."

"What happened?" Elric pushed the matted hair away from her face and offered her some of their wine. She drank gratefully.

"He took me to his palace and told me that he would marry me, that I should be his empress forever and rule beside him. But I was frightened. There was such pain in him—and such cruelty, too. I thought he must devour me, destroy me. Soon after my capture, I took the money and the boat and fled for the gateway, which he had told me about. . . ."

"You could find this gateway for us?" Elric asked.

"I think so. I have some knowledge of seamanship, learned from my father. But what would be the use, sir? He would find us again and drag us back. And he must be very near, even now."

"I have a little sorcery myself," Elric assured her, "and will pit it against Saxif D'Aan's, if I must." He turned to Count Smiorgan. "Can we get a sail aloft quickly?"

"Fairly quickly."

"Then let's hurry, Count Smiorgan Baldhead. I might have the means of getting us through this Crimson Gate and free from any further involvement in the dealings of the dead!"

4

While Count Smiorgan and Vassliss of Jharkor watched, Elric lowered himself to the deck, panting and pale. His first attempt to work sorcery in this world had failed and had exhausted him.

"I am further convinced," he told Smiorgan, "that we are in another plane of existence, for I should have worked my incantations with less effort."

"You have failed."

Elric rose with some difficulty. "I shall try again."

He turned his white face skyward; he closed his eyes; he stretched out his arms and his body tensed as he began the incantation again, his voice growing louder and louder, higher and higher, so that it resembled the shrieking of a gale.

He forgot where he was; he forgot his own identity; he forgot those who were with him as his whole mind concentrated upon the summoning. He sent his call out beyond the confines of the world, into that strange plane where the elementals dwelled—where the powerful creatures of the air could still be found—the *sylphs* of the breeze, and the *sharnahs,* who lived in the storms, and the most powerful of all, the *h'Haarshanns,* creatures of the whirlwind.

And now at last some of them began to come at his summons, ready to serve him as, by virtue of an ancient pact, the elementals had served his forefathers. And slowly the sail of the ship began to fill, and the timbers creaked, and Smiorgan raised the anchor, and the ship was sailing away from the island, through the rocky gap of the harbor, and out into the open sea, still beneath a strange blue sun.

Soon a huge wave was forming around them, lifting up the ship and carrying it across the ocean, so that Count Smiorgan and the girl marveled at the speed of their progress, while Elric, his crimson eyes open now, but blank and unseeing, continued to croon to his unseen allies.

Thus the ship progressed across the waters of the sea, and at last the island was out of sight and the girl, checking their position against the position of the sun, was able to give Count Smiorgan sufficient information for him to steer a course.

As soon as he could, Count Smiorgan went up to Elric, who still straddled the deck, still as stiff-limbed as before, and shook him.

"Elric! You will kill yourself with this effort. We need your friends no longer!"

At once the wind dropped and the wave dispersed and Elric, gasping, fell to the deck.

"It is harder here," he said. "It is so much harder here. It is as if I have to call across far greater gulfs than any I have known before."

And then Elric slept.

He lay in a warm bunk in a cool cabin. Through the porthole filtered diffused blue light. He sniffed. He caught the odor of hot food, and turning his head, saw that Vassliss stood there, a bowl of broth in her hands. "I was able to cook this," she said. "It will improve your health. As far as I can tell, we are nearing the Crimson Gate. The seas are always rough around the gate, so you will need your strength."

Elric thanked her pleasantly and began to eat the broth as she watched him.

"You are very like Saxif D'Aan," she said. "Yet harder in a way—and gentler, too. He is so remote. I know why that girl could never tell him that she loved him."

Elric smiled. "Oh, it's nothing more than a folktale, probably, the story I told you. This Saxif D'Aan could be another person altogether— or an impostor, even, who has taken his name—or a sorcerer. Some sorcerers take the names of other sorcerers, for they think it gives them more power."

There came a cry from above, but Elric could not make out the words.

The girl's expression became alarmed. Without a word to Elric, she hurried from the cabin.

Elric, rising unsteadily, followed her up the companionway.

Count Smiorgan Baldhead was at the wheel of his ship and he was pointing toward the horizon behind them. "What do you make of that, Elric?"

Elric peered at the horizon, but could see nothing. Often his eyes were weak, as now. But the girl said in a voice of quiet despair:

"It is a golden sail."

"You recognize it?" Elric asked her.

"Oh, indeed I do. It is the galleon of Earl Saxif D'Aan. He has found us. Perhaps he was lying in wait along our route, knowing we must come this way."

"How far are we from the gate?"

"I am not sure."

At that moment, there came a terrible noise from below, as if something sought to stave in the timbers of the ship.

"It's in the forward hatches!" cried Smiorgan. "See what it is, friend Elric! But take care, man!"

Cautiously Elric prised back one of the hatch covers and peered into the murky fastness of the hold. The noise of stamping and thumping continued on, and as his eyes adjusted to the light, he saw the source.

The white horse was there. It whinnied as it saw him, almost in greeting.

"How did it come aboard?" Elric asked. "I saw nothing. I heard nothing."

The girl was almost as white as Elric. She sank to her knees beside the hatch, burying her face in her arms.

"He has us! He has us!"

"There is still a chance we can reach the Crimson Gate in time," Elric reassured her. "And once in my own world, why, I can work much stronger sorcery to protect us."

"No," she sobbed, "it is too late. Why else would the white horse be here? He knows that Saxif D'Aan must soon board us."

"He'll have to fight us before he shall have you," Elric promised her.

"You have not seen his men. Cutthroats all. Desperate and wolfish! They'll show you no mercy. You would be best advised to hand me over to Saxif D'Aan at once and save yourselves. You'll gain nothing from trying to protect me. But I'd ask you a favor."

"What's that?"

"Find me a small knife to carry, that I may kill myself as soon as I know you two are safe."

Elric laughed, dragging her to her feet. "I'll have no such melodramatics from you, lass! We stand together. Perhaps we can bargain with Saxif D'Aan."

"What have you to barter?"

"Very little. But he is not aware of that."

"He can read your thoughts, seemingly. He has great powers!"

"I am Elric of Melniboné. I am said to possess a certain facility in the sorcerous arts, myself."

"But you are not as single-minded as Saxif D'Aan," she said simply. "Only one thing obsesses him—the need to make me his consort."

"Many girls would be flattered by the attention—glad to be an empress with a Melnibonéan emperor for a husband." Elric was sardonic.

She ignored his tone. "That is why I fear him so," she said in a murmur. "If I lost my determination for a moment, I could love him. I should be destroyed! It is what *she* must have known!"

5

The gleaming galleon, sails and sides all gilded so that it seemed the sun itself pursued them, moved rapidly upon them while the girl and Count Smiorgan watched aghast and Elric desperately attempted to recall his elemental allies, without success.

Through the pale blue light the golden ship sailed relentlessly in their wake. Its proportions were monstrous, its sense of power vast, its gigantic prow sending up huge, foamy waves on both sides as it sped silently toward them.

With the look of a man preparing himself to meet death, Count Smiorgan Baldhead of the Purple Towns unslung his battle-ax and loosened his sword in its scabbard, setting his little metal cap upon his bald pate. The girl made no sound, no movement at all, but she wept.

Elric shook his head and his long, milk-white hair formed a halo around his face for a moment. His moody crimson eyes began to focus on the world around him. He recognized the ship; it was of a pattern with the golden battle-barges of Melniboné—doubtless the ship in which Earl Saxif D'Aan had fled his homeland, searching for the Crimson Gate. Now Elric was convinced that this must be that same Saxif D'Aan and he knew less fear than did his companions, but considerably greater curiosity. Indeed, it was almost with nostalgia that he noted the ball of fire, like a natural comet, glowing with green light, come hissing and spluttering toward them, flung by the ship's forward catapult. He half expected to see a great dragon wheeling in the sky overhead, for it was with dragons and gilded battle-craft like these that Melniboné had once conquered the world.

The fireball fell into the sea a few inches from their bow and was evidently placed there deliberately, as a warning.

"Don't stop!" cried Vassliss. "Let the flames slay us! It will be better!"

Smiorgan was looking upward. "We have no choice. Look! He has banished the wind, it seems."

They were becalmed. Elric smiled a grim smile. He knew now what the folk of the Young Kingdoms must have felt when his ancestors had used these identical tactics against them.

"Elric?" Smiorgan turned to the albino. "Are these your people? That ship's Melnibonéan without question!"

"So are the methods," Elric told him. "I am of the blood royal of Melniboné. I could be emperor, even now, if I chose to claim my throne. There is some small chance that Earl Saxif D'Aan, though an ancestor, will recognize me and, therefore, recognize my authority. We are a conservative people, the folk of the Dragon Isle."

The girl spoke through dry lips, hopelessly: "He recognizes only the authority of the Lords of Chaos, who give him aid."

"All Melnibonéans recognize that authority," Elric told her with a certain humor.

From the forward hatch, the sound of the stallion's stamping and snorting increased.

"We're besieged by enchantments!" Count Smiorgan's normally ruddy features had paled. "Have you none of your own, Prince Elric, you can use to counter them?"

"None, it seems."

The golden ship loomed over them. Elric saw that the rails, high overhead, were crowded not with Imrryrian warriors but with cut-throats equally as desperate as those he had fought upon the island, and, apparently, drawn from the same variety of historical periods and nations. The galleon's long sweeps scraped the sides of the smaller vessel as they folded, like the legs of some water insect, to enable the grappling irons to be flung out. Iron claws bit into the timbers of the little ship and the brigandly crowd overhead cheered, grinning at them, menacing them with their weapons.

The girl began to run to the seaward side of the ship, but Elric caught her by the arm.

"Do not stop me, I beg you!" she cried. "Rather, jump with me and drown!"

"You think that death will save you from Saxif D'Aan?" Elric said. "If he has the power you say, death will only bring you more firmly into his grasp!"

"Oh!" The girl shuddered and then, as a voice called down to them from one of the tall decks of the gilded ship, she gave a moan and fainted into Elric's arms, so that, weakened as he was by his spell-working, it was all that he could do to stop himself falling with her to the deck.

The voice rose over the coarse shouts and guffaws of the crew. It was pure, lilting, and sardonic. It was the voice of a Melnibonéan, though it spoke the common tongue of the Young Kingdoms, a corruption, in itself, of the speech of the Bright Empire.

"May I have the captain's permission to come aboard?"

Count Smiorgan growled back: "You have us firm, sir! Don't try to disguise an act of piracy with a polite speech!"

"I take it I have your permission, then." The unseen speaker's tone remained exactly the same.

Elric watched as part of the rail was drawn back to allow a gangplank, studded with golden nails to give firmer footing, to be lowered from the galleon's deck to theirs.

A tall figure appeared at the top of the gangplank. He had the fine features of a Melnibonéan nobleman, was thin, proud in his bearing, clad in voluminous robes of cloth-of-gold, an elaborate helmet in gold and ebony upon his long auburn locks. He had gray-blue eyes, pale, slightly flushed skin, and he carried, so far as Elric could see, no weapons of any kind.

With considerable dignity, Earl Saxif D'Aan began to descend, his rascals at his back. The contrast between this beautiful intellectual and those he commanded was remarkable. Where he walked with straight back, elegant and noble, they slouched, filthy, degenerate, unintelligent, grinning with pleasure at their easy victory. Not a man among them showed any sign of human dignity; each was overdressed in tattered and unclean finery, each had at least three weapons upon his person, and there was much evidence of looted jewelry, of nose-rings, earrings, bangles, necklaces, toe- and finger-rings, pendants, cloak-pins, and the like.

"Gods!" murmured Smiorgan. "I've rarely seen such a collection of scum, and I thought I'd encountered most kinds in my voyages. How can such a man bear to be in their company?"

"Perhaps it suits his sense of irony," Elric suggested.

Earl Saxif D'Aan reached their deck and stood looking up at them to where they still positioned themselves, in the poop. He gave a slight bow. His features were controlled and only his eyes suggested something of the intensity of emotion dwelling within him, particularly as they fell upon the girl in Elric's arms.

"I am Earl Saxif D'Aan of Melniboné, now of the Islands Beyond the Crimson Gate. You have something with you which is mine. I would claim it from you."

"You mean the Lady Vassliss of Jharkor?" Elric said, his voice as steady as Saxif D'Aan's.

Saxif D'Aan seemed to note Elric for the first time. A slight frown crossed his brow and was quickly dismissed. "She is mine," he said. "You may be assured that she will come to no harm at my hands."

Elric, seeking some advantage, knew that he risked much when he next spoke, in the High Tongue of Melniboné, used between those of the blood royal. "Knowledge of your history does not reassure me, Saxif D'Aan."

Almost imperceptibly, the golden man stiffened and fire flared in his gray-blue eyes. "Who are you, to speak the Tongue of Kings? Who are you, who claims knowledge of my past?"

"I am Elric, son of Sadric, and I am the four-hundred-and-twenty-eighth emperor of the folk of R'lin K'ren A'a, who landed upon the Dragon Isle ten thousand years ago. I am Elric, your emperor, Earl Saxif D'Aan, and I demand your fealty." And Elric held up his right hand, upon which still gleamed a ring set with a single Actorios stone, the Ring of Kings.

Earl Saxif D'Aan now had firm control of himself again. He gave no sign that he was impressed. "Your sovereignty does not extend beyond your own world, noble emperor, though I greet you as a fellow monarch." He spread his arms so that his long sleeves rustled. "This world is mine. All that exists beneath the blue sun do I rule. You trespass, therefore, in my domain. I have every right to do as I please."

"Pirate pomp," muttered Count Smiorgan, who had understood nothing of the conversation but had gathered something of what passed by the tone. "Pirate braggadocio. What does he say, Elric?"

"He convinces me that he is not, in your sense, a pirate, Count Smiorgan. He claims that he is ruler of this plane. Since there is apparently no other, we must accept his claim."

"Gods! Then let him behave like a monarch and let us sail safely out of his waters!"

"We may—if we give him the girl."

Count Smiorgan shook his head. "I'll not do that. She's my passenger, in my charge. I must die rather than do that. It is the Code of the Sea-lords of the Purple Towns."

"You are famous for your adherence to that code," Elric said. "As for myself, I have taken this girl into my protection and, as hereditary emperor of Melniboné, I cannot allow myself to be browbeaten."

They had conversed in a murmur, but, somehow, Earl Saxif D'Aan had heard them.

"I must let you know," he said evenly, in the common tongue, "that the girl is mine. You steal her from me. Is that the action of an emperor?"

"She is not a slave," Elric said, "but the daughter of a free merchant in Jharkor. You have no rights upon her."

Earl Saxif D'Aan said, "Then I cannot open the Crimson Gate for you. You must remain in my world forever."

"You have closed the gate? Is it possible?"

"To me."

"Do you know that the girl would rather die than be captured by you, Earl Saxif D'Aan? Does it give you pleasure to instill such fear?"

The golden man looked directly into Elric's eyes as if he made some cryptic challenge. "The gift of pain has ever been a favorite gift among our folk, has it not? Yet it is another gift I offer her. She calls herself Vassliss of Jharkor, but she does not know herself. I know her. She is Gratyesha, Princess of Fwem-Omeyo, and I would make her my bride."

"How can it be that she does not know her own name?"

"She is reincarnated—soul and flesh are identical—that is how I know. And I have waited, Emperor of Melniboné, for many scores of years for her. Now I shall not be cheated of her."

"As you cheated yourself, two centuries past, in Melniboné?"

"You risk much with your directness of language, brother monarch!" There was a hint of a warning in Saxif D'Aan's tone, a warning much fiercer than any implied by the words.

"Well"—Elric shrugged—"you have more power than we do. My sorcery works poorly in your world. Your ruffians outnumber us. It should not be difficult for you to take her from us."

"You must give her to me. Then you may go free, back to your own world and your own time."

Elric smiled. "There is sorcery here. She is no reincarnation. You'd bring your lost love's spirit from the netherworld to inhabit this girl's body. Am I not right? That is why she must be given freely, or your sorcery will rebound upon you—or might—and you would not take the risk."

Earl Saxif D'Aan turned his head away so that Elric might not see his eyes. "She is the girl," he said, in the High Tongue. "I know that she is. I mean her soul no harm. I would merely give it back its memory."

"Then it is stalemate," said Elric.

"Have you no loyalty to a brother of the royal blood?" Saxif D'Aan murmured, still refusing to look at Elric.

"You claimed no such loyalty, as I recall, Earl Saxif D'Aan. If you accept me as your emperor, then you must accept my decisions. I keep the girl in my custody. Or you must take her by force."

"I am too proud."

"Such pride shall ever destroy love," said Elric, almost in sympathy. "What now, King of Limbo? What shall you do with us?"

Earl Saxif D'Aan lifted his noble head, about to reply, when from the hold the stamping and the snorting began again. His eyes widened. He looked questioningly at Elric, and there was something close to terror in his face.

"What's that? What have you in the hold?"

"A mount, my lord, that is all," said Elric equably.

"A horse? An ordinary horse?"

"A white one. A stallion, with bridle and saddle. It has no rider."

At once Saxif D'Aan's voice rose as he shouted orders for his men. "Take those three aboard our ship. This one shall be sunk directly. Hurry! Hurry!"

Elric and Smiorgan shook off the hands which sought to seize them and they moved toward the gangplank, carrying the girl between them, while Smiorgan muttered, "At least we are not slain, Elric. But what becomes of us now?"

Elric shook his head. "We must hope that we can continue to use Earl Saxif D'Aan's pride against him, to our advantage, though the gods alone know how we shall resolve the dilemma."

Earl Saxif D'Aan was already hurrying up the gangplank ahead of them.

"Quickly," he shouted. "Raise the plank!"

They stood upon the decks of the golden battle-barge and watched as the gangplank was drawn up, the length of rail replaced.

"Bring up the catapults," Saxif D'Aan commanded. "Use lead. Sink that vessel at once!"

The noise from the forward hold increased. The horse's voice echoed over ships and water. Hooves smashed at timber and then, suddenly, it came crashing through the hatch-covers, scrambling for purchase on the deck with its front hooves, and then standing there, pawing at the planks, its neck arching, its nostrils dilating, and its eyes glaring, as if ready to do battle.

Now Saxif D'Aan made no attempt to hide the terror on his face. His voice rose to a scream as he threatened his rascals with every sort of horror if they did not obey him with utmost speed. The catapults were dragged up and huge globes of lead were lobbed onto the decks of Smiorgan's ship, smashing through the planks like arrows through parchment so that almost immediately the ship began to sink.

"Cut the grappling hooks!" cried Saxif D'Aan, wrenching a blade from the hand of one of his men and sawing at the nearest rope. "Cast loose—quickly!"

Even as Smiorgan's ship groaned and roared like a drowning beast, the ropes were cut. The ship keeled over at once, and the horse disappeared.

"Turn about!" shouted Saxif D'Aan. "Back to Fhaligarn and swiftly, or your souls shall feed my fiercest demons!"

There came a peculiar, high-pitched neighing from the foaming water, as Smiorgan's ship, stern uppermost, gasped and was swallowed. Elric caught a glimpse of the white stallion, swimming strongly.

"Go below!" Saxif D'Aan ordered, indicating a hatchway. "The horse can smell the girl and thus is doubly difficult to lose."

"Why do you fear it?" Elric asked. "It is only a horse. It cannot harm you."

Saxif D'Aan uttered a laugh of profound bitterness. "Can it not, brother monarch? Can it not?"

As they carried the girl below, Elric was frowning, remembering a little more of the legend of Saxif D'Aan, of the girl he had punished so cruelly, and of her lover, Prince Carolak. The last he heard of Saxif D'Aan was the sorcerer crying:

"More sail! More sail!"

And then the hatch had closed behind them and they found themselves in an opulent Melnibonéan day-cabin, full of rich hangings, precious metal, decorations of exquisite beauty and, to Count Smiorgan, disturbing decadence. But it was Elric, as he lowered the girl to a couch, who noticed the smell.

"Augh! It's the smell of a tomb—of damp and mold. Yet nothing rots. It is passing peculiar, friend Smiorgan, is it not?"

"I scarcely noticed, Elric." Smiorgan's voice was hollow. "But I would agree with you on one thing. We are entombed. I doubt we'll live to escape this world now."

6

An hour had passed since they had been forced aboard. The door had been locked behind them, and it seemed Saxif D'Aan was too preoccupied with escaping the white stallion to bother with them. Peering through the lattice of a porthole, Elric could look back to where their ship had been sunk. They were many leagues distant already; yet he still thought, from time to time, that he saw the head and shoulders of the stallion above the waves.

Vassliss had recovered and sat pale and shivering upon the couch.

"What more do you know of that horse?" Elric asked her. "It would be helpful to me if you could recall anything you have heard."

She shook her head. "Saxif D'Aan spoke little of it, but I gather he fears the rider more than he does the horse."

"Ah!" Elric frowned. "I suspected it! Have you ever seen the rider?"

"Never. I think that Saxif D'Aan has never seen him, either. I think he believes himself doomed if that rider should ever sit upon the white stallion."

Elric smiled to himself.

"Why do you ask so much about the horse?" Smiorgan wished to know.

Elric shook his head. "I have an instinct, that is all. Half a memory. But I'll say nothing and think as little as I may, for there is no doubt Saxif D'Aan, as Vassliss suggests, has some power of reading the mind."

They heard a footfall above, descending to their door. A bolt was drawn and Saxif D'Aan, his composure fully restored, stood in the opening, his hands in his golden sleeves.

"You will forgive, I hope, the peremptory way in which I sent you here. There was danger which had to be averted at all costs. As a result, my manners were not all that they should have been."

"Danger to us?" Elric asked. "Or to you, Earl Saxif D'Aan?"

"In the circumstances, to all of us, I assure you."

"Who rides the horse?" Smiorgan asked bluntly. "And why do you fear him?"

Earl Saxif D'Aan was master of himself again, so there was no sign of a reaction. "That is very much my private concern," he said softly. "Will you dine with me now?"

The girl made a noise in her throat and Earl Saxif D'Aan turned piercing eyes upon her. "Gratyesha, you will want to cleanse yourself and make yourself beautiful again. I will see that facilities are placed at your disposal."

"I am not Gratyesha," she said. "I am Vassliss, the merchant's daughter."

"You will remember," he said. "In time, you will remember." There was such certainty, such obsessive power, in his voice that even Elric experienced a frisson of awe. "The things will be brought to you, and you may use this cabin as your own until we return to my palace on Fhaligarn. My lords . . ." He indicated that they should leave.

Elric said, "I'll not leave her, Saxif D'Aan. She is too afraid."

"She fears only the truth, brother."

"She fears you and your madness."

Saxif D'Aan shrugged insouciantly. "I shall leave first, then. If you would accompany me, my lords . . ." He strode from the cabin and they followed.

Elric said, over his shoulder, "Vassliss, you may depend upon my protection." And he closed the cabin doors behind him.

Earl Saxif D'Aan was standing upon the deck, exposing his noble face to the spray which was flung up by the ship as it moved with supernatural speed through the sea.

"You called me mad, Prince Elric? Yet you must be versed in sorcery, yourself."

"Of course. I am of the blood royal. I am reckoned knowledgeable in my own world."

"But here? How well does your sorcery work?"

"Poorly, I'll admit. The spaces between the planes seem greater."

"Exactly. But I have bridged them. I have time to learn how to bridge them."

"You are saying that you are more powerful than am I?"

"It is a fact, is it not?"

"It is. But I did not think we were about to indulge in sorcerous battles, Earl Saxif D'Aan."

"Of course. Yet, if you were to think of besting me by sorcery, you would think twice, eh?"

"I should be foolish to contemplate such a thing at all. It could cost me my soul. My life, at least."

"True. You are a realist, I see."

"I suppose so."

"Then we can progress on simpler lines, to settle the dispute between us."

"You propose a duel?" Elric was surprised.

Earl Saxif D'Aan's laughter was light. "Of course not—against your sword? That has power in all worlds, though the magnitude varies."

"I'm glad that you are aware of that," Elric said significantly.

"Besides," added Earl Saxif D'Aan, his golden robes rustling as he moved a little nearer to the rail, "you would not kill me—for only I have the means of your escaping this world."

"Perhaps we'd elect to remain," said Elric.

"Then you would be my subjects. But, no—you would not like it here. I am self-exiled. I could not return to my own world now, even if I wished to do so. It has cost me much, my knowledge. But I would found a dynasty here, beneath the blue sun. I must have my wife, Prince Elric. I must have Gratyesha."

"Her name is Vassliss," said Elric obstinately.

"She thinks it is."

"Then it is. I have sworn to protect her, as has Count Smiorgan. Protect her we shall. You will have to kill us all."

"Exactly," said Earl Saxif D'Aan with the air of a man who has been coaching a poor student toward the correct answer to a problem. "Exactly. I shall have to kill you all. You leave me with little alternative, Prince Elric."

"Would that benefit you?"

"It would. It would put a certain powerful demon at my service for a few hours."

"We should resist."

"I have many men. I do not value them. Eventually, they would overwhelm you. Would they not?"

Elric remained silent.

"My men would be aided by sorcery," added Saxif D'Aan. "Some would die, but not too many, I think."

Elric was looking beyond Saxif D'Aan, staring out to sea. He was sure that the horse still followed. He was sure that Saxif D'Aan knew, also.

"And if we gave up the girl?"

"I should open the Crimson Gate for you. You would be honored guests. I should see that you were borne safely through, even taken safely to some hospitable land in your own world, for even if you passed through the gate there would be danger. The storms."

Elric appeared to deliberate.

"You have only a little time to make your decision, Prince Elric. I had hoped to reach my palace, Fhaligarn, by now. I shall not allow you very much longer. Come, make your decision. You know I speak the truth."

"You know that I can work some sorcery in your world, do you not?"

"You summoned a few friendly elementals to your aid, I know. But at what cost? Would you challenge me directly?"

"It would be unwise of me," said Elric.

Smiorgan was tugging at his sleeve. "Stop this useless talk. He knows that we have given our word to the girl and that we *must* fight him!"

Earl Saxif D'Aan sighed. There seemed to be genuine sorrow in his voice. "If you are determined to lose your lives . . ." he began.

"I should like to know why you set such importance upon the speed with which we make up our minds," Elric said. "Why cannot we wait until we reach Fhaligarn?"

Earl Saxif D'Aan's expression was calculating, and again he looked full into Elric's crimson eyes. "I think you know," he said, almost inaudibly.

But Elric shook his head. "I think you give me too much credit for intelligence."

"Perhaps."

Elric knew that Saxif D'Aan was attempting to read his thoughts; he deliberately blanked his mind, and suspected that he sensed frustration in the sorcerer's demeanor.

And then the albino had sprung at his kinsman, his hand chopping at Saxif D'Aan's throat. The earl was taken completely off guard. He tried to call out, but his vocal chords were numbed. Another blow, and he fell to the deck, senseless.

"Quickly, Smiorgan," Elric shouted, and he had leaped into the rigging, climbing swiftly upward to the top yards. Smiorgan, bewildered, followed, and Elric had drawn his sword, even as he reached the crow's nest, driving upward through the rail so that the lookout was taken in the groin scarcely before he realized it.

Next, Elric was hacking at the ropes holding the mainsail to the yard. Already a number of Saxif D'Aan's ruffians were climbing after them.

The heavy golden sail came loose, falling to envelop the pirates and take several of them down with it.

Elric climbed into the crow's nest and pitched the dead man over the rail in the wake of his comrades. Then he had raised his sword over his head, holding it in his two hands, his eyes blank again, his head raised to the blue sun, and Smiorgan, clinging to the mast below, shuddered as he heard a peculiar crooning come from the albino's throat.

More of the cutthroats were ascending, and Smiorgan hacked at the rigging, having the satisfaction of seeing half a score go flying down to break their bones on the deck below, or be swallowed by the waves.

Earl Saxif D'Aan was beginning to recover, but he was still stunned. "Fool!" he was crying. "Fool!" But it was not possible to tell if he referred to Elric or to himself.

Elric's voice became a wail, rhythmical and chilling, as he chanted his incantation, and the strength from the man he had killed flowed into him and sustained him. His crimson eyes seemed to flicker with fires of another, nameless color, and his whole body shook as the strange runes shaped themselves in a throat which had never been made to speak such sounds.

His voice became a vibrant groan as the incantation continued, and

Smiorgan, watching as more of the crew made efforts to climb the mainmast, felt an unearthly coldness creep through him.

Earl Saxif D'Aan screamed from below:

"You would not dare!"

The sorcerer began to make passes in the air, his own incantation tumbling from his lips, and Smiorgan gasped as a creature made of smoke took shape only a few feet below him. The creature smacked its lips and grinned and stretched a paw, which became flesh even as it moved, toward Smiorgan. He hacked at the paw with his sword, whimpering.

"Elric!" cried Count Smiorgan, clambering higher so that he grasped the rail of the crow's nest. "Elric! He sends demons against us now!"

But Elric ignored him. His whole mind was in another world, a darker, bleaker world even than this one. Through gray mists, he saw a figure, and he cried a name. "Come!" he called in the ancient tongue of his ancestors. "Come!"

Count Smiorgan cursed as the demon became increasingly substantial. Red fangs clashed and green eyes glared at him. A claw stroked his boot and no matter how much he struck with his sword, the demon did not appear to notice the blows.

There was no room for Smiorgan in the crow's nest, but he stood on the outer rim, shouting with terror, desperate for aid. Still Elric continued to chant.

"Elric! I am doomed!"

The demon's paw grasped Smiorgan by his ankle.

"Elric!"

Thunder rolled out at sea; a bolt of lightning appeared for a second and then was gone. From nowhere there came the sound of a horse's hooves pounding, and a human voice shouting in triumph.

Elric sank back against the rail, opening his eyes in time to see Smiorgan being dragged slowly downward. With the last of his strength he flung himself forward, leaning far out to stab downward with Stormbringer. The runesword sank cleanly into the demon's right eye and it roared, letting go of Smiorgan, striking at the blade which drew its energy from it, and as that energy passed into the blade and thence to Elric, the albino grinned a frightful grin so that, for a second, Smiorgan became more frightened of his friend than he had been of the demon. The demon began to dematerialize, its only means of escape from the sword which drank its life-force, but more of Saxif D'Aan's rogues were behind it, and their blades rattled as they sought the pair.

Elric swung himself back over the rail, balanced precariously on the yard as he slashed at their attackers, yelling the old battle-cries of his people. Smiorgan could do little but watch. He noted that Saxif D'Aan was no longer on deck and he shouted urgently to Elric:

"Elric! Saxif D'Aan. He seeks out the girl."

Elric now took the attack to the pirates, and they were more than anxious to avoid the moaning runesword, some even leaping into the sea rather than encounter it. Swiftly the two leaped from yard to yard until they were again upon the deck.

"What does he fear? Why does he not use more sorcery?" panted Count Smiorgan, as they ran toward the cabin.

"I have summoned the one who rides the horse," Elric told him. "I had so little time—and I could tell you nothing of it, knowing that Saxif D'Aan would read my intention in your mind, if he could not in mine!"

The cabin doors were firmly secured from the inside. Elric began to hack at them with the black sword.

But the door resisted as it should not have resisted. "Sealed by sorcery and I've no means of unsealing it," said the albino.

"Will he kill her?"

"I don't know. He might try to take her into some other plane. We must—"

Hooves clattered on the deck and the white stallion reared behind them, only now it had a rider, clad in bright purple and yellow armor. He was bareheaded and youthful, though there were several old scars upon his face. His hair was thick and curly and blond and his eyes were a deep blue.

He drew tightly upon his reins, steadying the horse. He looked piercingly at Elric. "Was it you, Melnibonéan, who opened the pathway for me?"

"It was."

"Then I thank you, though I cannot repay you."

"You have repaid me," Elric told him, then drew Smiorgan aside as the rider leaned forward and spurred his horse directly at the closed doors, smashing through as though they were rotted cotton.

There came a terrible cry from within and then Earl Saxif D'Aan, hampered by his complicated robes of gold, rushed from the cabin, seizing a sword from the hand of the nearest corpse, darting Elric a look not so much of hatred but of bewildered agony, as he turned to face the blond rider.

The rider had dismounted now and came from the cabin, one arm around the shivering girl, Vassliss, one hand upon the reins of his horse, and he said, sorrowfully:

"You did me a great wrong, Earl Saxif D'Aan, but you did Gratyesha an infinitely more terrible one. Now you must pay."

Saxif D'Aan paused, drawing a deep breath, and when he looked up again, his eyes were steady, his dignity had returned.

"Must I pay in full?" he said.

"In full."

"It is all I deserve," said Saxif D'Aan. "I escaped my doom for many years, but I could not escape the knowledge of my crime. She loved me, you know. Not you."

"She loved us both, I think. But the love she gave you was her entire soul and I should not want that from any woman."

"You would be the loser, then."

"You never knew how much she loved you."

"Only—only afterward. . . ."

"I pity you, Earl Saxif D'Aan." The young man gave the reins of his horse to the girl, and he drew his sword. "We are strange rivals, are we not?"

"You have been all these years in Limbo, where I banished you—in that garden on Melniboné?"

"All these years. Only my horse could follow you. The horse of Tendric, my father, also of Melniboné, and also a sorcerer."

"If I had known that, then, I'd have slain you cleanly and sent the horse to Limbo."

"Jealously weakened you, Earl Saxif D'Aan. But now we fight as we should have fought then—man to man, with steel, for the hand of the one who loves us both. It is more than you deserve."

"Much more," agreed the sorcerer. And he brought up his sword to lunge at the young man who, Smiorgan guessed, could only be Prince Carolak himself.

The fight was predetermined. Saxif D'Aan knew that, if Carolak did not. Saxif D'Aan's skill in arms was up to the standard of any Melnibonéan nobleman, but it could not match the skill of a professional soldier, who had fought for his life time after time.

Back and forth across the deck, while Saxif D'Aan's rascals looked on in openmouthed astonishment, the rivals fought a duel which should have been fought and resolved two centuries before, while the girl they both plainly thought was the reincarnation of Gratyesha watched them with as much concern as might her original have watched when Saxif D'Aan first encountered Prince Carolak in the gardens of his palace, so long ago.

Saxif D'Aan fought well, and Carolak fought nobly, for on many occasions he avoided an obvious advantage, but at length Saxif D'Aan threw away his sword, crying: "Enough. I'll give you your vengeance,

Prince Carolak. I'll let you take the girl. But you'll not give me your damned mercy—you'll not take my pride."

And Carolak nodded, stepped forward, and struck straight for Saxif D'Aan's heart.

The blade entered clean and Earl Saxif D'Aan should have died, but he did not. He crawled along the deck until he reached the base of the mast, and he rested his back against it, while the blood pumped from the wounded heart. And he smiled.

"It appears," he said faintly, "that I cannot die, so long have I sustained my life by sorcery. I am no longer a man."

He did not seem pleased by this thought, but Prince Carolak, stepping forward and leaning over him, reassured him. "You will die," he promised, "soon."

"What will you do with her—with Gratyesha?"

"Her name is Vassliss," said Count Smiorgan insistently. "She is a merchant's daughter, from Jharkor."

"She must make up her own mind," Carolak said, ignoring Smiorgan.

Earl Saxif D'Aan turned glazed eyes on Elric. "I must thank you," he said. "You brought me the one who could bring me peace, though I feared him."

"Is that why, I wonder, your sorcery was so weak against me?" Elric said. "Because you wished Carolak to come and release you from your guilt?"

"Possibly, Elric. You are wiser in some matters, it seems, than am I."

"What of the Crimson Gate?" Smiorgan growled. "Can that be opened? Have you still the power, Earl Saxif D'Aan?"

"I think so." From the folds of his bloodstained garments of gold, the sorcerer produced a large crystal which shone with the deep colors of a ruby. "This will not only lead you to the gate, it will enable you to pass through, only I must warn you . . ." Saxif D'Aan began to cough. "The ship—" he gasped, "the ship—like my body—has been sustained by means of sorcery—therefore . . ." His head slumped forward. He raised it with a huge effort and stared beyond them at the girl who still held the reins of the white stallion. "Farewell, Gratyesha, Princess of Fwem-Omeyo. I loved you." The eyes remained fixed upon her, but they were dead eyes now.

Carolak turned back to look at the girl. "How do you call yourself, Gratyesha?"

"They call me Vassliss," she told him. She smiled up into his youthful, battle-scarred face. "That is what they call me, Prince Carolak."

"You know who I am?"

"I know you now."

"Will you come with me, Gratyesha? Will you be my bride, at last, in the strange new lands I have found, beyond the world?"

"I will come," she said.

He helped her up into the saddle of his white stallion and climbed so that he sat behind her. He bowed to Elric of Melniboné. "I thank you again, Sir Sorcerer, though I never thought to be helped by one of the royal blood of Melniboné."

Elric's expression was not without humor. "In Melniboné," he said, "I'm told it's tainted blood."

"Tainted with mercy, perhaps."

"Perhaps."

Prince Carolak saluted them. "I hope you find peace, Prince Elric, as I have found it."

"I fear my peace will more resemble that which Saxif D'Aan found," Elric said grimly. "Nonetheless, I thank you for your good words, Prince Carolak."

Then Carolak, laughing, had ridden his horse for the rail, leaped it, and vanished.

There was a silence upon the ship. The remaining ruffians looked uncertainly from one to the other. Elric addressed them:

"Know you this—I have the key to the Crimson Gate—and only I have the knowledge to use it. Help me sail the ship, and you'll have freedom from this world! What say you?"

"Give us our orders, Captain," said a toothless individual, and he cackled with mirth. "It's the best offer we've had in a hundred years or more!"

7

It was Smiorgan who first saw the Crimson Gate. He held the great red gem in his hand and pointed ahead.

"There! There, Elric! Saxif D'Aan has not betrayed us!"

The sea had begun to heave with huge, turbulent waves, and with the mainsail still tangled upon the deck, it was all that the crew could do to control the ship, but the chance of escape from the world of the blue sun made them work with every ounce of energy and, slowly, the golden battle-barge neared the towering crimson pillars.

The pillars rose from the gray, roaring water, casting a peculiar light upon tne crests of the waves. They appeared to have little substance, and yet stood firm against the battering of the tons of water lashing around them.

"Let us hope they are wider apart than they look," said Elric. "It would be a hard enough task steering through them in calm waters, let alone this kind of sea."

"I'd best take the wheel, I think," said Count Smiorgan, handing Elric the gem, and he strode back up the tilting deck, climbing to the covered wheelhouse and relieving the frightened man who stood there.

There was nothing Elric could do but watch as Smiorgan turned the huge vessel into the waves, riding the tops as best he could, but sometimes descending with a rush which made Elric's heart rise to his mouth. All around them, then, the cliffs of water threatened, but the ship was taking another wave before the main force of water could crash onto her decks. For all this, Elric was quickly soaked through and, though sense told him he would be best below, he clung to the rail, watching as Smiorgan steered the ship with uncanny sureness toward the Crimson Gate.

And then the deck was flooded with red light and Elric was half blinded. Gray water flew everywhere; there came a dreadful scraping sound, then a snapping as oars broke against the pillars. The ship shuddered and began to turn, sideways to the wind, but Smiorgan forced her around and suddenly the quality of the light changed subtly, though the sea remained as turbulent as ever and Elric knew, deep within him, that overhead, beyond the heavy clouds, a yellow sun was burning again.

But now there came a creaking and a crashing from within the bowels of the battle-barge. The smell of mold, which Elric had noted earlier, became stronger, almost overpowering.

Smiorgan came hurrying back, having handed over the wheel. His face was pale again. "She's breaking up, Elric," he called out, over the noise of the wind and the waves. He staggered as a huge wall of water struck the ship and snatched away several planks from the deck. "She's falling apart, man!"

"Saxif D'Aan tried to warn us of this!" Elric shouted back. "As he was kept alive by sorcery, so was his ship. She was old before he sailed her to that world. While there, the sorcery which sustained her remained strong—but on this plane it has no power at all. Look!" And he pulled at a piece of the rail, crumbling the rotten wood with his fingers. "We must find a length of timber which is still good."

At that moment a yard came crashing from the mast and struck the deck, bouncing, then rolling toward them.

Elric crawled up the sloping deck until he could grasp the spar and test it. "This one's still good. Use your belt or whatever else you can and tie yourself to it!"

The wind wailed through the disintegrating rigging of the ship; the sea smashed at the sides, driving great holes below the waterline.

The ruffians who had crewed her were in a state of complete panic, some trying to unship small boats which crumbled even as they swung them out, others lying flat against the rotted decks and praying to whatever gods they still worshiped.

Elric strapped himself to the broken yard as firmly as he could and Smiorgan followed his example. The next wave to hit the ship full on lifted them with it, cleanly over what remained of the rail and into the chilling, shouting waters of that terrible sea.

Elric kept his mouth tight shut against swallowing too much water and reflected on the irony of his situation. It seemed that, having escaped so much, he was to die a very ordinary death, by drowning.

It was not long before his senses left him and he gave himself up to the swirling and somehow friendly waters of the ocean.

He awoke, struggling.

There were hands upon him. He strove to fight them off, but he was too weak. Someone laughed, a rough, good-humored sound.

The water no longer roared and crashed around him. The wind no longer howled. Instead there was a gentler movement. He heard waves lapping against timber. He was aboard another ship.

He opened his eyes, blinking in warm, yellow sunlight. Red-cheeked Vilmirian sailors grinned down at him. "You're a lucky man—if man you be!" said one.

"My friend?" Elric sought for Smiorgan.

"He was in better shape than were you. He's down in Duke Avan's cabin now."

"Duke Avan?" Elric knew the name, but in his dazed condition could remember nothing to help him place the man. "You saved us?"

"Aye. We found you both drifting, tied to a broken yard carved with the strangest designs I've ever seen. A Melnibonéan craft, was she?"

"Yes, but rather old."

They helped him to his feet. They had stripped him of his clothes and wrapped him in woolen blankets. The sun was already drying his hair. He was very weak. He said:

"My sword?"

"Duke Avan has it, below."

"Tell him to be careful of it."

"We're sure he will."

"This way," said another. "The duke awaits you."

BOOK THREE

SAILING TO
THE PAST

1

Elric sat back in the comfortable, well-padded chair and accepted the wine-cup handed him by his host. While Smiorgan ate his fill of the hot food provided for them, Elric and Duke Avan appraised one another.

Duke Avan was a man of about forty, with a square, handsome face. He was dressed in a gilded silver breastplate, over which was arranged a white cloak. His britches, tucked into black knee-length boots, were of cream-colored doeskin. On a small sea-table at his elbow rested his helmet, crested with scarlet feathers.

"I am honored, sir, to have you as my guest," said Duke Avan. "I know you to be Elric of Melniboné. I have been seeking you for several months, ever since news came to me that you had left your homeland (and your power) behind and were wandering, as it were, incognito in the Young Kingdoms."

"You know much, sir."

"I, too, am a traveler by choice. I almost caught up with you in Pikarayd, but I gather there was some sort of trouble there. You left quickly and then I lost your trail altogether. I was about to give up looking for your aid when, by the greatest of good fortune, I found you floating in the water!" Duke Avan laughed.

"You have the advantage of me," said Elric, smiling. "You raise many questions."

"He's Avan Astran of Old Hrolmar," grunted Count Smiorgan from the other side of a huge ham bone. "He's well known as an adventurer —explorer—trader. His reputation's the best. We can trust him, Elric."

"I recall the name now," Elric told the duke. "But why should you seek my aid?"

The smell of the food from the table had at last impinged and Elric got up. "Would you mind if I ate something while you explained, Duke Avan?"

"Eat your fill, Prince Elric. I am honored to have you as a guest."

"You have saved my life, sir. I have never had it saved so courteously!"

Duke Avan smiled. "I have never before had the pleasure of, let us say, catching so courteous a fish. If I were a superstitious man, Prince

Elric, I should guess that some other force threw us together in this way."

"I prefer to think of it as coincidence," said the albino, beginning to eat. "Now, sir, tell me how I can aid you."

"I shall not hold you to any bargain, merely because I have been lucky enough to save your life," said Duke Avan Astran; "please bear that in mind."

"I shall, sir."

Duke Avan stroked the feathers of his helmet. "I have explored most of the world, as Count Smiorgan rightly says. I have been to your own Melniboné and I have even ventured east, to Elwher and the Unknown Kingdoms. I have been to Myyrrhn, where the Winged Folk live. I have traveled as far as World's Edge and hope one day to go beyond. But I have never crossed the Boiling Sea and I know only a small stretch of coast along the western continent—the continent that has no name. Have you been there, Elric, in your travels?"

The albino shook his head. "I seek experience of other cultures, other civilizations—that is why I travel. There has been nothing, so far, to take me there. The continent is largely uninhabited, and then, where it is inhabited, only by savages, is it not?"

"So we are told."

"You have other intelligence?"

"You know that there is some evidence," said Duke Avan in a deliberate tone, "that your own ancestors came originally from that mainland?"

"Evidence?" Elric pretended lack of interest. "A few legends, that is all."

"One of those legends speaks of a city older than dreaming Imrryr. A city that still exists in the deep jungles of the west."

Elric recalled his conversation with Earl Saxif D'Aan, and he smiled to himself. "You mean R'lin K'ren A'a?"

"Aye. A strange name." Duke Avan Astran leaned forward, his eyes alight with delighted curiosity. "You pronounce it more fluently than could I. You speak the secret tongue, the High Tongue, the Speech of Kings. . . ."

"Of course."

"You are forbidden to teach it to any but your own children, are you not?"

"You appear conversant with the customs of Melniboné, Duke Avan," Elric said, his lids falling so that they half covered his eyes. He leaned back in his seat as he bit into a piece of fresh bread with relish. "Do you know what the words mean?"

"I have been told that they mean simply 'Where the High Ones Meet' in the ancient speech of Melniboné," Duke Avan Astran told him.

Elric inclined his head. "That is so. Doubtless only a small town, in reality. Where local chiefs gathered, perhaps once a year, to discuss the price of grain."

"You believe that, Prince Elric?"

Elric inspected a covered dish. He helped himself to veal in a rich, sweet sauce. "No," he said.

"You believe, then, that there was an ancient civilization even before your own, from which your own culture sprang? You believe that R'lin K'ren A'a is still there, somewhere in the jungles of the west?"

Elric waited until he had swallowed. He shook his head.

"No," he said. "I believe that it does not exist at all."

"You are not curious about your ancestors?"

"Should I be?"

"They were said to be different in character from those who founded Melniboné. Gentler. . . ." Duke Avan Astran looked deep into Elric's face.

Elric laughed. "You are an intelligent man, Duke Avan of Old Hrolmar. You are a perceptive man. Oh, and indeed you are a cunning man, sir!"

Duke Avan grinned at the compliment. "And you know much more of the legends than you are admitting, if I am not mistaken."

"Possibly." Elric sighed as the food warmed him. "We are known as a secretive people, we of Melniboné."

"Yet," said Duke Avan, "you seem untypical. Who else would desert an empire to travel in lands where his very race was hated?"

"An emperor rules better, Duke Avan Astran, if he has close knowledge of the world in which he rules."

"Melniboné rules the Young Kingdoms no longer."

"Her power is still great. But that, anyway, was not what I meant. I am of the opinion that the Young Kingdoms offer something which Melniboné has lost."

"Vitality?"

"Perhaps."

"Humanity!" grunted Count Smiorgan Baldhead. "That is what your race has lost, Prince Elric. I say nothing of you—but look at Earl Saxif D'Aan. How can one so wise be such a simpleton? He lost everything—pride, love, power—because he had no humanity. And what humanity he had—why, it destroyed him."

"Some say it will destroy me," said Elric, "but perhaps 'humanity' is, indeed, what I seek to bring to Melniboné, Count Smiorgan."

"Then you will destroy your kindgom!" said Smiorgan bluntly. "It is too late to save Melniboné."

"Perhaps I can help you find what you seek, Prince Elric," said Duke Avan Astran quietly. "Perhaps there is time to save Melniboné, if you feel such a mighty nation is in danger."

"From within," said Elric. "But I speak too freely."

"For a Melnibonéan, that is true."

"How did you come to hear of this city?" Elric wished to know. "No other man I have met in the Young Kingdoms has heard of R'lin K'ren A'a."

"It is marked on a map I have."

Deliberately, Elric chewed his meat and swallowed it. "The map is doubtless a forgery."

"Perhaps. Do you recall anything else of the legend of R'lin K'ren A'a?"

"There is the story of the Creature Doomed to Live." Elric pushed the food aside and poured wine for himself. "The city is said to have received its name because the Lords of the Higher Worlds once met there to decide the rules of the Cosmic Struggle. They were overheard by the one inhabitant of the city who had not flown when they came. When they discovered him, they doomed him to remain alive forever, carrying the frightful knowledge in his head. . . ."

"I have heard that story, too. But the one that interests me is that the inhabitants of R'lin K'ren A'a never returned to their city. Instead they struck northward and crossed the sea. Some reached an island we now call Sorcerer's Isle while others went farther—blown by a great storm— and came at length to a larger island inhabited by dragons whose venom caused all it touched to burn . . . to Melniboné, in fact."

"And you wish to test the truth of that story. Your interest is that of a scholar?"

Duke Avan laughed. "Partly. But my main interest in R'lin K'ren A'a is more materialistic. For your ancestors left a great treasure behind them when they fled their city. Particularly they abandoned an image of Arioch, the Lord of Chaos—a monstrous image, carved in jade, whose eyes were two huge, identical gems of a kind unknown anywhere else in all the lands of the Earth. Jewels from another plane of existence. Jewels which could reveal all the secrets of the Higher Worlds, of the past and the future, of the myriad planes of the cosmos. . . ."

"All cultures have similar legends. Wishful thinking, Duke Avan, that is all. . . ."

"But the Melnibonéans had a culture unlike any others. The

Melnibonéans are not true men, as you well know. Their powers are superior, their knowledge far greater. . . ."

"It was once thus," Elric said. "But that great power and knowledge is not mine. I have only a fragment of it. . . ."

"I did not seek you in Bakshaan and later in Jadmar because I believed you could verify what I have heard. I did not cross the sea to Filkhar, then to Argimiliar and at last to Pikarayd because I thought you would instantly confirm all that I have spoken of—I sought you because I think you the only man who would wish to accompany me on a voyage which would give us the truth or falsehood to these legends once and for all."

Elric tilted his head and drained his wine-cup.

"Cannot you do that for yourself? Why should you desire my company on the expedition? From what I have heard of you, Duke Avan, you are not one who needs support in his venturings. . . ."

Duke Avan laughed. "I went alone to Elwher when my men deserted me in the Weeping Waste. It is not in my nature to know physical fear. But I have survived my travels this long because I have shown proper foresight and caution before setting off. Now it seems I must face dangers I cannot anticipate—sorcery, perhaps. It struck me, therefore, that I needed an ally who had some experience of fighting sorcery. And since I would have no truck with the ordinary kind of wizard such as Pan Tang spawns, you were my only choice. You seek knowledge, Prince Elric, just as I do. Indeed, it could be said that if it had not been for your yearning for knowledge, your cousin would never have attempted to usurp the Ruby Throne of Melniboné. . . ."

"Enough of that," Elric said bitterly. "Let's talk of this expedition. Where is the map?"

"You will accompany me?"

"Show me the map."

Duke Avan drew a scroll from his pouch. "Here it is."

"Where did you find it?"

"On Melniboné."

"You have been there recently?" Elric felt anger rise in him.

Duke Avan raised a hand. "I went there with a group of traders and I gave much for a particular casket which had been sealed, it seemed, for an eternity. Within that casket was this map." He spread out the scroll on the table. Elric recognized the style and the script—the old High Speech of Melniboné. It was a map of part of the western continent— more than he had ever seen on any other map. It showed a great river winding into the interior for a hundred miles or more. The river appeared to flow through a jungle and then divide into two rivers which later rejoined. The "island" of land thus formed had a black circle marked on it. Against this circle, in the involved writing of ancient Melniboné, was the name R'lin K'ren A'a. Elric inspected the scroll carefully. It did not seem to be a forgery.

"Is this all you found?" he asked.

"The scroll was sealed and this was embedded in the seal," Duke Avan said, handing something to Elric.

Elric held the object in his palm. It was a tiny ruby of a red so deep as to seem black at first, but when he turned it into the light he saw an image at the center of the ruby and he recognized that image. He frowned, then he said, "I will agree to your proposal, Duke Avan. Will you let me keep this?"

"Do you know what it is?"

"No. But I should like to find out. There is a memory somewhere in my head. . . ."

"Very well, take it. I will keep the map."

"When did you have it in mind to set off?"

Duke Avan's smile was sardonic. "We are already sailing around the southern coast to the Boiling Sea."

"There are few who have returned from that ocean," Elric murmured bitterly. He glanced across the table and saw that Smiorgan was imploring with his eyes for Elric not to have any part of Duke Avan's scheme. Elric smiled at his friend. "The adventure is to my taste."

Miserably, Smiorgan shrugged. "It seems it will be a little longer before I return to the Purple Towns."

2

The coast of Lormyr had disappeared in warm mist and Duke Avan Astran's schooner dipped its graceful prow toward the west and the Boiling Sea.

The Vilmirian crew of the schooner were used to a less demanding climate and more casual work than this and they went about their tasks, it seemed to Elric, with something of an aggrieved air.

Standing beside Elric in the ship's poop, Count Smiorgan Baldhead wiped sweat from his pate and growled: "Vilmirians are a lazy lot, Prince Elric. Duke Avan needs real sailors for a voyage of this kind. I could have picked him a crew, given the chance. . . ."

Elric smiled. "Neither of us was given the chance, Count Smiorgan. It was a fait accompli. He's a clever man, Duke Astran."

"It is not a cleverness I entirely respect, for he offered us no real choice. A free man is a better companion than a slave, says the old aphorism."

"Why did you not disembark when you had the chance, then, Count Smiorgan?"

"Because of the promise of treasure," said the black-bearded man frankly. "I would return with honor to the Purple Towns. Forget you not that I commanded the fleet that was lost. . . ."

Elric understood.

"My motives are straightforward," said Smiorgan. "Yours are much more complicated. You seem to desire danger as other men desire love-making or drinking—as if in danger you find forgetfulness."

"Is that not true of many professional soldiers?"

"You are not a mere professional soldier, Elric. That you know as well as I."

"Yet few of the dangers I have faced have helped me forget," Elric pointed out. "Rather they have strengthened the reminder of what I am —of the dilemma I face. My own instincts war against the traditions of my race." Elric drew a deep, melancholy breath. "I go where danger is because I think that an answer might lie there—some reason for all this tragedy and paradox. Yet I know I shall never find it."

"But it is why you sail to R'lin K'ren A'a, eh? You hope that your remote ancestors had the answer you need?"

"R'lin K'ren A'a is a myth. Even should the map prove genuine what shall we find but a few ruins? Imrryr has stood for ten thousand years and she was built at least two centuries after my people settled on Melniboné. Time will have taken R'lin K'ren A'a away."

"And this statue, this Jade Man, Avan spoke of?"

"If the statue ever existed, it could have been looted at any time in the past hundred centuries."

"And the Creature Doomed to Live?"

"A myth."

"But you hope, do you not, that it is all as Duke Avan says . . . ?" Count Smiorgan put a hand on Elric's arm. "Do you not?"

Elric stared ahead, into the writhing steam which rose from the sea. He shook his head.

"No, Count Smiorgan. I *fear* that it is all as Duke Avan says."

The wind blew whimsically and the schooner's passage was slow as the heat grew greater and the crew sweated still more and murmured fearfully. And upon each face, now, was a stricken look. Only Duke Avan seemed to retain his confidence. He called to them all to take heart; he told them that they should all be rich soon; and he gave orders for the oars to be unshipped, for the wind could no longer be trusted. They grumbled at this, stripping off their shirts to reveal skins as red as cooked lobsters. Duke Avan made a joke of that. But the Vilmirians no longer laughed at his jokes as they had done in the milder seas of their home waters.

Around the ship the sea bubbled and roared, and they navigated by their few instruments, for the steam obscured everything.

Once a green thing erupted from the sea and glared at them before disappearing.

They ate and slept little and Elric rarely left the poop. Count Smiorgan bore the heat silently and Duke Avan, seemingly oblivious to any discomfort, went cheerfully about the ship, calling encouragement to his men.

Count Smiorgan was fascinated by the waters. He had heard of them, but never crossed them. "These are only the outer reaches of this sea, Elric," he said in some wonder. "Think what it must be like at the middle."

Elric grinned. "I would rather not. As it is, I fear I'll be boiled to death before another day has passed."

Passing by, Duke Avan heard him and clapped him on the shoulder. "Nonsense, Prince Elric! The steam is good for you! There is nothing healthier!" Seemingly with pleasure, Duke Avan stretched his limbs. "It cleans all the poisons from the system."

Count Smiorgan offered him a glowering look and Duke Avan laughed. "Be of better cheer, Count Smiorgan. According to my charts —such as they are—a couple of days will see us nearing the coasts of the western continent."

"The thought fails to raise my spirits very greatly," said Count Smiorgan, but he smiled, infected by Avan's good humor.

But shortly thereafter the sea grew slowly less frenetic and the steam began to disperse until the heat became more tolerable.

At last they emerged into a calm ocean beneath a shimmering blue sky in which hung a red-gold sun.

But three of the Vilmirian crew had died to cross the Boiling Sea, and four more had a sickness in them which made them cough a great deal, and shiver, and cry out in the night.

For a while they were becalmed, but at last a soft wind began to blow and fill the schooner's sails and soon they had sighted their first land—a little yellow island where they found fruit and a spring of fresh water. Here, too, they buried the three men who had succumbed to the sickness of the Boiling Sea, for the Vilmirians had refused to have them buried in the ocean on the grounds that the bodies would be "stewed like meat in a pot."

While the schooner lay at anchor, just off the island, Duke Avan called Elric to his cabin and showed him, for a second time, that ancient map.

Pale golden sunlight filtered through the cabin's ports and fell upon the old parchment, beaten from the skin of a beast long since extinct, as Elric and Duke Avan Astran of Old Hrolmar bent over it.

"See," Duke Avan said, pointing. "This island's marked. The map's scale seems reasonably accurate. Another three days and we shall be at the mouth of the river."

Elric nodded. "But it would be wise to rest here for a while until our strength is fully restored and the morale of the crew is raised higher. There are reasons, after all, why men have avoided the jungles of the west over the centuries."

"Certainly there are savages there—some say they are not even human—but I'm confident we can deal with those dangers. I have much experience of strange territories, Prince Elric."

"But you said yourself you feared other dangers."

"True. Very well, we'll do as you suggest."

On the fourth day a strong wind began to blow from the east and they raised anchor. The schooner leaped over the waves under only half her canvas and the crew saw this as a good omen.

"They are mindless fools," Smiorgan said as they stood clinging to the rigging in the prow. "The time will come when they will wish they were suffering the cleaner hardships of the Boiling Sea. This journey, Elric, could benefit none of us, even if the riches of R'lin K'ren A'a are still there."

But Elric did not answer. He was lost in strange thoughts, unusual thoughts for him, for he was remembering his childhood, his mother and his father. They had been the last true rulers of the Bright Empire —proud, insouciant, cruel. They had expected him—perhaps because of his strange albinism—to restore the glories of Melniboné. Instead he threatened to destroy what was left of that glory. They, like himself, had had no real place in this new age of the Young Kingdoms, but they had refused to acknowledge it. This journey to the western continent, to the land of his ancestors, had a peculiar attraction for him. Here no new nations had emerged. The continent had, as far as he knew, remained the same since R'lin K'ren A'a had been abandoned. The jungles would be the jungles his folk had known, the land would be the land that had given birth to his peculiar race, molded the character of its people with their somber pleasures, their melancholy arts, and their dark delights. Had his ancestors felt this agony of knowledge, this impotence in the face of the understanding that existence had no point, no purpose, no hope? Was this why they had built their civilization in that particular pattern, why they had disdained the more placid, spiritual values of mankind's philosophers? He knew that many of the intellectuals of the Young Kingdoms pitied the powerful folk of Melniboné as mad. But if they had been mad and if they had imposed a madness upon the world that had lasted a hundred centuries, what had made them so? Perhaps the secret did lie in R'lin K'ren A'a—not in any tangible form, but in the ambience created by the dark jungles and the deep, old rivers. Perhaps here, at last, he would be able to feel at one with himself.

He ran his fingers through his milk-white hair and there was a kind of innocent anguish in his crimson eyes. He might be the last of his kind and yet he was unlike his kind. Smiorgan had been wrong. Elric knew that everything that existed had its opposite. In danger he might find peace. And yet, of course, in peace there was danger. Being an imperfect creature in an imperfect world he would always know paradox. And that was why in paradox there was always a kind of truth. That was why philosophers and soothsayers flourished. In a perfect world there would be no place for them. In an imperfect world the mysteries were always without solution and that was why there was always a great choice of solutions.

It was on the morning of the third day that the coast was sighted and the schooner steered her way through the sandbanks of the great delta and anchored, at last, at the mouth of the dark and nameless river.

3

Evening came and the sun began to set over the black outlines of the massive trees. A rich, ancient smell came from the jungle and through the twilight echoed the cries of strange birds and beasts. Elric was impatient to begin the quest up the river. Sleep—never welcome—was now impossible to achieve. He stood unmoving on the deck, his eyes hardly blinking, his brain barely active, as if expecting something to happen to him. The rays of the sun stained his face and threw black shadows over the deck and then it was dark and still under the moon and the stars. He wanted the jungle to absorb him. He wanted to be one with the trees and the shrubs and the creeping beasts. He wanted thought to disappear. He drew the heavily scented air into his lungs as if that alone would make him become what at that moment he desired to be. The drone of insects became a murmuring voice that called him into the heart of the old, old forest. And yet he could not move—could not answer. And at length Count Smiorgan came up on deck and touched his shoulder and said something and passively he went below to his bunk and wrapped himself in his cloak and lay there, still listening to the voice of the jungle.

Even Duke Avan seemed in a more introspective mood than usual when they upped anchor the next morning and began to row against the sluggish current. There were few gaps in the foliage above their heads and they had the impression that they were entering a huge, gloomy tunnel, leaving the sunlight behind with the sea. Bright plants twined among the vines that hung from the leafy canopy and caught in the ship's masts as they moved. Ratlike animals with long arms swung through the branches and peered at them with bright, knowing eyes. The river turned and the sea was no longer in sight. Shafts of sunlight filtered down to the deck and the light had a greenish tinge to it. Elric became more alert than he had ever been since he agreed to accompany Duke Avan. He took a keen interest in every detail of the jungle and the black river over which moved schools of insects like agitated clouds of mist and in which blossoms drifted like drops of blood in ink. Everywhere were rustlings, sudden squawks, barks and wet noises made by fish or river animals as they hunted the prey disturbed by the ship's oars which cut into the great clumps of weed and sent the things that hid there scurrying. The others began to complain of insect bites, but Elric was not troubled by them, perhaps because no insect could desire his deficient blood.

Duke Avan passed him on the deck. The Vilmirian slapped at his forehead. "You seem more cheerful, Prince Elric."

Elric smiled absently. "Perhaps I am."

"I must admit I personally find all this a bit oppressive. I'll be glad when we reach the city."

"You are still convinced you'll find it?"

"I'll be convinced otherwise when I've explored every inch of the island we're bound for."

So absorbed had he become in the atmosphere of the jungle that Elric was hardly aware of the ship or his companions. The ship beat very slowly up the river, moving at little more than walking speed.

A few days passed, but Elric scarcely noticed, for the jungle did not change—and then the river widened and the canopy parted and the wide, hot sky was suddenly full of huge birds crowding upward as the ship disturbed them. All but Elric were pleased to be under the open sky again and spirits rose. Elric went below.

The attack on the ship came almost immediately. There was a whistling noise and a scream and a sailor writhed and fell over clutching at a gray thin semicircle of something which had buried itsef in his stomach. An upper yard came crashing to the deck, bringing sail and rigging with it. A headless body took four paces toward the poop deck before collapsing, the blood pumping from the obscene hole that was its neck. And everywhere was the thin whistling noise. Elric heard the sounds from below and came back instantly, buckling on his sword. The first face he saw was Smiorgan's. The bald-pated man looked perturbed as he crouched against a rail on the starboard side. Elric had the impression of gray blurs whistling past, slashing into flesh and rigging, wood and canvas. Some fell to the deck and he saw that they were thin disks of crystalline rock, about a foot in diameter. They were being hurled from both banks of the river and there was no protection against them.

He tried to see who was throwing the disks and glimpsed something moving in the trees along the right bank. Then the disks ceased suddenly and there was a pause before some of the sailors dashed across the deck to seek better cover. Duke Avan suddenly appeared in the stern. He had unsheathed his sword.

"Get below. Get your bucklers and any armor you can find. Bring bows. Arm yourselves, men, or you're finished."

And as he spoke their attackers broke from the trees and began to wade into the water. No more disks came and it seemed likely they had exhausted their supply.

"By Chardros!" Avan gasped. "Are these real creatures or some sorcerer's conjurings?"

The things were essentially reptilian but with feathery crests and neck wattles, though their faces were almost human. Their forelegs were like the arms and hands of men, but their hindlegs were incredibly long and storklike. Balanced on these legs, their bodies towered over the water. They carried great clubs in which slits had been cut and doubtless these were what they used to hurl the crystalline disks. Staring at their faces, Elric was horrified. In some subtle way they reminded him of the characteristic faces of his own folk—the folk of Melniboné. Were these creatures his cousins? Or were they a species from which his people had evolved? He stopped asking the questions as an intense hatred for the creatures filled him. They were obscene: sight of them brought bile into his throat. Without thinking, he drew Stormbringer from its sheath.

The Black Sword began to howl and the familiar black radiance spilled from it. The runes carved into its blade pulsed a vivid scarlet which turned slowly to a deep purple and then to black once more.

The creatures were wading through the water on their stiltlike legs and they paused when they saw the sword, glancing at one another. And they were not the only ones unnerved by the sight, for Duke Avan and his men paled, too.

"Gods!" Avan yelled. "I know not which I prefer the look of—those who attack us or that which defends us!"

"Stay well away from that sword," Smiorgan warned. "It has the habit of killing more than its master chooses."

And now the reptilian savages were upon them, clutching at the ship's rails as the armed sailors rushed back on deck to meet the attack.

Clubs came at Elric from all sides, but Stormbringer shrieked and parried each blow. He held the sword in both hands, whirling it this way and that, plowing great gashes in the scaly bodies.

The creatures hissed and opened red mouths in agony and rage while their thick, black blood sank into the waters of the river. Although from the legs upward they were only slightly larger than a tall, well-built man, they had more vitality than any human and the deepest cuts hardly seemed to affect them, even when administered by Stormbringer. Elric was astonished at this resistance to the sword's power. Often a nick was enough for the sword to draw a man's soul from him. These things seemed immune. Perhaps they had no souls. . . .

He fought on, his hatred giving him strength.

But elsewhere on the ship the sailors were being routed. Rails were torn off and the great clubs crushed planks and brought down more rigging. The savages were intent on destroying the ship as well as the crew. And there was little doubt, now, that they would be successful.

Avan shouted to Elric. "By the names of all the gods, Prince Elric, can you not summon some further sorcery? We are doomed else!"

Elric knew Avan spoke truth. All around him the ship was being gradually pulled apart by the hissing reptilian creatures. Most of them had sustained horrible wounds from the defenders, but only one or two had collapsed. Elric began to suspect that they did, in fact, fight supernatural enemies.

He backed away and sought shelter beneath a half-crushed doorway as he tried to concentrate on a method of calling upon supernatural aid.

He was panting with exhaustion and he clung to a beam as the ship rocked back and forth in the water. He fought to clear his head.

And then the incantation came to him. He was not sure if it was appropriate, but it was the only one he could recall. His ancestors had made pacts, thousands of years before, with all the elementals who controlled the animal world. In the past he had summoned help from various of these spirits but never from the one he now sought to call. From his mouth began to issue the ancient, beautiful, and convoluted words of Melniboné's High Speech.

"King with Wings! Lord of all that work and are not seen, upon whose labors all else depends! Nnuuurrrr'c'c of the Insect Folk, I summon thee!"

Save for the motion of the ship, Elric ceased to be aware of all else happening around him. The sounds of the fight dimmed and were heard no more as he sent his voice out beyond his plane of the Earth into another—the plane dominated by King Nnuuurrrr'c'c of the Insects, paramount lord of his people.

In his ears now Elric heard a buzzing and gradually the buzzing formed itself in words.

"Who art thou, mortal? What right hast thou to summon me?"

"I am Elric, ruler of Melniboné. My ancestors aided thee, Nnuuurrrr'c'c."

"Aye—but long ago."

"And it is long ago that they last called on thee for thine aid!"

"True. What aid dost thou now require, Elric of Melniboné?"

"Look upon my plane. Thou wilt see that I am in danger. Canst thou abolish this danger, friend of the Insects?"

Now a filmy shape formed and could be seen as if through several layers of cloudy silk. Elric tried to keep his eyes upon it, but it kept leaving his field of vision and then returning for a few moments. He knew that he looked into another plane of the Earth.

"Canst thou help me, Nnuuurrrr'c'c?"

"Hast thou no patron of thine own species? Some Lord of Chaos who can aid thee?"

"My patron is Arioch and he is a temperamental demon at best. These days he aids me little."

"Then I must send thee allies, mortal. But call upon me no more when this is done."

"I shall not summon thee again, Nnuuurrrr'c'c."

The layers of film disappeared and with them the shape.

The noise of the battle crashed once again on Elric's consciousness and he heard with sharper clarity than before the screams of the sailors and the hissing of the reptilian savages and when he looked out from his shelter he saw that at least half the crew were dead.

As he came on deck Smiorgan ran up. "I thought you slain, Elric!

What became of you?" He was plainly relieved to see his friend still lived.

"I sought aid from another plane—but it does not seem to have materialized."

"I'm thinking we're doomed and had best try to swim downstream away from here and seek a hiding place in the jungle," Smiorgan said.

"What of Duke Avan? Is he dead?"

"He lives. But those creatures are all but impervious to our weapons. This ship will sink ere long." Smiorgan lurched as the deck tilted and he reached out to grab a trailing rope, letting his long sword dangle by its wrist-thong. "They are not attacking the stern at present. We can slip into the water there. . . ."

"I made a bargain with Duke Avan," Elric reminded the islander. "I cannot desert him."

"Then we'll all perish!"

"What's that?" Elric bent his head, listening intently.

"I hear nothing."

It was a whine which deepened in tone until it became a drone. Now Smiorgan heard it also and looked about him, seeking the source of the sound. And suddenly he gasped, pointing upward. "Is that the aid you sought?"

There was a vast cloud of them, black against the blue of the sky. Every so often the sun would flash on a dazzling color—a rich blue, green, or red. They came spiraling down toward the ship and now both sides fell silent, staring skyward.

The flying things were like huge dragonflies and the brightness and richness of their coloring was breathtaking. It was their wings which made the droning sound which now began to increase in loudness and heighten in pitch as the huge insects sped nearer.

Realizing that they were the object of the attack the reptile men stumbled backward on their long legs, trying to reach the shore before the gigantic insects were upon them.

But it was too late for flight.

The dragonflies settled on the savages until nothing could be seen of their bodies. The hissing increased and sounded almost pitiful as the insects bore their victims down to the surface and then inflicted on them whatever terrible death it was. Perhaps they stung with their tails—it was not possible for the watchers to see.

Sometimes a storklike leg would emerge from the water and thrash in the air for a moment. But soon, just as the reptiles were covered by the insect bodies, so were their cries drowned by the stange and blood-chilling humming that arose on all sides.

A sweating Duke Avan, sword still in hand, ran up the deck. "Is this your doing, Prince Elric?"

Elric looked on with satisfaction, but the others were plainly disgusted. "It was," he said.

"Then I thank you for your aid. This ship is holed in a dozen places and is letting in water at a terrible rate. It's a wonder we have not yet sunk. I've given orders to begin rowing and I hope we make it to the island in time." He pointed upstream. "There, you can just see it."

"What if there are more of those savages there?" Smiorgan asked.

Avan smiled grimly, indicating the farther shore. "Look." On their peculiar legs a dozen or more of the reptiles were fleeing into the jungle, having witnessed the fate of their comrades. "They'll be reluctant to attack us again, I think."

Now the huge dragonflies were rising into the air again and Avan turned away as he glimpsed what they had left behind. "By the gods, you work fierce sorcery, Prince Elric! Ugh!"

Elric smiled and shrugged. "It is effective, Duke Avan." He sheathed his runesword. It seemed reluctant to enter the scabbard and it moaned as if in resentment.

Smiorgan glanced at it. "That blade looks as if it will want to feast soon, Elric, whether you desire it or not."

"Doubtless it will find something to feed on in the forest," said the albino. He stepped over a piece of broken mast and went below.

Count Smiorgan Baldhead looked at the new scum on the surface of the water and he shuddered.

4

The wrecked schooner was almost awash when the crew clambered overboard with lines and began the task of dragging it up the mud that formed the banks of the island. Before them was a wall of foliage that seemed impenetrable. Smiorgan followed Elric, lowering himself into the shallows. They began to wade ashore.

As they left the water and set foot on the hard, baked earth, Smiorgan stared at the forest. No wind moved the trees and a peculiar silence had descended. No birds called from the trees, no insects buzzed, there were none of the barks and cries of animals they had heard on their journey upriver.

"Those supernatural friends of yours seem to have frightened more than the savages away," the black-bearded man murmured. "This place seems lifeless."

Elric nodded. "It is strange."

Duke Avan joined them. He had discarded his finery—ruined in the fight, anyway—and now wore a padded leather jerkin and doeskin breeches. His sword was at his side. "We'll have to leave most of our men behind with the ship," he said regretfully. "They'll make what repairs they can while we press on to find R'lin K'ren A'a." He tugged his light cloak about him. "Is it my imagination, or is there an odd atmosphere?"

"We have already remarked on it," Smiorgan said. "Life seems to have fled the island."

Duke Avan grinned. "If all we face is as timid, we have nothing further to fear. I must admit, Prince Elric, that had I wished you harm and then seen you conjure those monsters from thin air, I'd think twice about getting too close to you! Thank you, by the way, for what you did. We should have perished by now if it had not been for you."

"It was for my aid that you asked me to accompany you," Elric said wearily. "Let's eat and rest and then continue with our expedition."

A shadow passed over Duke Avan's face then. Something in Elric's manner had disturbed him.

Entering the jungle was no easy matter. Armed with axes the six members of the crew (all that could be spared) began to hack at the undergrowth. And still the unnatural silence prevailed. . . .

By nightfall they were less than half a mile into the forest and completely exhausted. The forest was so thick that there was barely room to pitch their tent. The only light in the camp came from the small, sputtering fire outside the tent. The crewmen slept where they could in the open.

Elric could not sleep, but now it was not the jungle which kept him awake. He was puzzled by the silence, for he was sure that it was not their presence which had driven all life away. There was not a single small rodent, bird, or insect anywhere to be seen. There were no traces of animal life. The island had been deserted of all but vegetation for a long while—perhaps for centuries or tens of centuries. He remembered another part of the old legend of R'lin K'ren A'a. It had been said that when the gods came to meet there not only the citizens fled, but also all the wildlife. Nothing had dared see the High Lords or listen to their conversation. Elric shivered, turning his white head this way and that on the rolled cloak that supported it, his crimson eyes tortured. If there were dangers on this island, they would be subtler dangers than those they had faced on the river.

The noise of their passage through the forest was the only sound to be heard on the island as they forced their way on the next morning.

With lodestone in one hand and map in the other, Duke Avan Astran sought to guide them, directing his men where to cut their path. But the going became even slower and it was obvious that no creatures had come this way for many ages.

By the fourth day they had reached a natural clearing of flat volcanic rock and found a spring there. Gratefully they made camp. Elric began to wash his face in the cool water when he heard a yell behind him. He sprang up. One of the crewmen was reaching for an arrow and fitting it to his bow.

"What is it?" Duke Avan called.

"I saw something, my lord!"

"Nonsense, there are no—"

"Look!" the man drew back the string and let fly into the upper terraces of the forest. Something did seem to stir then and Elric thought he saw a flash of gray among the trees.

"Did you see what kind of creature it was?" Smiorgan asked the man.

"No, master. I feared at first it was those reptiles again."

"They're too frightened to follow us onto this island," Duke Avan reassured him.

"I hope you're right," Smiorgan said nervously.

"Then what could it have been?" Elric wondered.

"I—I thought it was a man, master," the crewman stuttered.

Elric stared thoughtfully into the trees. "A man?"

Smiorgan asked, "You were hoping for this, Elric?"

"I am not sure. . . ."

Duke Avan shrugged. "More likely the shadow of a cloud passing over the trees. According to my calculations we should have reached the city by now."

"You think, after all, that it does not exist?" Elric said.

"I am beginning not to care, Prince Elric." The duke leaned against the bole of a huge tree, brushing aside a vine which touched his face. "Still there's naught else to do. The ship won't be ready to sail yet." He looked up into the branches. "I did not think I should miss those damned insects that plagued us on our way here. . . ."

The crewman who had shot the arrow suddenly shouted again. "There! I saw him! It is a man!"

While the others stared but failed to discern anything Duke Avan continued to lean against the tree. "You saw nothing. There is nothing here to see."

Elric turned toward him. "Give me the map and the lodestone, Duke Avan. I have a feeling I can find the way."

The Vilmirian shrugged, an expression of doubt on his square, handsome face. He handed the things over to Elric.

They rested the night and in the morning they continued, with Elric leading the way.

And at noon they broke out of the forest and saw the ruins of R'lin K'ren A'a.

5

Nothing grew among the ruins of the city. The streets were broken and the walls of the houses had fallen, but there were no weeds flowering in the cracks and it seemed that the city had but recently been brought down by an earthquake. Only one thing still stood intact, towering over the ruins. It was a gigantic statue of white, gray, and green jade—the statue of a naked youth with a face of almost feminine beauty that turned sightless eyes toward the north.

"The eyes!" Duke Avan Astran said. "They're gone!"

The others said nothing as they stared at the statue and the ruins surrounding it. The area was relatively small and the buildings had had little decoration. The inhabitants seemed to have been a simple, well-to-do folk—totally unlike the Melnibonéans of the Bright Empire. Elric could not believe that the people of R'lin K'ren A'a had been his ancestors. They had been too sane.

"The statue's already been looted," Duke Avan continued. "Our damned journey's been in vain!"

Elric laughed. "Did you really think you would be able to prise the Jade Man's eyes from their sockets, my lord?"

The statue was as tall as any tower of the Dreaming City and the head alone must have been the size of a reasonably large building. Duke Avan pursed his lips and refused to listen to Elric's mocking voice. "We may yet find the journey worth our while," he said. "There were other treasures in R'lin K'ren A'a. Come. . . ."

He led the way into the city.

Very few of the buildings were even partially standing, but they were nonetheless fascinating if only for the peculiar nature of their building materials, which were of a kind the travelers had never seen before.

The colors were many, but faded by time—soft reds and yellows and blues—and they flowed together to make almost infinite combinations.

Elric reached out to touch one wall and was surprised at the cool feel of the smooth material. It was neither stone nor wood nor metal. Perhaps it had been brought here from another plane?

He tried to visualize the city as it had been before it was deserted. The streets had been wide, there had been no surrounding wall, the houses had been low and built around large courtyards. If this was, indeed, the original home of his people, what had happened to change them from the peaceful citizens of R'lin K'ren A'a to the insane builders of Imrryr's bizarre and dreaming towers? Elric had thought he might find a solution to a mystery here, but instead he had found another mystery. It was his fate, he thought, shrugging to himself.

And then the first crystal disk hummed past his head and smashed against a collapsing wall.

The next disk split the skull of a crewman and a third nicked Smiorgan's ear before they had thrown themselves flat among the rubble.

"They're vengeful, those creatures," Avan said with a hard smile. "They'll risk much to pay us back for their comrades' deaths!"

Terror was on the face of each surviving crewman and fear had begun to creep into Avan's eyes.

More disks clattered nearby, but it was plain that the party was temporarily out of sight of the reptiles. Smiorgan coughed as white dust rose from the rubble and caught in his throat.

"You'd best summon those monstrous allies of yours again, Elric."

Elric shook his head. "I cannot. My ally said he would not serve me a second time." He looked to his left where the four walls of a small house still stood. There seemed to be no door, only a window.

"Then call something," Count Smiorgan said urgently. "Anything."

"I am not sure. . . ."

Then Elric rolled over and sprang for the shelter, flinging himself through the window to land on a pile of masonry that grazed his hands and knees.

He staggered upright. In the distance he could see the huge blind statue of the god dominating the city. This was said to be an image of Arioch—though it resembled no image of Arioch Elric had ever seen manifested. Did that image protect R'lin K'ren A'a—or did it threaten it? Someone screamed. He glanced through the opening and saw that a disk had landed and chopped through a man's forearm.

He drew Stormbringer and raised it, facing the jade statue.

"Arioch!" he cried. "Arioch—aid me!"

Black light burst from the blade and it began to sing, as if joining in Elric's incantation.

"Arioch!"

Would the demon come? Often the patron of the kings of Melniboné refused to materialize, claiming that more urgent business called him— business concerning the eternal struggle between Law and Chaos.

"Arioch!"

Sword and man were now wreathed in a palpitating black mist and Elric's white face was flung back, seeming to writhe as the mist writhed.

"Arioch! I beg thee to aid me! It is Elric who calls thee!"

And then a voice reached his ears. It was a soft, purring, reasonable voice. It was a tender voice.

"Elric, I am fondest of thee. I love thee more than any other mortal —but aid thee I cannot—not yet."

Elric cried desperately: "Then we are doomed to perish here!"

"Thou canst escape this danger. Flee alone into the forest. Leave the others while thou hast time. Thou hast a destiny to fulfill elsewhere and elsewhen. . . ."

"I will not desert them."

"Thou art foolish, sweet Elric."

"Arioch—since Melniboné's founding thou hast aided her kings. Aid her last king this day!"

"I cannot dissipate my energies. A great struggle looms. And it would cost me much to return to R'lin K'ren A'a. Flee now. Thou shalt be saved. Only the others will die."

And then the Duke of Hell had gone. Elric sensed the passing of his presence. He frowned, fingering his belt pouch, trying to recall something he had once heard. Slowly, he resheathed the reluctant sword. Then there was a thump and Smiorgan stood panting before him.

"Well, is aid on the way?"

"I fear not." Elric shook his head in despair. "Once again Arioch refuses me. Once again he speaks of a greater destiny—a need to conserve his strength."

"Your ancestors could have picked a more tractable demon as their patron. Our reptilian friends are closing in. Look. . . ." Smiorgan pointed to the outskirts of the city. A band of about a dozen stilt-legged creatures were advancing, their huge clubs at the ready.

There was a scuffling noise from the rubble on the other side of the wall and Avan appeared, leading his men through the opening. He was cursing.

"No extra aid is coming, I fear," Elric told him.

The Vilmirian smiled grimly. "Then the monsters out there knew more than did we!"

"It seems so."

"We'll have to try to hide from them," Smiorgan said without much conviction. "We'd not survive a fight."

The little party left the ruined house and began to inch its way through what cover it could find, moving gradually nearer to the center of the city and the statue of the Jade Man.

A sharp hiss from behind them told them that the reptile warriors had sighted them again and another Vilmirian fell with a crystal disk protruding from his back. They broke into a panicky run.

Ahead now was a red building of several stories which still had its roof.

"In there!" Duke Avan shouted.

With some relief they dashed unhesitatingly up worn steps and through a series of dusty passages until they paused to catch their breath in a great, gloomy hall.

The hall was completely empty and a little light filtered through cracks in the wall.

"This place has lasted better than the others," Duke Avan said. "I wonder what its function was. A fortress, perhaps."

"They seem not to have been a warlike race," Smiorgan pointed out. "I suspect the building had some other function."

The three surviving crewmen were looking fearfully about them. They looked as if they would have preferred to have faced the reptile warriors outside.

Elric began to cross the floor and then paused as he saw something painted on the far wall.

Smiorgan saw it too. "What's that, friend Elric?"

Elric recognized the symbols as the written High Speech of old Melniboné, but it was subtly different and it took him a short time to decipher its meaning.

"Know you what it says, Elric?" Duke Avan murmured, joining them.

"Aye—but it's cryptic enough. It says: 'If thou hast come to slay me, then thou art welcome. If thou hast come without the means to awaken the Jade Man, then begone. . . .'"

"Is it addressed to us, I wonder," Avan mused, "or has it been there for a long while?"

Elric shrugged. "It could have been inscribed at any time during the past ten thousand years. . . ."

Smiorgan walked up to the wall and reached out to touch it. "I would say it was fairly recent," he said. "The paint still being wet."

Elric frowned. "Then there are inhabitants here still. Why do they not reveal themselves?"

"Could those reptiles out there be the denizens of R'lin K'ren A'a?" Avan said. "There is nothing in the legends that says they were humans who fled this place. . . ."

Elric's face clouded and he was about to make an angry reply when Smiorgan interrupted.

"Perhaps there is just one inhabitant. Is that what you are thinking, Elric? The Creature Doomed to Live? Those sentiments could be his. . . ."

Elric put his hands to his face and made no reply.

"Come," Avan said. "We've no time to debate on legends." He strode across the floor and entered another doorway, beginning to descend steps. As he reached the bottom they heard him gasp.

The others joined him and saw that he stood on the threshold of another hall. But this one was ankle-deep in fragments of stuff that had been thin leaves of a metallic material which had the flexibility of parchment. Around the walls were thousands of small holes, rank upon rank, each with a character painted over it.

"What is it?" Smiorgan asked.

Elric stooped and picked up one of the fragments. This had half a Melnibonéan character engraved on it. There had even been an attempt to obliterate this.

"It was a library," he said softly. "The library of my ancestors. Someone has tried to destroy it. These scrolls must have been virtually indestructible, yet a great deal of effort has gone into making them indecipherable." He kicked at the fragments. "Plainly our friend—or friends—is a consistent hater of learning."

"Plainly," Avan said bitterly. "Oh, the *value* of those scrolls to the scholar! All destroyed!"

Elric shrugged. "To Limbo with the scholar—their value to me was quite considerable!"

Smiorgan put a hand on his friend's arm and Elric shrugged it off. "I had hoped . . ."

Smiorgan cocked his bald head. "Those reptiles have followed us into the building, by the sound of it."

They heard the distant sound of strange footsteps in the passages behind them.

The little band of men moved as silently as they could through the ruined scrolls and crossed the hall until they entered another corridor which led sharply upward.

Then, suddenly, daylight was visible.

Elric peered ahead. "The corridor has collapsed ahead of us and is blocked, by the look of it. The roof has caved in and we may be able to escape through the hole."

They clambered upward over the fallen stones, glancing warily behind them for signs of their pursuers.

At last they emerged in the central square of the city. On the far sides of this square were placed the feet of the great statue, which now towered high above their heads.

Directly before them were two peculiar constructions which, unlike the rest of the buildings, were completely whole. They were domed and faceted and were made of some glasslike substance which defracted the rays of the sun.

From below they heard the reptile men advancing down the corridor.

"We'll seek shelter in the nearest of those domes," Elric said. He broke into a trot, leading the way.

The others followed him through the irregularly shaped opening at the base of the dome.

Once inside, however, they hesitated, shielding their eyes and blinking heavily as they tried to discern their way.

"It's like a maze of mirrors!" Smiorgan gasped. "By the gods, I've never seen a better. Was that its function, I wonder."

Corridors seemed to go off in all directions—yet they might be nothing more than reflections of the passage they were in. Cautiously Elric began to continue farther into the maze, the five others following him.

"This smells of sorcery to me," Smiorgan muttered as they advanced. "Have we been forced into a trap, I wonder."

Elric drew his sword. It murmured softly—almost querulously.

Everything shifted suddenly and the shapes of his companions grew dim.

"Smiorgan! Duke Avan!"

He heard voices murmuring, but they were not the voices of his friends.

"Count Smiorgan!"

But then the burly sea-lord faded away altogether and Elric was alone.

6

He turned and a wall of red brilliance struck his eyes and blinded him.

He called out and his voice was turned into a dismal wail which mocked him.

He tried to move, but he could not tell whether he remained in the same spot or walked a dozen miles.

Now there was someone standing a few yards away, seemingly obscured by a screen of multicolored transparent gems. He stepped forward and made to dash away the screen, but it vanished and he stopped suddenly.

He looked on a face of infinite sorrow.

And the face was his own face, save that the man's coloring was normal and his hair was black.

"What are you?" Elric said thickly.

"I have had many names. One is Erekosë. I have been many men. Perhaps I am all men."

"But you are like me!"

"I am you."

"No!"

The phantom's eyes held tears as it stared in pity at Elric.

"Do not weep for me!" Elric roared. "I need no sympathy from you!"

"Perhaps I weep for myself, for I know our fate."

"And what is that?"

"You would not understand."

"Tell me."

"Ask your gods."

Elric raised his sword. Fiercely he said, "No—I'll have my answer from you!"

And the phantom faded away.

Elric shivered. Now the corridor was populated by a thousand such phantoms. Each murmured a different name. Each wore different clothes. But each had his face, if not his coloring.

"Begone!" he screamed. "Oh, Gods, what is this place?"

And at his command they disappeared.

"Elric?"

The albino whirled, sword ready. But it was Duke Avan Astran of Old Hrolmar. He touched his own face with trembling fingers, but said levelly, "I must tell you that I believe I am losing my sanity, Prince Elric. . . ."

"What have you seen?"

"Many things. I cannot describe them."

"Where are Smiorgan and the others?"

"Doubtless each went his separate way, as we did."

Elric raised Stormbringer and brought the blade crashing against a crystal wall. The Black Sword moaned, but the wall merely changed its position.

But through a gap now Elric saw ordinary daylight. "Come, Duke Avan—there is escape!"

Avan, dazed, followed him and they stepped out of the crystal and found themselves in the central square of R'lin K'ren A'a.

But there were noises. Carts and chariots moved about the square. Stalls were erected on one side. People moved peacefully about. And the Jade Man did not dominate the sky above the city. Here, there was no Jade Man at all.

Elric looked at the faces. They were the eldritch features of the folk of Melniboné. Yet these had a different cast to them which he could not at first define. Then he recognized what they had. It was tranquillity. He reached out his hand to touch one of the people.

"Tell me, friend, what year . . . ?"

But the man did not hear him. He walked by.

Elric tried to stop several of the passersby, but not one could see or hear him.

"How did they lose this peace?" Duke Avan asked wonderingly. "How did they become like you, Prince Elric?"

Elric almost snarled as he turned sharply to face the Vilmirian. "Be silent!"

Duke Avan shrugged. "Perhaps this is merely an illusion."

"Perhaps," Elric said sadly, "but I am sure this is how they lived—until the coming of the High Ones."

"You blame the gods, then?"

"I blame the despair that the gods brought."

Duke Avan nodded gravely. "I understand."

He turned back toward the great crystal and then stood listening. "Do you hear that voice, Prince Elric? What is it saying?"

Elric heard the voice. It seemed to be coming from the crystal. It was speaking the old tongue of Melniboné, but with a strange accent. "This way," it said. "This way."

Elric paused. "I have no liking to return there."

Avan said, "What choice have we?"

They stepped together through the entrance.

Again they were in the maze that could be one corridor or many and the voice was clearer. "Take two paces to your right," it instructed.

Avan glanced at Elric. "What was that?" Elric told him. "Shall we obey?" Avan asked.

"Aye." There was resignation in the albino's voice.

They took two paces to their right.

"Now four to your left," said the voice.

They took four paces to their left.

"Now one forward."

They emerged into the ruined square of R'lin K'ren A'a.

Smiorgan and one Vilmirian crewman stood there.

"Where are the others?" Avan demanded.

"Ask him," Smiorgan said wearily, gesturing with the sword in his right hand.

They stared at the man who was either an albino or a leper. He was completely naked and he bore a distinct likeness to Elric. At first Elric thought this was another phantom, but then he saw that there were also several differences in their faces. There was something sticking from the man's side, just above the third rib. With a shock, Elric recognized it as the broken shaft of a Vilmirian arrow.

The naked man nodded. "Aye—the arrow found its mark. But it could not slay me, for I am J'osui C'reln Reyr. . . ."

"You believe yourself to be the Creature Doomed to Live," Elric murmured.

"I am he." The man gave a bitter smile. "Do you think I try to deceive you?"

Elric glanced at the arrow shaft and then shook his head.

"You are ten thousand years old?" Avan stared at him.

"What does he say?" asked J'osui C'reln Reyr of Elric. Elric translated.

"Is that all it has been?" The man sighed. Then he looked intently at Elric. "You are of my race?"

"It seems so."

"Of what family?"

"Of the royal line."

"Then you have come at last. I, too, am of that line."

"I believe you."

"I notice that the Olab seek you."

"The Olab?"

"Those primitives with the clubs."

"Aye. We encountered them on our journey upriver."

"I will lead you to safety. Come."

Elric allowed J'osui C'reln Reyr to take them across the square to where part of a tottering wall still stood. The man then lifted a flagstone and showed them the steps leading down into darkness. They followed him, descending cautiously as he caused the flagstone to lower itself above their heads. And then they found themselves in a room lit by crude oil lamps. Save for a bed of dried grasses the room was empty.

"You live sparely," Elric said.

"I have need for nothing else. My head is sufficiently furnished. . . ."

"Where do the Olab come from?" Elric asked.

"They are but recently arrived in these parts. Scarcely a thousand years ago—or perhaps half that time—they came from farther upriver after some quarrel with another tribe. They do not usually come to the island. You must have killed many of them for them to wish you such harm."

"We killed many."

J'osui C'reln Reyr gestured at the others who were staring at him in some discomfort. "And these? Primitives, also, eh? They are not of our folk."

"There are few of our folk left."

"What does he say?" Duke Avan asked.

"He says that those reptile warriors are called the Olab," Elric told him.

"And was it these Olab who stole the Jade Man's eyes?"

When Elric translated the question the Creature Doomed to Live was astonished. "Did you not know, then?"

"Know what?"

"Why, you have been *in* the Jade Man's eyes! Those great crystals in which you wandered—that is what they are!"

7

When Elric offered this information to Duke Avan, the Vilmirian burst into laughter. He flung his head back and roared with mirth while the others looked gloomily on. The cloud that had fallen across his features of late suddenly cleared and he became again the man whom Elric had first met.

Smiorgan was the next to smile and even Elric acknowledged the irony of what had happened to them.

"Those crystals fell from his face like tears soon after the High Ones departed," continued J'osui C'reln Reyr.

"So the High Ones did come here."

"Aye—the Jade Man brought the message and all the folk departed, having made their bargain with him."

"The Jade Man was not built by your people?"

"The Jade Man is Duke Arioch of Hell. He strode from the forest one day and stood in the square and told the people what was to come about—that our city lay at the center of some particular configuration and that it was only there that the Lords of the Higher Worlds could meet."

"And the bargain?"

"In return for their city, our royal line might in the future increase their power with Arioch as their patron. He would give them great knowledge and the means to build a new city elsewhere."

"And they accepted this bargain without question?"

"There was little choice, kinsman."

Elric lowered his eyes to regard the dusty floor. "And thus they were corrupted," he murmured.

"Only I refused to accept the pact. I did not wish to leave this city and I mistrusted Arioch. When all others set off down the river, I remained here—where we are now—and I heard the Lords of the Higher Worlds arrive and I heard them speak, laying down the rules under which Law and Chaos would fight thereafter. When they had gone, I emerged. But Arioch—the Jade Man—was still here. He looked down on me through his crystal eyes and he cursed me. When that was done the crystals fell and landed where you now see them. Arioch's spirit departed, but his jade image was left behind."

"And you still retain all memory of what transpired between the Lords of Law and Chaos?"

"That is my doom."

"Perhaps your fate was less harsh than that which befell those who left," Elric said quietly. "I am the last inheritor of that particular doom. . . ."

J'osui C'reln Reyr looked puzzled and then he stared into Elric's eyes and an expression of pity crossed his face. "I had not thought there was a worse fate—but now I believe there might be. . . ."

Elric said urgently, "Ease my soul, at least. I must know what passed between the High Lords in those days. I must understand the nature of my existence—as you, at least, understand yours. Tell me, I beg you!"

J'osui C'reln Reyr frowned and he stared deeply into Elric's eyes. "Do you not know all my story, then?"

"Is there more?"

"I can only *remember* what passed between the High Lords—but when I try to tell my knowledge aloud or try to write it down, I cannot.
. . ."

Elric grasped the man's shoulder. "You must try! You must try!"

"I know that I cannot."

Seeing the torture in Elric's face, Smiorgan came up to him. "What is it, Elric?"

Elric's hand clutched his head. "Our journey has been useless." Unconsciously he used the old Melnibonéan tongue.

"It need not be," said J'osui C'reln Reyr. "For me, at least." He paused. "Tell me, how did you find this city? Was there a map?"

Elric produced the map. "This one."

"Aye, that is the one. Many centuries ago I put it into a casket which I placed in a small trunk. I launched the trunk into the river, hoping that it would follow my people and they would know what it was."

"The casket was found in Melniboné, but no one had bothered to open it," Elric explained. "That will give you an idea of what happened to the folk who left here. . . ."

The strange man nodded gravely. "And was there still a seal upon the map?"

"There was. I have it."

"An image of one of the manifestations of Arioch, embedded in a small ruby?"

"Aye. I thought I recognized the image, but I could not place it."

"The Image in the Gem," murmured J'osui C'reln Reyr. "As I prayed, it has returned—borne by one of the royal line!"

"What is its significance?"

Smiorgan interrupted. "Will this fellow help us to escape, Elric? We are becoming somewhat impatient. . . ."

"Wait," the albino said. "I will tell you everything later."

"The Image in the Gem could be the instrument of my release," said the Creature Doomed to Live. "If he who possesses it is of the royal line, then he can command the Jade Man."

"But why did you not use it?"

"Because of the curse that was put on me. I had the power to command, but not to summon the demon. It was a joke, I understand, of the High Lords."

Elric saw bitter sadness in the eyes of J'osui C'reln Reyr. He looked at the white, naked flesh and the white hair and the body that was neither old nor young, at the shaft of the arrow sticking out above the third rib on the left side.

"What must I do?" he asked.

"You must summon Arioch and then you must command him to enter his body again and recover his eyes so that he may see to walk away from R'lin K'ren A'a."

"And when he walks away?"

"The curse goes with him."

Elric was thoughtful. If he did summon Arioch—who was plainly reluctant to come—and then commanded him to do something he did not wish to do, he stood the chance of making an enemy of that powerful, if unpredictable entity. Yet they were trapped here by the Olab warriors, with no means of escaping them. If the Jade Man walked, the Olab would almost certainly flee and there would be time to get back to the ship and reach the sea. He explained everything to his companions. Both Smiorgan and Avan looked dubious and the remaining Vilmirian crewman looked positively terrified.

"I must do it," Elric decided, "for the sake of this man. I must call Arioch and lift the doom that is on R'lin K'ren A'a."

"And bring a greater doom to us!" Duke Avan said, putting his hand automatically upon his sword-hilt. "No. I think we should take our chances with the Olab. Leave this man—he is mad—he raves. Let's be on our way."

"Go if you choose," Elric said. "But I will stay with the Creature Doomed to Live."

"Then you will stay here forever. You cannot believe his story!"

"But I do believe it."

"You must come with us. Your sword will help. Without it, the Olab will certainly destroy us."

"You saw that Stormbringer has little effect against the Olab."

"And yet it has some. Do not desert me, Elric!"

"I am not deserting you. I must summon Arioch. That summoning will be to your benefit, if not to mine."

"I am unconvinced."

"It was my sorcery you wanted on this venture. Now you shall have my sorcery."

Avan backed away. He seemed to fear something more than the Olab, more than the summoning. He seemed to read a threat in Elric's face of which even Elric was unaware.

"We must go outside," said J'osui C'reln Reyr. "We must stand beneath the Jade Man."

"And when this is done," Elric asked suddenly, "how will we leave R'lin K'ren A'a?"

"There is a boat. It has no provisions, but much of the city's treasure is on it. It lies at the west end of the island."

"That is some comfort," Elric said. "And you could not use it yourself?"

"I could not leave."

"Is that part of the curse?"

"Aye—the curse of my timidity."

"Timidity has kept you here ten thousand years?"

"Aye. . . ."

They left the chamber and went out into the square. Night had fallen and a huge moon was in the sky. From where Elric stood it seemed to frame the Jade Man's sightless head like a halo. It was completely silent. Elric took the Image in the Gem from his pouch and held it between the forefinger and thumb of his left hand. With his right he drew Stormbringer. Avan, Smiorgan, and the Vilmirian crewman fell back.

He stared up at the huge jade legs, the genitals, the torso, the arms, the head, and he raised his sword in both hands and screamed:

"Arioch!"

Stormbringer's voice almost drowned his. It pulled in his hands; it threatened to leave his grasp altogether as it howled.

"Arioch!"

All the watchers saw now was the throbbing, radiant sword, the white face and hands of the albino and his crimson eyes glaring through the blackness.

"Arioch!"

And then a voice which was not Arioch's came to Elric's ears and it seemed that the sword itself spoke.

"Elric—Arioch must have blood and souls. Blood and souls, my lord. . . ."

"No. These are my friends and the Olab cannot be harmed by Stormbringer. Arioch must come without the blood, without the souls."

"Only those can summon him for certain!" said a voice, more clearly now. It was sardonic and it seemed to come from behind him. He turned, but there was nothing there.

He saw Duke Avan's nervous face, and as his eyes fixed on the Vilmirian's countenance, the sword swung around, twisting against Elric's grip, and plunging toward the duke.

"No!" cried Elric. "Stop!"

But Stormbringer would not stop until it had plunged deep into Duke Avan's heart and quenched its thirst. The crewman stood transfixed as he watched his master die.

Duke Avan writhed. "Elric! What treachery do you . . . ?" He screamed. "Ah, no!"

He jerked. "Please . . ."

He quivered. "My soul . . ."

He died.

Elric withdrew the sword and cut the crewman down as he ran to his master's aid. The action had been without thought.

"Now Arioch has his blood and his souls," he said coldly. "Let Arioch come!"

Smiorgan and the Creature Doomed to Live had retreated, staring at the possessed Elric in horror. The albino's face was cruel.

"Let Arioch come!"

"I am here, Elric."

Elric whirled and saw that something stood in the shadow of the statue's legs—a shadow within a shadow.

"Arioch—thou must return to this manifestation and make it leave R'lin K'ren A'a forever."

"I do not choose to, Elric."

"Then I must command thee, Duke Arioch."

"Command? Only he who possesses the Image in the Gem may command Arioch—and then only once."

"I have the Image in the Gem." Elric held up the tiny object. "See."

The shadow within a shadow swirled for a moment as if in anger.

"If I obey your command, you will set in motion a chain of events which you might not desire," Arioch said, speaking suddenly in Low Melnibonéan as if to give extra gravity to his words.

"Then let it be. I command you to enter the Jade Man and pick up its eyes so that it might walk again. Then I command you to leave here and take the curse of the High Ones with you."

Arioch replied, "When the Jade Man ceases to guard the place where the High Ones meet, then the great struggle of the Upper Worlds begins on this plane."

"I command thee, Arioch. Go into the Jade Man!"

"You are an obstinate creature, Elric."

"Go!" Elric raised Stormbringer. It seemed to sing in monstrous glee and it seemed at that moment to be more powerful than Arioch himself, more powerful than all the Lords of the Higher Worlds.

The ground shook. Fire suddenly blazed around the form of the great statue. The shadow within a shadow disappeared.

And the Jade Man stooped.

Its great bulk bent over Elric and its hands reached past him and it groped for the two crystals that lay on the ground. Then it found them and took one in each hand, straightening its back.

Elric stumbled toward the far corner of the square where Smiorgan and J'osui C'reln Reyr already crouched in terror.

A fierce light now blazed from the Jade Man's eyes and the jade lips parted.

"It is done, Elric!" said a huge voice.

J'osui C'reln Reyr began to sob.

"Then go, Arioch."

"I go. The curse is lifted from R'lin K'ren A'a and from J'osui C'reln Reyr—but a greater curse now lies upon your whole plane."

"What is this, Arioch? Explain yourself!" Elric cried.

"Soon you will have your explanation. Farewell!"

The enormous legs of jade moved suddenly and in a single step had cleared the ruins and had begun to crash through the jungle. In a moment the Jade Man had disappeared.

Then the Creature Doomed to Live laughed. It was a strange joy that he voiced. Smiorgan blocked his ears.

"And now!" shouted J'osui C'reln Reyr. "Now your blade must take my life. I can die at last!"

Elric passed his hand across his face. He had hardly been aware of any of the recent events. "No," he said in a dazed tone. "I cannot. . . ."

And Stormbringer flew from his hand—flew to the body of the Creature Doomed to Live and buried itself in its chest.

And as he died, J'osui C'reln Reyr laughed. He fell to the ground and his lips moved. A whisper came from them. Elric stepped nearer to hear.

"The sword has my knowledge now. My burden has left me."

The eyes closed.

J'osui C'reln Reyr's ten-thousand-year life-span had ended.

Weakly, Elric withdrew Stormbringer and sheathed it. He stared down at the body of the Creature Doomed to Live and then he looked up, questioningly, at Smiorgan.

The burly sea-lord turned away.

The sun began to rise. Gray dawn came. Elric watched the corpse of J'osui C'reln Reyr turn to powder that was stirred by the wind and mixed with the dust of the ruins. He walked back across the square to where Duke Avan's twisted body lay and he fell to his knees beside it.

"You were warned, Duke Avan Astran of Old Hrolmar, that ill befell those who linked their fortunes with Elric of Melniboné. But you thought otherwise. Now you know." With a sigh he got to his feet.

Smiorgan stood beside him. The sun was now touching the taller parts of the ruins. Smiorgan reached out and gripped his friend's shoulder.

"The Olab have vanished. I think they've had their fill of sorcery."

"Another man has been destroyed by me, Smiorgan. Am I forever to be tied to this cursed sword? I must discover a way to rid myself of it or my heavy conscience will bear me down so that I cannot rise at all."

Smiorgan cleared his throat, but was otherwise silent.

"I will lay Duke Avan to rest," Elric said. "You go back to where we left the ship and tell the men that we come."

Smiorgan began to stride across the square toward the east.

Elric tenderly picked up the body of Duke Avan and went toward the opposite side of the square, to the underground room where the Creature Doomed to Live had lived out his life for ten thousand years.

It seemed so unreal to Elric now, but he knew that it had not been a dream, for the Jade Man had gone. His tracks could be seen through the jungle. Whole clumps of trees had been flattened.

He reached the place and descended the stairs and laid Duke Avan down on the bed of dried grasses. Then he took the duke's dagger and, for want of anything else, dipped it in the duke's blood and wrote on the wall above the corpse:

This was Duke Avan Astran of Old Hrolmar. He explored the world and brought much knowledge and treasure back to Vilmir, his land. He dreamed and became lost in the dream of another and so died. He enriched the Young Kingdoms—and thus encouraged another dream. He died so that the Creature Doomed to Live might die, as he desired. . . .

Elric paused. Then he threw down the dagger. He could not justify his own feelings of guilt by composing a high-sounding epitaph for the man he had slain.

He stood there, breathing heavily, then once again picked up the dagger.

He died because Elric of Melniboné desired a peace and a knowledge he could never find. He died by the Black Sword.

Outside in the middle of the square, at noon, still lay the lonely body of the last Vilmirian crewman. Nobody had known his name. Nobody felt grief for him or tried to compose an epitaph for him. The dead Vilmirian had died for no high purpose, followed no fabulous dream. Even in death his body would fulfill no function. On this island there was no carrion to feed. In the dust of the city there was no earth to fertilize.

Elric came back into the square and saw the body. For a moment, to

Elric it symbolized everything that had transpired here and would tran-
spire later.

"There is no purpose," he murmured.

Perhaps his remote ancestors had, after all, realized that, but had not
cared. It had taken the Jade Man to make them care and then go mad
in their anguish. The knowledge had caused them to close their minds
to much.

"Elric!"

It was Smiorgan returning. Elric looked up.

"The Olab dealt with the crew and the ship before they came after us.
They're all slain. The boat is destroyed."

Elric remembered something the Creature Doomed to Live had told
him. "There is another boat," he said. "On the east side of the island."

It took them the rest of the day and all of that night to discover
where J'osui C'reln Reyr had hidden his boat. They pulled it down to
the water in the diffused light of the morning and they inspected it.

"It's a sturdy boat," said Count Smiorgan approvingly. "By the look
of it, it's made of that same strange material we saw in the library of
R'lin K'ren A'a." He climbed in and searched through the lockers.

Elric was staring back at the city, thinking of a man who might have
become his friend, just as Count Smiorgan had become his friend. He
had no friends, save Cymoril, in Melniboné. He sighed.

Smiorgan had opened several lockers and was grinning at what he
saw there. "Pray the gods I return safe to the Purple Towns—we have
what I sought! Look, Elric! Treasure! We have benefited from this venture, after all!"

"Aye. . . ." Elric's mind was on other things. He forced himself to
think of more practical matters. "But the jewels will not feed us, Count
Smiorgan," he said. "It will be a long journey home."

"Home?" Count Smiorgan straightened his great back, a bunch of
necklaces in either fist. "Melniboné?"

"The Young Kingdoms. You offered to guest me in your house, as I
recall."

"For the rest of your life, if you wish. You saved my life, friend Elric
—now you have helped me save my honor."

"These past events have not disturbed you? You saw what my blade
can do—to friends as well as enemies."

"We do not brood, we of the Purple Towns," said Count Smiorgan
seriously. "And we are not fickle in our friendships. You know an anguish, Prince Elric, that I'll never feel—never understand—but I have
already given you my trust. Why should I take it away again? That is

not how we are taught to behave in the Purple Towns." Count Smiorgan brushed at his black beard and he winked. "I saw some cases of
provisions among the wreckage of Avan's schooner. We'll sail around
the island and pick them up."

Elric tried to shake the black mood from himself, but it was hard, for
he had slain a man who had trusted him, and Smiorgan's talk of trust
only made the guilt heavier.

Together they launched the boat into the weed-thick water and Elric
looked back once more at the silent forest and a shiver passed through
him. He thought of all the hopes he had entertained on the journey
upriver and he cursed himself for a fool.

He tried to think back, to work out how he had come to be in this
place, but too much of the past was confused with those singularly
graphic dreams to which he was prone. Had Saxif D'Aan and the world
of the blue sun been real? Even now, it faded. Was this place real? There
was something dreamlike about it. It seemed to him he had sailed on
many fateful seas since he had fled from Pikarayd. Now the promise of
the peace of the Purple Towns was very dear to him.

Soon the time must come when he must return to Cymoril and the
Dreaming City, to decide if he was ready to take up the responsibilities
of the Bright Empire of Melniboné, but until that moment he would
guest with his new friend, Smiorgan, and learn the ways of the simpler,
more direct folk of Menii.

As they raised the sail and began to move with the current, Elric said
to Smiorgan suddenly, "You trust me, then, Count Smiorgan?"

The sea-lord was a little surprised by the directness of the question.
He fingered his beard. "Aye," he said at length, "as a man. But we live
in cynical times, Prince Elric. Even the gods have lost their innocence,
have they not?"

Elric was puzzled. "Do you think that I shall ever betray you—as—
as I betrayed Avan, back there?"

Smiorgan shook his head. "It's not in my nature to speculate upon
such matters. You are loyal, Prince Elric. You feign cynicism, yet I
think I've rarely met a man so much in need of a little real cynicism."
He smiled. "Your sword betrayed you, did it not?"

"To serve me, I suppose."

"Aye. There's the irony of it. Man may trust man, Prince Elric, but
perhaps we'll never have a truly sane world until men learn to trust
mankind. That would mean the death of magic, I think."

And it seemed to Elric, then, that his runesword trembled at his side,
and moaned very faintly, as if it were disturbed by Count Smiorgan's
words.

THE WEIRD OF THE
WHITE WOLF

THE WEIRD OF THE WHITE WOLF

To the memory of Ted Carnell, editor of *New Worlds* and of *Science Fantasy,* who published all the early Elric stories and at whose suggestion I first began to write the series. A kind and generous man who gave me much encouragement in my early years and without whom these stories would never have been written.

CONTENTS

PROLOGUE

THE DREAM OF EARL AUBEC

In which we learn something of how the Age of the Young Kingdoms emerged and of the part played by the Dark Lady, Myshella, whose fate would later be intertwined with that of Elric of Melniboné . . .

From the glassless window of the stone tower it was possible to see the wide river winding off between loose, brown banks, through the heaped terrain of solid green copses which blended very gradually into the mass of the forest proper. And out of the forest, the cliff rose, grey and light-green, up and up, the rock darkening, lichen-covered, to merge with the lower, and even more massive, stones of the castle. It was the castle which dominated the countryside in three directions, drawing the eye from river, rock, or forest. Its walls were high and of thick granite, with towers; a dense field of towers, grouped so as to shadow one another.

Aubec of Malador marvelled and wondered how human builders could ever have constructed it, save by sorcery. Brooding and mysterious, the castle seemed to have a defiant air, for it stood on the very edge of the world.

At this moment the lowering sky cast a strange, deep-yellow light against the western sides of the towers, intensifying the blackness untouched by it. Huge billows of blue sky rent the general racing greyness above, and mounds of red cloud crept through to blend and produce more and subtler colourings. Yet, though the sky was impressive, it could not take the gaze away from the ponderous series of man-made crags that were Castle Kaneloon.

Earl Aubec of Malador did not turn from the window until it was completely dark outside; forest, cliff, and castle but shadowy tones against the overall blackness. He passed a heavy, knotted hand over his almost bald scalp and thoughtfully went towards the heap of straw which was his intended bed.

The straw was piled in a niche created by a buttress and the outer wall and the room was well-lighted by Malador's lantern. But the air was cold as he lay down on the straw with his hand close to the two-handed broadsword of prodigious size. This was his only weapon. It looked as if it had been forged for a giant—Malador was virtually that himself—with its wide crosspiece and heavy, stone-encrusted hilt and five-foot blade, smooth and broad. Beside it was Malador's old, heavy armour, the casque balanced on top with its somewhat tattered black plumes waving slightly in a current of air from the window.

Malador slept.

His dreams, as usual, were turbulent; of mighty armies surging across the blazing landscapes, curling banners bearing the blazons of a hundred nations, forests of shining lance-tips, seas of tossing helmets, the brave, wild blasts of the war-horns, the clatter of hooves, and the songs and cries and shouts of soldiers. These were dreams of earlier times, of his youth when, for Queen Eloarde of Klant, he had conquered all the Southern nations—almost to the edge of the world. Only Kaneloon, on the very edge, had he not conquered, and this because no army would follow him there.

For one of so martial an appearance, these dreams were surprisingly unwelcome, and Malador woke several times that night, shaking his head in an attempt to rid himself of them.

He would rather have dreamed of Eloarde, though she was the cause of his restlessness, but he saw nothing of her in his sleep; nothing of her soft, black hair that billowed around her pale face, nothing of her green eyes and red lips and her proud, disdainful posture. Eloarde had assigned him to this quest and he had not gone willingly, though he had no choice, for as well as his mistress she was also his Queen. The Champion was traditionally her lover—and it was unthinkable to Earl Aubec that any other condition should exist. It was his place, as Champion of Klant, to obey and go forth from her palace to seek Castle Kaneloon alone and conquer it and declare it part of her Empire, so that it could be said Queen Eloarde's domain stretched from the Dragon Sea to World's Edge.

Nothing lay beyond World's Edge—nothing save the swirling stuff of unformed Chaos which stretched away from the Cliffs of Kaneloon for eternity, roiling and broiling, multicoloured, full of monstrous half-shapes—for Earth alone was Lawful and constituted of ordered matter, drifting in the sea of Chaos-stuff as it had done for aeons.

In the morning, Earl Aubec of Malador extinguished the lantern which he had allowed to remain alight, drew greaves and hauberk on to him, placed his black plumed helm upon his head, put his broadsword over his shoulder and sallied out of the stone tower which was all that remained whole of some ancient edifice.

His leathern-shod feet stumbled over stones that seemed partially dissolved, as if Chaos had once lapped here instead of against the towering Cliffs of Kaneloon. That, of course, was quite impossible, since Earth's boundaries were known to be constant.

Castle Kaneloon had seemed closer the night before and that, he now realised, was, because it was so huge. He followed the river, his feet sinking in the loamy soil, the great branches of the trees shading him from the increasingly hot sun as he made his way towards the cliffs

Kaneloon was now out of sight, high above him. Every so often he used his sword as an axe to clear his way through the places where the foliage was particularly thick.

He rested several times, drinking the cold water of the river and mopping his face and head. He was unhurried, he had no wish to visit Kaneloon, he resented the interruption to his life with Eloarde which he thought he had earned. Also he, too, had a superstitious dread of the mysterious castle, which was said to be inhabited only by one human occupant—the Dark Lady, a sorceress without mercy who commanded a legion of demons and other Chaos-creatures.

He regarded the cliffs at midday and regarded the path leading upward with a mixture of wariness and relief. He had expected to have to scale the cliffs. He was not one, however, to take a difficult route where an easy one presented itself, so he looped a cord around his sword and slung in over his back, since it was too long and cumbersome to carry at his side. Then, still in bad humour, he began to climb the twisting path.

The lichen-covered rocks were evidently ancient, contrary to the speculations of certain philosophers who asked why Kaneloon had only been heard of a few generations since. Maladcr believed in the general answer to this question—that explorers had never ventured this far until fairly recently. He glanced back down the path and saw the tops of the trees below him, their foliage moving slightly in the breeze. The tower in which he'd spent the night was just visible in the distance and, beyond that, he knew, there was no civilisation, no outpost of Man for many days' journey North, East, or West—could Chaos lie to the South? He had never been so close to the edge of the world before and wondered how the sight of unformed matter would affect his brain.

At length he clambered to the top of the cliff and stood, arms akimbo, staring up at Castle Kaneloon which soared a mile away, its highest towers hidden in the clouds, its immense walls rooted on the rock and stretching away, limited on both sides only by the edge of the cliff. And, on the other side of the cliff, Malador watched the churning, leaping Chaos-substance, predominantly grey, blue, brown, and yellow at this moment, though its colours changed constantly, spew like the sea-spray a few feet from the castle.

He became filled with a feeling of such indescribable profundity that he could only remain in this position for a long while, completely overwhelmed by a sense of his own insignificance. It came to him, eventually, that if anyone did dwell in the Castle Kaneloon, then they must have a robust mind or else must be insane, and then he sighed and strode on towards his goal, noting that the ground was perfectly flat, without blemish, green, obsidian, and reflecting imperfectly the dancing Chaos-stuff from which he averted his eyes as much as he could.

Kaneloon had many entrances, all dark and unwelcoming, and had they all not been of regular size and shape they might have been so many cave-mouths.

Malador paused before choosing which to take, and then walked with outward purposefulness towards one. He went into blackness which appeared to stretch away forever. It was cold; it was empty and he was alone.

He was soon lost. His footsteps made no echo, which was unexpected; then the blackness began to give way to a series of angular outlines, like the walls of a twisting corridor—walls which did not reach the unsensed roof, but ended several yards above his head. It was a labyrinth, a maze. He paused and looked back and saw with horror that the maze wound off in many directions, though he was sure he had followed a straight path from the outside.

For an instant, his mind became diffused and madness threatened to engulf him, but he battened it down, unslung his sword, shivering. Which way? He pressed on, unable to tell, now, whether he went forward or backward.

The madness lurking in the depths of his brain filtered out and became fear and, immediately following the sensation of fear, came the shapes. Swift-moving shapes, darting from several different directions, gibbering, fiendish, utterly horrible.

One of these creatures kept at him and he struck at it with his blade. It fled, but seemed unwounded. Another came and another and he forgot his panic as he smote around him, driving them back until all had fled. He paused and leaned, panting, on his sword. Then, as he stared around him, the fear began to flood back into him and more creatures appeared—creatures with wide, blazing eyes and clutching talons, creatures with malevolent faces, mocking him, creatures with half-familiar faces, some recognisable as those of old friends and relatives, yet twisted into horrific parodies. He screamed and ran at them, whirling his huge sword, slashing, hacking at them, rushing past one group to turn a bend in the labyrinth and encounter another.

Malicious laughter coursed through the twisting corridors, following him and preceding him as he ran. He stumbled and fell against a wall. At first the wall seemed of solid stone, then, slowly it became soft and he sank through it, his body lying half in one corridor, half in another. He hauled himself through, still on hands and knees, looked up and saw Eloarde, but an Eloarde whose face grew old as he watched.

'I am mad,' he thought. *'Is this reality or fantasy—or both?'*
He reached out a hand, *'Eloarde!'*
She vanished but was replaced by a crowding horde of demons. He raised himself to his feet and flailed around him with his blade, but they skipped outside his range and he roared at them as he advanced. Momentarily, while he thus exerted himself, the fear left him again and, with the disappearance of the fear, so the visions vanished until he realised that the fear preceded the manifestations and he tried to control it.

He almost succeeded, forcing himself to relax, but it welled up again and the creatures bubbled out of the walls, their shrill voices full of malicious mirth.

This time he did not attack them with his sword, but stood his ground as calmly as he could and concentrated upon his own mental condition. As he did so, the creatures began to fade away and then the walls of the labyrinth dissolved and it seemed to him that he stood in a peaceful valley, calm and idyllic. Yet, hovering close to his consciousness, he seemed to see the walls of the labyrinth faintly outlined, and disgusting shapes moving here and there along the many passages.

He realised that the vision of the valley was as much an illusion as the labyrinth and, with this conclusion, both valley and labyrinth faded and he stood in the enormous hall of a castle which could only be Kaneloon.

The hall was unoccupied though well-furnished, and he could not see the source of the light, which was bright and even. He strode towards a table, on which were heaped scrolls, and his feet made a satisfying echo. Several great metal-studded doors led off from the hall, but for the moment he did not investigate them, intent on studying the scrolls and seeing if they could help him unravel Kaneloon's mystery.

He propped his sword against the table and took up the first scroll.

It was a beautiful thing of red vellum, but the black letters upon it meant nothing to him and he was astounded for, though dialects varied from place to place, there was only one language in all the lands of the Earth. Another scroll bore different symbols still, and a third he unrolled carried a series of highly stylised pictures which were repeated here and there so that he guessed they formed some kind of alphabet. Disgusted, he flung the scroll down, picked up his sword, drew an immense breath, and shouted:

'Who dwells here? Let them know that Aubec, Earl of Malador, Champion of Klant and Conqueror of the South claims this castle in the name of Queen Eloarde, Empress of all the Southlands!'

In shouting these familiar words, he felt somewhat more comfortable, but he received no reply. He lifted his casque a trifle and scratched his neck. Then he picked up his sword, balanced it over his shoulder, and made for the largest door.

Before he reached it, it sprang open and a huge, manlike thing with hands like grappling irons grinned at him.

He took a pace backward and then another until, seeing that the thing did not advance, stood his ground observing it.

It was a foot or so taller than he, with oval, multifaceted eyes that, by their nature, seemed blank. Its face was angular and had a grey, metallic sheen. Most of its body was comprised of burnished metal, jointed in the manner of armour. Upon its head was a tight-fitting hood, studded with brass. It had about it an air of tremendous and insensate power, though it did not move.

'A golem!' Malador exclaimed for it seemed to him that he remembered such man-made creatures from legends. 'What sorcery created *you!*'

The golem did not reply but its hands—which were in reality comprised of four spikes of metal apiece—began slowly to flex themselves; and still the golem grinned.

This thing, Malador knew, did not have the same amorphous quality of his earlier visions. This was solid, this was real and strong, and even Malador's manly strength, however much he exerted it, could not defeat such a creature. Yet neither could he turn away.

With a scream of metal joints, the golem entered the hall and stretched its burnished hands towards the earl.

Malador could attack or flee, and fleeing would be senseless. He attacked.

His great sword clasped in both hands, he swung it sideways at the golem's torso, which seemed to be its weakest point. The golem lowered an arm and the sword shuddered against metal with a mighty clang that set the whole of Malador's body quaking. He stumbled backward. Remorselessly, the golem followed him.

Malador looked back and searched the hall in the hope of finding a weapon more powerful than his sword, but saw only shields of an ornamental kind upon the wall to his right. He turned and ran to the wall, wrenching one of the shields from its place and slipping it on to his arm. It was an oblong thing, very light, and comprising several layers of cross-grained wood. It was inadequate, but it made him feel a trifle better as he whirled again to face the golem.

The golem advanced, and Malador thought he noticed something familiar about it, just as the demons of the labyrinth had seemed familiar, but the impression was only vague. Kaneloon's weird sorcery was affecting his mind, he decided.

The creature raised the spikes on its right arm and aimed a swift blow at Malador's head. He avoided it, putting up his sword as protection. The spikes clashed against the sword and then the left arm pistoned forward, driving at Malador's stomach. The shield stopped the blow, though the spikes pierced it deeply. He yanked the buckler off the spikes, slashing at the golem's leg-joints as he did so.

Still staring into the middle-distance, with apparently no real interest in Malador, the golem advanced like a blind man as the earl turned and leapt on to the table, scattering the scrolls. Now he brought his huge sword down upon the golem's skull, and the brass studs sparked and the hood and head beneath it was dented. The golem staggered and then grasped the table, heaving it off the floor so that Malador was forced to leap to the ground. This time he made for the door and tugged at its latch-ring, but the door would not open.

His sword was chipped and blunted. He put his back to the door as the golem reached him and brought its metal hand down on the top edge of the shield. The shield shattered and a dreadful pain shot up Malador's arm. He lunged at the golem, but he was unused to handling the big sword in this manner and the stroke was clumsy.

Malador knew that he was doomed. Force and fighting skill were not enough against the golem's insensate strength. At the golem's next blow he swung aside, but was caught by one of its spike-fingers which ripped through his armour and drew blood, though at that moment he felt no pain.

He scrambled up, shaking away the grip and fragments of wood which remained of the shield, grasping his sword firmly.

'The soulless demon has no weak spot,' he thought, *'and since it has no true intelligence, it cannot be appealed to. What would a golem fear?'*

The answer was simple. The golem would only fear something as strong or stronger than itself.

He must use cunning.

He ran for the upturned table with the golem after him, leaped over the table and wheeled as the golem stumbled but did not, as he'd hoped, fall. However, the golem was slowed by its encounter, and Aubec took advantage of this to rush for the door through which the golem had entered. It opened. He was in a twisting corridor, darkly shadowed, not unlike the labyrinth he had first found in Kaneloon. The door closed, but he could find nothing to bar it with. He ran up the corridor as the golem tore the door open and came lumbering swiftly after him.

The corridor writhed about in all directions, and, though he could not always see the golem, he could hear it and had the sickening fear that he would turn a corner at some stage and run straight into it. He did not—but he came to a door and, upon opening it and passing through it, found himself again in the hall of Castle Kaneloon.

He almost welcomed this familiar sight as he heard the golem, its metal parts screeching, continue to come after him. He needed another shield, but the part of the hall in which he now found himself had no wall-shields—only a large, round mirror of bright, clear-polished metal. It would be too heavy to be much use, but he seized it, tugging it from its hook. It fell with a clang and he hauled it up, dragging it with him as he stumbled away from the golem which had emerged into the room once more.

Using the chains by which the mirror had hung, he gripped it before him and, as the golem's speed increased and the monster rushed upon him, he raised this makeshift shield.

The golem shrieked.

Malador was astounded. The monster stopped dead and cowered away from the mirror. Malador pushed it towards the golem and the thing turned its back and fled, with a metallic howl, through the door it had entered by.

Relieved and puzzled, Malador sat down on the floor and studied the mirror. There was certainly nothing magical about it, though its quality was good. He grinned and said aloud:

'The creature *is* afraid of something. It is afraid of itself!'

He threw back his head and laughed loudly in his relief. Then he frowned. 'Now to find the sorcerers who created him and take vengeance on them!' He pushed himself to his feet, twisted the chains of the mirror more securely about his arm and went to another door, concerned lest the golem complete its circuit of the maze and return through the door. This door would not budge, so he lifted his sword and hacked at the latch for a few moments until it gave. He strode into a well-lit passage with what appeared to be another room at its far end—the door open.

A musky scent came to his nostrils as he progressed along the passage—the scent that reminded him of Eloarde and the comforts of Klant.

When he reached the circular chamber, he saw that it was a bedroom —a woman's bedroom full of the perfume he had smelled in the passage. He controlled the direction his mind took, thought of loyalty and Klant, and went to another door which led off from the room. He lugged it open and discovered a stone staircase winding upward. This he mounted, passing windows that seemed glazed with emerald or ruby, beyond which shadow-shapes flickered so that he knew he was on the side of the castle overlooking Chaos.

The staircase seemed to lead up into a tower, and when he finally reached the small door at its top he was feeling out of breath and paused before entering. Then he pushed the door open and went in.

A huge window was set in one wall, a window of clear glass through which he could see the ominous stuff of Chaos leaping. A woman stood by this window as if awaiting him.

'You are indeed a champion, Earl Aubec,' said she with a smile that might have been ironic.

'How do you know my name?'

'No sorcery gave it me, Earl of Malador—you shouted it loudly enough when you first saw the hall in its true shape.'

'Was not *that*, then, sorcery,' he said ungraciously, 'the labyrinth, the demons—even the valley? Was not the golem made by sorcery? Is not this whole cursed castle of a sorcerous nature?'

She shrugged. 'Call it so if you'd rather not have the truth. Sorcery, in your mind at least, is a crude thing which only hints at the true powers existing in the universe.'

He did not reply, being somewhat impatient of such statements. He had learned, by observing the philosophers of Klant, that mysterious words often disguised commonplace things and ideas. Instead, he looked at her sulkily and over-frankly.

She was fair, with green-blue eyes and a light complexion. Her long robe was of a similar colour to her eyes. She was, in a secret sort of way, very beautiful and, like all the denizens of Kaneloon he'd encountered, a trifle familiar.

'You recognise Kaneloon?' she asked.

He dismissed her question. 'Enough of this—take me to the masters of this place!'

'There is none but me, Myshella the Dark Lady—and I am the mistress.'

He was disappointed. 'Was it just to meet you that I came through such perils?'

'It was—and greater perils even than you think, Earl Aubec. Those were but the monsters of your own imagination!'

'Taunt me not, lady.'

She laughed. 'I speak in good faith. The castle creates its defences out of your own mind. It is a rare man who can face and defeat his own imagination. Such a one has not found me here for two hundred years. All since have perished by fear—until now.'

She smiled at him. It was a warm smile.

'And what is the prize for so great a feat?' he said gruffly.

She laughed again and gestured towards the window which looked out upon the edge of the world and Chaos beyond. 'Out there nothing exists as yet. If you venture into it, you will be confronted again by creatures of your hidden fancy, for there is nothing else to behold.'

She gazed at him admiringly and he coughed in his embarrassment. 'Once in a while,' she said, 'there comes a man to Kaneloon who can withstand such an ordeal. Then may the frontiers of the world be extended, for when a man stands against Chaos it must recede and new lands spring into being!'

'So that is the fate you have in mind for me, sorceress!'

She glanced at him almost demurely. Her beauty seemed to increase as he looked at her. He clutched at the hilt of his sword, gripping it tight as she moved gracefully towards him and touched him, as if by accident. 'There is a reward for your courage.' She looked into his eyes and said no more of the reward, for it was clear what she offered. 'And after—do my bidding and go against Chaos.'

'Lady, know you not that ritual demands of Klant's Champion that he be the queen's faithful consort? I would not betray my word and trust!' He gave a hollow laugh. 'I came here to remove a menace to my queen's kingdom—not to be your lover and lackey!'

'There is no menace here.'

'That seems true . . .'

She stepped back as if appraising him anew. For her this was unprecedented—never before had her offer been refused. She rather liked this solid man who also combined courage and imagination in his character. It was incredible, she thought, how in a few centuries such traditions could grow up—traditions which could bind a man to a woman he probably did not even love. She looked at him as he stood there, his body rigid, his manner nervous.

'Forget Klant,' she said, 'think of the power you might have—the power of true creation!'

'Lady, I claim this castle for Klant. This is what I came to do and that is what I do now. If I leave here alive, I shall be judged the conqueror and you must comply.'

She hardly heard him. She was thinking of various plans to convince him that her cause was superior to his. Perhaps she could still seduce him? Or use some drug to bewitch him? No, he was too strong for either, she must think of some other stratagem.

She felt her breasts heaving involuntarily as she looked at him. She would have preferred to have seduced him. It had always been as much her reward as the heroes who had earlier won over the dangers of Kaneloon. And then, she thought, she knew what to say.

'Think, Earl Aubec,' she whispered. 'Think—new lands for your queen's Empire!'

He frowned.

'Why not extend the Empire's boundaries farther?' she continued. 'Why not *make* new territories?'

She watched him anxiously as he took off his helm and scratched his heavy, bald head. 'You have made a point at last,' he said dubiously.

'Think of the honours you would receive in Klant if you succeeded in winning not merely Kaneloon—but that which lies *beyond!*'

Now he rubbed his chin. 'Aye,' he said, 'Aye . . .' His great brows frowned deeply.

'New plains, new mountains, new seas—new populations, even— whole cities full of people fresh-sprung and yet with the memory of generations of ancestors behind them! All this can be done by *you,* Earl of Malador—for Queen Eloarde and Lormyr!'

He smiled faintly, his imagination fired at last. 'Aye! If I can defeat such dangers here—then I can do the same out there! It will be the greatest adventure in history! My name will become a legend— Malador, Master of Chaos!'

She gave him a tender look, though she had half-cheated him.

He swung his sword up on to his shoulder. 'I'll try this, lady.'

She and he stood together at the window, watching the Chaos-stuff whispering and rolling for eternity before them. To her it had never been wholly familiar, for it changed all the time. Now its tossing colours were predominantly red and black. Tendrils of mauve and orange spiralled out of this and writhed away.

Weird shapes flitted about in it, their outlines never clear, never quite recognisable.

He said to her: 'The Lords of Chaos rule this territory. What will they have to say?'

'They can say nothing, do little. Even they have to obey the Law of the Cosmic Balance which ordains that if man can stand against Chaos, then it shall be his to order and make Lawful. Thus the Earth grows, slowly.'

'How do I enter it?'

She took the opportunity to grasp his heavily muscled arm and point through the window. 'See—there—a causeway leads down from this tower to the cliff.' She glanced at him sharply. 'Do you see it?'

'Ah—yes—I had not, but now I do. Yes, a causeway.'

Standing behind him, she smiled a little to herself. 'I will remove the barrier,' she said.

He straightened his helm on his head. 'For Klant and Eloarde and only those do I embark upon this adventure.'

She moved towards the wall and raised the window. He did not look at her as he strode down the causeway into the multicoloured mist.

As she watched him disappear, she smiled to herself. How easy it was to beguile the strongest man by pretending to go his way! He might add lands to his Empire, but he might find their populations unwilling to accept Eloarde as their Empress. In fact, if Aubec did his work well, then he would be creating more of a threat to Klant than ever Kaneloon had been.

Yet she admired him, she was attracted to him, perhaps, because he was not so accessible, a little more than she had been to that earlier hero who had claimed Aubec's own land from Chaos barely two hundred years before. Oh, he had been a man! But he, like most before him, had needed no other persuasion than the promise of her body.

Earl Aubec's weakness had lain in his strength, she thought. By now he had vanished into the heaving mists.

She felt a trifle sad that this time the execution of the task given her by the Lords of Law had not brought her the usual pleasure.

Yet perhaps, she thought, she felt a more subtle pleasure in his steadfastness and the means she had used to convince him.

For centuries had the Lords of Law entrusted her with Kaneloon and its secrets. But the progress was slow, for there were few heroes who could survive Kaneloon's dangers—few who could defeat self-created perils.

Yet, she decided with a slight smile on her lips, the task had its various rewards. She moved into another chamber to prepare for the transition of the castle to the new edge of the world.

Thus were the seeds sown of the Age of the Young Kingdoms, the Age of Men, which was to produce the downfall of Melniboné.

BOOK ONE

THE DREAMING CITY

Which tells how Elric came back to Imrryr, what he did there, and how, at last, his weird fell upon him . . .

1

'What's the hour?' The black-bearded man wrenched off his gilded helmet and flung it from him, careless of where it fell. He drew off his leathern gauntlets and moved closer to the roaring fire, letting the heat soak into his frozen bones.

'Midnight is long past,' growled one of the other armoured men who gathered around the blaze. 'Are you still sure he'll come?'

'It's said that he's a man of his word, if that comforts you.'

It was a tall, pale-faced youth who spoke. His thin lips formed the words and spat them out maliciously. He grinned a wolf-grin and stared the new arrival in the eyes, mocking him.

The newcomer turned away with a shrug. 'That's so—for all your irony, Yaris. He'll come.' He spoke as a man does when he wishes to reassure himself.

There were six men, now, around the fire. The sixth was Smiorgan—Count Smiorgan Baldhead of the Purple Towns. He was a short, stocky man of fifty years with a scarred face partially covered with a thick, black growth of hair. His eyes smouldered morosely and his lumpy fingers plucked nervously at his rich-hilted longsword. His pate was hairless, giving him his name, and over his ornate, gilded armour hung a loose woollen cloak, dyed purple.

Smiorgan said thickly, 'He has no love for his cousin. He has become bitter. Yyrkoon sits on the Ruby Throne in his place and has proclaimed him an outlaw and a traitor. Elric needs us if he would take his throne and his bride back. We can trust him.'

'You're full of trust tonight, Count,' Yaris smiled thinly, 'a rare thing to find in these troubled times. I say this—' He paused and took a long breath, staring at his comrades, summing them up. His gaze flicked from lean-faced Dharmit of Jharkor to Fadan of Lormyr who pursed his podgy lips and looked into the fire.

'Speak up, Yaris,' petulantly urged the patrician-featured Vilmirian, Naclon. 'Let's hear what you have to say, lad, if it's worth hearing.'

Yaris looked towards Jiku the dandy, who yawned impolitely and scratched his long nose.

'Well!' Smiorgan was impatient. 'What d'you say, Yaris?'

'I say that we should start now and waste no more time waiting on Elric's pleasure! He's laughing at us in some tavern a hundred miles from here—or else plotting with the Dragon Princes to trap us. For years we have planned this raid. We have little time in which to strike—our fleet is too big, too noticeable. Even if Elric has not betrayed us, then spies will soon be running eastwards to warn the Dragons that there is a fleet massed against them. We stand to win a fantastic fortune —to vanquish the greatest merchant city in the world—to reap immeasurable riches—or horrible death at the hands of the Dragon Princes, if we wait overlong. Let's bide our time no more and set sail before our prize hears of our plan and brings up reinforcements!'

'You always were too ready to mistrust a man, Yaris.' King Naclon of Vilmir spoke slowly, carefully—distastefully eyeing the taut-featured youth. 'We could not reach Imrryr without Elric's knowledge of the maze-channels which lead to its secret ports. If Elric will not join us— then our endeavour will be fruitless—hopeless. We need him. We must wait for him—or else give up our plans and return to our homelands.'

'At least I'm willing to take a risk,' yelled Yaris, anger lancing from his slanting eyes. 'You're getting old—all of you. Treasures are not won by care and forethought but by swift slaying and reckless attack.'

'Fool!' Dharmit's voice rumbled around the fire-flooded hall. He laughed wearily. 'I spoke thus in my youth—and lost a fine fleet soon after. Cunning and Elric's knowledge will win us Imrryr—that and the mightiest fleet to sail the Sighing Sea since Melniboné's banners fluttered over all the nations of the Earth. Here we are—the most powerful Sea Lords in the world, masters, every one of us, of more than a hundred swift vessels. Our names are feared and famous—our fleets ravage the coasts of a score of lesser nations. We hold *power!*' He clenched his great fist and shook it in Yaris' face. His tone became more level and he smiled viciously, glaring at the youth and choosing his words with precision.

'But all this is worthless—meaningless—without the power which Elric has. That is the power of knowledge—of sorcery, if I must use the cursed word. His fathers knew of the maze which guards Imrryr from sea-attack. And his fathers passed that secret on to him. Imrryr, the Dreaming City, dreams in peace—and will continue to do so unless we have a guide to help us steer a course through the treacherous waterways which lead to her harbours. We *need* Elric—we know it, and he knows it. That's the truth!'

'Such confidence, gentlemen, is warming to the heart.' There was irony in the heavy voice which came from the entrance to the hall. The heads of the six Sea Lords jerked towards the doorway.

Yaris' confidence fled from him as he met the eyes of Elric of Melniboné. They were old eyes in a fine featured, youthful face. Crimson eyes which stared into eternity. Yaris shuddered, turned his back on Elric, preferring to look into the bright glare of the fire.

Elric smiled warmly as Count Smiorgan gripped his shoulder. There was a certain friendship between the two. He nodded condescendingly to the other four and walked with lithe grace towards the fire. Yaris stood aside and let him pass. Elric was tall, broad-shouldered and slim-hipped. He wore his long hair bunched and pinned at the nape of his neck and, for an obscure reason, affected the dress of a Southern barbarian. He had long, knee-length boots of soft doe-leather, a breastplate of strangely wrought silver, a jerkin of chequered blue and white linen, britches of scarlet wool and a cloak of rustling green velvet. At his hip rested his runesword of black iron—the feared Stormbringer, forged by ancient and alien sorcery.

His bizarre dress was tasteless and gaudy, and did not match his sensitive face and long-fingered, almost delicate hands, yet he flaunted it since it emphasised the fact that he did not belong in any company— that he was an outsider and an outcast. But, in reality, he had little need to wear such outlandish gear—for his eyes and skin were enough to mark him.

Elric, Last Lord of Melniboné, was a pure albino who drew his power from a secret and terrible source.

Smiorgan sighed. 'Well, Elric, when do we raid Imrryr?'

Elric shrugged. 'As soon as you like; I care not. Give me a little time in which to do certain things.'

'Tomorrow? Shall we sail tomorrow?' Yaris said hesitantly, conscious of the strange power dormant in the man he had earlier accused of treachery.

Elric smiled, dismissing the youth's statement. 'Three days' time,' he said. 'Three—or more.'

'Three days! But Imrryr will be warned of our presence by then!' Fat, cautious Fadan spoke.

'I'll see that your fleet's not found,' Elric promised. 'I have to go to Imrryr first—and return.'

'You won't do the journey in three days—the fastest ship could not make it.' Smiorgan gaped.

'I'll be in the Dreaming City in less than a day,' Elric said softly, with finality.

Smiorgan shrugged. 'If you say so, I'll believe it—but why this necessity to visit the city ahead of the raid?'

'I have my own compunctions, Count Smiorgan. But worry not—I shan't betray you. I'll lead the raid myself, be sure of that.' His dead-white face was lighted eerily by the fire and his red eyes smouldered. One lean hand firmly gripped the hilt of his runesword and he appeared to breathe more heavily. 'Imrryr fell, in spirit, five hundred years ago— she will fall completely soon—for ever! I have a little debt to settle. This is my only reason for aiding you. As you know I have made only a few conditions—that you raze the city to the ground and a certain man and woman are not harmed. I refer to my cousin Yyrkoon and his sister Cymoril . . .'

Yaris' thin lips felt uncomfortably dry. Much of his blustering manner resulted from the early death of his father. The old sea-king had died—leaving young Yaris as the new ruler of his lands and his fleets. Yaris was not at all certain that he was capable of commanding such a vast kingdom—and tried to appear more confident than he actually felt. Now he said: 'How shall we hide the fleet, Lord Elric?'

The Melnibonéan acknowledged the question. 'I'll hide it for you,' he promised. 'I go now to do this—but make sure all your men are off the ships first—will you see to it, Smiorgan?'

'Aye,' rumbled the stocky count.

He and Elric departed from the hall together, leaving five men behind; five men who sensed an air of icy doom hanging about the overheated hall.

'How could he hide such a mighty fleet when we, who know this fjord better than any, could find nowhere?' Dharmit of Jharkor said bewilderedly.

None answered him.

They waited, tensed and nervous, while the fire flickered and died untended. Eventually Smiorgan returned, stamping noisily on the boarded floor. There was a haunted haze of fear surrounding him; an almost tangible aura, and he was shivering, terribly. Tremendous, racking undulations swept up his body and his breath came short.

'Well? Did Elric hide the fleet—all at once? What did he do?' Dharmit spoke impatiently, choosing not to heed Smiorgan's ominous condition.

'He has hidden it.' That was all Smiorgan said, and his voice was thin, like that of a sick man, weak from fever.

Yaris went to the entrance and tried to stare beyond the fjord slopes where many campfires burned, tried to make out the outlines of ships' masts and rigging, but he could see nothing.

'The night mist's too thick,' he murmured, 'I can't tell whether our ships are anchored in the fjord or not.' Then he gasped involuntarily as a white face loomed out of the clinging fog. 'Greetings, Lord Elric,' he stuttered, noting the sweat on the Melnibonéan's strained features.

Elric staggered past him, into the hall. 'Wine,' he mumbled, 'I've done what's needed and it's cost me hard.'

Dharmit fetched a jug of strong Cadsandrian wine and with a shaking hand poured some into a carved wooden goblet. Wordlessly he passed the cup to Elric who quickly drained it. 'Now I will sleep,' he said, stretching himself into a chair and wrapping his green cloak around him. He closed his disconcerting crimson eyes and fell into a slumber born of utter weariness.

Fadan scurried to the door, closed it and pulled the heavy iron bar down.

None of the six slept much that night and, in the morning, the door was unbarred and Elric was missing from the chair. When they went outside, the mist was so heavy that they soon lost sight of one another, though scarcely two feet separated any of them.

Elric stood with his legs astraddle on the shingle of the narrow beach. He looked back at the entrance to the fjord and saw, with satisfaction, that the mist was still thickening, though it lay only over the fjord itself, hiding the mighty fleet. Elsewhere, the weather was clear and overhead a pale winter sun shone sharply on the black rocks of the rugged cliffs which dominated the coastline. Ahead of him the sea rose and fell monotonously, like the chest of a sleeping water-giant, grey and pure, glinting in the cold sunlight. Elric fingered the raised runes on the hilt of his black broadsword and a steady north wind blew into the voluminous folds of his dark green cloak, swirling it around his tall, lean frame.

The albino felt fitter than he had done on the previous night when he had expended all his strength in conjuring the mist. He was well-versed in the art of nature-wizardry, but he did not have the reserves of power which the Sorcerer Emperors of Melniboné had possessed when they had ruled the world. His ancestors had passed their knowledge down to him—but not their mystic vitality and many of the spells and secrets that he had were unusable, since he did not have the reservoir of strength, either of soul or of body, to work them. But for all that, Elric knew of only one other man who matched his knowledge—his cousin Yyrkoon. His hand gripped the hilt tighter as he thought of the cousin who had twice betrayed his trust, and he forced himself to concentrate on his present task—the speaking of spells to aid him on his voyage to the Isle of the Dragon Masters whose only city, Imrryr the Beautiful, was the object of the Sea Lords' massing.

Drawn up on the beach, a tiny sailing-boat lay—Elric's own small ship, sturdy and far stronger, far older, than it appeared. The brooding sea flung surf around its timbers as the tide withdrew, and Elric realised that he had little time in which to work his helpful sorcery.

His body tensed and he blanked his conscious mind, summoning secrets from the dark depths of his soul. Swaying, his eyes staring unseeingly, his arms jerking out ahead of him and making unholy signs in the air, he began to speak in a sibilant monotone. Slowly the pitch of his voice rose, resembling the scarcely heard shriek of a distant gale as it comes closer—then, quite suddenly, the voice rose higher until it was howling wildly to the skies and the air began to tremble and quiver. Shadow-shapes began slowly to form and they were never still but darted around Elric's body as, stiff-legged, he started forward towards his boat.

His voice was inhuman as it howled insistently, summoning the wind elementals—the *sylphs* of the breeze; the *sharnahs,* makers of gales; the *h'Haarshanns,* builders of whirlwinds—hazy and formless, they eddied around him as he summoned their aid with the alien words of his forefathers who had, ages before, made unthinkable pacts with the elementals in order to procure their services.

Still stiff-limbed, Elric entered the boat and, like an automaton, his fingers ran up the sail and set it. Then a great wave erupted out of the placid sea, rising higher and higher until it towered over the vessel. With a surging crash, the water smashed down on the boat, lifted it and bore it out to sea. Sitting blank-eyed in the stern, Elric still crooned his hideous song of sorcery as the spirits of the air plucked at the sail and sent the boat flying over the water faster than any mortal ship could speed. And all the while, the deafening, unholy shriek of the released elementals filled the air about the boat as the shore vanished and open sea was all that was visible.

2

So it was, with wind-demons for shipmates, that Elric, last Prince of the Royal line of Melniboné, returned to the last city still ruled by his own race—the last city and the final remnant of Melnibonéan architecture. The cloudy pink and subtle yellow tints of her nearer towers came into sight within a few hours of Elric's leaving the fjord and just off-shore of the Isle of the Dragon Masters the elementals left the boat and fled back to their secret haunts among the peaks of the highest mountains in the world. Elric awoke, then, from his trance, and regarded with fresh wonder the beauty of his own city's delicate towers which were visible even so far away, guarded still by the formidable sea-wall with its great gate, the five-doored maze and the twisting, high-walled channels, of which only one led to the inner harbour of Imrryr.

Elric knew that he dare not risk entering the harbour by the maze, though he knew the route perfectly. He decided, instead, to land the boat further up the coast in a small inlet of which he had knowledge. With sure, capable hands, he guided the little craft towards the hidden inlet which was obscured by a growth of shrubs loaded with ghastly blue berries of a type decidedly poisonous to men since their juice first turned one blind and then slowly mad. This berry, the *nodoil,* grew only on Imrryr as did other rare and deadly plants.

Light, low-hanging cloud wisps streamed slowly across the sun-painted sky, like fine cobwebs caught by a sudden breeze. All the world seemed blue and gold and green and white, and Elric, pulling his boat up on the beach, breathed the clean, sharp air of winter and savoured the scent of decaying leaves and rotting undergrowth. Somewhere a bitch-fox barked her pleasure to her mate and Elric regretted the fact that his depleted race no longer appreciated natural beauty, preferring to stay close to their city and spend many of their days in drugged slumber. It was not the city which dreamed, but its overcivilised inhab-

itants. Elric, smelling the rich, clean winterscents, was wholly glad that
he had given up his birthright and did not rule the city as he had been
born to do.

Instead, Yyrkoon, his cousin, sprawled on the Ruby Throne of Imrr-
ryr the Beautiful and hated Elric because he knew that the albino, for
all his disgust with crowns and rulership, was still the rightful King of
the Dragon Isle and that he, Yyrkoon, was an usurper, not elected by
Elric to the throne, as Melnibonéan tradition demanded.

But Elric had better reasons for hating his cousin. For those reasons
the ancient capital would fall in all its magnificent splendour and the
last fragment of a glorious Empire would be obliterated as the pink, the
yellow, the purple and white towers crumbled—if Elric had his way and
the Sea Lords were successful.

On foot, Elric strode inland, towards Imrryr, and as he covered the
miles of soft turf, the sun cast an ochre pall over the land and sank,
giving way to a dark and moonless night, brooding and full of evil
portent.

At last he came to the city. It stood out in stark black silhouette, a
city of fantastic magnificence, in conception and in execution. It was the
oldest city in the world, built by artists and conceived as a work of art
rather than a functional dwelling place, but Elric knew that squalor
lurked in many narrow streets and that the Lords of Imrryr left many
of the towers empty and uninhabited rather than let the bastard population of the city dwell therein. There were few Dragon Masters left; few
who would claim Melnibonéan blood.

Built to follow the shape of the ground, the city had an organic
appearance, with winding lanes spiralling to the crest of the hill where
stood the castle, tall and proud and many-spired, the final, crowning
masterpiece of the ancient, forgotten artist who had built it. But there
was no life-sound emanating from Imrryr the Beautiful, only a sense of
soporific desolation. The city slept—and the Dragon Masters and their
ladies and their special slaves dreamed drug-induced dreams of gran-
deur and incredible horror while the rest of the population, ordered by
curfew, tossed on tawdry mattresses and tried not to dream at all.

Elric, his hand ever near his sword-hilt, slipped through an unguarded gate in the city wall and began to walk cautiously through the
unlighted streets, moving upwards, through the winding lanes, towards
Yyrkoon's great palace.

Wind sighed through the empty rooms of the Dragon towers and
sometimes Elric would have to withdraw into places where the shadows
were deeper when he heard the tramp of feet and a group of guards
would pass, their duty being to see that the curfew was rigidly obeyed.

Often he would hear wild laughter echoing from one of the towers, still ablaze with bright torchlight which flung strange, disturbing shadows on the walls; often, too, he would hear a chilling scream and a frenzied, idiot's yell as some wretch of a slave died in obscene agony to please his master.

Elric was not appalled by the sounds and the dim sights. He appreciated them. He was still a Melnibonéan—their rightful leader if he chose to regain his powers of kingship—and though he had an obscure urge to wander and sample the less sophisticated pleasures of the outside world, ten thousand years of a cruel, brilliant and malicious culture was behind him and the pulse of his ancestry beat strongly in his deficient veins.

Elric knocked impatiently upon the heavy, black-wood door. He had reached the palace and now stood by a small back entrance, glancing cautiously around him, for he knew that Yyrkoon had given the guards orders to slay him if he entered Imrryr.

A bolt squealed on the other side of the door and it moved silently inwards. A thin, seamed face confronted Elric.

'Is it the king?' whispered the man, peering out into the night. He was a tall, extremely thin individual with long, gnarled limbs which shifted awkwardly as he moved nearer, straining his beady eyes to get a glimpse of Elric.

'It's Prince Elric,' the albino said. 'But you forget, Tanglebones, my friend, that a new king sits on the Ruby Throne.'

Tanglebones shook his head and his sparse hair fell over his face. With a jerking movement he brushed it back and stood aside for Elric to enter. 'The Dragon Isle has but one king—and his name is Elric, whatever usurper would have it otherwise.'

Elric ignored this statement, but he smiled thinly and waited for the man to push the bolt back into place.

'She still sleeps, sire,' Tanglebones murmured as he climbed unlit stairs, Elric behind him.

'I guessed that,' Elric said. 'I do not underestimate my good cousin's powers of sorcery.'

Upwards, now, in silence, the two men climbed until at last they reached a corridor which was aflare with dancing torchlight. The marble walls reflected the flames and showed Elric, crouching with Tanglebones behind a pillar, that the room in which he was interested was guarded by a massive archer—a eunuch by the look of him—who was alert and wakeful. The man was hairless and fat, his blue-black gleaming armour tight on his flesh, but his fingers were curled around the string of his short, bone bow and there was a slim arrow resting on the string. Elric guessed that this man was one of the crack eunuch archers, a member of the Silent Guard, Imrryr's finest company of warriors.

Tanglebones, who had taught the young Elric the arts of fencing and archery, had known of the guard's presence and had prepared for it. Earlier he had placed a bow behind the pillar. Silently he picked it up and, bending it against his knee, strung it. He fitted an arrow to the string, aimed it at the right eye of the guard and let fly—just as the eunuch turned to face him. The shaft missed. It clattered against the man's gorget and fell harmlessly to the reed-strewn stones of the floor.

So Elric acted swiftly, leaping forward, his runesword drawn and its alien power surging through him. It howled in a searing arc of black steel and cut through the bone bow which the eunuch had hoped would deflect it. The guard was panting and his thick lips were wet as he drew breath to yell. As he opened his mouth, Elric saw what he had expected, the man was tongueless and was a mute. His own shortsword came out and he just managed to parry Elric's next thrust. Sparks flew from the iron and Stormbringer bit into the eunuch's finely edged blade; he staggered and fell back before the nigromantic sword which appeared to be endowed with a life of its own. The clatter of metal echoed loudly up and down the short corridor and Elric cursed the fate which had made the man turn at the crucial moment. Grimly, swiftly, he broke down the eunuch's clumsy guard.

The eunuch saw only a dim glimpse of his opponent behind the black, whirling blade which appeared to be so light and which was twice the length of his own stabbing sword. He wondered, frenziedly, who his attacker could be and he thought he recognised the face. Then a scarlet eruption obscured his vision, he felt searing agony clutch at his face and then, philosophically, for eunuchs are necessarily given to a certain fatalism, he realised that he was to die.

Elric stood over the eunuch's bloated body and tugged his sword from the corpse's skull, wiping the mixture of blood and brains on his late opponent's cloak. Tanglebones had wisely vanished. Elric could hear the clatter of sandalled feet rushing up the stairs. He pushed the door open and entered the room which was lit by two small candles placed at either end of a wide, richly tapestried bed. He went to the bed and looked down at the raven-haired girl who lay there.

Elric's mouth twitched and bright tears leapt into his strange red eyes. He was trembling as he turned back to the door, sheathed his sword and pulled the bolts into place. He returned to the bedside and knelt down beside the sleeping girl. Her features were as delicate and of a similar mould as Elric's own, but she had an added, exquisite beauty.

She was breathing shallowly, in a sleep induced not by natural weariness but by her own brother's evil sorcery.

Elric reached out and tenderly took one fine-fingered hand in his. He put it to his lips and kissed it.

'Cymoril,' he murmured, and an agony of longing throbbed in that name. 'Cymoril—wake up.'

The girl did not stir, her breathing remained shallow and her eyes remained shut. Elric's white features twisted and his red eyes blazed as he shook in terrible and passionate rage. He gripped the hand, so limp and nerveless, like the hand of a corpse; gripped it until he had to stop himself for fear that he would crush the delicate fingers.

A shouting soldier began to beat at the door.

Elric replaced the hand on the girl's firm breast and stood up. He glanced uncomprehendingly at the door.

A sharper, colder voice interrupted the soldier's yelling.

'What is happening—has someone tried to see my poor sleeping sister?'

'Yyrkoon, the black hellspawn,' said Elric to himself.

Confused babblings from the soldier and Yyrkoon's voice raised as he shouted through the door. 'Whoever is in there—you will be destroyed a thousand times when you are caught. You cannot escape. If my good sister is harmed in any way—then you will never die, I promise you that. But you will pray to your Gods that you could!'

'Yyrkoon, you paltry rabble—you cannot threaten one who is your equal in the dark arts. It is I, Elric—your rightful master. Return to your rabbit hole before I call down every evil power upon, above, and under the Earth to blast you!'

Yyrkoon laughed hesitantly. 'So you have returned again to try to waken my sister. Any such attempt will not only slay her—it will send her soul into the deepest hell—where you may join it, willingly!'

'By Arnara's six breasts—you it will be who samples the thousand deaths before long.'

'Enough of this.' Yyrkoon raised his voice. 'Soldiers—I command you to break this door down—and take that traitor alive. Elric—there are two things you will never again have—my sister's love and the Ruby Throne. Make what you can of the little time available to you, for soon you will be grovelling to me and praying for release from your soul's agony!'

Elric ignored Yyrkoon's threats and looked at the narrow window to the room. It was just large enough for a man's body to pass through. He bent down and kissed Cymoril upon the lips, then he went to the door and silently withdrew the bolts.

There came a crash as a soldier flung his weight against the door. It swung open, pitching the man forward to stumble and fall on his face. Elric drew his sword, lifted it high and chopped at the warrior's neck. The head sprang from its shoulders and Elric yelled loudly in a deep, rolling voice.

'*Arioch! Arioch!* I give you blood and souls—only aid me now! This man I give you, mighty King of Hell—aid your servant, Elric of Melniboné!'

Three soldiers entered the room in a bunch. Elric struck at one and sheared off half his face. The man screamed horribly.

'Arioch, Lord of the Darks—I give you blood and souls. Aid me, evil one!'

In the far corner of the gloomy room, a blacker mist began slowly to form. But the soldiers pressed closer and Elric was hard put to hold them back.

He was screaming the name of Arioch, Lord of the Higher Hell, incessantly, almost unconsciously as he was pressed back further by the weight of the warriors' numbers. Behind them, Yyrkoon mouthed in rage and frustration, urging his men, still, to take Elric alive. This necessity gave Elric some small advantage—that and the runesword Stormbringer which was glowing with a strange black luminousness, and the shrill howling it gave out was grating into the ears of those who heard it. Two more corpses now littered the carpeted floor of the chamber, their blood soaking into the fine fabric.

'*Blood and souls for my lord Arioch!*'

The dark mist heaved and began to take shape, Elric spared a look towards the corner and shuddered despite his inurement to hell-born horror. The warriors now had their backs to the thing in the corner and Elric was by the window. The amorphous mass that was a less than pleasant manifestation of Elric's fickle patron God heaved again, and Elric made out its intolerably alien shape. Bile flooded into his mouth and as he drove the soldiers towards the thing which was sinuously flooding forward he fought against madness.

Suddenly, the soldiers seemed to sense that there was something behind them. They turned, four of them, and each screamed insanely as the black horror made one final rush to engulf them. Arioch crouched over them, sucking out their souls. Then, slowly, their bones began to give and snap and still shrieking bestially the men flopped like obnoxious invertebrates upon the floor; their spines broken, they still lived. Elric turned away, thankful for once that Cymoril slept, and leapt to the window ledge. He looked down and realised with despair that he was not going to escape by that route after all. Several hundred feet lay between him and the ground. He rushed to the door where Yyrkoon, his eyes wide with fear, was trying to drive Arioch back. Arioch was already fading.

Elric pushed past his cousin, spared a final glance for Cymoril, then ran the way he had come, his feet slipping on blood. Tanglebones met him at the head of the dark stairway.

'What has happened, King Elric—what's in there?'

Elric seized Tanglebones by his lean shoulder and made him descend the stairs. 'No time,' he panted, 'but we must hurry while Yyrkoon is still engaged with his current problem. In five days' time Imrryr will experience a new phase in her history—perhaps the last. I want you to make sure that Cymoril is safe. Is that clear?'

'Aye, Lord, but . . .'

They reached the door and Tanglebones shot the bolts and opened it.

'There is no time for me to say anything else. I must escape while I can. I will return in five days—with companions. You will realise what I mean when that time comes. Take Cymoril to the Tower of D'a'rputna —and await me there.'

Then Elric was gone, soft-footed, running into the night with the shrieks of the dying still ringing through the blackness after him.

3

Elric stood unspeaking in the prow of Count Smiorgan's flagship. Since his return to the fjord and the fleet's subsequent sailing for open sea, he had spoken only orders, and those in the tersest of terms. The Sea Lords muttered that a great hate lay in him, that it festered his soul and made him a dangerous man to have as comrade or enemy; and even Count Smiorgan avoided the moody albino.

The reaver prows struck eastward and the sea was black with light ships dancing on the bright water in all directions; they looked like the shadow of some enormous sea-bird flung on the water. Nearly half a thousand fighting ships stained the ocean—all of them of similar form, long and slim and built for speed rather than battle, since they were for coast-raiding and trading. Sails were caught by the pale sun; bright colours of fresh canvas—orange, blue, black, purple, red, yellow, light green or white. And every ship had sixteen or more rowers—each rower a fighting man. The crews of the ships were also the warriors who would attack Imrryr—there was no wastage of good man-power since the sea-nations were underpopulated, losing hundreds of men each year in their regular raids.

In the centre of the great fleet, certain larger vessels sailed. These carried great catapults on their decks and were to be used for storming the sea wall of Imrryr. Count Smiorgan and the other Lords looked at their ships with pride, but Elric only stared ahead of him, never sleeping, rarely moving, his white face lashed by salt spray and wind, his white hand tight upon his swordhilt.

The reaver ships ploughed steadily eastwards—forging towards the Dragon Isle and fantastic wealth—or hellish horror. Relentlessly, doom-driven, they beat onwards, their oars splashing in unison, their sails bellying taut with a good wind.

Onwards they sailed, towards Imrryr the Beautiful, to rape and plunder the world's oldest city.

Two days after the fleet had set sail, the coastline of the Dragon Isle was sighted and the rattle of arms replaced the sound of oars as the mighty fleet hove to and prepared to accomplish what sane men thought impossible.

Orders were bellowed from ship to ship and the fleet began to mass into battle formation, then the oars creaked in their grooves and ponderously, with sails now furled, the fleet moved forward again.

It was a clear day, cold and fresh, and there was a tense excitement about all the men, from Sea Lord to galley hand, as they considered the immediate future and what it might bring. Serpent prows bent towards the great stone wall which blocked off the first entrance to the harbour. It was nearly a hundred feet high and towers were built upon it—more functional than the lace-like spires of the city which shimmered in the distance, behind them. The ships of Imrryr were the only vessels allowed to pass through the great gate in the centre of the wall and the route through the maze—the exact entrance even—was a well-kept secret from outsiders.

On the sea wall, which now loomed tall above the fleet, amazed guards scrambled frantically to their posts. To them, threat of attack was well-nigh unthinkable, yet here it was—a great fleet, the greatest they had ever seen—come against Imrryr the Beautiful! They took to their posts, their yellow cloaks and kilts rustling, their bronze armour rattling, but they moved with bewildered reluctance as if refusing to accept what they saw. And they went to their posts with desperate fatalism, knowing that even if the ships never entered the maze itself, they would not be alive to witness the reavers' failure.

Dyvim Tarkan, Commander of the Wall, was a sensitive man who loved life and its pleasures. He was highbrowed and handsome, with a thin wisp of beard and a tiny moustache. He looked well in the bronze armour and high-plumed helmet; he did not want to die. He issued terse orders to his men and, with well-ordered precision, they obeyed him. He listened with concern to the distant shouts from the ships and he wondered what the first move of the reavers would be. He did not wait long for his answer.

A catapult on one of the leading vessels twanged throatily and its throwing arm rushed up, releasing a great rock which sailed, with every appearance of leisurely grace, towards the wall. It fell short and splashed into the sea which frothed against the stones of the wall.

Swallowing hard and trying to control the shake in his voice, Dyvim Tarkan ordered his own catapult to discharge. With a thudding crash the release rope was cut and a retaliatory iron ball went hurtling towards the enemy fleet. So tight-packed were the ships that the ball could not miss—it struck full on the deck of the flagship of Dharmit of Jharkor and crushed the timbers in. Within seconds, accompanied by the cries of maimed and drowning men, the ship had sunk and Dharmit with it. Some of the crew were taken aboard other vessels but the wounded were left to drown.

Another catapult sounded and this time a tower full of archers was squarely hit. Masonry erupted outwards and those who still lived fell sickeningly to die in the foam-tipped sea lashing the wall. This time, angered by the deaths of their comrades, Imrryrian archers sent back a stream of slim arrows into the enemy's midst. Reavers howled as red-fletched shafts buried themselves thirstily in flesh. But reavers returned the arrows liberally and soon only a handful of men were left on the wall as further catapult rocks smashed into towers and men, destroying their only war-machine and part of the wall besides.

Dyvim Tarkan still lived, though red blood stained his yellow tunic and an arrow shaft protruded from his left shoulder. He still lived when the first ram-ship moved intractably towards the great wooden gate and smashed against it, weakening it. A second ship sailed in beside it and, between them, they stove in the gate and glided through the entrance; the first non-Imrryrian ships ever to do such a thing. Perhaps it was outraged horror that tradition had been broken which caused poor Dyvim Tarkan to lose his footing at the edge of the wall and fall screaming down to break his neck on the deck of Count Smiorgan's flagship as it sailed triumphantly through the gate.

Now the ram-ships made way for Count Smiorgan's craft, for Elric had to lead the way through the maze. Ahead of them loomed five tall entrances, black gaping maws all alike in shape and size. Elric pointed to the third from the left and with short strokes the oarsmen began to paddle the ship into the dark mouth of the entrance. For some minutes, they sailed in darkness.

'Flares!' shouted Elric. 'Light the flares!'

Torches had already been prepared and these were now lighted. The men saw that they were in a vast tunnel hewn out of natural rock which twisted tortuously in all directions.

'Keep close,' Elric ordered and his voice was magnified a score of times in the echoing cavern. Torchlight blazed and Elric's face was a mask of shadow and frisking light as the torches threw up long tongues of flame to the bleak roof. Behind him, men could be heard muttering in awe and, as more craft entered the maze and lit their own torches, Elric could see some torches waver as their bearers trembled in superstitious fear. Elric felt some discomfort as he glanced through the flickering shadows and his eyes, caught by torchflare, gleamed fever-bright.

With dreadful monotony, the oars splashed onwards as the tunnel widened and several more cavemouths came into sight. 'The middle entrance,' Elric ordered. The steersman in the stern nodded and guided the ship towards the entrance Elric had indicated. Apart from the muted murmur of some men and the splash of oars, there was a grim and ominous silence in the towering cavern.

Elric stared down at the cold, dark water and shuddered.

Eventually they moved once again into bright sunlight and the men looked upwards, marvelling at the height of the great walls above them. Upon those walls squatted more yellow-clad, bronze-armoured archers and as Count Smiorgan's vessel led the way out of the black caverns, the torches still burning in the cool winter air, arrows began to hurtle down into the narrow canyon, biting into throats and limbs.

'Faster!' howled Elric. 'Row faster—speed is our only weapon now!'

With frantic energy the oarsmen bent to their sweeps and the ships began to pick up speed even though Imrryrian arrows took heavy toll of the reaver crewmen. Now the high-walled channel ran straight and Elric saw the quays of Imrryr ahead of him.

'Faster! Faster! Our prize is in sight!'

Then, suddenly, the ship broke past the walls and was in the calm waters of the harbour, facing the warriors drawn up on the quay. The ship halted, waiting for reinforcements to plunge out of the channel and join them. When twenty ships were through, Elric gave the command to attack the quay and now Stormbringer howled from its scabbard. The flagship's port side thudded against the quay as arrows rained down upon it. Shafts whistled all around Elric but, miraculously, he was unscathed as he led a bunch of yelling reavers on to land. Imrryrian axe-men bunched forward and confronted the reavers, but it was plain that they had little spirit for the fight—they were too disconcerted by the course which events had taken.

Elric's black blade struck with frenzied force at the throat of the leading axe-man and sheared off his head. Howling demoniacally now that it had again tasted blood, the sword began to writhe in Elric's grasp, seeking fresh flesh in which to bite. There was a hard, grim smile on the albino's colourless lips and his eyes were narrowed as he struck without discrimination at the warriors.

He planned to leave the fighting to those he had led to Imrryr, for he had other things to do—and quickly. Behind the yellow-garbed soldiers, the tall towers of Imrryr rose, beautiful in their soft and scintillating colours of coral pink and powdery blue, of gold and pale yellow, white and subtle green. One such tower was Elric's objective—the tower of D'a'rputna where he had ordered Tanglebones to take Cymoril, knowing that in the confusion this would be possible.

Elric hacked a blood-drenched path through those who attempted to halt him and men fell back, screaming horribly as the runesword drank their souls.

Now Elric was past them, leaving them to the bright blades of the reavers who poured on to the quayside, and was running up through the twisting streets, his sword slaying anyone who attempted to stop him. Like a white-faced ghoul he was, his clothing tattered and bloody, his armour chipped and scratched, but he ran speedily over the cobblestones of the twisting streets and came at last to the slender tower of hazy blue and soft gold—the Tower of D'a'rputna. Its door was open, showing that someone was inside, and Elric rushed through it and entered the large ground-floor chamber. No one greeted him.

'Tanglebones!' he yelled, his voice roaring loudly even in his own ears. 'Tanglebones—are you here?' He leapt up the stairs in great bounds, calling his servant's name. On the third floor he stopped suddenly, hearing a low groan from one of the rooms. 'Tanglebones—is that you?' Elric strode towards the room, hearing a strangled gasping. He pushed open the door and his stomach seemed to twist within him as he saw the old man lying upon the bare floor of the chamber, striving vainly to stop the flow of blood which gouted from a great wound in his side.

'What's happened man—where's Cymoril?'

Tanglebones' old face twisted in pain and grief. 'She—I—I brought her here, master, as you ordered. But—' he coughed and blood dribbled down his wizened chin, 'but—Prince Yyrkoon—he—he apprehended me—must have followed us here. He—struck me down and took Cymoril back with him—said she'd be—safe in the Tower of B'aal'nezbett. Master—I'm sorry . . .'

'So you should be,' Elric retorted savagely. Then his tone softened. 'Do not worry, old friend—I'll avenge you and myself. I can still reach Cymoril now I know where Yyrkoon has taken her. Thank you for trying, Tanglebones—may your long journey down the last river be uneventful.'

He turned abruptly on his heel and left the chamber, running down the stairs and out into the street again.

The Tower of B'aal'nezbett was the highest tower in the Royal Palace. Elric knew it well, for it was there that his ancestors had studied their dark sorceries and conducted frightful experiments. He shuddered as he thought what Yyrkoon might be doing to his own sister.

The streets of the city seemed hushed and strangely deserted, but Elric had no time to ponder why this should be so. Instead he dashed towards the palace, found the main gate unguarded and the main entrance to the building deserted. This too was unique, but it constituted luck for Elric as he made his way upwards, climbing familiar ways towards the topmost tower.

Finally, he reached a door of shimmering black crystal which had no bolt or handle to it. Frenziedly, Elric struck at the crystal with his sorcerous blade but the crystal appeared only to flow and re-form. His blows had no effect.

Elric racked his mind, seeking to remember the single alien word which would make the door open. He dared not put himself in the trance which would have, in time, brought the word to his lips, instead he had to dredge his subconscious and bring the word forth. It was dangerous but there was little else he could do. His whole frame trembled as his face twisted and his brain began to shake. The word was coming as his vocal chords jerked in his throat and his chest heaved.

He coughed the word out and his whole mind and body ached with the strain. Then he cried:

'I command thee—open!'

He knew that once the door opened, his cousin would be aware of his presence, but he had to risk it. The crystal expanded, pulsating and seething, and then began to flow *out*. It flowed into nothingness, into something beyond the physical universe, beyond time. Elric breathed thankfully and passed into the Tower of B'aal'nezbett. But now an eerie fire, chilling and mind-shattering, was licking around Elric as he struggled up the steps towards the central chamber. There was a strange music surrounding him, uncanny music which throbbed and sobbed and pounded in his head.

Above him he saw a leering Yyrkoon, a black runesword also in his hand, the mate of the one in Elric's own grasp.

'Hellspawn!' Elric said thickly, weakly, 'I see you have recovered Mournblade—well, test its powers against its brother if you dare. I have come to destroy you, cousin.'

Stormbringer was giving forth a peculiar moaning sound which sighed over the shrieking, unearthly music accompanying the licking, chilling fire. The runesword writhed in Elric's fist and he had difficulty in controlling it. Summoning all his strength he plunged up the last few steps and aimed a wild blow at Yyrkoon. Beyond the eerie fire bubbled yellow-green lava, on all sides, above and beneath. The two men were surrounded only by the misty fire and the lava which lurked beyond it

—they were outside the Earth and facing one another for a final battle. The lava seethed and began to ooze inwards, dispersing the fire.

The two blades met and a terrible shrieking roar went up. Elric felt his whole arm go numb and it tingled sickeningly. Elric felt like a puppet. He was no longer his own master—the blade was deciding his actions for him. The blade, with Elric behind it, roared past its brother sword and cut a deep wound in Yyrkoon's left arm. He howled and his eyes widened in agony. Mournblade struck back at Stormbringer, catching Elric in the very place he had wounded his cousin. He sobbed in pain, but continued to move upwards, now wounding Yyrkoon in the right side with a blow strong enough to have killed any other man. Yyrkoon laughed then—laughed like a gibbering demon from the foulest depths of Hell. His sanity had broken at last and Elric now had the advantage. But the great sorcery which his cousin had conjured was still in evidence and Elric felt as if a giant had grasped him, was crushing him as he pressed his advantage, Yyrkoon's blood spouting from the wound and covering Elric, also. The lava was slowly withdrawing and now Elric saw the entrance to the central chamber. Behind his cousin another form moved. Elric gasped. Cymoril had awakened and, with horror on her face, was shrieking at him.

The sword still swung in a black arc, cutting down Yyrkoon's brother blade and breaking the usurper's guard.

'Elric!' cried Cymoril desperately. 'Save me—save me now, else we are doomed for eternity.'

Elric was puzzled by the girl's words. He could not understand the sense of them. Savagely he drove Yyrkoon upwards towards the chamber.

'Elric—put Stormbringer away. Sheath your sword or we shall part again.'

But even if he could have controlled the whistling blade, Elric would not have sheathed it. Hate dominated his being and he would sheathe it in his cousin's evil heart before he put it aside.

Cymoril was weeping, now, pleading with him. But Elric could do nothing. The drooling, idiot thing which had been Yyrkoon of Imrryr, turned at its sister's cries and stared leeringly at her. It cackled and reached out one shaking hand to seize the girl by her shoulder. She struggled to escape, but Yyrkoon still had his evil strength. Taking advantage of his opponent's distraction, Elric cut deep through his body, almost severing the trunk from the waist.

And yet, incredibly, Yyrkoon remained alive, drawing his vitality from the blade which still clashed against Elric's own rune-carved sword. With a final push he flung Cymoril forward and she died screaming on the point of Stormbringer.

Then Yyrkoon laughed one final cackling shriek and his black soul went howling down to hell.

The tower resumed its former proportions, all fire and lava gone. Elric was dazed—unable to marshal his thoughts. He looked down at the dead bodies of the brother and the sister. He saw them, at first, only as corpses—a man's and a woman's.

Then dark truth dawned on his clearing brain and he moaned in grief, like an animal. He had slain the girl he loved. The runesword fell from his grasp, stained by Cymoril's lifeblood, and clattered unheeded down the stairs. Sobbing now, Elric dropped beside the dead girl and lifted her in his arms.

'Cymoril,' he moaned, his whole body throbbing. 'Cymoril—I have slain you.'

4

Elric looked back at the roaring, crumbling, tumbling, flame-spewing ruins of Imrryr and drove his sweating oarsmen faster. The ship, sail still unfurled, bucked as a contrary current of wind caught it and Elric was forced to cling to the ship's side lest he be tossed overboard. He looked back at Imrryr and felt a tightness in his throat as he realised that he was truly rootless, now; a renegade and a woman-slayer, though involuntarily the latter. He had lost the only woman he had loved in his blind lust for revenge. Now it was finished—everything was finished. He could envisage no future, for his future had been bound up with his past and now, effectively, that past was flaming in ruins behind him. Dry sobs eddied in his chest and he gripped the ship's rail yet more firmly.

His mind reluctantly brooded on Cymoril. He had laid her corpse upon a couch and had set fire to the Tower. Then he had gone back to find the reavers successful, straggling back to their ships loaded with loot and girl-slaves, jubilantly firing the tall and beautiful buildings as they went.

He had caused to be destroyed the last tangible sign that the grandiose, magnificent Bright Empire had ever existed. He felt that most of himself was gone with it.

Elric looked back at Imrryr and suddenly a greater sadness overwhelmed him as a tower, as delicate and as beautiful as fine lace, cracked and toppled with flames leaping about it.

He had shattered the last great monument to the earlier race—his own race. Men might have learned again, one day, to build strong, slender towers like those of Imrryr, but now the knowledge was dying with the thundering chaos of the fall of the Dreaming City and the fast-diminishing race of Melniboné.

But what of the Dragon Masters? Neither they nor their golden ships had met the attacking reavers—only their foot-soldiers had been there to defend the city. Had they hidden their ships in some secret waterway and fled inland when the reavers overran the city? They had put up too short a fight to be truly beaten. It had been far too easy. Now that the ships were retreating, were they planning some sudden retaliation? Elric felt that they might have such a plan—perhaps a plan concerning dragons. He shuddered. He had told the others nothing of the beasts which Melnibonéans had controlled for centuries. Even now, someone might be unlocking the gates of the underground Dragon Caves. He turned his mind away from the unnerving prospect.

As the fleet headed towards open sea, Elric's eyes were still looking sadly towards Imrryr as he paid silent homage to the city of his forefathers and the dead Cymoril. He felt hot bitterness sweep over him again as the memory of her death upon his own sword-point came sharply to him. He recalled her warning, when he had left her to go adventuring in the Young Kingdoms, that by putting Yyrkoon on the Ruby Throne as Regent, by relinquishing his power for a year, he doomed them both. He cursed himself. Then a muttering, like a roll of distant thunder, spread through the fleet and he wheeled sharply, intent on discovering the cause of the consternation.

Thirty golden-sailed Melnibonéan battle barges had appeared on both sides of the harbour, issuing from two mouths of the maze. Elric realised that they must have hidden in the other channels, waiting to attack the fleet when they returned, satiated and depleted. Great war-galleys they were, the last ships of Melniboné, and the secret of their building was unknown. They had a sense of age and slumbering might about them as they rowed swiftly, each with four or five banks of great sweeping oars, to encircle the raven ships.

Elric's fleet seemed to shrink before his eyes until it seemed as though it were a bobbing collection of wood-shavings against the towering splendour of the shimmering battle barges. They were well-equipped and fresh for a fight, whereas the weary reavers were intensely battle-tired. There was only one way to save a small part of the fleet, Elric knew. He would have to conjure a witch-wind for sailpower. Most of the flagships were around him and he now occupied that of Yaris, for the youth had got himself wildly drunk and had died by the knife of a Melnibonéan slave wench. Next to Elric's ship was Count Smiorgan's and the stocky Sea Lord was frowning, knowing full well that he and his ships, for all their superior numbers, would not stand up to a sea-fight.

But the conjuring of winds great enough to move many vessels was a dangerous thing, for it released colossal power and the elementals who controlled the winds were apt to turn upon the sorcerer himself if he was not more than careful. But it was the only chance, otherwise the rams which sent ripples from the golden prows would smash the reaver ships to driftwood.

Steeling himself, Elric began to speak the ancient and terrible, many-vowelled names of the beings who existed in the air. Again, he could not risk the trance-state, for he had to watch for signs of the elementals turning upon him. He called to them in a speech that was sometimes high like the cry of a gannet, sometimes rolling like the roar of shore-bound surf, and the dim shapes of the Powers of the Wind began to flit before his blurred gaze. His heart throbbed horribly in his ribs and his legs felt weak. He summoned all his strength and conjured a wind which shrieked wildly and chaotically about him, rocking even the huge Melnibonéan ships back and forth. Then he directed the wind and sent it into the sails of some forty of the reaver ships. Many he could not save for they lay outside even his wide range.

But forty of the craft escaped the smashing rams and, amidst the sound of howling wind and sundered timbers, leapt on the waves, their masts creaking as the wind cracked into their sails. Oars were torn from the hands of the rowers, leaving a wake of broken wood on the white salt trail which boiled behind each of the reaver ships.

Quite suddenly, they were beyond the slowly closing circle of Mel-nibonéan ships and careering madly across the open sea, while all the crews sensed a difference in the air and caught glimpses of strange, soft-shaped forms around them. There was a discomforting sense of evil about the beings which aided them, an awesome alienness.

Smiorgan waved to Elric and grinned thankfully.

'We're safe, thanks to you, Elric!' he yelled across the water. 'I knew you'd bring us luck!'

Elric ignored him.

Now the Dragon Lords, vengeance-bent, gave chase. Almost as fast as the magic-aided reaver fleet were the golden barges of Imrryr, and some reaver galleys, whose masts cracked and split beneath the force of the wind driving them, were caught.

Elric saw mighty grappling hooks of dully gleaming metal swing out from the decks of the Imrryrian galleys and thud with a moan of wrenched timber into those of the fleet which lay broken and powerless behind him. Fire leapt from catapults upon the Dragon Lords' ships and careered towards many a fleeing reaver craft. Searing, foul-stinking flame hissed like lava across the decks and ate into planks like vitriol into paper. Men shrieked, beating vainly at brightly burning clothes, some leaping into water which would not extinguish the fire. Some sank beneath the sea and it was possible to trace their descent as, flaming even below the surface, men and ships fluttered to the bottom like blazing, tired moths.

Reaver decks, untouched by fire, ran red with reaver blood as the enraged Imrryrian warriors swung down the grappling ropes and dropped among the raiders, wielding great swords and battle-axes and wrecking havoc amongst the sea-ravens. Imrryrian arrows and Imrryrian javelins swooped from the towering decks of Imrryrian galleys and tore into the panicky men on the smaller ships.

All this Elric saw as he and his vessels began slowly to overhaul the leading Imrryrian ship, flag-galley of Admiral Magum Colim, commander of the Melnibonéan fleet.

Now Elric spared a word for Count Smiorgan. 'We've outrun them!' he shouted above the howling wind to the next ship where Smiorgan stood staring wide-eyed at the sky. 'But keep your ships heading westwards or we're finished!'

But Smiorgan did not reply. He still looked skyward and there was horror in his eyes; in the eyes of a man who, before this, had never known the quivering bite of fear. Uneasily, Elric let his own eyes follow the gaze of Smiorgan. Then he saw them.

They were dragons, without doubt! The great reptiles were some miles away, but Elric knew the stamp of the huge flying beasts. The average wingspan of these near-extinct monsters was some thirty feet across. Their snake-like bodies, beginning in a narrow-snouted head and terminating in a dreadful whip of a tail, were forty feet long and although they did not breathe the legendary fire and smoke, Elric knew that their venom was combustible and could set fire to wood or fabric on contact.

Imrryrian warriors rode the dragon backs. Armed with long, spearlike goads, they blew strangely shaped horns which sang out curious notes over the turbulent sea and calm blue sky. Nearing the golden fleet, now half-a-league away, the leading dragon sailed down and circled towards the huge golden flag-galley, its wings making a sound like the crack of lightning as they beat through the air.

The grey-green, scaled monster hovered over the golden ship as it heaved in the white-foamed turbulent sea. Framed against the cloudless sky, the dragon was in sharp perspective and it was possible for Elric to get a clear view of it. The goad which the Dragon Master waved to Admiral Magum Colim was a long, slim spear upon which the strange pennant of black and yellow zig-zag lines was, even at this distance, noticeable. Elric recognised the insignia on the pennant.

Dyvim Tvar, friend of Elric's youth, Lord of the Dragon Caves, was leading his charges to claim vengeance for Imrryr the Beautiful.

Elric howled across the water to Smiorgan. 'These are your main danger, now. Do what you can to stave them off!' There was a rattle of iron as the men prepared, near-hopelessly, to repel the new menace. Witch-wind would give little advantage over the fast-flying dragons. Now Dyvim Tvar had evidently conferred with Magum Colim and his goad lashed out at the dragon throat. The huge reptile jerked upwards and began to gain altitude. Eleven other dragons were behind it, joining it now.

With seeming slowness, the dragons began to beat relentlessly towards the reaver fleet as the crewmen prayed to their own Gods for a miracle.

They were doomed. There was no escaping the fact. Every reaver ship was doomed and the raid had been fruitless.

Elric could see the despair in the faces of the men as the masts of the reaver ships continued to bend under the strain of the shrieking witch-wind. They could do nothing, now, but die . . .

Elric fought to rid his mind of the swirling uncertainty which filled it. He drew his sword and felt the pulsating, evil power which lurked in rune-carved Stormbringer. But he hated that power now—for it had caused him to kill the only human he had cherished. He realised how much of his strength he owed to the black-iron sword of his fathers and how weak he might be without it. He was an albino and that meant that he lacked the vitality of a normal human being. Savagely, futilely, as the mist in his mind was replaced by red fear, he cursed the pretensions of revenge he had held, cursed the day when he had agreed to lead the raid on Imrryr and most of all he bitterly vilified dead Yyrkoon and his twisted envy which had been the cause of the whole doom-ridden course of events.

But it was too late now for curses of any kind. The loud slapping of beating dragon wings filled the air and the monsters loomed over the fleeting reaver craft. He had to make some kind of decision—though he had no love for life, he refused to die by the hands of his own people. When he died, he promised himself, it would be by his own hand. He made his decision, hating himself.

He called off the witch-wind as the dragon venom seared down and struck the last ship in line.

He put all his powers into sending a stronger wind into the sails of his own boat while his bewildered comrades in the suddenly becalmed ships called over the water, inquiring desperately the reason for his act.

Elric's ship was moving fast, now, and might just escape the dragons. He hoped so.

He deserted the man who had trusted him, Count Smiorgan, and watched as venom poured from the sky and engulfed him in blazing green and scarlet flame. Elric fled, keeping his mind from thoughts of the future, and sobbed aloud, that proud prince of ruins; and he cursed the malevolent Gods for the black day when idly, for their amusement, they had spawned men.

Behind him, the last reaver ships flared into sudden appalling brightness and, although half-thankful that they had escaped the fate of their comrades, the crew looked at Elric accusingly. He sobbed on, not heeding them, great griefs racking his soul.

A night later, off the coast of an island called Pan Tang, when the ship was safe from the dreadful recriminations of the Dragon Masters and their beasts, Elric stood brooding in the stern while the men eyed him with fear and hatred, muttering of betrayal and heartless cowardice. They appeared to have forgotten their own fear and subsequent safety.

Elric brooded, and he held the black runesword in his two hands. Stormbringer was more than an ordinary battle-blade, this he had known for years, but now he realised that it was possessed of more sentience than he had imagined. The frightful thing had used its wielder and had made Elric destroy Cymoril. Yet he was horribly dependent upon it; he realised this with soul-rending certainty. But he feared and resented the sword's power—hated it bitterly for the chaos it had wrought in his brain and spirit. In an agony of uncertainty he held the blade in his hands and forced himself to weigh the factors involved. Without the sinister sword, he would lose pride—perhaps even life— but he might know the soothing tranquillity of pure rest; with it he would have power and strength—but the sword would guide him into a doom-racked future. He would savour power—but never peace.

He drew a great, sobbing breath and, blind misgiving influencing him, threw the sword into the moon-drenched sea.

Incredibly, it did not sink. It did not even float on the water. It fell point forwards into the sea and *stuck* there, quivering as if it were embedded in timber. It remained throbbing in the water, six inches of its blade immersed, and began to give off a weird devil-scream—a howl of horrible malevolence.

With a choking curse Elric stretched out his slim, whitely gleaming hand, trying to recover the sentient hellblade. He stretched further, leaning far out over the rail. He could not grasp it—it lay some feet from him, still. Gasping, a sickening sense of defeat overwhelming him, he dropped over the side and plunged into the bone-chilling water, striking out with strained, grotesque strokes, towards the hovering sword. He was beaten—the sword had won.

He reached it and put his fingers around the hilt. At once it settled in his hand and Elric felt strength seep slowly back into his aching body. Then he realised that he and the sword were interdependent, for though he needed the blade, Stormbringer, parasitic, required a user—without a man to wield it, the blade was also powerless.

'We must be bound to one another then,' Elric murmured despairingly. 'Bound by hell-forged chains and fate-haunted circumstance. Well, then—let it be thus so—and men will have cause to tremble and flee when they hear the names of Elric of Melniboné and Stormbringer, his sword. We are two of a kind—produced by an age which has deserted us. Let us give this age *cause* to hate us!'

Strong again, Elric sheathed Stormbringer and the sword settled against his side; then, with powerful strokes, he began to swim towards the island while the men he left on the ship breathed with relief and speculated whether he would live or perish in the bleak waters of that strange and nameless sea . . .

BOOK TWO

WHILE THE GODS LAUGH

I, while the gods laugh, the world's vortex am;
Maelstrom of passions in that hidden sea
Whose waves of all-time lap the coasts of me,
And in small compass the dark waters cram.

Mervyn Peake, *Shapes and Sounds*,
1941.

1

One night, as Elric sat moodily drinking alone in a tavern, a wingless woman of Myyrrhn came gliding out of the storm and rested her lithe body against him.

Her face was thin and frail-boned, almost as white as Elric's own albino skin, and she wore flimsy pale-green robes which contrasted well with her dark red hair.

The tavern was ablaze with candle-flame and alive with droning argument and gusty laughter, but the words of the woman of Myyrrhn came clear and liquid, carrying over the zesty din.

'I have sought you twenty days,' she said to Elric who regarded her insolently through hooded crimson eyes and lazed in a high-backed chair; a silver wine-cup in his long-fingered right hand and his left on the pommel of his sorcerous runesword Stormbringer.

'Twenty days,' murmured the Melnibonéan softly, speaking as if to himself; deliberately rude. 'A long time for a beautiful and lonely woman to be wandering the world.' He opened his eyes a trifle wider and spoke to her directly: 'I am Elric of Melniboné, as you evidently know. I grant no favours and ask none. Bearing this in mind, tell me why you have sought me for twenty days.'

Equably, the woman replied, undaunted by the albino's supercilious tone. 'You are a bitter man, Elric; I know this also—and you are grief-haunted for reasons which are already legend. I ask you no favours— but bring you myself and a proposition. What do you desire most in the world?'

'Peace,' Elric told her simply. Then he smiled ironically and said: 'I am an evil man, lady, and my destiny is hell-doomed, but I am not unwise, nor unfair. Let me remind you a little of the truth. Call this legend if you prefer—I do not care.

'A woman died a year ago, on the blade of my trusty sword.' He patted the blade sharply and his eyes were suddenly hard and self-mocking. 'Since then I have courted no woman and desired none. Why should I break such secure habits? If asked, I grant you that I could speak poetry to you, and that you have a grace and beauty which moves me to interesting speculation, but I would not load any part of my dark burden upon one as exquisite as you. Any relationship between us, other than formal, would necessitate my unwilling shifting of part of that burden.' He paused for an instant and then said slowly: 'I should admit that I scream in my sleep sometimes and am often tortured by incommunicable self-loathing. Go while you can, lady, and forget Elric for he can bring only grief to your soul.'

With a quick movement he turned his gaze from her and lifted the silver wine-cup, draining it and replenishing it from a jug at his side.

'No,' said the wingless woman of Myyrrhn calmly, 'I will not. Come with me.'

She rose and gently took Elric's hand. Without knowing why, Elric allowed himself to be led from the tavern and out into the wild, rainless storm which howled around the Filkharian city of Raschil. A protective and cynical smile hovered about his mouth as she drew him towards the sea-lashed quayside where she told him her name. Shaarilla of the Dancing Mist, wingless daughter of a dead necromancer—a cripple in her own strange land, and an outcast.

Elric felt uncomfortably drawn to this calm-eyed woman who wasted few words. He felt a great surge of emotion well within him; emotion he had never thought to experience again, and he wanted to take her finely moulded shoulders and press her slim body to his. But he quelled the urge and studied her marble delicacy and her wild hair which flowed in the wind about her head.

Silence rested comfortably between them while the chaotic wind howled mournfully over the sea. Here, Elric could ignore the warm stink of the city and he felt almost relaxed. At last, looking away from him towards the swirling sea, her green robe curling in the wind, she said: 'You have heard, of course, of the Dead Gods' Book?'

Elric nodded. He was interested, despite the need he felt to disassociate himself as much as possible from his fellows. The mythical book was believed to contain knowledge which could solve many problems that had plagued men for centuries—it held a holy and mighty wisdom which every sorcerer desired to sample. But it was believed destroyed, hurled into the sun when the Old Gods were dying in the cosmic wastes which lay beyond the outer reaches of the solar system. Another legend, apparently of later origin, spoke vaguely of the dark ones who had interrupted the Book's sunward coursing and had stolen it before it could be destroyed. Most scholars discounted this legend, arguing that, by this time, the book would have come to light if it did still exist.

Elric made himself speak flatly so that he appeared to be disinterested when he answered Shaarilla. 'Why do you mention the Book?'

'I know that it exists,' Shaarilla replied intensely, 'and I know where it is. My father acquired the knowledge just before he died. Myself—and the book—you may have if you will help me get it.'

Could the secret of peace be contained in the book? Elric wondered. Would he, if he found it, be able to dispense with Stormbringer?

'If you want it so badly that you seek my help,' he said eventually, 'why do you not wish to keep it?'

'Because I would be afraid to have such a thing perpetually in my custody—it is not a book for a woman to own, but you are possibly the last mighty nigromancer left in the world and it is fitting that you should have it. Besides, you might kill me to obtain it—I would never be safe with such a volume in my hands. I need only one small part of its wisdom.'

'What is that?' Elric inquired, studying her patrician beauty with a new pulse stirring within him.

Her mouth set and the lids fell over her eyes. 'When we have the book in our hands—then you will have your answer. Not before.'

'This answer is good enough,' Elric remarked quickly, seeing that he would gain no more information at that stage. 'And the answer appeals to me.' Then, half before he realised it, he seized her shoulders in his slim, pale hands and pressed his colourless lips to her scarlet mouth.

Elric and Shaarilla rode westwards, towards the Silent Land, across the lush plains of Shazaar where their ship had berthed two days earlier. The border country between Shazaar and the Silent Land was a lonely stretch of territory, unoccupied even by peasant dwellings; a no-man's land, though fertile and rich in natural wealth. The inhabitants of Shazaar had deliberately refrained from extending their borders further, for though the dwellers in the Silent Land rarely ventured beyond the Marshes of the Mist, the natural borderline between the two lands, the inhabitants of Shazaar held their unknown neighbours in almost superstitious fear.

The journey had been clean and swift, though ominous, with several persons who should have known nothing of their purpose warning the travellers of nearing danger. Elric brooded, recognising the signs of doom but choosing to ignore them and communicate nothing to Shaarilla who, for her part, seemed content with Elric's silence. They

spoke little in the day and so saved their breath for the wild love-play of
the night.

The thud of the two horses' hooves on the soft turf, the muted creak
and clatter of Elric's harness and sword, were the only sounds to break
the stillness of the clear winter day as the pair rode steadily, nearing the
quaking, treacherous trails of the Marshes of the Mist.

One gloomy night, they reached the borders of the Silent Land,
marked by the marsh, and they halted and made camp, pitching their
silk tent on a hill overlooking the mist-shrouded wastes.

Banked like black pillows against the horizon, the clouds were ominous. The moon lurked behind them, sometimes piercing them sufficiently to send a pale tentative beam down on to the glistening marsh or
its ragged, grassy frontiers. Once, a moonbeam glanced off silver, illu-
minating the dark silhouette of Elric, but, as if repelled by the sight of a
living creature on that bleak hill, the moon once again slunk behind its
cloud-shield, leaving Elric thinking deeply. Leaving Elric in the darkness he desired.

Thunder rumbled over distant mountains, sounding like the laughter
of far-off Gods. Elric shivered, pulled his blue cloak more tightly about
him, and continued to stare over the misted lowlands.

Shaarilla came to him soon, and she stood beside him, swathed in a
thick woollen cloak which could not keep out all the damp chill in the
air.

'The Silent Land,' she murmured. 'Are all the stories true, Elric? Did
they teach you of it in old Melniboné?'

Elric frowned, annoyed that she had disturbed his thoughts. He
turned abruptly to look at her, staring blankly through his crimson-
irised eyes for a moment and then saying flatly:

'The inhabitants are unhuman and feared. This I know. Few men
ventured into their territory, ever. None have returned, to my knowledge. Even in the days when Melniboné was a powerful Empire, this
was one nation my ancestors never ruled—nor did they desire to do so.
The denizens of the Silent Land are said to be a dying race, far more
evil than my ancestors ever were, who enjoyed dominion over the Earth
long before men gained any sort of power. They rarely venture beyond
the confines of their territory, nowadays, encompassed as it is by marsh-
land and mountains.'

Shaarilla laughed, then, with little humour. 'So they are unhuman are
they, Elric? Then what of my people, who are related to them? What of
me, Elric?'

'You're human enough for me,' replied Elric insouciantly, looking her in the eyes. She smiled.

'No compliment,' she said, 'but I'll take it for one—until your glib tongue finds a better.'

That night they slept restlessly and, as he had predicted, Elric screamed agonisingly in his turbulent, terror-filled sleep and he called a name which made Shaarilla's eyes fill with pain and jealousy. That name was Cymoril. Wide-eyed in his grim sleep, Elric seemed to be staring at the one he named, speaking other words in a sibilant language which made Shaarilla block her ears and shudder.

The next morning, as they broke camp, folding the rustling fabric of the yellow silk tent between them, Shaarilla avoided looking at Elric directly but later, since he made no move to speak, she asked him a question in a voice which shook somewhat.

It was a question which she needed to ask, but one which came hard to her lips. 'Why do you desire the Dead Gods' Book, Elric? What do you believe you will find in it?'

Elric shrugged, dismissing the question, but she repeated her words less slowly, with more insistence.

'Very well then,' he said eventually. 'But it is not easy to answer you in a few sentences. I desire, if you like, to know one of two things.'

'And what is that, Elric?'

The tall albino dropped the folded tent to the grass and sighed. His fingers played nervously with the pommel of his runesword. 'Can an ultimate God exist—or not? That is what I need to know, Shaarilla, if my life is to have any direction at all.

'The Lords of Law and Chaos now govern our lives. But is there some being greater than them?'

Shaarilla put a hand on Elric's arm. 'Why must you know?' she said.

'Despairingly, sometimes, I seek the comfort of a benign God, Shaarilla. My mind goes out, lying awake at night, searching through black barrenness for something—anything—which will take me to it, warm me, protect me, tell me that there is order in the chaotic tumble of the universe; that it is consistent, this precision of the planets, not simply a brief, bright spark of sanity in an eternity of malevolent anarchy.'

Elric sighed and his quiet tones were tinged with hopelessness. 'Without some confirmation of the order of things, my only comfort is to accept the anarchy. This way, I can revel in chaos and know, without fear, that we are all doomed from the start—that our brief existence is both meaningless and damned. I can accept, then, that we are more than forsaken, because there was never anything there to forsake us. I have weighed the proof, Shaarilla, and must believe that anarchy prevails, in spite of all the laws which seemingly govern our actions, our sorcery, our logic. I see only chaos in the world. If the Book we seek tells me otherwise, then I shall gladly believe it. Until then, I will put my trust only in my sword and myself.'

Shaarilla stared at Elric strangely. 'Could not this philosophy of yours have been influenced by recent events in your past? Do you fear the consequences of your murder and treachery? Is it not more comforting for you to believe in deserts which are rarely just?'

Elric turned on her, crimson eyes blazing in anger, but even as he made to speak, the anger fled him and he dropped his eyes towards the ground, hooding them from her gaze.

'Perhaps,' he said lamely. 'I do not know. That is the only *real* truth, Shaarilla. *I do not know.*'

Shaarilla nodded, her face lit by an enigmatic sympathy; but Elric did not see the look she gave him, for his own eyes were full of crystal tears which flowed down his lean, white face and took his strength and will momentarily from him.

'I am a man possessed,' he groaned, 'and without this devil-blade I carry I would not be a man at all.'

2

They mounted their swift, black horses and spurred them with abandoned savagery down the hillside towards the Marsh, their cloaks whipping behind them as the wind caught them, lashing them high into the air. Both rode with set, hard faces, refusing to acknowledge the aching uncertainty which lurked within them.

And the horses' hooves had splashed into quaking bogland before they could halt.

Cursing, Elric tugged hard on his reins, pulling his horse back on to firm ground. Shaarilla, too, fought her own panicky stallion and guided the beast to the safety of the turf.

'How do we cross?' Elric asked her impatiently.

'There was a map—' Shaarilla began hesitantly.

'Where is it?'

'It—it was lost. I lost it. But I tried hard to memorise it. I think I'll be able to get us safely across.'

'How did you lose it—and why didn't you tell me of this before?' Elric stormed.

'I'm sorry, Elric—but for a whole day, just before I found you in that tavern, my memory was gone. Somehow, I lived through a day without knowing it—and when I awoke, the map was missing.'

Elric frowned. 'There is some force working against us, I am sure,' he muttered, 'but what it is, I do not know.' He raised his voice and said to her: 'Let us hope that your memory is not too faulty, now. These Marshes are infamous the world over, but by all accounts, only natural hazards wait for us.' He grimaced and put his fingers around the hilt of his runesword. 'Best go first, Shaarilla, but stay close. Lead the way.'

She nodded, dumbly, and turned her horse's head towards the north, galloping along the bank until she came to a place where a great, tapering rock loomed. Here, a grassy path, four feet or so across, led out into the misty marsh. They could only see a little distance ahead, because of the clinging mist, but it seemed that the trail remained firm for some way. Shaarilla walked her horse on to the path and jolted forward at a slow trot, Elric following immediately behind her.

Through the swirling, heavy mist which shone whitely, the horses moved hesitantly and their riders had to keep them on short, tight rein. The mist padded the marsh with silence and the gleaming, watery fens around them stank with foul putrescence. No animal scurried, no bird shrieked above them. Everywhere was a haunting, fear-laden silence which made both horses and riders uneasy.

With panic in their throats, Elric and Shaarilla rode on, deeper and deeper into the unnatural Marshes of the Mist, their eyes wary and even their nostrils quivering for scent of danger in the stinking morass.

Hours later, when the sun was long past its zenith, Shaarilla's horse reared, screaming and whinnying. She shouted for Elric, her exquisite features twisted in fear as she stared into the mist. He spurred his own bucking horse forwards and joined her.

Something moved, slowly, menacingly in the clinging whiteness. Elric's right hand whipped over to his left side and grasped the hilt of Stormbringer.

The blade shrieked out of its scabbard, a black fire gleaming along its length and alien power flowing from it into Elric's arm and through his body. A weird, unholy light leapt into Elric's crimson eyes and his mouth was wrenched into a hideous grin as he forced the frightened horse further into the skulking mist.

'Arioch, Lord of the Seven Darks, be with me now!' Elric yelled as he made out the shifting shape ahead of him. It was white, like the mist, yet somehow *darker*. It stretched high above Elric's head. It was nearly eight feet tall and almost as broad. But it was still only an outline, seeming to have no face or limbs—only movement: darting, malevolent movement! But Arioch, his patron god, chose not to hear.

Elric could feel his horse's great heart beating between his legs as the beast plunged forward under its rider's iron control. Shaarilla was screaming something behind him, but he could not hear the words. Elric hacked at the white shape, but his sword met only mist and it howled angrily. The fear-crazed horse would go no further and Elric was forced to dismount.

'Keep hold of the steed,' he shouted behind him to Shaarilla and moved on light feet towards the darting shape which hovered ahead of him, blocking his path.

Now he could make out some of its saliencies. Two eyes, the colour of thin, yellow wine, were set high in the thing's body, though it had no separate head. A mouthing, obscene slit, filled with fangs, lay just beneath the eyes. It had no nose or ears that Elric could see. Four appendages sprang from its upper parts and its lower body slithered along the ground, unsupported by any limbs. Elric's eyes ached as he looked at it. It was incredibly disgusting to behold and its amorphous body gave off a stench of death and decay. Fighting down his fear, the albino inched forward warily, his sword held high to parry any thrust the thing might make with its arms. Elric recognised it from a description in one of his grimoires. It was a Mist Giant—possibly the only Mist Giant, Bellbane. Even the wisest wizards were uncertain how many existed—one or many. It was a ghoul of the swamp-lands which fed off the souls and the blood of men and beasts. But the Marshes of this Mist were far to the east of Bellbane's reputed haunts.

Elric ceased to wonder why so few animals inhabited that stretch of the swamp. Overhead the sky was beginning to darken.

Stormbringer throbbed in Elric's grasp as he called the names of the ancient Demon-Gods of his people. The nauseous ghoul obviously recognised the names. For an instant, it wavered backwards. Elric made his legs move towards the thing. Now he saw that the ghoul was not white at all. But it had no colour to it that Elric could recognise. There was a suggestion of orangeness dashed with sickening greenish yellow, but he did not see the colours with his eyes—he only *sensed* the alien, unholy tinctures.

Then Elric rushed towards the thing, shouting the names which now had no meaning to his surface consciousness. '*Balaan—Marthim! Aesma! Alastor! Saebos! Verdelet! Nizilfkm! Haborym!* Haborym of the Fires Which Destroy!' His whole mind was torn in two. Part of him wanted to run, to hide, but he had no control over the power which now gripped him and pushed him to meet the horror. His sword blade hacked and slashed at the shape. It was like trying to cut through water —sentient, pulsating water. But Stormbringer had effect. The whole shape of the ghoul quivered as if in dreadful pain. Elric felt himself plucked into the air and his vision went. He could see nothing—do nothing but hack and cut at the thing which now held him.

Sweat poured from him as, blindly, he fought on.

Pain which was hardly physical—a deeper, horrifying pain, filled his being as he howled now in agony and struck continually at the yielding bulk which embraced him and was pulling him slowly towards its gaping maw. He struggled and writhed in the obscene grasp of the thing. With powerful arms, it was holding him, almost lasciviously, drawing him closer as a rough lover would draw a girl. Even the mighty power intrinsic in the runesword did not seem enough to kill the monster.

Though its efforts were somewhat weaker than earlier, it still drew Elric nearer to the gnashing, slavering mouth-slit.

Elric cried the names again, while Stormbringer danced and sang an evil song in his right hand. In agony, Elric writhed, praying, begging and promising, but still he was drawn inch by inch towards the grinning maw.

Savagely, grimly, he fought and again he screamed for Arioch. A mind touched his—sardonic, powerful, evil—and he knew Arioch responded at last! Almost imperceptibly, the Mist Giant weakened. Elric pressed his advantage and the knowledge that the ghoul was losing its strength gave him more power. Blindly, agony piercing every nerve of his body, he struck and struck.

Then, quite suddenly, he was falling.

He seemed to fall for hours, slowly, weightlessly until he landed upon a surface which yielded beneath him. He began to sink.

Far off, beyond time and space, he heard a distant voice calling to him. He did not want to hear it; he was content to lie where he was as the cold, comforting stuff in which he lay dragged him slowly into itself.

Then some sixth sense made him realise that it was Shaarilla's voice calling him and he forced himself to make sense out of her words.

'Elric—the marsh! You're in the marsh. Don't move!'

He smiled to himself. Why should he move? Down he was sinking, slowly, calmly—down into the welcoming marsh . . . *Had there been another time like this; another marsh?*

With a mental jolt, full awareness of the situation came back to him and he jerked his eyes open. Above him was mist. To one side a pool of unnamable colouring was slowly evaporating, giving off a foul odour. On the other side he could just make out a human form, gesticulating wildly. Beyond the human form were the barely discernible shapes of two horses. Shaarilla was there. Beneath him—

Beneath him was the marsh.

Thick, stinking slime was sucking him downwards as he lay spread-eagled upon it, half-submerged already. Stormbringer was still in his right hand. He could just see it if he turned his head. Carefully, he tried to lift the top half of his body from the sucking morass. He succeeded, only to feel his legs sink deeper. Sitting upright, he shouted to the girl.

'Shaarilla! Quickly—a rope!'

'There is no rope, Elric!' She was ripping off her top garment, frantically tearing it into strips.

Still Elric sank, his feet finding no purchase beneath them.

Shaarilla hastily knotted the strips of cloth. She flung the makeshift rope inexpertly towards the sinking albino. It fell short. Fumbling in her haste, she threw it again. This time his groping left hand found it. The girl began to haul on the fabric. Elric felt himself rise a little and then stop.

'It's no good, Elric—I haven't the strength.'

Cursing her, Elric shouted: 'The horse—tie it to the horse!'

She ran towards one of the horses and looped the cloth around the pommel of the saddle. Then she tugged at the beast's reins and began to walk it away.

Swiftly, Elric was dragged from the sucking bog and, still gripping Stormbringer was pulled to the inadequate safety of the strip of turf.

Gasping, he tried to stand, but found his legs incredibly weak beneath him. He rose, staggered, and fell. Shaarilla knelt down beside him.

'Are you hurt?'

Elric smiled in spite of his weakness. 'I don't think so.'

'It was dreadful. I couldn't see properly what was happening. You seemed to disappear and then—then you screamed that—that name!' She was trembling, her face pale and taut.

'What name?' Elric was genuinely puzzled. 'What name did I scream?'

She shook her head. 'It doesn't matter—but whatever it was—it saved you. You reappeared soon afterwards and fell into the marsh . . .'

Stormbringer's power was still flowing into the albino. He already felt stronger.

With an effort, he got up and stumbled unsteadily towards his horse.

'I'm sure that the Mist Giant does not usually haunt this marsh—it was sent here. By what—or whom—I don't know, but we must get to firmer ground while we can.'

Shaarilla said: 'Which way—back or forward?'

Elric frowned. 'Why, forward, of course. Why do you ask?'

She swallowed and shook her head. 'Let's hurry, then,' she said.

They mounted their horses and rode with little caution until the marsh and its cloak of mist was behind them.

Now the journey took on a new urgency as Elric realised that some force was attempting to put obstacles in their way. They rested little and savagely rode their powerful horses to a virtual standstill.

On the fifth day they were riding through barren, rocky country and a light rain was falling.

The hard ground was slippery so that they were forced to ride more slowly, huddled over the sodden necks of their horses, muffled in cloaks which only inadequately kept out the drizzling rain. They had ridden in silence for some time before they heard a ghastly cackling baying ahead of them and the rattle of hooves.

Elric motioned towards a large rock looming to their right. 'Shelter there,' he said. 'Something comes towards us—possibly more enemies. With luck, they'll pass us.' Shaarilla mutely obeyed him and together they waited as the hideous baying grew nearer.

'One rider—several other beasts,' Elric said, listening intently. 'The beasts either follow or pursue the rider.'

Then they were in sight—racing through the rain. A man frantically spurring an equally frightened horse—and behind him, the distance decreasing, a pack of what at first appeared to be dogs. But these were not dogs—they were half-dog and half-bird, with the lean, shaggy bodies and legs of dogs but possessing birdlike talons in place of paws and savagely curved beaks which snapped where muzzles should have been.

'The hunting dogs of the Dharzi!' gasped Shaarilla. 'I thought that they, like their masters, were long extinct!'

'I, also,' Elric said. 'What are they doing in these parts? There was never contact between the Dharzi and the dwellers of this Land.'

'Brought here—by *something,*' Shaarilla whispered. 'Those devil-dogs will scent us to be sure.'

Elric reached for his runesword. 'Then we can lose nothing by aiding their quarry,' he said, urging his mount forward. 'Wait here, Shaarilla.'

By this time, the devil-pack and the man they pursued were rushing past the sheltering rock, speeding down a narrow defile. Elric spurred his horse down the slope.

'Ho there!' he shouted to the frantic rider. 'Turn and stand, my friend —I'm here to aid you!'

His moaning runesword lifted high, Elric thundered towards the snapping, howling devil-dogs and his horse's hooves struck one with an impact which broke the unnatural beast's spine. There were some five or six of the weird dogs left. The rider turned his horse and drew a long sabre from a scabbard at his waist. He was a small man, with a broad ugly mouth. He grinned in relief.

'A lucky chance, this meeting, good master!'

This was all he had time to remark before two of the dogs were leaping at him and he was forced to give his whole attention to defending himself from their slashing talons and snapping beaks.

The other three dogs concentrated their vicious attention upon Elric. One leapt high, its beak aimed at Elric's throat. He felt foul breath on his face and hastily brought Stormbringer round in an arc which chopped the dog in two. Filthy blood spattered Elric and his horse and the scent of it seemed to increase the fury of the other dogs' attack. But the blood made the dancing black runesword sing an almost ecstatic tune and Elric felt it writhe in his grasp and stab at another of the hideous dogs. The point caught the beast just below its breastbone as it reared up at the albino. It screamed in terrible agony and turned its beak to seize the blade. As the beak connected with the lambent black metal of the sword, a foul stench, akin to the smell of burning, struck Elric's nostrils and the beast's scream broke off sharply.

Engaged with the remaining devil-dog, Elric caught a fleeting glimpse of the charred corpse. His horse was rearing high, lashing at the last alien animal with flailing hooves. The dog avoided the horse's attack and came at Elric's unguarded left side. The albino swung in the saddle and brought his sword hurtling down to slice into the dog's skull and spill brains and blood on the wetly gleaming ground. Still somehow alive, the dog snapped feebly at Elric, but the Melnibonéan ignored its futile attack and turned his attention to the little man who had dispensed with one of his adversaries, but was having difficulty with the second. The dog had grasped the sabre with its beak, gripping the sword near the hilt.

Talons raked towards the little man's throat as he strove to shake the dog's grip. Elric charged forward, his runesword aimed like a lance to where the devil-dog dangled in mid-air, its talons slashing, trying to reach the flesh of its former quarry. Stormbringer caught the beast in its lower abdomen and ripped upwards, slitting the thing's underparts from crutch to throat. It released its hold on the small man's sabre and fell writhing to the ground. Elric's horse trampled it into the rocky ground. Breathing heavily, the albino sheathed Stormbringer and warily regarded the man he had saved. He disliked unnecessary contact with anyone and did not wish to be embarrassed by a display of emotion on the little man's part.

He was not disappointed, for the wide, ugly mouth split into a cheerful grin and the man bowed in the saddle as he returned his own curved blade to its scabbard.

'Thanks, good sir,' he said lightly. 'Without your help, the battle might have lasted longer. You deprived me of good sport, but you meant well. Moonglum is my name.'

'Elric of Melniboné, I,' replied the albino, but saw no reaction on the little man's face. This was strange, for the name of Elric was now infamous throughout most of the world. The story of his treachery and the slaying of his cousin Cymoril had been told and elaborated upon in taverns throughout the Young Kingdoms. Much as he hated it, he was used to receiving some indication of recognition from those he met. His albinoism was enough to mark him.

Intrigued by Moonglum's ignorance, and feeling strangely drawn towards the cocky little rider, Elric studied him in an effort to discover from what land he came. Moonglum wore no armour and his clothes were of faded blue material, travel-stained and worn. A stout leather belt carried the sabre, a dirk and a woollen purse. Upon his feet, Moonglum wore angle-length boots of cracked leather. His horse-furniture was much used but of obviously good quality. The man himself, seated high in the saddle, was barely more than five feet tall, with legs too long, in proportion, to the rest of his slight body. His nose was short and uptilted, beneath grey-green eyes, large and innocent-seeming. A mop of vivid red hair fell over his forehead and down his neck, unrestrained. He sat his horse comfortably, still grinning but looking now behind Elric to where Shaarilla rode to join them.

Moonglum bowed elaborately as the girl pulled her horse to a halt.

Elric said coldly, 'The Lady Shaarilla—Master Moonglum of—?'

'Of Elwher,' Moonglum supplied, 'The mercantile capital of the East —the finest city in the world.'

Elric recognised the name. 'So you are from Elwher, Master Moonglum. I have heard of the place. A new city, is it not? Some few centuries old. You have ridden far.'

'Indeed I have, sir. Without knowledge of the language used in these parts, the journey would have been harder, but luckily the slave who inspired me with tales of his homeland taught me the speech thoroughly.'

'But why do you travel these parts—have you not heard the legends?' Shaarilla spoke incredulously.

'Those very legends were what brought me hence—and I'd begun to discount them, until those unpleasant pups set upon me. For what reason they decided to give chase, I will not know, for I gave them no cause to take a dislike to me. This is, indeed, a barbarous land.'

Elric was uncomfortable. Light talk of the kind which Moonglum seemed to enjoy was contrary to his own brooding nature. But in spite of this, he found that he was liking the man more and more.

It was Moonglum who suggested that they travel together for a while. Shaarilla objected, giving Elric a warning glance, but he ignored it.

'Very well then, friend Moonglum, since three are stronger than two, we'd appreciate your company. We ride towards the mountains.' Elric himself, was feeling in a more cheerful mood.

'And what do you seek there?' Moonglum inquired.

'A secret,' Elric said, and his new-found companion was discreet enough to drop the question.

3

So they rode, while the rainfall increased and splashed and sang among the rocks with the sky like dull steel above them and the wind crooning a dirge about their ears. Three small figures riding swiftly towards the black mountain barrier which rose over the world like a brooding God. And perhaps it was a God that laughed sometimes as they neared the foothills of the range, or perhaps it was the wind whistling through the dark mystery of canyons and precipices and the tumble of basalt and granite which climbed towards lonely peaks. Thunder clouds formed around those peaks and lightning smashed downwards like a monster finger searching the earth for grubs. Thunder rattled over the range and Shaarilla spoke her thoughts at last to Elric; spoke them as the mountains came in sight.

'Elric—let us go back, I beg you. Forget the Book—there are too many forces working against us. Take heed of the signs, Elric, or we are doomed!'

But Elric was grimly silent, for he had long been aware that the girl was losing her enthusiasm for the quest she had started.

'Elric—please. We will never reach the Book. Elric, turn back.'

She rode beside him, pulling at his garments until impatiently he shrugged himself clear of her grasp and said:

'I am intrigued too much to stop now. Either continue to lead the way—or tell me what you know and stay here. You desired to sample the Book's wisdom once—but now a few minor pitfalls on our journey have frightened you. What was it you needed to learn, Shaarilla?'

She did not answer him, but said instead: 'And what was it you desired, Elric? Peace, you told me. Well, I warn you, you'll find no peace in those grim mountains—if we reach them at all.'

'You have not been frank with me, Shaarilla,' Elric said coldly, still looking ahead of him at the black peaks. 'You know something of the forces seeking to stop us.'

She shrugged. 'It matters not—I know little. My father spoke a few vague warnings before he died, that is all.'

'What did he say?'

'He said that He who guards the Book would use all his power to stop mankind from using its wisdom.'

'What else?'

'Nothing else. But it is enough, now that I see that my father's warning was truly spoken. It was this guardian who killed him, Elric—or one of the guardian's minions. I do not wish to suffer that fate, in spite of what the Book might do for me. I had thought you powerful enough to aid me—but now I doubt it.'

'I have protected you so far,' Elric said simply. 'Now tell me what you seek from the Book?'

'I am too ashamed.'

Elric did not press the question, but eventually she spoke softly, almost whispering. 'I sought my wings,' she said.

'Your wings—you mean the Book might give you a spell so that you could grow wings!' Elric smiled ironically. 'And that is why you seek the vessel of the world's mightiest wisdom!'

'If you were thought deformed in your own land—it would seem important enough to you,' she shouted defiantly.

Elric turned his face towards her, his crimson-irised eyes burning with a strange emotion. He put a hand to his dead white skin and a crooked smile twisted his lips. 'I, too, have felt as you do,' he said quietly. That was all he said and Shaarilla dropped behind him again, shamed.

They rode on in silence until Moonglum, who had been riding discreetly ahead, cocked his overlarge skull on one side and suddenly drew rein.

Elric joined him. 'What is it, Moonglum?'

'I hear horses coming this way,' the little man said. 'And voices which are disturbingly familiar. More of those devil-dogs, Elric—and this time accompanied by riders!'

Elric, too, heard the sounds, now, and shouted a warning to Shaarilla.

'Perhaps you were right,' he called. 'More trouble comes towards us.'

'What now?' Moonglum said, frowning.

'Ride for the mountains,' Elric replied, 'and we may yet outdistance them.'

They spurred their steeds into a fast gallop and sped towards the hills.

But their flight was hopeless. Soon a black pack was visible on the horizon and the sharp birdlike baying of the devil-dogs drew nearer. Elric stared backward at their pursuers. Night was beginning to fall, and visibility was decreasing with every passing moment but he had a vague impression of the riders who raced behind the pack. They were swathed in dark cloaks and carried long spears. Their faces were invisible, lost in the shadow of the hoods which covered their heads.

Now Elric and his companions were forcing their horses up a steep incline, seeking the shelter of the rocks which lay above.

'We'll halt here,' Elric ordered, 'and try to hold them off. In the open they could easily surround us.'

Moonglum nodded affirmatively, agreeing with the good sense contained in Elric's words. They pulled their sweating steeds to a standstill and prepared to join battle with the howling pack and their dark-cloaked masters.

Soon the first of the devil-dogs were rushing up the incline, their beak-jaws slavering and their talons rattling on stone. Standing between two rocks, blocking the way between with their bodies, Elric and Moonglum met the first attack and quickly dispatched three of the animals. Several more took the place of the dead and the first of the riders was visible behind them as night crept closer.

'Arioch!' swore Elric, suddenly recognising the riders. 'These are the Lords of Dharzi—dead these ten centuries. We're fighting dead men, Moonglum, and the too-tangible ghosts of their dogs. Unless I can think of a sorcerous means to defeat them, we're doomed!'

The zombie-men appeared to have no intention of taking part in the attack for the moment. They waited, their dead eyes eerily luminous, as the devil-dogs attempted to break through the swinging network of steel with which Elric and his companion defended themselves. Elric was racking his brains—trying to dredge a spoken spell from his memory which would dismiss these living dead. Then it came to him, and hoping that the forces he had to invoke would decide to aid him, he began to chant:

> 'Let the Laws which govern all things
> Not so lightly be dismissed;
> Let the Ones who flout the Earth Kings
> With a fresher death be kissed.'

Nothing happened. 'I've failed.' Elric muttered hopelessly as he met the attack of a snapping devil-dog and spitted the thing on his sword.

But then—the ground rocked and seemed to *seethe* beneath the feet of the horses upon whose backs the dead men sat. The tremor lasted a few seconds and then subsided.

'The spell was not powerful enough,' Elric sighed.

The earth trembled again and small craters formed in the ground of the hillside upon which the dead Lords of Dharzi impassively waited. Stones crumbled and the horses stamped nervously. Then the earth rumbled.

'Back!' yelled Elric warningly. 'Back—or we'll go with them!' They retreated—backing towards Shaarilla and their waiting horses as the ground sagged beneath their feet. The Dharzi mounts were rearing and snorting and the remaining dogs turned nervously to regard their masters with puzzled, uncertain eyes. A low moan was coming from the lips of the living dead. Suddenly, a whole area of the surrounding hillside split into cracks, and yawning crannies appeared in the surface. Elric and his companions swung themselves on to their horses as, with a frightful multi-voiced scream, the dead Lords were swallowed by the earth, returning to the depths from which they had been summoned.

A deep unholy chuckle arose from the shattered pit. It was the mocking laughter of the Earth Kings taking their rightful prey back into their keeping. Whining, the devil-dogs slunk towards the edge of the pit, sniffing around it. Then, with one accord, the black pack hurled itself down into the chasm, following its masters to whatever cold doom awaited them.

Moonglum shuddered. 'You are on familiar terms with the strangest people, friend Elric,' he said shakily and turned his horse towards the mountains again.

They reached the black mountains on the following day and nervously Shaarilla led them along the rocky route she had memorised. She no longer pleaded with Elric to return—she was resigned to whatever fate awaited them. Elric's obsession was burning within him and he was filled with impatience—certain that he would find, at last, the ultimate truth of existence in the Dead Gods' Book. Moonglum was cheerfully sceptical, while Shaarilla was consumed with foreboding.

Rain still fell and the storm growled and crackled above them. And, as the driving rainfall increased with fresh insistence, they came, at last, to the black, gaping mouth of a huge cave.

'I can lead you no further,' Shaarilla said wearily. 'The Book lies somewhere beyond the entrance to this cave.'

Elric and Moonglum looked uncertainly at one another, neither of them sure what move to make next. To have reached their goal seemed somehow anticlimactic—for nothing blocked the cave entrance—and nothing appeared to guard it.

'It is inconceivable,' said Elric, 'that the dangers which beset us were not engineered by something, yet here we are—and no one seeks to stop us entering. Are you sure this is the *right* cave, Shaarilla?'

The girl pointed upwards to the rock above the entrance. Engraved in it was a curious symbol which Elric instantly recognised.

'The sign of Chaos!' Elric exclaimed. 'Perhaps I should have guessed.'

'What does it mean, Elric?' Moonglum asked.

'That is the symbol of everlasting disruption and anarchy,' Elric told him. 'We are standing in territory presided over by the Lords of Entropy or one of their minions. So that is who our enemy is! This can only mean one thing—the Book is of extreme importance to the order of things on this plane—possibly all the myriad planes of the universe. It was why Arioch was reluctant to aid me—he, too, is a Lord of Chaos!'

Moonglum stared at him in puzzlement. 'What do you mean, Elric?'

'Know you not that two forces govern the world—fighting an eternal battle?' Elric replied. 'Law and Chaos. The upholders of Chaos state that in such a world as they rule, all things are possible. Opponents of Chaos—those who ally themselves with the forces of Law—say that without Law *nothing* material is possible.

'Some stand apart, believing that a balance between the two is the proper state of things, but we cannot. We have become embroiled in a dispute between the two forces. The Book is valuable to either faction, obviously, and I could guess that the minions of Entropy are worried what power we might release if we obtain this Book. Law and Chaos rarely interfere directly in Men's lives—that is why we have not been fully aware of their presence. Now, perhaps, I will discover at last the answer to the one question which concerns me—does an ultimate force rule over the opposing factions of Law and Chaos?'

Elric stepped through the cave entrance, peering into the gloom while the others hesitantly followed him.

'The cave stretches back a long way. All we can do is press on until we find its far wall,' Elric said.

'Let's hope that its far wall lies not *downwards,*' Moonglum said ironically as he motioned Elric to lead on.

They stumbled forward as the cave grew darker and darker. Their voices were magnified and hollow to their own ears as the floor of the cave slanted sharply down.

'This is no cave,' Elric whispered, 'it's a *tunnel*—but I cannot guess where it leads.'

For several hours they pressed onwards in pitch darkness, clinging to one another as they reeled forward, uncertain of their footing and still aware that they were moving down a gradual incline. They lost all sense of time and Elric began to feel as if he were living through a dream. Events seemed to have become so unpredictable and beyond his control that he could no longer cope with thinking about them in ordinary terms. The tunnel was long and dark and wide and cold. It offered no comfort and the floor eventually became the only thing which had any reality. It was firmly beneath his feet. He began to feel that possibly he was not moving—that the floor, after all, was moving and he was re- maining stationary. His companions clung to him but he was not aware of them. He was lost and his brain was numb. Sometimes he swayed and felt that he was on the edge of a precipice. Sometimes he fell and his groaning body met hard stone, disproving the proximity of the gulf down which he half-expected to fall.

All the while he made his legs perform walking motions, even though he was not at all sure whether he was actually moving forward. And time meant nothing—became a meaningless concept with relation to nothing.

Until, at last, he was aware of a faint, blue glow ahead of him and he knew that he had been moving forward. He began to run down the incline, but found that he was going too fast and had to check his speed. There was a scent of alien strangeness in the cool air of the cave tunnel and fear was a fluid force which surged over him, something separate from himself.

The others obviously felt it, too, for though they said nothing, Elric could sense it. Slowly they moved downward, drawn like automatons towards the pale blue glow below them.

And then they were out of the tunnel, staring awestruck at the un- earthly vision which confronted them. Above them, the very air seemed of the strange blue colour which had originally attracted them. They were standing on a jutting slab of rock and, although it was still some- how *dark,* the eerie blue glow illuminated a stretch of glinting silver beach beneath them. And the beach was lapped by a surging dark sea which moved restlessly like a liquid giant in disturbed slumber. Scat- tered along the silver beach were the dim shapes of wrecks—the bones of peculiarly designed boats, each of a different pattern from the rest. The sea surged away into darkness and there was no horizon—only blackness. Behind them, they could see a sheer cliff which was also lost in darkness beyond a certain point. And it was cold—bitterly cold, with an unbelievable sharpness. For though the sea threshed beneath them, there was no dampness in the air—no smell of salt. It was a bleak and awesome sight and, apart from the sea, they were the only things that moved—the only things to make sound, for the sea was horribly silent in its restless movement.

'What now, Elric?' whispered Moonglum, shivering.

Elric shook his head and they continued to stand there for a long time until the albino—his white face and hands ghastly in the alien light said: 'Since it is impracticable to return—we shall venture over the sea.'

His voice was hollow and he spoke as one who was unaware of his words.

Steps, cut into the living rock, led down towards the beach and now Elric began to descend them. The others allowed him to lead them staring around them, their eyes lit by a terrible fascination.

4

Their feet profaned the silence as they reached the silver beach of crystalline stones and crunched across it. Elric's crimson eyes fixed upon one of the objects littering the beach and he smiled. He shook his head savagely from side to side, as if to clear it. Trembling, he pointed to one of the boats, and the pair saw that it was intact, unlike the others. It was yellow and red—vulgarly gay in this environment and nearing it they observed that it was made of wood, yet unlike any wood they had seen. Moonglum ran his stubby fingers along its length.

'Hard as iron,' he breathed. 'No wonder it has not rotted as the others have.' He peered inside and shuddered. 'Well the owner won't argue if we take it,' he said wryly.

Elric and Shaarilla understood him when they saw the unnaturally twisted skeleton which lay at the bottom of the boat. Elric reached inside and pulled the thing out, hurling it on to the stones. It rattled and rolled over the gleaming shingle, disintegrating as it did so, scattering bones over a wide area. The skull came to rest by the edge of the beach, seeming to stare sightlessly out over the disturbing ocean.

As Elric and Moonglum strove to push and pull the boat down the beach towards the sea, Shaarilla moved ahead of them and squatted down, putting her hand into the wetness. She stood up sharply, shaking the stuff from her hand.

'This is not water as I know it,' she said. They heard her, but said nothing.

'We'll need a sail,' Elric murmured. The cold breeze was moving out over the ocean. 'A cloak should serve.' He stripped off his cloak and knotted it to the mast of the vessel. 'Two of us will have to hold this at either edge,' he said. 'That way we'll have some slight control over the direction the boat takes. It's makeshift—but the best we can manage.'

They shoved off, taking care not to get their feet in the sea.

The wind caught the sail and pushed the boat out over the ocean, moving at a faster pace than Elric had at first reckoned. The boat began to hurtle forward as if possessed of its own volition and Elric's and Moonglum's muscles ached as they clung to the bottom ends of the sail.

Soon the silver beach was out of sight and they could see little—the pale blue light above them scarcely penetrating the blackness. It was then that they heard the dry flap of wings over their heads and looked up.

Silently descending were three massive ape-like creatures, borne on great leathery wings. Shaarilla recognised them and gasped.

'*Clakars!*'

Moonglum shrugged as he hurriedly drew his sword—'A name only —what are they?' But he received no answer for the leading winged ape descended with a rush, mouthing and gibbering, showing long fangs in a slavering snout. Moonglum dropped his portion of the sail and slashed at the beast but it veered away, its huge wings beating, and sailed upwards again.

Elric unsheathed Stormbringer—and was astounded. The blade remained silent, its familiar howl of glee muted. The blade shuddered in his hand and instead of the rush of power which usually flowed up his arm, he felt only a slight tingling. He was panic-stricken for a moment —without the sword, he would soon lose all vitality. Grimly fighting down his fear, he used the sword to protect himself from the rushing attack of one of the winged apes.

The ape gripped the blade, bowling Elric over, but it yelled in pain as the blade cut through one knotted hand, severing fingers which lay twitching and bloody on the narrow deck. Elric gripped the side of the boat and hauled himself upright once more. Shrilling its agony, the winged ape attacked again, but this time with more caution. Elric summoned all his strength and swung the heavy sword in a two-handed grip, ripping off one of the leathery wings so that the mutilated beast flopped about the deck. Judging the place where its heart should be, Elric drove the blade in under the breast-bone. The ape's movements subsided.

Moonglum was lashing wildly at two of the winged apes which were attacking him from both sides. He was down on one knee, vainly hacking at random. He had opened up the whole side of a beast's head but, though in pain, it still came at him. Elric hurled Stormbringer through the darkness and it struck the wounded beast in the throat, point first. The ape clutched with clawing fingers at the steel and fell overboard. Its corpse floated on the liquid but slowly began to sink. Elric grabbed with frantic fingers at the hilt of his sword, reaching far over the side of the boat. Incredibly, the blade was sinking with the beast. Knowing Storm-bringer's properties as he did, Elric was amazed—once when he had hurled the runesword into the ocean, it had refused to sink. Now it was being dragged beneath the surface as any ordinary blade would be dragged. He gripped the hilt and hauled the sword out of the winged ape's carcass.

His strength was seeping swiftly from him. It was incredible. What alien laws governed this cavern world? He could not guess—and all he was concerned with was regaining his waning strength. Without the runesword's power, this was impossible!

Moonglum's curved blade had disembowelled the remaining beast and the little man was busily tossing the dead thing over the side. He turned, grinning triumphantly, to Elric.

'A good fight,' he said.

Elric shook his head. 'We must cross this sea speedily,' he replied, 'else we're lost—finished. My power is gone.'

'How? Why?'

'I know not—unless the forces of Entropy rule more strongly here. Make haste—there is no time for speculation.'

Moonglum's eyes were disturbed. He could do nothing but act as Elric said.

Elric was trembling in his weakness, holding the billowing sail with draining strength. Shaarilla moved to help him, her thin hands close to his, her deep-set eyes bright with sympathy.

'What *were* those things?' Moonglum gasped, his teeth naked and white beneath his back-drawn lips, his breath coming short.

'Clakars,' Shaarilla replied. 'They are the primeval ancestors of my people, older in origin than recorded time. My people are thought the oldest inhabitants of this planet.'

'Whoever seeks to stop us in this quest of yours had best find some—original means.' Moonglum grinned. 'The old methods don't work.' But the other two did not smile, for Elric was half-fainting and the woman was concerned only with his plight. Moonglum shrugged, staring ahead.

When he spoke again, sometime later, his voice was excited. 'We're nearing land!'

Land it was, and they were traveling fast towards it. Too fast. Elric heaved himself upright and spoke heavily and with difficulty. 'Drop the sail!' Moonglum obeyed him. The boat sped on, struck another stretch of silver beach and ground up it, the prow ploughing a dark scar through the glinting shingle. It stopped suddenly, tilting violently to one side so that the three were tumbled against the boat's rail.

Shaarilla and Moonglum pulled themselves upright and dragged the limp and nerveless albino on to the beach. Carrying him between them, they struggled up the beach until the crystalline shingle gave way to thick, fluffy moss, padding their footfalls. They laid the albino down and stared at him worriedly, uncertain of their next actions.

Elric strained to rise, but was unable to do so. 'Give me time,' he gasped. 'I won't die—but already my eyesight is fading. I can only hope that the blade's power will return on dry land.'

With a mighty effort, he pulled Stormbringer from its scabbard and he smiled in relief as the evil runesword moaned faintly and then, slowly, its song increased in power as black flame flickered along its length. Already the power was flowing into Elric's body, giving him renewed vitality. But even as strength returned, Elric's crimson eyes flared with terrible misery.

'Without this black blade,' he groaned, 'I am nothing, as you see. But what is it making of me? Am I to be bound to it forever?'

The others did not answer him and they were both moved by an emotion they could not define—an emotion blended of fear, hate and pity—linked with something else . . .

Eventually, Elric rose, trembling, and silently led them up the mossy hillside towards a more natural light which filtered from above. They could see that it came from a wide chimney, leading apparently to the upper air. By means of the light, they could soon make out a dark, irregular shape which towered in the shadow of the gap.

As they neared the shape, they saw that it was a castle of black stone —a sprawling pile covered with dark green crawling lichen which curled over its ancient bulk with an almost sentient protectiveness. Towers appeared to spring at random from it and it covered a vast area. There seemed to be no windows in any part of it and the only orifice was a rearing doorway blocked by thick bars of a metal which glowed with dull redness, but without heat. Above this gate, in flaring amber, was the sign of the Lords of Entropy, representing eight arrows radiating from a central hub in all directions. It appeared to hang in the air without touching the black, lichen-covered stone.

'I think our quest ends here,' Elric said grimly. 'Here, or nowhere.'

'Before I go further, Elric, I'd like to know what it is you seek,' Moonglum murmured. 'I think I've earned the right.'

'A book,' Elric said carelessly. 'The Dead Gods' Book. It lies within those castle walls—of that I'm certain. We have reached the end of our journey.'

Moonglum shrugged. 'I might not have asked,' he smiled, 'for all your words mean to me. I hope that I will be allowed some small share of whatever treasure it represents.'

Elric grinned, in spite of the coldness which gripped his bowels, but he did not answer Moonglum.

'We need to enter the castle, first,' he said instead.

As if the gates had heard him, the metal bars flared to a pale green and then their glow faded back to red and finally dulled into non-existence. The entrance was unbarred and their way apparently clear.

'I like not *that,'* growled Moonglum. 'Too easy. A trap awaits us—are we to spring it at the pleasure of whoever dwells within the castle confines?'

'What else can we do?' Elric spoke quietly.

'Go back—or forward. Avoid the castle—do not tempt He who guards the Book!' Shaarilla was gripping the albino's right arm, her whole face moving with fear, her eyes pleading. 'Forget the Book, Elric!'

'Now?' Elric laughed humourlessly. 'Now—after this journey? No, Shaarilla, not when the truth is so close. Better to die than never to have tried to secure the wisdom in the Book when it lies so near.'

Shaarilla's clutching fingers relaxed their grip and her shoulders slumped in hopelessness. 'We cannot do battle with the minions of Entropy . . .'

'Perhaps we will not have to.' Elric did not believe his own words but his mouth was twisted with some dark emotion, intense and terrible. Moonglum glanced at Shaarilla.

'Shaarilla is right,' he said with conviction. 'You'll find nothing but bitterness, possibly death, inside those castle walls. Let us, instead, climb yonder steps and attempt to reach the surface.' He pointed to some twisting steps which led towards the yawning rent in the cavern roof.

Elric shook his head. 'No. You go if you like.'

Moonglum grimaced in perplexity. 'You're a stubborn one, friend Elric. Well, if it's all or nothing—then I'm with you. But personally, I have always preferred compromise.'

Elric began to walk slowly forward towards the dark entrance of the bleak and towering castle.

In a wide, shadowy courtyard a tall figure, wreathed in scarlet fire, stood awaiting them.

Elric marched on, passing the gateway. Moonglum and Shaarilla nervously followed.

Gusty laughter roared from the mouth of the giant and the scarlet fire fluttered about him. He was naked and unarmed, but the power which flowed from him almost forced the three back. His skin was scaly and of smoky purple colouring. His massive body was alive with rippling muscle as he rested lightly on the balls of his feet. His skull was long, slanting sharply backwards at the forehead and his eyes were like slivers of blue steel, showing no pupil. His whole body shook with mighty, malicious joy.

'Greetings to you, Lord Elric of Melniboné—I congratulate you for your remarkable tenacity!'

'Who are you?' Elric growled, his hand on his sword.

'My name is Orunlu the Keeper and this is a stronghold of the Lords of Entropy.' The giant smiled cynically. *'You need not finger your puny blade so nervously, for you should know that I cannot harm you now. I gained power to remain in your realm only by making that vow.'*

Elric's voice betrayed his mounting excitement. 'You cannot stop us?'

'I do not dare to—since my oblique efforts have failed. But your foolish endeavours perplex me somewhat, I'll admit. The Book is of importance to us—but what can it mean to you? I have guarded it for three hundred centuries and have never been curious enough to seek to discover why my Masters place so much importance upon it—why they bothered to rescue it on its sunward course and incarcerate it on this boring ball of earth populated by the capering, briefly-lived clowns called Men?'

'I seek in it the Truth,' Elric said guardedly.

'There is no Truth but that of Eternal struggle,' the scarlet-flamed giant said with conviction.

'What rules above the forces of Law and Chaos?' Elric asked. 'What controls your destinies as it controls mine?'

The giant frowned.

'That question, I cannot answer. I do not know. There is only the Balance.'

'Then perhaps the Book will tell us who holds it.' Elric said purposefully. 'Let me pass—tell me where it lies.'

The giant moved back, smiling ironically. *'It lies in a small chamber in the central tower. I have sworn never to venture there, otherwise I might even lead the way. Go if you like—my duty is over.'*

Elric, Moonglum and Shaarilla stepped towards the entrance of the castle, but before they entered, the giant spoke warningly from behind them.

'I have been told that the knowledge contained in the Book could swing the balance on the side of the forces of Law. This disturbs me—but, it appears, there is another possibility which disturbs me even more.'

'What is that?' Elric said.

'It could create such a tremendous impact on the multiverse that complete entropy would result. My Masters do not desire that—for it could

mean the destruction of all matter in the end. We exist only to fight—not to win, but to preserve the eternal struggle.'

'I care not,' Elric told him. 'I have little to lose, Orunlu the Keeper.'

'Then go.' The giant strode across the courtyard into blackness.

Inside the tower, light of a pale quality illuminated winding steps leading upwards. Elric began to climb them in silence, moved by his own doom-filled purpose. Hesitantly, Moonglum and Shaarilla followed in his path, their faces set in hopeless acceptance.

On and upward the steps mounted, twisting tortuously towards their goal, until at last they came to the chamber, full of blinding light, many-coloured and scintillating, which did not penetrate outwards at all but remained confined to the room which housed it.

Blinking, shielding his red eyes with his arm, Elric pressed forward and, through slitted pupils saw the source of the light lying on a small stone dais in the centre of the room.

Equally troubled by the bright light, Shaarilla and Moonglum followed him into the room and stood in awe at what they saw.

It was a huge book—the Dead Gods' Book, its covers encrusted with alien gems from which the light sprang. It gleamed, it *throbbed* with light and brilliant colour.

'At last,' Elric breathed, 'At last—the Truth!'

He stumbled forward like a man made stupid with drink, his pale hands reaching for the thing he had sought with such savage bitterness. His hands touched the pulsating cover of the Book and, trembling, turned it back.

'Now, I shall learn,' he said, half-gloatingly.

With a crash, the cover fell to the floor, sending the bright gems skipping and dancing over the paving stones.

Beneath Elric's twitching hands lay nothing but a pile of yellowish dust.

'No!' His scream was anguished, unbelieving. 'No!' Tears flowed down his contorted face as he ran his hands through the fine dust. With a groan which racked his whole being, he fell forward, his face hitting the disintegrated parchment. Time had destroyed the Book—untouched, possibly forgotten, for three hundred centuries. Even the wise and powerful Gods who had created it had perished—and now its knowledge followed them into oblivion.

They stood on the slopes of the high mountain, staring down into the green valleys below them. The sun shone and the sky was clear and blue. Behind them lay the gaping hole which led into the stronghold of the Lords of Entropy.

Elric looked with sad eyes across the world and his head was lowered beneath a weight of weariness and dark despair. He had not spoken since his companions had dragged him sobbing from the chamber of the Book. Now he raised his pale face and spoke in a voice tinged with self-mockery, sharp with bitterness—a lonely voice: the calling of hungry seabirds circling cold skies above bleak shores.

'Now,' he said, 'I will live my life without ever knowing why I live it —whether it has purpose or not. Perhaps the Book could have told me. But would I have believed it, even then? I am the eternal sceptic—never *sure* that my actions are my own; never certain that an ultimate entity is not guiding me.

'I envy those who know. All I can do now is to continue my quest and hope, without hope, that before my span is ended, the truth will be presented to me.'

Shaarilla took his limp hands in hers and her eyes were wet.

'Elric—let me comfort you.'

The albino sneered bitterly. 'Would that we'd never met, Shaarilla of the Dancing Mist. For a while, you gave me hope—I had thought to be at last at peace with myself. But, because of you, I am left more hopeless than before. There is no salvation in this world—only malevolent doom. Goodbye.'

He took his hands away from her grasp and set off down the mountainside.

Moonglum darted a glance at Shaarilla and then at Elric. He took something from his purse and put it in the girl's hand.

'Good luck,' he said, and then he was running after Elric until he caught him up.

Still striding, Elric turned at Moonglum's approach and, despite his brooding misery said: 'What is it, friend Moonglum? Why do you follow me?'

'I've followed you thus far, Master Elric, and I see no reason to stop,' grinned the little man. 'Besides, unlike yourself, I'm a materialist. We'll need to eat, you know.'

Elric frowned, feeling a warmth growing within him. 'What do you mean, Moonglum?'

Moonglum chuckled. 'I take advantage of situations of any kind, where I may,' he answered. He reached into his purse and displayed something on his outstretched hand which shone with a dazzling brilliancy. It was one of the jewels from the cover of the Book. 'There are more in my purse,' he said, 'And each one worth a fortune.' He took Elric's arm.

'Come, Elric—what new lands shall we visit so that we may change these baubles into wine and pleasant company?'

Behind them, standing stock still on the hillside, Shaarilla stared miserably after them until they were no longer visible. The jewel Moonglum had given her dropped from her fingers and fell, bouncing and bright, until it was lost amongst the heather. Then she turned—and the dark mouth of the cavern yawned before her.

BOOK THREE

THE SINGING CITADEL

In which Elric has his first dealings with Pan Tang, Yishana of Jharkor, the sorcerer Theleb K'aarna, and learns something more of the Higher Worlds . . .

1

The turquoise sea was peaceful in the golden light of early evening, and the two men at the rail of the ship stood in silence, looking north to the misty horizon. One was tall and slim, wrapped in a heavy black cloak, its cowl flung back to reveal his long, milk-white hair; the other was short and red-headed.

'She was a fine woman and she loved you,' said the short man at length. 'Why did you leave her so abruptly?'

'She was a fine woman,' the tall one replied, 'but she would have loved me to her cost. Let her seek her own land and stay there. I have already slain one woman whom I loved, Moonglum. I would not slay another.'

Moonglum shrugged. 'I sometimes wonder, Elric, if this grim destiny of yours is the figment of your own guilt-ridden mood.'

'Perhaps,' Elric replied carelessly. 'But I do not care to test the theory. Let's speak no more of this.'

The sea foamed and rushed by as the oars disrupted the surface, driving the ship swiftly towards the port of Dhakos, capital of Jharkor, one of the most powerful of the Young Kingdoms. Less than two years previously Jharkor's king, Dharmit, had died in the ill-fated raid on Imrryr, and Elric had heard that the men of Jharkor blamed him for the young king's death, though this was not the case. He cared little whether they blamed him or not, for he was still disdainful of the greater part of mankind.

'Another hour will see nightfall, and it's unlikely we'll sail at night,' Moonglum said. 'I'll to bed, I think.'

Elric was about to reply when he was interrupted by a high-pitched shout from the crowsnest.

'Sail on larboard stern!'

The lookout must have been half asleep, for the ship bearing down on them could easily be made out from the deck. Elric stepped aside as the captain, a dark-faced Tarkeshite, came running along the deck.

'What's the ship, captain?' called Moonglum.

'A Pan Tang trireme—a warship. They're on ramming course.' The captain ran on, yelling orders to the helm to turn the ship aside.

Elric and Moonglum crossed the deck to see the trireme better. She was a black-sailed ship, painted black and heavily gilded, with three rowers to an oar as against their two. She was big and yet elegant, with a high curving stern and a low prow. Now they could see the waters broken by her big, brass-sheathed ram. She had two lateen-rigged sails, and the wind was in her favour.

The rowers were in a panic as they sweated to turn the ship according to the helmsman's orders. Oars rose and fell in confusion and Moonglum turned to Elric with a half-smile.

'They'll never do it. Best ready your blade, friend.'

Pan Tang was an isle of sorcerers, fully human, who sought to emulate the old power of Melniboné. Their fleets were among the best in the Young Kingdoms and raided with little discrimination. The Theocrat of Pan Tang, chief of the priest-aristocracy, was Jagreen Lern, who was reputed to have a pact with the powers of Chaos and a plan to rule the world.

Elric regarded the men of Pan Tang as upstarts who could never hope to mirror the glory of his ancestors, but even he had to admit that this ship was impressive and would easily win a fight with the Tarkeshite galley.

Soon the great trireme was bearing down on them and captain and helmsman fell silent as they realised they could not evade the ram. With a harsh sound of crushed timbers, the ram connected with the stern, holing the galley beneath the waterline.

Elric stood immobile, watching as the trireme's grappling irons hurtled towards their galley's deck. Somewhat half-heartedly, knowing they were no match for the well-trained and well-armoured Pan Tang crew, the Tarkeshites ran towards the stern, preparing to resist the boarders.

Moonglum cried urgently: 'Elric—we must help!'

Reluctantly Elric nodded. He was loathe to draw the runesword from its scabbard at his side. Of late its power seemed to have increased.

Now the scarlet-armoured warriors were swinging towards where the Tarkeshites waited. The first wave, armed with broadswords and battle-axes, hit the sailors, driving them back.

Now Elric's hand fell to the hilt of Stormbringer. As he gripped it and drew it, the blade gave an odd, disturbing moan, as if of anticipation, and a weird black radiance flickered along its length. Now it throbbed in Elric's hand like something alive as the albino ran forward to aid the Tarkeshite sailors.

Already half the defenders had been hewed down and as the rest retreated, Elric, with Moonglum at his heels, moved forward. The scarlet-armoured warriors' expressions changed from grim triumph to startlement as Elric's great black blade shrieked up and down and clove through a man's armour from shoulder to lower ribs.

Evidently they recognized him and the sword, for both were legendary. Though Moonglum was a skilled swordsman, they all but ignored him as they realised that they must concentrate all their strength on bringing Elric down if they were to survive.

The old, wild killing-lust of his ancestors now dominated Elric as the blade reaped souls. He and the sword became one and it was the sword, not Elric, that was in control. Men fell on all sides, screaming more in horror than in pain as they realised what the sword had drawn from them. Four came at him with axes whistling. He sliced off one's head, cut a deep gash in another's midriff, lopped off an arm, and drove the blade point first into the heart of the last. Now the Tarkeshites were cheering, following after Elric and Moonglum as they cleared the sinking galley's decks of attackers.

Howling like a wolf, Elric grabbed a rope—part of the black and gold trireme's rigging—and swung towards the enemy's decks.

'Follow him!' Moonglum yelled. 'This is our only chance—this ship's doomed!'

The trireme had raised decks fore and aft. On the foredeck stood the captain, splendid in scarlet and blue, his face aghast at this turn of events. He had expected to get his prize effortlessly, now it seemed *he* was to be the prize!

Stormbringer sang a wailing song as Elric pressed towards the foredeck, a song that was at once triumphant and ecstatic. The remaining warriors no longer rushed at him, and concentrated on Moonglum, who was leading the Tarkeshite crew, leaving Elric's path to the captain clear.

The captain, a member of the theocracy, would be harder to vanquish than his men. As Elric moved towards him, he noted that the man's armour had a peculiar glow to it—it had been sorcerously treated.

The captain was typical of his kind—stocky, heavily-bearded, with malicious black eyes over a strong, hooked nose. His lips were thick and red and he was smiling a little as, with axe in one hand and sword in the other, he prepared to meet Elric, who was running up the steps.

Elric gripped Stormbringer in both hands and lunged for the captain's stomach, but the man stepped sideways and parried with his sword, swinging the axe left-handed at Elric's unprotected head. The albino had to sway to one side, staggered, and fell to the deck, rolling as the broadsword thudded into the deck, just missing his shoulder. Stormbringer seemed to rise of its own accord to block a further axe blow and then chopped upwards to sheer off the head near the handle. The captain cursed and discarded the handle, gripped his broadsword in both hands and raised it. Again Stormbringer acted a fraction sooner than Elric's own reactions. He drove the blade up towards the man's heart. The magic-treated armour stopped it for a second; but then Stormbringer shrilled a chilling, wailing song, shuddered as if summoning more strength, slipped on the armour again. And then the magic armour split like a nutshell, leaving Elric's opponent bare-chested, his arms still raised for the strike. His eyes widened. He backed away, his sword forgotten, his gaze fixed on the evil runeblade as it struck him under the breast-bone and drove in. He grimaced, whimpered, and dropped his sword, clutching instead at the blade, which was sucking out his soul.

'By Chardros—not—not—aahhh!'

He died knowing that even his soul was not safe from the hell-blade borne by the wolf-faced albino.

Elric wrenched Stormbringer from the corpse, feeling his own vitality increase as the sword passed on its stolen energy, refusing to consider the knowledge that he needed the sword the more he used it.

On the deck of the trireme, only the galley-slaves were left alive. But the deck was tilting badly, for the trireme's ram and grapples still tied it to the sinking Tarkeshite ship.

'Cut the grappling ropes and back water—quickly!' Elric yelled. Sailors, realising what was happening, leapt forward to do as he ordered. The slaves backed water, and the ram came out with a groan of split wood. The grapples were cut and the doomed galley set adrift.

Elric counted the survivors. Less than half the crew were alive, and their captain had died in the first onslaught. He addressed the slaves.

'If you'd have your freedom, row well towards Dhakos,' he called. The sun was setting, but now that he was in command he decided to sail through the night by the stars.

Moonglum shouted incredulously: 'Why offer them their freedom? We could sell them in Dhakos and thus be paid for today's exertion!'

Elric shrugged. 'I offer them freedom because I choose to, Moonglum.'

The redhead sighed and turned to supervise the throwing of the dead and wounded overboard. He would never understand the albino, he decided. It was probably for the best.

And that was how Elric came to enter Dhakos in some style, when he had originally intended to slip into the city without being recognised.

Leaving Moonglum to negotiate the sale of the trireme and divide the money between the crew and himself, Elric drew his hood over his head and pushed through the crowd which had collected, making for an inn he knew of by the west gate of the city.

2

Later that night, when Moonglum had gone to bed, Elric sat in the tavern room drinking. Even the most enthusiastic of the night's roisterers had left when they had noticed with whom they shared the room; and now Elric sat alone, the only light coming from a guttering reed torch over the outside door.

Now the door opened and a richly-dressed youth stood there, staring in.

'I seek the White Wolf,' he said, his head at a questioning angle. He could not see Elric clearly.

'I'm sometimes called that name in these parts,' Elric said calmly. 'Do you seek Elric of Melniboné?'

'Aye. I have a message.' The youth came in, keeping his cloak wrapped about him, for the room was cold though Elric did not notice it.

'I am Count Yolan, deputy-commander of the city guard,' the youth said arrogantly, coming up to the table at which Elric sat and studying the albino rudely. 'You are brave to come here so openly. Do you think the folk of Jharkor have such short memories they can forget that you led their king into a trap scarce two years since?'

Elric sipped his wine, then said from behind the rim of his cup: 'This is rhetoric, Count Yolan. What is your message?'

Yolan's assured manner left him; he made a rather weak gesture. 'Rhetoric to you, perhaps—but I for one feel strongly on the matter. Would not King Dharmit be here today if you had not fled from the battle that broke the power of the Sea Lords and your own folk? Did you not use your sorcery to aid you in your flight, instead of using it to aid the men who thought they were your comrades?'

Elric sighed. 'I know your purpose here was not to bait me in this manner. Dharmit died on board his flagship during the first attack on Imrryr's sea-maze, not in the subsequent battle.'

'You sneer at my questions and then proffer lame lies to cover your own cowardly deed,' Yolan said bitterly. 'If I had my way you'd be fed to your hell-blade there—I've heard what happened earlier.'

Elric rose slowly. 'Your taunts tire me. When you feel ready to deliver your message, give it to the inn-keeper.'

He walked around the table, moving towards the stairs, but stopped as Yolan turned and plucked at his sleeve.

Elric's corpse-white face stared down at the young noble. His crimson eyes flickered with a dangerous emotion. 'I am not used to such familiarity, young man.'

Yolan's hand fell away. 'Forgive me. I was self-indulgent and should not have let my emotions override diplomacy. I came on a matter of discretion—a message from Queen Yishana. She seeks your help.'

'I'm as disinclined to help others as I am to explain my actions,' Elric spoke impatiently. 'In the past my help has not always been to the advantage of those who've sought it. Dharmit, your queen's half-brother, discovered that.'

Yolan said sullenly: 'You echo my own warnings to the queen, sir. For all that, she desires to see you in private—tonight . . .' he scowled and looked away. 'I would point out that I could have you arrested should you refuse.'

'Perhaps.' Elric moved again towards the steps. 'Tell Yishana that I stay the night here and move on at dawn. She may visit me if her request is so urgent.' He climbed the stairs, leaving a gape-mouthed Yolan sitting alone in the quiet of the tavern.

Theleb K'aarna scowled. For all his skill in the black arts, he was a fool in love; and Yishana, sprawled on her fur-rich bed, knew it. It pleased her to have power over a man who could destroy her with a simple incantation if it were not for his love-weakness. Though Theleb K'aarna stood high in the hierarchy of Pan Tang, it was clear to her that she was in no danger from the sorcerer. Indeed, her intuition informed her that this man who loved to dominate others also needed to be dominated. She filled this need for him—with relish.

Theleb K'aarna continued to scowl at her. 'How can that decadent spell-singer help you where I cannot?' he muttered, sitting down on the bed and stroking her bejewelled foot.

Yishana was not a young woman, neither was she pretty. Yet there was an hypnotic quality about her tall, full body, her lush black hair, and her wholly sensuous face. Few of the men she had singled out for her pleasure had been able to resist her.

Neither was she sweet-natured, just, wise, nor self-sacrificing. The historians would append no noble soubriquet to her name. Still, there was something so self-sufficient about her, something denying the usual standards by which a person was judged, that all who knew her admired her, and she was well-loved by those she ruled—loved rather as a wilful child is loved, yet loved with firm loyalty.

Now she laughed quietly, mockingly at her sorcerer lover.

'You're probably right, Theleb K'aarna, but Elric is a legend—the most spoken-of, least-known man in the world. This is my opportunity to discover what others have only speculated on—his true character.'

Theleb K'aarna made a pettish gesture. He stroked his long black beard and got up, walking to a table bearing fruit and wine. He poured wine for them both. 'If you seek to make me jealous again, you are succeeding, of course. I hold little hope for your ambition. Elric's ancestors were half-demons—his race is not human and cannot be judged by our yardsticks. To us, sorcery is learned after years of study and sacrifice—to Elric's kind, sorcery is intuitive—natural. You may not live to learn his secrets. Cymoril, his beloved cousin, died on his blade—and she was his betrothed!'

'Your concern is touching.' She lazily accepted the goblet he handed to her. 'But I'll continue with my plan, none the less. After all, you can hardly claim to have had much success in discovering the nature of this citadel!'

'There are subtleties I have not properly plumbed as yet!'

'Then perhaps Elric's intuition will provide answers where you fail,' she smiled. Then she got up and looked through the window at the sky where the full moon hung in a clear sky over the spires of Dhakos. 'Yolan is late. If all went properly, he should have brought Elric here by now.'

'Yolan was a mistake. You should not have sent such a close friend of Dharmit's. For all we know, he's challenged Elric and killed him!'

Again she couldn't resist laughter. 'Oh, you wish too hard—it clouds your reason. I sent Yolan because I knew he would be rude to the albino and perhaps weaken his usual insouciance—arouse his curiosity. Yolan was a kind of bait to bring Elric to us!'

'Then possibly Elric sensed this?'

'I am not overly intelligent, my love—but I think my instincts rarely betray me. We shall see soon.'

A little later there was a discreet scratch at the door and a handmaiden entered.

'Your Highness, Count Yolan has returned.'

'Only Count Yolan?' There was a smile on Theleb K'aarna's face. It was to disappear in a short while as Yishana left the room, garbed for the street.

'You are a fool!' he snarled as the door slammed. He flung down his goblet. Already he had been unsuccessful in the matter of the citadel and, if Elric displaced him, he could lose everything. He began to think very deeply, very carefully.

3

Though he claimed lack of conscience, Elric's tormented eyes belied the claim as he sat at his window, drinking strong wine and thinking on the past. Since the sack of Imrryr, he had quested the world, seeking some purpose to his existence, some meaning to his life.

He had failed to find the answer in the Dead God's Book. He had failed to love Shaarilla, the wingless woman of Myyrrhn, failed to forget Cymoril, who still inhabited his nightmares. And there were memories of other dreams—of a fate he dare not think upon.

Peace, he thought, was all he sought. Yet even peace in death was denied him. It was in this mood that he continued to brood until his reverie was broken by a soft scratching at the door.

Immediately his expression hardened. His crimson eyes took on a guarded look, his shoulders lifted so that when he stood up he was all cool arrogance. He placed the cup on the table and said lightly:

'Enter!'

A woman entered, swathed in a dark red cloak, unrecognisable in the gloom of the room. She closed the door behind her and stood there, motionless and unspeaking.

When at length she spoke, her voice was almost hesitant, though there was some irony in it, too.

'You sit in darkness, Lord Elric, I had thought to find you asleep . . .'

'Sleep, madam, is the occupation that bores me most. But I will light a torch if you find the darkness unattractive.' He went to the table and removed the cover from the small bowl of charcoal which lay there. He reached for a thin wooden spill and placed one end in the bowl, blowing gently. Soon the charcoal glowed, and the taper caught, and he touched it to a reed torch that hung in a bracket on the wall above the table.

The torch flared and sent shadows skipping around the small chamber. The woman drew back her cowl and the light caught her dark, heavy features and the masses of black hair which framed them. She contrasted strongly with the slender, aesthetic albino who stood a head taller, looking at her impassively.

She was unused to impassive looks and the novelty pleased her.

'You sent for me, Lord Elric—and you see I am here.' She made a mock curtsey.

'Queen Yishana,' he acknowledged the curtsey with a slight bow. Now that she confronted him, she sensed his power—a power that perhaps attracted even more strongly than her own. And yet, he gave no hint that he responded to her. She reflected that a situation she had expected to be interesting might, ironically, become frustrating. Even this amused her.

Elric, in turn, was intrigued by this woman in spite of himself. His jaded emotions hinted that Yishana might restore their edge. This excited him and perturbed him at once.

He relaxed a little and shrugged. 'I have heard of you, Queen Yishana, in other lands than Jharkor. Sit down if you wish.' He indicated a bench and seated himself on the edge of the bed.

'You are more courteous than your summons suggested,' she smiled as she sat down, crossed her legs, and folded her arms in front of her. 'Does this mean that you will listen to a proposition I have?'

He smiled back. It was a rare smile for him, a little grim, but without the usual bitterness. 'I think so. You are an unusual woman, Queen Yishana. Indeed, I would suspect that you had Melnibonéan blood if I did not know better.'

'Not all your Young Kingdom "upstarts" are quite as unsophisticated as you believe, my lord.'

'Perhaps.'

'Now that I see you at last, face to face, I find your dark legend a little hard to credit in parts—and yet, on the other hand,' she put her head on one side and regarded him frankly, 'it would seem that the legends speak of a less subtle man than the one I see before me.'

'That is the way with legends.'

'Ah,' she half-whispered, 'what a force we could be together, you and I . . .'

'Speculation of that sort irritates me, Queen Yishana. What is your purpose in coming here?'

'Very well, I did not expect you to listen, even.'

'I'll listen—but expect nothing more.'

'Then listen. I think the story will be appreciated, even by you.'

Elric listened and, as Yishana had suspected, the tale she told began
to catch his interest . . .

Several months ago, Yishana told Elric, peasants in the Gharavian
province of Jharkor began to talk of some mysterious riders who were
carrying off young men and women from the villages.

Suspecting bandits, Yishana had sent a detachment of her White
Leopards, Jharkor's finest fighting men, to the province to put down the
brigands.

None of the White Leopards had returned. A second expedition had
found no trace of them but, in a valley close to the town of Thokora,
they had come upon a strange citadel. Descriptions of the citadel were
confused. Suspecting that the White Leopards had attacked and been
defeated, the officer in charge had used discretion, left a few men to
watch the citadel and report anything they saw, and returned at once to
Dhakos. One thing was certain—the citadel had not been in the valley a
few months before.

Yishana and Theleb K'aarna had led a large force to the valley. The
men left behind had disappeared but, as soon as he saw the citadel,
Theleb K'aarna had warned Yishana not to attack.

'It was a marvellous sight, Lord Elric,' Yishana continued. 'The citadel scintillated with shining, rainbow colours—colours that were constantly altering, changing. The whole building looked unreal—sometimes it stood out sharply; sometimes it seemed misty, as if about to
vanish. Theleb K'aarna said its nature was sorcerous, and we did not
doubt him. Something from the Realm of Chaos, he said, and that
seemed likely.' She got up.

She spread her hands. 'We are not used to large-scale manifestations
of sorcery in these parts. Theleb K'aarna was familiar enough with
sorcery—he comes from the City of Screaming Statues on Pan Tang,
and such things are seen frequently—but even he was taken aback.'

'So you withdrew,' Elric prompted impatiently.

'We were about to—in fact Theleb K'aarna and myself were already
riding back at the head of the army when the music came . . . It was
sweet, beautiful, unearthly, painful—Theleb K'aarna shouted to me to
ride as swiftly as I could away from it. I dallied, attracted by the music,
but he slapped the rump of my horse and we rode, fast as dragons in
flight, away from there. Those nearest us also escaped—but we saw the
rest turn and move back towards the citadel, drawn by the music.
Nearly two hundred men went back—and vanished.'

'What did you do then?' Elric asked as Yishana crossed the floor and
sat down beside him. He moved to give her more room.

'Theleb K'aarna has been trying to investigate the nature of the citadel—its purpose and its controller. So far, his divinations have told him little more than he guessed: that the Realm of Chaos has sent the citadel to the Realm of Earth and is slowly extending its range. More and more of our young men and women are being abducted by the minions of Chaos.'

'And these minions?' Yishana had moved a little closer, and this time Elric did not move away.

'None who has sought to stop them has succeeded—few have lived.'

'And what do you seek of me?'

'Help.' She looked closely into his face and reached out a hand to touch him. 'You have knowledge of both Chaos and Law—old knowledge, instinctive knowledge if Theleb K'aarna is right. Why, your very Gods are Lords of Chaos.'

'That is exactly true, Yishana—and because our patron Gods are of Chaos, it is not in my interest to fight against any one of them.'

Now he moved towards her and he was smiling, looking into her eyes. Suddenly, he took her in his arms. 'Perhaps you will be strong enough,' he said enigmatically, just before their lips met. 'And as for the other matter—we can discuss that later.'

In the deep greenness of a dark mirror, Theleb K'aarna saw something of the scene in Elric's room and he glowered impotently. He tugged at his beard as the scene faded for the tenth time in a minute. None of his mutterings could restore it. He sat back in his chair of serpent skulls and planned vengeance. That vengeance could take time maturing, he decided; for, if Elric could be useful in the matter of the citadel, there was no point in destroying him yet. . . .

4

Next afternoon, three riders set off for the town of Thokora. Elric and Yishana rode close together; but the third rider, Theleb K'aarna, kept a frowning distance. If Elric was at all embarrassed by this display on the part of the man he had ousted in Yishana's affections, he did not show it.

Elric, finding Yishana more than attractive in spite of himself, had agreed at least to inspect the citadel and suggest what it might be and how it might be fought. He had exchanged a few words with Moonglum before setting off.

They rode across the beautiful grasslands of Jharkor, golden beneath a hot sun. It was two days' ride to Thokora, and Elric intended to enjoy it.

Feeling less than miserable, he galloped along with Yishana, laughing with her in her enjoyment. Yet, buried deeper than it would normally have been, there was a deep forboding in his heart as they neared the mysterious citadel, and he noted that Theleb K'aarna occasionally looked satisfied when he should have looked disgruntled.

Sometimes Elric would shout to the sorcerer. 'Ho, old spell-maker, do you feel no joyful release from the cares of the court out here amidst the beauties of nature? Your face is long, Theleb K'aarna—breathe in the untainted air and laugh with us!' Then Theleb K'aarna would scowl and mutter, and Yishana would laugh at him and glance brightly at Elric.

So they came to Thokora and found it a smouldering pit that stank like a midden of hell.

Elric sniffed. 'This is Chaos work. You were right enough there, Theleb K'aarna. Whatever fire destroyed such a large town, it was not natural fire. Whoever is responsible for this is evidently increasing his power. As you know, sorcerer, the Lords of Law and Chaos are usually in perfect balance, neither tampering directly with our Earth. Evidently the balance has tipped a little way to one side, as it sometimes does, favouring the Lords of Disorder—allowing them access to our realm. Normally it is possible for an earthly sorcerer to summon aid from Chaos or Law for a short time, but it is rare for either side to establish itself so firmly as our friend in the citadel evidently has. What is more disturbing—for you of the Young Kingdoms, at least—is that, once such power is gained, it is possible to increase it, and the Lords of Chaos could in time conquer the Realm of Earth by gradual increase of their strength here.'

'A terrible possibility,' muttered the sorcerer, genuinely afraid. Even though he could sometimes summon help from Chaos, it was in no human being's interest to have Chaos ruling over him.

Elric climbed back into his saddle. 'We'd best make speed to the valley,' he said.

'Are you sure it is wise, after witnessing this?' Theleb K'aarna was nervous.

Elric laughed. 'What? And you a sorcerer from Pan Tang—that isle that claims to know as much of sorcery as my ancestors, the Bright Emperors! No, no— besides, I'm not in a cautious mood today!'

'Nor am I,' cried Yishana, clapping her steed's sides. 'Come, gentlemen—to the Citadel of Chaos!'

By late afternoon, they had topped the range of hills surrounding the valley and looked down at the mysterious citadel.

Yishana had described it well—but not perfectly. Elric's eyes ached as he looked at it, for it seemed to extend beyond the Realm of Earth into a different plane, perhaps several.

It shimmered and glittered and all Earthly colours were there, as well as many which Elric recognised as belonging to other planes. Even the basic outline of the citadel was uncertain. In contrast, the surrounding valley was a sea of dark ash, which sometimes seemed to eddy, to undulate and send up spurting geysers of dust, as if the basic elements of nature had been disturbed and warped by the presence of the supernatural citadel.

'Well?' Theleb K'aarna tried to calm his nervous horse as it backed away from the citadel. 'Have you seen the like in the world before?'

Elric shook his head. 'Not in this world, certainly; but I've seen it before. During my final initiation into the arts of Melniboné, my father took me with him in astral form to the Realm of Chaos, there to receive the audience of my patron the Lord Arioch of the Seven Darks . . .'

Theleb K'aarna shuddered. 'You have been to Chaos? It is Arioch's citadel, then?'

Elric laughed in disdain. 'That! No, it is a hovel compared to the palaces of the Lords of Chaos.'

Impatiently, Yishana said; 'Then who dwells *there?*'

'As I remember, the one who dwelt in the citadel when I passed through the Chaos Realm in my youth—he was no Lord of Chaos, but a kind of servant to the Lords. Yet,' he frowned, 'not exactly a servant. . . .'

'*Ach!* You speak in riddles.' Theleb K'aarna turned his horse to ride down the hills, away from the citadel. 'I know you Melnibonéans! Starving, you'd rather have a paradox than food!'

Elric and Yishana followed him some distance, then Elric stopped. Elric pointed behind him.

'The one who dwells yonder is a paradoxical sort of fellow. He's a kind of Jester to the Court of Chaos. The Lords of Chaos respect him—perhaps fear him slightly—even though he entertains them. He delights them with cosmic riddles, with farcical satires purporting to explain the nature of the Cosmic Hand that holds both Chaos and Law in balance, he juggles enigmas like baubles, laughs at what Chaos holds dear, takes seriously that which they mock at . . .' He paused and shrugged. 'So I have heard, at least.'

'Why should he be here?'

'Why should he be anywhere? I could guess at the motives of Chaos or Law and probably be right. But not even the Lords of the Higher Worlds can understand the motives of Balo the Jester. It is said that he is the only one allowed to move between the Realms of Chaos and Law at will, though I have never heard of him coming to the Realm of Earth before. Neither, for that matter, have I ever heard him credited with such acts of destruction as that which we've witnessed. It is a puzzle to me—one which would no doubt please him if he knew.'

'There would be one way of discovering the purpose of his visit,' Theleb K'aarna said with a faint smile. 'If someone entered the citadel . . .'

'Come now, sorcerer,' Elric mocked. 'I've little love for life, to be sure, but there are some things of value to me—my soul, for one!'

Theleb K'aarna began to ride on down the hill, but Elric remained thoughtfully where he was, Yishana beside him.

'You seem more troubled by this than you should be, Elric,' she said.

'It *is* disturbing. There is a hint here that, if we investigate the citadel further, we should become embroiled in some dispute between Balo and his masters—perhaps even the Lords of Law, too. To become so involved could easily mean our destruction, since the forces at work are more dangerous and powerful than anything we are familiar with on Earth.'

'But we cannot simply watch this Balo laying our cities waste, carrying off our fairest, threatening to rule Jharkor himself within a short time!'

Elric sighed, but did not reply.

'Have you no sorcery, Elric, to send Balo back to Chaos where he belongs, to seal the breach he has made in our Realm?'

'Even Melnibonéans cannot match the power of the Lords of the Higher Worlds—and my forefathers knew much more of sorcery than do I. My best allies serve neither Chaos nor Law, they are elementals: lords of fire, earth, air, and water, entities with affinities with beasts and plants. Good allies in an earthly battle—but of no great use when matched against one such as Balo. I must think. . . . At least, if I opposed Balo it would not necessarily incur the wrath of my patron Lords. Something, I suppose. . . .'

The hills rolled green and lush to the grasslands at their feet, the sun beat down from a clear sky on the infinity of grass stretching to the horizon. Above them a large predatory bird wheeled; and Theleb K'aarna was a tiny figure, turning in the saddle to call to them in a thin voice, but his words could not be heard.

Yishana seemed dispirited. Her shoulders slightly slumped, and she did not look at Elric as she began to guide her horse slowly down towards the sorcerer of Pan Tang. Elric followed, conscious of his own indecision, yet half-careless of it. What did it matter to him if . . . ?

The music began, faintly at first, but beginning to swell with an attractive, poignant sweetness, evoking nostalgic memories, offering peace and giving life a sharp meaning, all at once. If the music came from instruments, then they were not earthly. It produced in him a yearning to turn about and discover its source, but he resisted it. Yishana, on the other hand, was evidently not finding the music so easily resisted. She had wheeled completely round, her face radiant, her lips trembling and tears shining in her eyes.

Elric, in his wanderings in unearthly realms, had heard music like it before—it echoed many of the bizarre symphonies of old Melniboné—and it did not draw him as it drew Yishana. He recognised swiftly that she was in danger, and as she came past him, spurring her horse, he reached out to grab her bridle.

Her whip slashed at his hand and, cursing with unexpected pain, he dropped the bridle. She went past him, galloping up to the crest of the hill and vanishing over it in an instant.

'Yishana!' He shouted at her desperately, but his voice would not carry over the pulsing music. He looked back, hoping that Theleb K'aarna would lend help, but the sorcerer was riding rapidly away. Evidently, on hearing the music, he had come to a swift decision.

Elric raced after Yishana, screaming for her to turn back. His own horse reached the top of the hill and he saw her bent over her steed's neck as she goaded it towards the shining citadel.

'Yishana! You go to your doom!'

Now she had reached the outer limits of the citadel, and her horse's feet seemed to strike off shimmering waves of colour as they touched the Chaos-disturbed ground surrounding the place. Although he knew it was too late to stop her, Elric continued to speed after her, hoping to reach her before she entered the citadel itself.

But, even as he entered the rainbow swirl, he saw what appeared to be a dozen Yishanas going through a dozen gateways into the citadel. Oddly refracted light created the illusion and made it impossible to tell which was the real Yishana.

With Yishana's disappearance the music stopped and Elric thought he heard a faint whisper of laughter following it. His horse was by this time becoming increasingly difficult to control, and he did not trust himself to it. He dismounted, his legs wreathed in radiant mist, and let the horse go. It galloped off, snorting its terror.

Elric's left hand moved to the hilt of his runesword, but he hesitated to draw it. Once pulled from its scabbard, the blade would demand souls before it allowed itself to be resheathed. Yet it was his only weapon. He withdrew his hand, and the blade seemed to quiver angrily at his side.

'Not yet, Stormbringer. There may be forces within who are stronger even than you!'

He began to wade through the faintly-resisting light swirls. He was half-blinded by the scintillating colours around him, which sometimes shone dark blue, silver, and red; sometimes gold, light green, amber. He also felt the sickening lack of any sort of orientation—distance, depth, breadth were meaningless. He recognised what he had only experienced in an astral form—the odd, timeless, spaceless quality that marked a Realm of the Higher Worlds.

He drifted, pushing his body in the direction in which he guessed Yishana had gone, for by now he had lost sight of the gateway or any of its mirage images.

He realised that, unless he was doomed to drift here until he starved, he must draw Stormbringer; for the runeblade could resist the influence of Chaos.

This time, when he gripped the sword's hilt, he felt a shock run up his arm and infuse his body with vitality. The sword came free from the scabbard. From the huge blade, carved with strange old runes, a black radiance poured, meeting the shifting colours of Chaos and dispersing them.

Now Elric shrieked the age-old battle-ululation of his folk and pressed on into the citadel, slashing at the intangible images that swirled on all sides. The gateway was ahead, and Elric knew it now, for his sword had shown him which were the mirages. It was open as Elric reached the portal. He paused for a moment, his lips moving as he remembered an invocation that he might need later. Arioch, Lord of Chaos, patron god-demon of his ancestors, was a negligent power and whimful—he could not rely on Arioch to aid him here, unless . . .

In slow graceful strides, a golden beast with eyes of ruby-fire was loping down the passage that led from the portal. Bright though the eyes were, they seemed blind, and its huge, doglike muzzle was closed. Yet its path could only lead it to Elric and, as it neared him, the mouth suddenly gaped showing coral fangs. In silence it came to a halt, the blind eyes never once settling on the albino, and then sprang!

Elric staggered back, raising the sword in defence. He was flung to the ground by the beast's weight and felt its body cover him. It was cold, cold, and it made no attempt to savage him—just lay on top of him and let the cold permeate his body.

Elric began to shiver as he pushed at the chilling body of the beast. Stormbringer moaned and murmured in his hand, and then it pierced some part of the beast's body, and a horrible cold strength began to fill the albino. Reinforced by the beast's own life-force, he heaved upwards. The beast continued to smother him, though now a thin, barely audible sound was coming from it. Elric guessed that Stormbringer's small wound was hurting the creature.

Desperately, for he was shaking and aching with cold, he moved the sword and stabbed again. Again the thin sound from the beast; again cold energy flooded through him, and again he heaved. This time the beast was flung off and crawled back towards the portal. Elric sprang up, raised Stormbringer high, and brought the sword down on the golden creature's skull. The skull shattered as ice might shatter.

Elric rang forward into the passage and, once within, the place became filled with roars and shrieks that echoed and were magnified. It was as if the voice that the cold beast had lacked outside was shouting its death-agonies here.

Now the floor rose until he was running up a spiral ramp. Looking down, he shuddered, for he looked into an infinite pit of subtle, dangerous colours that swam about in such a way that he could hardly take his eyes from them. He even felt his body begin to leave the ramp and go towards the pit, but he strengthened his grip on the sword and disciplined himself to climb on.

Upwards, as he looked, was the same as downwards. Only the ramp had any kind of constancy, and this began to take on the appearance of a thinly-cut jewel, through which he could see the pit and in which it was reflected.

Greens and blues and yellows predominated, but there were also traces of dark red, black, and orange, and many other colours not in an ordinary human spectrum.

Elric knew he was in some province of the Higher Worlds and guessed that it would not be long before the ramp led him to new danger.

Danger did not seem to await him when at last he came to the end of the ramp and stepped on to a bridge of similar stuff, which led over the scintillating pit to an archway that shone with a steady blue light.

He crossed the bridge cautiously and as cautiously entered the arch. Everything was blue-tinged here, even himself; and he trod on, the blue becoming deeper and deeper as he progressed.

Then Stormbringer began to murmur and, either warned by the sword or by some sixth sense of his own, Elric wheeled to his right. Another archway had appeared there and from this there began to shine a light as deep red as the other was blue. Where the two met was a purple of fantastic richness and Elric stared at this, experiencing a similar hypnotic pull as he had had when climbing the ramp. Again his mind was stronger, and he forced himself to enter the red arch. At once another arch appeared to his left, sending a beam of green light to merge with the red, and another to his left brought yellow light, one ahead brought mauve until he seemed trapped within the criss-cross of beams. He slashed at them with Stormbringer, and the black radiance reduced the beams for a moment to streamers of light, which reformed again. Elric continued to move forward.

Now, looming through the confusion of colour, a shape appeared and Elric thought it was that of a man.

Man it was in shape—but not in size it seemed. Yet, when it drew closer, it was no giant—less than Elric's height. Still it gave the *impression* of vast proportions, rather as if it *were* a giant and Elric had grown to its size.

It blundered towards Elric and went *through* him. It was not that the man was intangible—it was Elric who felt the ghost. The creature's mass seemed of incredible density. The creature was turning, its huge hands reaching out, its face a mocking grimace. Elric struck at it with

Stormbringer and was astonished as the runesword was halted, making no impression on the creature's bulk.

Yet when it grasped Elric, its hands went through him. Elric backed away, grinning now in relief. Then he saw with some terror that the light was gleaming through him. He had been right—*he* was the ghost!

The creature reached out for him again, grabbed him again, failed to hold him.

Elric, conscious that he was in no physical danger from the monster, yet also highly conscious that his sanity was about to be permanently impaired, turned and fled.

Quite suddenly he was in a hall, the walls of which were of the same unstable, shifting colours as the rest of the place. But sitting on a stool in the centre of the hall, holding in his hands some tiny creatures that seemed to be running about on his palm, was a small figure who looked up at Elric and grinned merrily.

'Welcome, King of Melniboné. And how fares the last ruler of my favourite earthly race?'

The figure was dressed in shimmering motley. On his head was a tall, spiked crown—a travesty of and a comment upon the crowns of the mighty. His face was angular and his mouth wide.

'Greetings, Lord Balo,' Elric made a mock bow. 'Strange hospitality you offer in your welcome.'

'Ahaha—it did not amuse you, eh? Men are so much harder to please than gods—you would not think it, would you?'

'Men's pleasures are rarely so elaborate. Where is Queen Yishana?'

'Allow me my pleasures also, mortal. Here she is, I think.' Balo plucked at one of the tiny creatures on his palm. Elric stepped forward and saw that Yishana was indeed there, as were many of the lost soldiers. Balo looked up at him and winked. 'They are so much easier to handle in this size.'

'I do not doubt it, though I wonder if it is not we who are larger rather than they who are smaller. . . .'

'You are astute, mortal. But can you guess how this came to be?'

'Your creature back there—your pits and colours and archways— somehow they warp—what?'

'*Mass,* King Elric. But you would not understand such concepts. Even the Lords of Melniboné, most godlike and intelligent of mortals, only learned how to manipulate the elements in ritual, invocation, and spell, but never understood what they manipulated—that is where the Lords of the Higher Worlds score, whatever their differences.'

'But I survived without need for spells. I survived by disciplining my mind!'

'That helped, for certain—but you forget your greatest asset—that disturbing blade there. You use it in your petty problems to aid you, and you never realise that it is like making use of a mighty war galley to catch a sprat. That sword represents power in *any* Realm, King Elric!'

'Aye, so it might. This does not interest me. Why are you here, Lord Balo?'

Balo chuckled, his laughter rich and musical. 'Oho, I am in disgrace. I quarrelled with my masters, who took exception to a joke of mine about their insignificance and egotism, about their destiny and their pride. Bad taste to them, King, is any hint of their own oblivion. I made a joke in bad taste. I fled from the Higher Worlds to Earth, where, unless invoked, the Lords of Law or Chaos can rarely interfere. You will like my intention, Elric, as would any Melnibonéan—I intend to establish my own Realm on Earth—the Realm of Paradox. A little from Law, a little from Chaos—a Realm of opposites, of curiosities and jokes.'

'I'm thinking we already have such a world as you describe, Lord Balo, with no need for you to create it!'

'Earnest irony, King Elric, for an insouciant man of Melniboné.'

'Ah, that it may be. I am a boor on occasions such as these. Will you release Yishana and myself?'

'But you and I are giants—I have given you the status and appearance of a god. You and I could be partners in this enterprise of mine!'

'Unfortunately, Lord Balo, I do not possess your range of humour and am unfitted for such an exalted role. Besides,' Elric grinned suddenly, 'it is in my mind that the Lords of the Higher Worlds will not easily let drop the matter of your ambition, since it appears to conflict so strongly with theirs.'

Balo laughed but said nothing.

Elric also smiled, but it was an attempt to hide his racing thoughts. 'What do you intend to do if I refuse?'

'Why, Elric, you would not refuse! I can think of many subtle pranks that I could play on you . . .'

'Indeed? And the Black Swords?'

'Ah, yes . . .'

'Balo, in your mirth and obsessions you have not considered everything thoroughly. You should have exerted more effort to vanquish me before I came here.'

Now Elric's eyes gleamed hot and he lifted the sword, crying:

'*Arioch! Master! I invoke thee, Lord of Chaos!*'

Balo started. 'Cease that, King Elric!'

'*Arioch—here is a soul for you to claim!*'

'Quiet, I say!'

'Arioch! Hear me!' Elric's voice was loud and desperate.

Balo let his tiny playthings fall and rose hurriedly, skipping towards Elric.

'Your invocation is unheeded!' He laughed, reaching out for Elric. But Stormbringer moaned and shuddered in Elric's hand and Balo withdrew his hand. His face became serious and frowning.

'Arioch of the Seven Darks—your servant calls you!'

The walls of flame trembled and began to fade. Balo's eyes widened and jerked this way and that.

'Oh, Lord Arioch—come reclaim your straying Balo!'

'You cannot!' Balo scampered across the room where one section of the flame had faded entirely, revealing darkness beyond.

'Sadly for you, little jester, he can . . .' The voice was sardonic and yet beautiful. From the darkness stepped a tall figure, no longer the shapeless gibbering thing that had, until now, been Arioch's favoured manifestation when visiting the Realm of Earth. Yet the great beauty of the newcomer, filled as it was with a kind of compassion mingled with pride, cruelty, and sadness, showed at once that he could not be human. He was clad in doublet of pulsing scarlet, hose of ever-changing hue, a long golden sword at his hips. His eyes were large, but slanted high, his hair was long and as golden as the sword, his lips were full and his chin pointed like his ears.

'Arioch!' Balo stumbled backwards as the Lord of Chaos advanced.

'It was your mistake, Balo,' Elric said from behind the jester. 'Did you not realise only the Kings of Melniboné may invoke Arioch and bring him to the Realm of Earth? It has been their age-old privilege.'

'And much have they abused it,' said Arioch, smiling faintly as Balo grovelled. 'However, this service you have done us, Elric, will make up for past misuses. I was not amused by the matter of the Mist Giant . . .'

Even Elric was awed by the incredibly powerful presence of the Chaos Lord. He also felt much relieved, for he had not been sure that Arioch could be summoned in this way.

Now Arioch stretched an arm down towards Balo and lifted the jester by his collar so that he jerked and struggled in the air, his face writhing in fear and consternation.

Arioch took hold of Balo's head and squeezed it. Elric looked on in amazement as the head began to shrink. Arioch took Balo's legs and bent them in, folding Balo up and kneading him in his slender, inhuman hands until he was a small, solid ball. Arioch then popped the ball into his mouth and swallowed it.

'I have not eaten him, Elric,' he said with another faint smile. 'It is merely the easiest way of transporting him back to the Realms from which he came. He has transgressed and will be punished. All this'—he waved an arm to indicate the citadel—'is unfortunate and contradicts the plans we of Chaos have for Earth—plans which will involve you, our servant, and make you mighty.'

Elric bowed to his master. 'I am honoured, Lord Arioch, though I seek no favours.'

Arioch's silvery voice lost some of its beauty and his face seemed to cloud for a second. 'You are pledged to serve Chaos, Elric, as were your ancestors. You *will* serve Chaos! The time draws near when both Law and Chaos will battle for the Realm of Earth—and Chaos shall win! Earth will be incorporated into our Realm and you will join the hierarchy of Chaos, become immortal as we are!'

'Immortality offers little to me, my lord.'

'Ah, Elric, have the men of Melniboné become as the half-apes who now dominate Earth with their puny "civilisations"? Are you no better than these Young Kingdom upstarts? Think what we offer!'

'I shall, my lord, when the time you mention comes.' Elric's head was still lowered.

'You shall indeed,' Arioch raised his arms. 'Now to transport this toy of Balo's to its proper Realm, and redress the trouble he has caused, lest some hint reaches our opponents before the proper time.'

Arioch's voice swelled like the singing of a million brazen bells and Elric sheathed his sword and clapped his hands over his ears to stop the pain.

Then Elric felt his body seem to *shred* apart, swell and stretch until it became like smoke drifting on air. Then, faster, the smoke began to be drawn together, becoming denser and denser and he seemed to be shrinking now. All around him were rolling banks of colour, flashes and indescribable noises. Then came a vast blackness and he closed his eyes against the images that seemed reflected in the blackness.

When he opened them he stood in the valley and the singing citadel was gone. Only Yishana and a few surprised-looking soldiers stood there. Yishana ran towards him.

'Elric—was it you who saved us?'

'I must claim only part of the credit,' he said.

'Not all my soldiers are here,' she said, inspecting the men. 'Where are the rest—and the villagers abducted earlier?'

'If Balo's tastes are like his masters', then I fear they now have the honour of being part of a demigod. The Lords of Chaos are not flesh-eaters, of course, being of the Higher Worlds, but there is something they savour in men which satisfies them . . .'

Yishana hugged her body as if in cold. 'He was huge—I cannot believe that his citadel could contain his bulk!'

'The citadel was more than a dwelling-place, that was obvious. Somehow it changed size, shape—and other things I cannot describe. Arioch of Chaos transported it and Balo back to where they belong.'

'Arioch! But he is one of the Greatest Six! How did he come to Earth?'

'An old pact with my remote ancestors. By calling him they allow him to spend a short time in our realm, and he repays them with some favour. This was done.'

'Come, Elric,' she took his arm. 'Let's away from the valley.'

Elric was weak and enfeebled by the efforts of summoning Arioch, and the experiences he had had before and since the episode. He could hardly walk; and soon it was Yishana who supported him as they made slow progress, the dazed warriors following in their wake, towards the nearest village, where they could obtain rest and horses to take them back to Dhakos.

5

As they staggered past the blasted ruins of Thokara, Yishana pointed suddenly at the sky.

'What is that?'

A great shape was winging its way towards them. It had the appearance of a butterfly, but a butterfly with wings so huge they blotted out the sun.

'Can it be some creature of Balo's left behind?' she speculated.

'Hardly likely,' he replied. 'This has the appearance of a monster conjured by a human sorcerer.'

'Theleb K'aarna!'

'He has surpassed himself,' Elric said wryly. 'I did not think him capable.'

'It is his vengeance on us, Elric!'

'That seems reasonable. But I am weak, Yishana—and Stormbringer needs souls if it is to replenish my strength.' He turned a calculating eye on the warriors behind him who were gaping up at the creature as it came nearer. Now they could see it had a man's body, covered with hairs or feathers hued like a peacock's.

The air whistled as it descended, its fifty-foot wings dwarfing the seven feet of head and body. From its head grew two curling horns, and its arms terminated in long talons.

'We are doomed, Elric!' cried Yishana. She saw that the warriors were fleeing and she cried after them to come back. Elric stood there passively, knowing that alone he could not defeat the butterfly-creature.

'Best go with them, Yishana,' he murmured. 'I think it will be satisfied with me.'

'No!'

He ignored her and stepped towards the creature as it landed and began to glide over the ground in his direction. He drew a quiescent

Stormbringer, which felt heavy in his hand. A little strength flowed into him, but not enough. His only hope was to strike a good blow at the creature's vitals and draw some of its own life-force into himself.

The creature's voice shrilled at him, and the strange, insane face twisted as he approached. Elric realised that this was no true supernatural denizen of the nether worlds, but a once-human creature warped by Theleb K'aarna's sorcery. At least it was mortal, and he had only physical strength to contend with. In better condition it would have been easy for him—but now . . .

The wings beat at the air as the taloned hands grasped at him. He took Stormbringer in both hands and swung the runeblade at the thing's neck. Swiftly the wings folded in to protect its neck and Stormbringer became entangled in the strange, sticky flesh. A talon caught Elric's arm, ripping it to the bone. He yelled in pain and yanked the sword from the enfolding wing.

He tried to steady himself for another blow, but the monster grabbed his wounded arm and began drawing him towards its now lowered head —and the horns that curled from it.

He struggled, hacking at the thing's arms with the extra strength that came with the threat of death.

Then he heard a cry from behind him and saw a figure from the corner of his eye, a figure that leapt forward with two blades gleaming in either hand. The swords slashed at the talons and with a shriek the creature turned on Elric's would-be rescuer.

It was Moonglum. Elric fell backwards, breathing hard, as he watched his little red-headed friend engage the monster.

But Moonglum would not survive for long, unless aided.

Elric racked his brain for some spell that would help; but he was too weak, even if he could think of one, to raise the energy necessary to summon supernatural help.

And then it came to him! Yishana! She was not as exhausted as he. But could she do it?

He turned as the air moaned to the beating of the creature's wings. Moonglum was only just managing to hold it off, his two swords flashing rapidly as he parried every effort to grasp him.

'Yishana!' croaked the albino.

She came up to him and placed a hand on his. 'We could leave, Elric —perhaps hide from that thing.'

'No. I must help Moonglum. Listen—you realise how desperate our position is, do you not? Then keep that in mind while you recite this rune with me. Perhaps together we may succeed. There are many kinds of lizards in these parts, are there not?'

'Aye—many.'

'Then this is what you must say—and remember that we shall all perish by Theleb K'aarna's servant if you are not successful.'

In the half worlds, where dwelt the master-types of all creatures other than Man, an entity stirred, hearing its name. The entity was called Haaashaastaak; and it was scaly and cold, with no true intellect, such as men and gods possessed, but an *awareness,* which served it as well if not better. It was brother, on this plane, to such entities as Meerclar, Lord of the Cats, Roofdrak, Lord of the Dogs, Nuru-ah, Lord of the Cattle, and many, many others. This was Haaashaastaak, Lord of the Lizards. It did not really hear words in the exact sense, but it heard rhythms which meant much to it, even though it did not know why. The rhythms were being repeated over and over again, but seemed too faint to be worth much attention. It stirred and yawned, but did nothing . . .

> *'Haaashaastaak, Lord of Lizards,*
> *Your children were fathers of men,*
> *Haaashaastaak, Prince of Reptiles.*
> *Come aid a grandchild now!*
>
> *'Haaashaastaak, Father of Scales,*
> *Cold-blooded bringer of life . . .'*

It was a bizarre scene, with Elric and Yishana desperately chanting the rune over and over again as Moonglum fought on, slowly losing strength.

Haaashaastaak quivered and became more curious. The rhythms were no stronger, yet they seemed more insistent. He would travel, he decided, to that place where those he watched over dwelt. He knew that if he answered the rhythms, he would have to obey whatever source they had. He was not, of course, aware that such decisions had been implanted into him in a far distant age—the time before the creation of Earth, when the Lords of Law and Chaos, then inhabitants of a single realm and known by another name, had watched over the forming of things and laid down the manner and logic in which things should behave, following their great edict from the voice of the Cosmic Balance—the voice which had never spoken since.

Haaashaastaak betook himself, a little slothfully, to Earth.

Elric and Yishana were still chanting hoarsely, as Haaashaastaak made his sudden appearance. He had the look of a huge iguana, and his eyes were many-coloured, many faceted jewels, his scales seeming of gold, silver, and other rich metals. A slightly hazy outline surrounded him, as if he had brought part of his own environment with him.

Yishana gasped and Elric breathed a deep sigh. As a child he had learned the languages of all animal-masters, and now he must recall the simple language of the lizard-master, Haaashaastaak.

His need fired his brain, and the words came suddenly.

'Haaashaastaak,' he cried pointing at the butterfly-creature, 'mokik ankkuh!'

The lizard lord turned its jewelled eyes on the creature and its great tongue suddenly shot out towards it, curling around the monster. It shrilled in terror as it was drawn towards the lizard lord's great maw. Legs and arms kicked as the mouth closed on it. Several gulps and Haaashaastaak had swallowed Theleb K'aarna's prize creation. Then it turned its head uncertainly about for a few moments and vanished.

Pain began to throb now through Elric's torn arm as Moonglum staggered towards him, grinning in relief.

'I followed behind you at a distance as you requested,' he said, 'since you suspected treachery from Theleb K'aarna. But then I spied the sorcerer coming this way and followed him to a cave in yonder hills,' he pointed. 'But when the deceased,' he laughed shakily, 'emerged from the cave, I decided that it would be best to chase that, for I had the feeling it was going in your direction.'

'I am glad you were so astute,' Elric said.

'It was your doing, really,' Moonglum replied. 'For, if you hadn't anticipated treachery from Theleb K'aarna, I might not have been here at the right moment.' Moonglum suddenly sank to the grass, leaned back, grinned, and fainted.

Elric felt very dazed himself. 'I do not think we need fear anything more from your sorcerer just yet, Yishana,' he said. 'Let us rest here and refresh ourselves. Perhaps then your cowardly soldiers will have returned, and we can send them to a village to get us some horses.'

They stretched out on the grass and, lying in each other's arms, went to sleep.

Elric was astonished to wake in a bed, a soft bed. He opened his eyes and saw Yishana and Moonglum smiling down at him.

'How long have I been here?'

'More than two days. You did not wake when the horses came, so we had the warriors construct a stretcher to bear you to Dhakos. You are in my palace.'

Elric cautiously moved his stiff, bandaged arm. It was still painful. 'Are my belongings still at the inn?'

'Perhaps, if they have not been stolen. Why?'

'I have a pouch of herbs there, which will heal this arm quickly and also supply me with a little strength, which I need badly.'

'I will go and see if they are still there,' Moonglum said and walked from the chamber.

Yishana stroked Elric's milk-white hair. 'I have much to thank you for, wolf,' said she. 'You have saved my kingdom—perhaps all the Young Kingdoms. In my eyes you are redeemed for my brother's death.'

'Oh, I thank you, madam,' said Elric with a mocking tone.

She laughed. 'You are still a Melnibonéan.'

'Still that, aye.'

'A strange mixture, however. Sensitive and cruel, sardonic and loyal to your little friend Moonglum. I look forward to knowing you better my lord.'

'As to that, I am not sure if you will have the opportunity.'

She gave him a hard look. 'Why?'

'Your résumé of my character was incomplete, Queen Yishana—you should have added "careless of the world—and yet vengeful." I wish to be revenged on your pet wizard.'

'But he is spent, surely—you said so yourself.'

'I am, as you remarked, still a Melnibonéan! My arrogant blood calls vengeance on an upstart!'

'Forget Theleb K'aarna. I will have him hunted by my White Leopards. Even his sorcery will not win against such savages as they are!'

'Forget him? Oh, no!'

'Elric, Elric—I will give you my kingdom, declare you ruler of Jharkor, if you will let me be your consort.'

He reached out and stroked her bare arm with his good hand.

'You are unrealistic, queen. To take such an action would bring wholesale rebellion in your land. To your folk, I am still the Traitor of Imrryr.'

'Not now—now you are the Hero of Jharkor.'

'How so? They did not know of their peril and thus will feel no gratitude. It were best that I settled my debt with your wizard and went on my way. The streets must already be full of rumours that you have taken your brother's murderer to your bed. Your popularity with your subjects must be at its lowest, madam.'

'I do not care.'

'You will if your nobles lead the people in insurrection and crucify you naked in the city square.'

'You are familiar with our customs.'

'We Melnibonéans are a learned folk, queen.'

'Well versed in all the arts.'

'All of them.' Again he felt his blood race as she rose and barred the door. At that moment he felt no need for the herbs which Moonglum had gone to find.

When he tiptoed from the room that night, he found Moonglum waiting patiently in the antechamber. Moonglum proffered the pouch with a wink. But Elric's mood was not light. He took bunches of herbs from the pouch and selected what he needed.

Moonglum grimaced as he watched Elric chew and swallow the stuff. Then together they stole from the palace.

Armed with Stormbringer and mounted, Elric rode slightly behind his friend as Moonglum led the way towards the hills beyond Dhakos.

'If I know the sorcerers of Pan Tang,' murmured the albino, 'then Theleb K'aarna will be more exhausted than was I. With luck we will come upon him sleeping.'

'I shall wait outside the cave in that case,' said Moonglum, for he now had some experience of Elric's vengeance-taking and did not relish watching Theleb K'aarna's slow death.

They galloped speedily until the hills were reached and Moonglum showed Elric the cave mouth.

Leaving his horse, the albino went soft-footed into the cave, his runesword ready.

Moonglum waited nervously for Theleb K'aarna's first shrieks, but none came. He waited until dawn began to bring the first faint light and then Elric, face frozen with anger, emerged from the cave.

Savagely he grasped his horse's reins and swung himself into the saddle.

'Are you satisfied?' Moonglum asked tentatively.

'Satisfied, no! The dog has vanished!'

'Gone—but . . .'

'He was more cunning than I thought. There are several caves and I sought him in all of them. In the farthest I discovered traces of sorcerous runes on the walls and floor. He has transported himself somewhere and I could not discover where, in spite of deciphering most of the runes! Perhaps he went to Pan Tang.'

'Ah, then our quest has been futile. Let us return to Dhakos and enjoy a little more of Yishana's hospitality.'

'No—we go to Pan Tang.'

'But, Elric, Theleb K'aarna's brother sorcerers dwell there in strength; and Jagreen Lern, the theocrat, forbids visitors!'

'No matter. I wish to finish my business with Theleb K'aarna.'

'You have no proof that he is there!'

'No matter!'

And then Elric was spurring his horse away, riding like a man possessed or fleeing from dreadful peril—and perhaps he was both possessed and fleeing. Moonglum did not follow at once but thoughtfully watched his friend gallop off. Not normally introspective, he wondered if Yishana had perhaps affected the albino more strongly than he would have wished. He did not think that vengeance on Theleb K'aarna was Elric's prime desire in refusing to return to Dhakos.

Then he shrugged and clapped his heels to his steed's flanks, racing to catch up with Elric as the cold dawn rose, wondering if they would continue towards Pan Tang once Dhakos was far enough behind.

But Elric's head contained no thoughts, only emotion flooded him—emotion he did not wish to analyse. His white hair streaming behind him, his dead-white, handsome face set, his slender hands tightly clutching the stallion's reins, he rode. And only his strange, crimson eyes reflected the misery and conflict within him.

In Dhakos that morning, other eyes held misery, but not for too long. Yishana was a pragmatic queen.